STRANDS

OF

BRONZE

AND

GOLD

STRANDS

OF

BRONZE

AND

GOLD

JANE NICKERSON

ALFRED A. KNOPF
NEW YORK

THIS IS A BORZOI BOOK PUBLISHED BY ALFRED A. KNOPF

All rights reserved. Published in the United States by Alfred A. Knopf, an imprint of Random House Children's Books, a division of Random House, Inc., New York.

Knopf, Borzoi Books, and the colophon are registered trademarks of Random House, Inc.

Visit us on the Web! randomhouse.com/teens

Educators and librarians, for a variety of teaching tools, visit us at RHTeachersLibrarians.com

Library of Congress Cataloging-in-Publication Data
Nickerson, Jane.
  Strands of bronze and gold / Jane Nickerson — 1st ed.
    p. cm.
  Summary: After the death of her father in 1855, seventeen-year-old Sophia goes to live with her wealthy and mysterious godfather at his gothic mansion, Wyndriven Abbey, in Mississippi, where many secrets lie hidden.
  ISBN 978-0-307-97598-0 (trade) — ISBN 978-0-375-97118-1 (lib. bdg.) — ISBN 978-0-307-97606-2 (ebook)
  [1. Orphans—Fiction. 2. Slavery—Fiction. 3. Plantation life—Mississippi—Fiction. 4. Ghosts—Fiction. 5. Mississippi—History—19th century—Fiction.] I. Title.
PZ7.N55812Str 2013
[Fic]—dc23   2012001041

The text of this book is set in 13.15-point LTC Metropolitan.

Printed in the United States of America
March 2013
10 9 8 7 6 5 4 3 2 1

First Edition

To my Stella,
whose way with words
amazes me.

CONTENTS

ONCE UPON A TIME . . .

there lived a very powerful lord, the owner of estates, farms and a great splendid castle, and his name was Bluebeard. . . . He was very handsome and charming, but, if the truth be told, there was something about him that made you feel respect, and a little uneasy.

FROM "BLUEBEARD" IN
TALES FROM THE BROTHERS GRIMM

CHAPTER 1

THE FAIRY TALE BEGINS

You see, I had a fabulously wealthy godfather. That was why anything was possible for me.

I couldn't remember a time when thoughts of him didn't send a silvery little thrill through my body. He was a mystery and a magician and all my family's hopes for the future rolled into one. Soon, when the carriage covered the last miles of our journey, I would meet him at last—my godfather and guardian, Monsieur Bernard de Cressac.

And his wife, of course, but I tended to forget about her.

The wildwood we had plunged into might easily have been the setting for the thief's lair in "The Robber Bridegroom," so tangled and murky and haunted it seemed. However—I smashed a mosquito against my neck and my own blood spurted out—fairy-tale forests would never have been this itchy or this sweltering. Perspiration dripped off my nose before my handkerchief could catch it. Inside my bonnet my curls were plastered to my head.

My godfather had referred to my hair as "bronze" in one of his letters when I was younger—a letter featuring a delightfully spun story about a princess with tresses the shade of my own, *strands of bronze and gold*. . . .

M. de Cressac's last letter lay in my lap, its ivory paper limp from much handling. As always, at sight of the bold black handwriting, my chest tightened. A few months earlier, while my family had been going about the sad business of mourning the death of our father, M. de Cressac had been thinking of me, had been penning this invitation to his home, Wyndriven Abbey. Telling me he could not return to his "solemn duties" until he had asked me to come to him so I might "sweeten the atmosphere of an old man's dwelling" with my "companionship, youth, and beauty."

My brother Harry had snorted at that last part.

In that letter M. de Cressac called himself an old man. This conflicted with the image I had always held of the saint, soldier, explorer. The adventurer I had fantasized about had been old, of course, since he was a friend of my father's—forty at least—but muscular and hearty. Well, shortly I would know everything. Shortly my godfather would take his place in my life as a real, solid person, rather than a misty figure of daydreams.

On and on we twisted and snaked beneath arched branches in dim green leaf light, swallowed whole by trees. My eyes grew tired of the sporadic, flickering patches of pale sunshine. It was getting late, but evidently in Mississippi, summer heat didn't fade with the day.

Surely we'd get there soon.

I pulled down my bonnet's crinkly mourning crape veil and

shoved down my long, tight sleeves just as the trees thinned. We rounded a curve—and there it stood.

The magnificence of the building whooshed at me like a blast of icy wind. Wyndriven Abbey loomed in the center of spreading lawns and gardens and terraces as though it had stood in that spot for centuries. The drive widened as it approached the great edifice, which seemed more of a town than a house. It was toothed with crenellations and spiky with pinnacles and spires and turrets, the setting sun rosily staining the stone and lighting fires in a myriad of mullioned windows.

It was ridiculously vast and grim and terrifying. I loved it already.

As we drove down a gravel driveway edged with dark cedars, though, we passed an eyesore—an ancient, gnarled oak thrust among the cedars, pressing close overhead. It was shrouded with poison ivy (leaves of three, let them be!) and diseased with great misshapen nodules bulging on the trunk. A flock of crows burst out of the branches in a cacophony of cawing and beating wings.

It was not an ill omen.

The carriage pulled into a courtyard, and the very tall footman jumped down to help me alight. The coachman and the footman were both Africans, but they seemed elegantly European in their coats of resplendent sapphire velvet.

Surely I wasn't actually shrinking as I climbed stone steps to massive, iron-shod doors. As per habit, I pinched my cheeks and bit my lips to bring on more color, forgetting that I was probably already flushed from the heat. The de Cressacs must be pleased with my appearance, or at least not appalled.

I tugged at the rope of an iron bell. The echoes of its clanging still sounded when the door was answered by another very young, very tall footman.

"I am Miss Sophia Petheram," I said in a tight little voice, "come to stay with the de Cressac family."

"Yes," the footman said, opening the door wider and gesturing with a flourish for me to enter. "You're expected, Miss."

He spoke formally, but I must have looked frightened because he flashed a reassuring grin. He was young enough that he had not yet learned to be perfectly impassive.

In the lofty hall, whose arched and vaulted ceiling disappeared into shadows, candles already glittered in sconces and an immense candelabra blazed away on a center table. Beeswax tapers, they must be, from the clear, clean light. Of course gaslight would not yet have reached this place, so deep in the wilds. An expanse of black-and-white marble led to the grand staircase, wide and splendidly balustraded, seemingly hung in space. In the gloom the brilliant trompe l'œil decorations painted on the wall behind deceived me for a moment into thinking the staircase was a mere painting as well.

The footman's eyes went past my shoulder. "Mr. Ling, the butler, will take you to the master."

Outwardly I barely flinched when a figure glided forward from the wall just behind me.

"I hope I did not startle you," said a deep, quiet voice.

My chest still thudded. Yes, definitely startled.

Mr. Ling was a Chinese man, the first I had ever met, wrinkled like a walnut shell and with a long gray beard, wearing a high-collared black brocade tunic and skirt. Something to tell my siblings. His eyes were incredibly weary. He bowed. I flipped back my veil and curtsied, not caring that one probably shouldn't curtsy to servants. He was so very old, and his eyes . . .

"Come this way, Miss Petheram," he said. He spoke excellent English. He led me through a long gallery with adjoining anterooms and salons. It was a kaleidoscope of dazzling opulence—gold leaf and stamped leather, rich tapestries and ornate paintings. Only I was out of place.

I fingered the hair brooch at my throat—brown strands from my father and coppery strands from my mother—plaited by my sister, Anne, into a heart shape.

On the journey I had whiled away the moments, hours, days by designing dresses in my mind. It was a weakness of mine that often I'd get so enmeshed in my musings I would forget reality. In my imaginary meeting with M. de Cressac, I had worn a gown of emerald green silk with jet beads embroidered in the skirt that clicked as I walked. I could hear it. I could feel it—the weight of the beads. I looked down. Surprise! Still ugly black bombazine. Never had I imagined I would meet my guardian swathed in a fabric so dark and dull it swallowed the light of every room.

By the time Mr. Ling threw back double doors, announcing my name, my mouth was dry as cotton and my hands sticky as they clutched my reticule.

My godfather rose from a chair, and we stood looking at each other. Everything in me seemed to spiral. This person standing before me was the most handsome man I had ever laid eyes upon.

His hair and beard were black with a few silver threads that gave them almost a bluish cast. His features were finely chiseled, with laugh lines around the eyes. To my delight (and dismay), he sported small silver hoops in his ears, like a pirate. I had always adored pirates. Tall and powerfully built, his buff linen coat fit his figure superbly and he carried himself with the natural grace of an athlete as he strode toward me.

I curtsied and he bowed slightly.

He took my small hands in his large ones and looked down into my face without speaking. His eyes were the color of honey.

Time to launch into the words I had prepared. "I am pleased to meet you at last, sir. You are most kind to let me come and live in your beautiful home."

"*Enchanté, Mademoiselle.*" His tone was grave, but amusement flashed across his features at my polite little speech. He held my hand to his lips and kissed it, still watching my face.

"My—my family sends their good wishes and compliments."

M. de Cressac laughed outright now. "Do they indeed? After I have stolen away their sister? My little Sophia, at last you come to me. Let me see you better." He pushed back my bonnet so it hung by its ribbons from my neck.

I looked him bravely in the eye without blinking as he studied me.

"*Oui,*" he said softly. "Yes." His hand smoothed my damp, rumpled hair. "Do you know—no, how could you?—that the one time I saw you, you were a babe in your dear mother's arms. She was ill, and died soon after, but still a beauty. She had a certain fey quality, as though she were not quite of this world, and I suspected you would look just like her when you were grown."

The story was that as a scrawny, squalling infant, red of face and hair (my brother Harry's description), I had enchanted M. de Cressac, although no one could imagine why. It must have been my mother who did the enchanting.

"And—and is Madame de Cressac at home?" I asked.

"I am, alas, a widower."

A widower. My father had said Madame de Cressac was a French lady. A lovely French lady. "I didn't know—I'm so sorry. Papa should . . . he should have told us."

"He probably did not know. I am afraid I did not communicate with Martin much these last years."

As my godfather spoke, an elderly woman with an unfortunate nose and an immense silver tray shuffled into the room, a chatelaine jingling from her waist. She paused, regarding me with an anxious scrutiny.

"Ah," M. de Cressac said, taking the tray from her hands, "Mrs. Duckworth, allow me to present my goddaughter, Sophia Petheram. Sophia, Mrs. Duckworth is the housekeeper here and worth her weight in gold."

The lady beamed first at M. de Cressac and then at me. Her eyes nearly squinted shut. Her skin was doughy, with large pores. "You're very welcome, I'm sure." She had a British accent and her voice was pitched unusually high.

"Mrs. Duckworth's greatest pleasure is looking after people," M. de Cressac said. "If there is anything you should want, let her know, and she will see to it that you get it. Unless, of course, I notice and give it to you first." He winked at me. "Be assured we intend to spoil you."

"That we do." The housekeeper nodded so enthusiastically that the gold brooch on her ample bosom bobbed. "Now, Miss, sit you down and have a nice glass of cold lemonade and some refreshment, and then I will show you to your room."

"I will accompany you both," M. de Cressac said. "I want to see Sophia's face when she first sets eyes on her bedchamber."

My last qualms were put to flight by this reception. Obviously Mrs. Duckworth was respectability itself, even if there was no longer a Madame de Cressac in the household.

The tea tray was mounded with lemon tarts, maids of honor, jam cake with burnt sugar glaze, coconut cake with divinity icing, cream buns, and cheesecakes. I sipped lemonade (mint was sprinkled on it, making it taste like grass, only in a pleasing way) and nibbled a cream bun, trying not to let cream ooze everywhere, while my god-father inquired about my journey.

"Your carriage was wonderful," I said, swallowing quickly. "I've never been in one as well sprung. I could sink back into the cushions and rest and even read without the swaying and bumping making me ill. And all the blooming magnolia trees in the town are lovely. So Southern-looking."

"Yes, Chicataw, Mississippi, is indeed 'Southern-looking.'"

"People nearly fell out of their windows staring as we drove by. They must have recognized your crest on the door."

"Naturally they are eaten up with curiosity. Although I have been here twenty-five years, I am still the strange foreigner. We have few dealings in the town." He noticed me dab my forehead with my handkerchief. "When first I came to the South, the heat was oppressive, but I am used to it now."

"I'll become used to it too," I said. "You should have seen the suspicious character I rode with in the coach on the way to Memphis. As we drove, I thought up all sorts of stories explaining him. He wore a greatcoat and a hat pulled down over his ears. While the rest of us shoved up our sleeves and fanned ourselves with everything we could lay our hands on—newspapers and handkerchiefs and, of course, real fans if we could find ours—and took off anything we were allowed to take off, he only unfastened the top button of his coat. First his collar wilted, then his tie went crooked, and then he simply gave up and leaned back and slept, snoring. The sweat pooled in his ears and a fly crawled across his nose. It was dreadful to behold a human being dissolve before my very eyes."

"Certainly it would be disturbing," my godfather said. "Dear me, what dangerous and grueling adventures you have been through! And yet you appear charmingly unscathed."

He told about his estate. His voice melted around me like warm chocolate. He had just enough French accent to add to his charm. "The main house was a real English abbey. One that housed medieval monks and nuns. Are you disappointed it is not a new house? That it is so . . . well used?"

"Oh, no! I love antique places, and this one is amazing. I used to pass the old section in Boston and feel envious. There was one house in particular that dated from the mid-1600s and it—it was intriguing." I compressed my lips to keep from launching into a long story. M. de Cressac had an odd and contradictory effect on me. I had never been a chatterbox, but the way he watched me, as if fascinated, stimulated me to keep talking on and on. However, it was not because he made me comfortable; indeed, a certain tension quivered in the air, and I sat bolt upright on the edge of my chair.

"Bah! Boston!" He dismissed the city with a flick of one long hand. "Two hundred puny years is nothing. But I am happy you consider the abbey 'amazing.' Many were amazed when I brought it over here block by block and put it back together in this setting. I added wings designed to blend perfectly with the ancient."

Mrs. Duckworth chimed in often, her face wreathed with smiles.

As I answered their questions, I tried to absorb the—yes, *amazing*—room in which we sat. It was a witness to my godfather's powers of enchantment that I hadn't noticed it earlier. Three walls and the ceiling were covered with painted mythological figures, some of which seemed to stride out disconcertingly or peer at me over M. de Cressac's shoulder.

My godfather ceased whatever he was saying in midsentence. "I see you are admiring this room, Sophia. It is called the Heaven chamber. An apt name, is it not?"

"It's glorious. Quite breathtaking, although . . ."

"Although what? In what way does my Heaven room displease you? I will have it changed immediately to be more to your taste."

I blushed. "It's only—oh, I'm so silly—it's only that I wish more of the bodies were clothed."

Both my godfather and his housekeeper burst into peals of laughter.

"And I had *so* hoped to impress you with my lovely room. Foolish me. So you do not like all the rolls of rosy, naked flesh?" M. de Cressac pinched my chin. "Ah, *mon ange,* you are a delightful inno-cent. Would you have me paint a top hat and frock coat on Zeus? A dowager's shawl and bonnet on Hera?"

I made myself join in with a weak giggle. "Perhaps a riding habit on Diana?"

"Yes! Yes!" M. de Cressac slapped his thigh. Soon I was really laughing. Everything was more comfortable once we had laughed together.

CHAPTER 2

KNOWING THINGS

My godfather flung open the doors to my bedroom. I could feel his eyes on my face, gauging my reaction. I entered the room, prepared to appear delighted. There was no need for pretense. Obviously I was not to be treated as a pitiful, unwanted relation. I turned to M. de Cressac and tried to say the words "Thank you," but no sound came out.

He nodded, smiling. He understood.

A world of underwater fantasy stretched before us. The bed, shaped like a gigantic opalescent seashell, was raised on a dais and swathed in a velvet coverlet the color of sea foam. Curtains of filmy green-blue, shot through with silver, hung about it, as well as mosquito netting that could be held down by posts in the footboard. The floor was of mottled blue marble, polished and slick as glass, while white-paneled walls held niches showcasing statues of dolphins and sea gods. Above the mantel, which was held up by alabaster mermaids, soared an undersea mosaic featuring starfish and seaweed done all in luminous blue, gray, and lavender mother-of-pearl, and in front of the fireplace squatted a massive round otto-man upholstered in crushed white velvet, tufted with pearls.

I had always craved luxury, so this room was a delight, although my Puritan ancestors might well be turning over in their graves. I dashed from one beautiful item to another. I could scarcely believe I was now the proud owner of a dressing table stocked with a marble-backed hand mirror, combs, and brushes, as well as a glit-tering array of faceted crystal bottles and jars and pots of ointments and powders and perfumes. What would my brother Harry think if he saw me using these artifices? He used to tease that I was vain because he caught me gazing at myself in the mirror once. Perhaps he was right—certainly it was lovely to be young and fortunate and have my godfather say I resembled my mother, who had been a "beauty."

M. de Cressac might have been reading my mind because he said suddenly, "You favor your mother in more ways than hair and fea-tures. Your voice, the way you move, even your expression—as if you are thinking delightful, secret thoughts. I once called her *mon rayon de soleil*—a ray of sunshine."

"How well did you know her?"

"Not as well as I wished."

"Won't you tell me more about her? No one would ever answer my questions satisfactorily."

"Someday. When I am in the mood."

I lifted a pearl-handled pen shaped like a feather from the dainty lady's desk. Every consideration had been prepared. "You're too good, sir!" I cried. He was, indeed, too good, and I intended to enjoy every bit of it.

He beamed down from his imposing height. "Allow me to be generous. I have lived too long without my . . . goddaughter." He hesitated over the last word, lightly brushing a stray wisp of hair from my cheek. "Mrs. Duckworth will show you your powder closet and the wardrobes, which are stocked with a few ready-made frocks to make do until Madame Duclos can supply you with new ones."

"Surely I have enough for right now." I felt I should protest at least a little. "After all, I'm in mourning still for my father."

"Ah, that is where I hope you will humor me." He clasped his hands together beneath his chin. "Your father was a good friend to me. You know he was my attorney when I was in great trouble, and I mourn his death. However, I cannot bear to see you always drooping in black like a sad little starling. Will you not oblige me by coming out of mourning now? No one here will judge us for our breach of etiquette. You can honor your father in other ways. You must remember the happy times and tell me of them."

"I suppose I can do that," I said doubtfully. If only my sister, Anne, were here to help me know if it were right. Or my eldest brother, Junius, who felt it his duty to instruct everyone in proper manners. I didn't wish to be disrespectful to our father's memory, but then again, M. de Cressac now stood in my father's place, and surely what he'd asked, while not customary, was not actually inappropriate.

"Of course you can." He nodded encouragement. "You will join me for supper in the banquet hall in forty-five minutes." He strode from the room.

Mrs. Duckworth puffed and wheezed over to the paneling beside the fireplace and pressed a cunningly hidden spring. The panel whispered open, revealing an alcove lined with tall wardrobes. In the center stood a hip bath, shaped like a great shell. I should be Venus emerging from the sea on her half shell when I stood in it.

Suddenly exhaustion washed over me like a tidal wave. I yearned to take a bath right now and then go straight to bed. But I mustn't be unsociable on my first evening.

The housekeeper was sympathetic. "It's all a great deal to take in, isn't it? I tried to tell the master you might like a light supper in your room and then bed, but he would have none of it. You never can tell him anything when he's excited about something. Many's the time when he was small, I reminded him, 'Now, Master Bernard, waited-for pleasures are all the more precious for the waiting,' but he never would listen."

"You were here with M. de Cressac when he was a child?"

"Not here. But yes. I was his nurse over in France. My father had been in the wars with Napoleon, and Mother and I followed him about, first to Portugal and then to Southern France, where the de Cressacs hired me. They wanted an English nurse, you see, so Master Bernard would grow up speaking both French and English."

How odd to think of this comfortable, simple woman, who seemed as if she should like nothing better than a cozy English cottage fireside, traipsing about in foreign places.

"His English is perfect," I commented.

"Yes, indeed. I took such pains with him. And we were that fond of each other that he kept me on as housekeeper in his French estate, and when he brought Wyndriven Abbey over—oh, the crazy ways of the very rich!—he insisted I come along. Ling and Achal, the master's valet, and Alphonse, the cook, are the only other staff who have been with the master since France. Mr. Bass, the agent, came to him soon after. He's a Southerner. All the rest of the servants were purchased here."

I winced at the word "purchased," but she didn't notice. An ornate little sofa stood at an angle near the bath. I lowered myself to it now and touched the seat beside me. "Won't you sit for a minute and tell me more about everything? I've waited so long to come here, and you must know all about my godfather and this place."

Mrs. Duckworth needed no further urging. She settled herself down comfortably and continued. "Of course, I'm not familiar with the workers on the master's plantation. Wyndriven Plantation, it's called. 'Tis on the other side of Chicataw, and we haven't much to do with them."

"Master Bernard must have been a wonderful little boy for you to be so attached to him."

There followed a long description of Mrs. Duckworth's affection for, and the wonders of, dear young Master Bernard, of his French home, his seat on a pony, and his skills at fencing.

I mused that she must have loved the little boy as my family loved me. I had been spoiled too, perhaps—not materially, except for my godfather's gifts, but with an abundance of affection and attention partly because everyone wanted to make up for the fact that I never knew my mother.

Mrs. Duckworth was about to launch into a description of Master Bernard's *father's* seat on his horse and *his* accomplishments when she stopped in midsentence. "Goodness me, we'd better hurry, hadn't we? The master said forty-five minutes, and it must be nearly that now. We don't want him waiting."

I wished she hadn't stopped. I loved *knowing* things.

Mrs. Duckworth threw back the doors of one of the wardrobes. I had only a moment to gain an impression of a rainbow of dresses hanging inside before she pulled out one of muted rose plaid taffeta, trimmed with strips of black velvet.

"Either I or one of the housemaids will help you dress," she said, "until your French maid arrives."

"Oh, please. I can dress myself." In spite of my long-held belief that I was destined for luxury, it was still hard to change the habits of my lifetime.

"Dress yourself? What would Master Bernard say to that? And who would tighten your laces and button you in the back? And style your hair and look after your frocks and hose and jewelry and bags and fans? No, indeed. You'll have your maid, and someone else will help till then. She was to have been here by now, but there were complications bringing her over from France."

"Well, if I must have a lady's maid, can't I use one of the housemaids? You see, I speak little French, and an English speaker would be more comfortable for me."

"As to that, you may talk to the master, but he has strong opinions about things, and I doubt it would do you any good."

I held on to the bedpost while she pulled my laces tight. I didn't protest as I would have with Anne. Mrs. Duckworth secured my hoops and slipped the dress over my head. It was nearly sleeveless, with the merest wisp of ruffle over my shoulders, and a far lower décolletage than I had ever before worn. Of course, in high society, evening frocks were more formal than at home, and I'd grow accustomed to the top of my bosom showing and not feel so exposed, but thank goodness Harry and Junius weren't here to see. I had to admit, though, that I looked stylish and pretty.

Mrs. Duckworth opened a drawer filled with confections such as silk stockings and handkerchiefs, lacy gloves and mitts, and drew out a pair of hose. As she lowered herself painfully to her knees to help me draw them on, I touched her shoulder. "It's kind of you to help like this. And to prepare this lovely room. Was it all done over just for me?"

She looked quickly down to the stocking in her hand, but not before a shadow passed over her face. For a moment she didn't answer. Then, "The rooms were actually decorated eleven years ago by Master's wife—Madame Tatiana. She had lovely taste, but she died soon after the rooms were complete."

"I'm so sorry. Monsieur de Cressac never mentioned her death in any of his letters."

"No, well, he wouldn't have, would he, plunged in grief as he was? The master hasn't had luck with marriage. Madame Tatiana was a sweet girl, and my favorite. Russian, you know, and spoke little English, but genteel in her own foreign way. She died in childbirth and the baby went too."

My father must have been mistaken about Madame de Cressac being French. "I'm so sorry," I said again.

I stepped into satin slippers, pulled on black lace mitts, and Mrs. Duckworth led me down the winding corridors and great staircase to the echoing banquet hall.

CHAPTER 3

DINNER WITH MONSIEUR

M. de Cressac sat in a thronelike chair at the end of the refectory table, and as I entered the banquet hall, I was struck again by how good-looking he was. He waved his hand toward a seat just around the corner from him. We huddled alone together at the end of what seemed a highly polished, mile-long surface.

He gestured upward to the ceiling, two stories high. "Perhaps these walls and ceiling will be more to your liking than the so lewd ones in the Heaven chamber."

Heat rushed to my cheeks at the reminder of my *faux pas.* "Sir, forgive me for being silly. It's a beautiful room. Pray, don't—"

"No, no. Do not apologize. I am wicked to tease you. But look. Look up."

I leaned my head back and squinted. The walls were covered with tapestries—hunters and knights and court scenes. Above them, the stone of the ceiling appeared blackened and sooty and the massive beams charred. I wasn't sure what he wanted me to observe. "Was there . . . a fire here?"

"Three hundred years ago. And you can still see the effects. This is part of the original abbey. It suffered from the great monastic plunder of the sixteenth century—the abbot was so incautious as to make an unflattering remark about Anne Boleyn, and the abbey was torched. Luckily most of it was stone, so it survived. Do you see why I wanted it brought here? This country has no history. I wanted a house with history in a land where people are allowed to be who they are, without having to bow down to centuries of tradition. A delightful paradox. This new world is the perfect place."

I did not mention that I would have scrubbed the soot from the ceiling stones while they were handily down and dismantled, nor that for his slaves the new world was not at all a perfect place. "The tapestries are lovely. I admire fine needlework. Embroidery is a favorite pastime of mine." I twisted my ring around my finger. It was of chased silver and had once adorned my mother's hand. "Perhaps I could stitch you a tapestry someday? A small one, of course," I said shyly.

His attractive smile lit his face. "I am touched. I should like that of all things. It pleases me that you are a young lady of such accomplishments."

Above us was suspended a great fan attached to a rope. A small black boy pulled on the rope, causing the air to waft downward. Another boy shooed insects away from the table by means of a stick tied with flapping strips of rags. I smiled at them, but they took their jobs seriously and ignored me.

The two footmen now stood on either side of a vast fireplace. I was told their names were Charles and George. My lips twitched, although I managed not to laugh, because, as they flanked the mantel, they appeared to be bookends. Both were the same height, which was easily over six feet, had the same livery, the same coffee-colored skin, and both stared forward, expressionless, in between serving the different courses.

They offered onion soup, followed by fish; tripe with white sauce; roast suckling pig; white asparagus; game hens with sweet sauce; mutton chops; cold baked ham; a calf's head, boiled and grilled, with the brains mashed inside; and spiced pears in brandy.

Each course was accompanied by its particular spirits, served by Ling—sherry with the soup, Chablis with the fish, claret with the chops. I did not care to drink, as it was not my family's custom. Also, this place was too dreamlike and M. de Cressac confused me too much to risk addling my wits with alcohol. He and his surroundings were far outside my experience, but then, so was most everything in the world if one didn't count the places I had gone and the people I had known through books and daydreams.

I nibbled a bit of this and that and pushed food around on my plate to make it appear as if I had eaten more. Not only had I always been a picky eater, but also I feared that in this great, echoing hall my chewing would be too loud.

Evidently M. de Cressac noticed my food-shuffling. "You must be exhausted, but do try one thing," he said. "For my sake. The tripe. It is a great favorite of mine."

He laughed when I wrinkled my nose.

"The problem, you see," he said, drawing conspiratorially closer, "is that my chef, Alphonse, who, I assure you, is an *artiste,* will be offended if you do not sample his way with the sauce. He might end up prostrate on his bed, unable to cook tomorrow, and that would be a tragedy of mammoth proportions."

When he leaned so close, I feared he could see down my gown. I put my hand over my chest. He didn't appear to notice. Or—was his *not* looking a bit deliberate?

Hurriedly I said, "All right, I'll try it. A tiny bit."

He nodded to Charles, the younger footman who had grinned at me upon my arrival this afternoon, and Charles served up a sympathetic dab.

Somehow I managed to swallow some of the rubbery gray stuff without chewing. It made me cough, so my godfather offered a sip of wine, which made me choke all the more.

Once recovered from my coughing fit, to distract him from the fact that I still was hardly eating, I commented on the novelty of the foods. "We have just one servant who does most of the cooking. Bridget would be amazed how even the ham is served so beautifully, with fancy little parsley wings, as if it will fly off any moment. And so much I've never seen before. Where does it all come from?"

"Shipped from all across the world. I am so happy to be the one to introduce you to these delights. Now," he said, holding up his fork, "has Mrs. Duckworth already regaled you with tales of my youthful escapades?"

"Not escapades, precisely. More how perfect you were in every way."

"Dear old Ducky. When I was small, she saved me from a great deal of well-deserved punishment. I was too spirited for my own good, but, perhaps wrongly, she could not bear that I should ever be disciplined."

"She does believe you hung the moon." I toyed with a bit of mutton, cutting it into tiny pieces, eating a little, and scattering the rest.

In a flash my godfather made a quick move and tossed me a lustrous green, heart-shaped fruit from an immense silver compote. Somehow I caught it.

"That is soursop," he said. "I developed a taste for it in Africa, and my chief gardener has grown a productive tree here in the orangery. I built the orangery because I desire my flowers and fruits year-round. Perhaps you will like the soursop, even if you do not care for the rest of my food." His smile took away any sting there might have been in his remark.

I clutched at the napkin in my lap. "It's all wonderful, sir. Really it is, and a feast fit for royalty. But the fact is, I don't eat a great deal of heavy food. I'm sorry."

He threw his hands into the air. "Bah, what does it matter? Try the soursop."

I bit warily into the fruit for fear it would be sour, with that name, but I needn't have worried. Its flesh was firm and tasted like a combination of strawberry and pineapple, with an underlying creamy flavor. "Ambrosia," I said.

"I am happy to have pleased you."

"Oh, Monsieur, you please me in everything. Everything is perfect, just perfect."

He looked up at me through thick, dark eyelashes. "I am glad. By the way," he said softly, holding my gaze, "you have a charming speaking voice. So light and breathy."

I murmured my thanks for the compliment. Now I'd be trying to listen to myself all evening. In spite of the great fan, perspiration trickled down my chest into my cleavage. I snatched up a napkin and dabbed at it.

Naturally my godfather took note. "We battle the heat with lukewarm baths and ice and fans, but even a king would have no way to stay cool here in June." He clapped his hands. "George, bring Mademoiselle Sophia an ice. Quickly!"

George hurried from the room.

He returned shortly with a cut-glass bowl of ice cream with peaches, the first I had ever eaten. More ambrosia.

"I store the ice in a hole fifty feet down at the plantation," M. de Cressac said, a look of pleasure on his face as he watched me eat. "Someday I will take you there. It is like a crystal palace. And believe it or not, it does freeze occasionally in northern Mississippi in wintertime. When the cold comes, we must get you a set of white furs so you may be a snow queen."

I pictured myself in a fluffy white hat and muff and gave a shiver of anticipation. "You always have known what gifts would please me most. Through the years we all used to wait eagerly to see what would come next. You see, we never had much money, so when I look back on birthdays and Christmases and such, the things you sent shine in my memory like miracles."

Once we grew too old for glorious and ingenious toys, the inappropriateness of the gifts my godfather thought appropriate for our simple lifestyle had also provided amusement, but I didn't mention that. Although I myself loved lavish, pretty things, and would stroke the sumptuous fabrics and finger the jewelry, my siblings used to laugh at how excessive everything was. M. de Cressac seemed to delight in the ornate and opulent. If a brooch should have two curlicues, the one he sent me would have six. If a pair of kid half boots should have one rosette, the ones he gave me would be spotted with them.

I wondered if I ought not to speak of our poverty. But surely M. de Cressac must have known all about it. Throughout my life, the fretting regarding money had draped over my family like layers of cobweb, delicate but intrusive.

I sighed and decided to speak the complete truth. "Anne says our trouble is that we're genteel, but only in a theoretical way."

He leaned forward. "What does she mean?"

"Theoretically, we know how to wear our clothes and order dinners and—and how to ride, that sort of thing, but in practice we can't afford decent dressmakers or fine food or horses. Thank you, though, for paying for my riding lessons. I enjoyed them." I paused as I reflected on the effect our theoretic gentility had on us— endless frustration and endless yearning for those things we could not have. "But please," I continued quickly, "don't think we did without necessities or were unhappy. On the contrary, we did very well. I only wanted you to know how we appreciated your kindness."

"*Pauvre petite.*" His voice was gentle. "I worried about you. I could do so little. I would have done more, but I feared your father would not have liked it. I tried to send money once, long after his attorney fees were paid, and he returned it. His pride, you know."

Darling Papa, so gentle and weak and lovable; occasionally, however, the iron would enter his soul and he would be surprisingly stubborn about certain things.

My eyes blurred as they still often did when I thought of him.

M. de Cressac squeezed my hand. His own hand was very warm. "Ah, see how the tears yet come. Your father was a good man. I am sorry I saw him so little in late years and that he is now gone, although it brought you to me. I know I cannot replace him or be worthy to be your father, but will you allow me to be your dear friend and companion? Will you let me share my world with you and will you confide in me?"

"Of course."

He held my hand palm up to study.

"This," he said, "is a fine-boned hand made for true gentility and not the theoretical type of which you speak. It is so small and delicate; how can you even hold anything?"

I smiled and drew it back. "I promise, my hands are completely functional."

His eyes twinkled. He lifted his fork but paused with it in midair. "Ah, I nearly forgot. We must continue your lesson in cuisine. Some delectable calf brains." He started to signal for Charles.

"No, thank you!" I hastened to exclaim.

My godfather looked at me for a moment and then gave a great barking laugh. "I shall so enjoy having you here. And shall relish the challenge of teaching you about the good things in life. Do you know, you remind me of a ballerina I once met in Russia. She . . ."

He regaled me with a charming story, and I listened mesmerized, forgetting to be tired, especially since I reminded him of the beautiful ballerina in question. Had I truly not drunk any spirits? I felt intoxicated.

At the end of the tale he called over the fan and insect boys, who had also obviously been listening. "Now, Sir Tater Bug and Sir Reuben, what do you expect for your gallant efforts at keeping the mosquitoes and heat at bay?"

The boys grinned. "Candy, sir," one of them said stoutly.

M. de Cressac laughed and rubbed the boy's head. "What? No requests for calf brains from you either? Well, you are good boys and deserve your reward. Here, then."

He dug in his pocket and drew out a handful of lemon drops for each of them.

"Now," he said, "off to bed with the both of you. It is getting late, and we must manage without your services."

The boys scampered away, and I smiled at my godfather.

"His name really is Tater Bug," M. de Cressac explained. "At least I have never heard him called anything else." Suddenly he banged his fist on the table, causing me to start. "I am remiss," he said. "I have not yet thanked you for discarding the black."

I nodded in acknowledgment. "But, sir, there's no need for thanks. I must admit I was happy to have an excuse to wear pretty clothes. Black is a ghastly color on me."

He laughed again, although I wasn't sure what I had said that was funny.

"Now," he said, patting my shoulder in a fatherly way, "will you oblige me with one more thing?"

Again I nodded, waiting.

"This 'sir' business—must we stand on formality? May we not be good friends? I call you Sophia; won't you call me by my given name, Bernard, *s'il vous plaît?* Yes, I am your godfather, but you make me feel an old, old man when you look up with those great, trusting blue eyes and address me as 'Monsieur' this and 'sir' that in an oh-so-deferential tone. You make me seem at least eighty. Do I appear to be eighty to you?"

"Now, you know you don't. How absurd! Why, I don't believe you can be much above—thirty." I switched from saying "forty" at the last moment, since I had no idea how old he actually was and didn't wish to offend. Although it had been he who had called himself an old man in his invitation letter. "And you appear to be strong and in excellent health."

"Diplomatically put," he said wryly. "My gout and lumbago rarely keep me crippled long. And I am very strong indeed, as I might perhaps show you someday."

I peeked up at him and was relieved that his amber eyes danced.

"But tell me," he continued, "will you not call me Bernard?"

"I should like to oblige, sir, but would it be fitting when you stand in place of a father to me?"

"The devil with 'fitting.' It is what I wish, and I warn you I am persistent in getting what I want."

"Then you have been very spoiled," I said sternly, and immediately wondered if I should have. I was teasing, but some people wouldn't have understood. I simply had no practice in how to behave out in the world. I considered myself a modern girl, and back in our home I was allowed to be more spirited and free-speaking than my mother would have been at my age. However, I still believed in abiding by society's traditional rules as long as I understood the reason for them. Of course the world was a much nicer place when people practiced respect and consideration and morality. Thankfully, my godfather was smiling at my words, so he was not offended. Onward, then. I tossed my head. "And why 'warn' me? Should I be wary of your wishes?"

"Hopefully not." His voice was soft.

I looked to see if he was still smiling. Now he was not.

Suddenly he shrugged. "Besides, you are too young to be concerned with what is 'fitting.' You should be enjoying life. There is a poem in Latin by the great Horace: *Carpe diem, quam minimum credula postero.* Translated it means: 'Pluck the day, trusting as little as possible in the future.' Plucking the day is my philosophy."

I made no comment on this way of thinking, since it sounded quite irresponsible. "Perhaps I might address you as Uncle Bernard. Would that do?"

" 'Uncle.' No. I will not be called your *uncle*. Dashed if I'll be an uncle!" His eyes flashed with pretend indignation.

It might be as much fun to tease and be teased by my godfather as it was with my brother Harry. "Then perhaps *Monsieur* Bernard," I suggested.

"*Mais oui,* an excellent solution. For now."

The dinner lasted till nearly eleven o'clock.

"Oh, *mon chaton,*" he said at last. "My poor sleepy kitten can barely keep her eyes open. Come and kiss me good night, then, and Charles will show you back to your room."

I leaned in to him a little stiffly since he was still practically a stranger, and I bravely kissed his cheek. It was not terrible, being the extraordinarily attractive cheek it was, after all. Quite the opposite.

Charles led me to my chamber, where a yawning housemaid waited. The girl helped me undress and don a rather revealing but beautiful silken night shift. She braided my hair without comment, except to tell me her name was Talitha. She was a pretty girl in an exotic way, tall and willowy, with golden undertones to her dark skin, wearing a simple black dress along with a snowy apron and head kerchief.

"You must be worn out by this time of night," I said. "Do they work you awfully hard?"

She seemed startled to be asked such a question. She paused before speaking, as if weighing how she ought to answer. "It ain't too bad," she said finally. "Better than pulling out joint grass from the cotton fields."

"Oh, yes," I said. "If that's the other choice. But I'm sorry to have kept you up late."

I had watched the field hands on my way here. The heat-hazed landscape had been dotted with bent figures of women and girls wearing faded prints and rags on their heads, of men and boys in homespun shirtsleeves and limp hats, hoeing and pulling weeds and picking off bugs. I pitied them for their hard work in this heat. I pitied them for their ghastly clothing.

This Talitha must be close to my age. Could we talk to each other sometimes? At least a little bit? I tried again. "Having your hair up in a kerchief must be much cooler than the way I do mine. Mine is so hot on the neck."

She didn't vouchsafe this attempt with any comment. She simply raised her beautifully arched eyebrows slightly to acknowledge my words and turned back the covers of the bed. When I was tucked in, she pulled the mosquito netting canopy down to the bedposts.

A great buzzing swelled from outside. I bolted straight up. "What's that sound?"

Talitha's lips quirked in what appeared to be amusement. "Them be cicadas. A kind of bug in the trees."

"They're going to drive me insane."

She shrugged. "You get used to them."

"Good night," I said, but she was already sweeping regally from the room.

Instantly I clambered from bed, getting myself tangled in the netting on the way. I turned the key in the door. I needed the security of a lock between myself and that vast maze of rooms.

I heaved a sigh of relief, as if I had accomplished a great feat to be standing there, prepared for bed. I had left the bosom of my family to travel by rail and by coach, had seen new sights, eaten new foods, and made a few new acquaintances. It was indeed an achievement for a girl such as me who had always been sheltered from the outside world.

While I knelt by the bed to pray, I absently twisted the ring on my finger. It fell jingling to the marble floor and bounced under the bedstead. I lowered the lamp to reveal it lying there deep in the recesses. By wriggling myself partially under, I reached it, and was edging back out when something caught my eye. I peered closer at the inner leg of the bed. There, scratched into the opalescent paint, was a name—Adele.

But wasn't M. Bernard's wife named Tatiana? Maybe a house-maid had done it, might have scratched her own name. What a foolish thing—anyone seeing it would know who the culprit was, and she would be promptly punished.

I blew out the lamp and slipped between fragrant sheets, silky to the touch. My toes glided instead of catching on the fabric as they had at home. *Fine-twined linen,* I thought. That was in the Bible. Unless it was in Shakespeare. Who could keep them straight?

Outside, the incessant cicadas droned. Inside, some large insect fluttered against the netting.

What were my family's cozy evenings like now in our gaunt, gray stone house, without their little sister to tell them funny stories or to tease Harry about his dandy's clothes or to play the piano while they sang? I had always been surrounded by people who cherished me. Homesick tears welled behind my closed eyelids. I wiped them on the fine-twined linen. I must remember I was here for my sib-lings' sake as much as for my own.

The smell from the waxy, whiter-than-white camellias on the mantel was too strong. Their scent cloyed. Suffocated. Once again I dislodged myself from the netting, careful not to let the insect in. I padded across cool, smooth marble and then sank into the velvety plush of the rug, removed the vase, set it outside on my balcony, and returned to bed.

It was too hot. I kicked off the covers. Now I was too exposed and vulnerable. At last I compromised by pulling the sheet across my middle but leaving legs and arms bare.

CHAPTER 4

UNLOCKED DOORS

"*Bonjour,* Sophia."

Below me, my godfather had stepped out onto the terrace and was gazing up at my balcony. He was in his shirtsleeves, with the collar open. A lock of black hair fell across his forehead. In the sunlight he looked young and energetic and so handsome my limbs went weak.

I realized I still wore my meager night shift and quickly crossed my arms over the front. I had been so transfixed by the view it hadn't occurred to me that anyone might observe me.

Evidently my prudish actions amused him because there was laughter in his voice when he called up, "It is a beautiful morning, no? The picture of a June day. I regret I shall not be joining you until tonight. Too much business, alas. Mortgages and stock yields. Bah! But I will see you at supper. Make yourself at home, *ma chérie.*"

He disappeared back into the house.

Once he strode safely out of sight, the vista, which I had stepped out to see, drew from me an exclamation of delight.

Directly below lay a terrace with blood-red roses swarming over the stone balustrade. Beyond that, set out in a variety of shades of green, was a topiary garden, the dense foliage sculpted into amazing shapes. The largest were a life-sized elephant, a giraffe, and a lion, but dozens of other figures spiked up in frames of boxwood— human figures, obelisks and pyramids, cones and tapering swirls. The people shapes were a bit disturbing—alive yet not alive, and eyeless. What could I give them for eyes? I thought of roses, and the image made me laugh.

Pristine flower gardens reached down to a little lake, spotted with swans and spanned by a Palladian bridge, with columns and classical symmetry. Beyond the vast expanse of lake and lawn and parkland, trees stretched on forever. The estate was ringed with a wall of wildwood that crouched, waiting its chance to take over the cleared land once again.

The sky was still tinted pinky gold from dawn. A mockingbird landed, singing, on the rail nearby, and I breathed in a lungful of already-warm air perfumed by roses and pine needles. This was a beautiful place, and I was happy, happy, happy.

I went inside, leaving my doors open to sun and sweet air. What to do now? I had no idea how a day here began. I should have slept in longer, since, from all the novels and serial stories I had read, that was the way of ladies of leisure. But I was too excited to drift off again.

My trunk waited beside the fireplace. I unlocked the door in case the maid should come, and I began unpacking my belongings, spreading them about. My books went on the desk. I touched the tooled blue leather cover, stamped in silver, of *Grimm's Fairy Tales.*

Wyndriven Abbey might well be the castle in any one of them. My mother's miniature belonged on the night table and my workbasket beside a chair. Perhaps they weren't so fine and didn't match the underwater grotto theme, but they made the lovely room seem more truly my own. I needed pieces of home in this place.

The tall jewelry box, a long-ago gift from my godfather, now stood on a chest of drawers. It was of Chinese design in black and gold lacquer, with drawers behind latched doors. In it glittered the jewelry he had sent me throughout the years, a few small childhood treasures, my godfather's epistles to me, and the only love letters I had ever received. I opened the bottom drawer to make sure I had indeed tucked in Felix's letters.

Felix, my father's young law clerk, had been sweet on me the year I was fifteen. There were several notes. I didn't care for him in that way, but I didn't discourage him because I liked having an admirer and he was the only boy I knew. At last, taking pity on him, Anne made me write, instructing me to tell "the poor mooncalf" that I was too young for such things. But I reread his words sometimes, and in spite of the fact that Felix was only a couple of years older and equally inexperienced in the ways of romance, they were precious to me. He waxed awkwardly lyrical about my midnight blue eyes and skin like peaches and cream. A girl couldn't help but be flattered. Especially a girl who worried about her complexion. He had scrawled his notes on scraps of legal paper, which amused me at the time, as the *Ladies' Monthly Assistant* assured that "for love letters good paper is indispensable." What would the worthy Mrs. Ophelia Taylor think of poor Felix's missives?

As for "peaches and cream," I placed my two jars of Dew of

Venus lotion on the dressing table. I had bought them months ago in hopes they would erase my scattered freckles, but at home I never remembered to slather it on. Here I would remember. This was my chance to improve myself. To become elegant and gracious. And interesting.

"Who will I be here?" The words jarred the muggy air. My hand flew over my mouth as Talitha, the housemaid from last night, entered.

"Master say I am to help you dress and take you down to breakfast, Miss."

She brought water for a sponge bath and then assisted me into fresh drawers and chemise. She laced up my corset and topped it with a camisole trimmed with *broderie anglaise.*

I tried to engage her in conversation once again. "Have you any family, Talitha?"

"A sister," she said shortly. "But not here."

Next came stockings and garters and a flounced petticoat topped by my hoop, and finally a morning frock. As she dressed me, I made a few more attempts to get her talking, but she answered either in monosyllables or not at all.

The dress was so roomy that Talitha had to find a sash to pull it in, while the pair of beaded slippers she held out pinched my feet. Whoever had purchased my wardrobe had bought in several sizes. The maid brushed back my hair in two smooth wings over my ears, although the humidity would soon make it frizz, then plaited and coiled it and tucked it into a snood. My grooming was completed with pearl earrings and a ribbon about my neck.

Mrs. Duckworth joined me for breakfast in a small (for this

house) morning room. "Normally I eat in my own quarters, but I thought you might like a bit of company for your first breakfast here," she said.

Gay sunshine poured in through floor-to-ceiling windows, sending lights twinkling through cut crystal and silver and sparkling in the jarred jams and jellies on the sideboard. The walls were covered in hand-painted Chinese silk, with blue and green landscapes composed of mist-shrouded mountains and waterfalls, willow trees and winding paths. I wondered what lay at the end of those alluring roads.

Through the glass doors beckoned a glorious day for exploration.

"It's so pretty outside," I told Mrs. Duckworth. "I'm going to stroll through the grounds after breakfast." Imagine living in a house with "grounds."

"I don't expect you'll have time today," she said. "Master Bernard's orders are that I am to give you a tour of the house this morning. The parts I can, of course, for I haven't all the keys, but there's still more than enough to boggle the mind. And then, this afternoon, Madame Duclos will arrive. She's traveled all the way from New Orleans to measure you for your wardrobe."

I lifted my hands in a helpless gesture. "Really and truly, Mrs. Duckworth, I've got more than enough. My head's all in a twirl."

"Oh, no, no, my dear." She shook her head violently. "You cannot disappoint the master in his plans. Only think—morning dresses and walking dresses and evening dresses. A whole long list Master Bernard has made."

"Well then, do you think the dressmaker will allow me to help a little with the designing and sewing? I'm quite good at it."

Mrs. Duckworth was scandalized. "Certainly not. She'll take your measurements and show you fabrics and trims and fashion plates, but then she'll bundle the whole kit and kaboodle back to New Orleans and you won't see it until it's done."

I seated myself and reached for a beaten biscuit and saucer of marmalade. "My sister, Anne, and I used to laugh at all the specific outfits a high-society lady is expected to own. We would pore over fashion plates and read them aloud. Receiving dresses for the morning and receiving dresses for the afternoon and promenading dresses for walking in the park and promenading dresses for walking at the seaside. Wouldn't it be nice to have nothing to do but change clothes? Why, do you suppose I ought to be wearing a marmalade gown in which to eat marmalade?"

Mrs. Duckworth didn't crack a smile. She remained serious, concerned lest I not appreciate the delights in store for me.

"Master Bernard says you are even to have a ball gown."

"Oh? Truly? Will there be a ball? Does Monsieur de Cressac entertain much?"

"No, no, not now, but back in France . . . such interesting festivities he hosted. Once he held a soiree in honor of some Grecian marbles he had acquired. All the guests wore gauzy togas and powdered their skin and hair pure white. Like statues themselves, you see? Some who did not understand might have thought their costumes too scanty, but oh, it was a sight! Master Bernard resembled one of those Grecian gods. With a wreath of leaves in his hair." She nodded in reminiscence, then remembered our subject. "But he's ordered a gown for you, which makes me wonder if he's planning a ball at which to present you to local society."

She offered this last with a smile that completely closed her eyes, as though she expected the prospect of a ball would be the *pièce de résistance* for all my girlish hopes and dreams. As it should be for a seventeen-year-old girl, and as indeed, once I recovered from the picture of my godfather decked out in leaves, it was for me. I rewarded her expectations by giving my shoulders a delighted shiver. "I'm so happy to be here. Monsieur de Cressac is kindness itself. I shall hardly know how to go on with so many new clothes—it will quite turn my head. And a ball! Do you really think he might hold a ball?"

"I should think it likely for your sake. You're very young, and he knows you would enjoy such a thing, though in all the years he's lived in Mississippi, it's never before happened. I've never seen him like this, even—but that's neither here nor there. The master isn't fond of local society; he says the Southern aristocracy is without true culture, and according to him, all Mississippi gentlemen do is drink whiskey and hunt and play poker."

"And chew tobacco," I chimed in. "The hem of my traveling skirt is gummed up with brown tobacco juice from the floor of the stage-coach I rode on in Tennessee. Disgusting. It was as if the men didn't care where they spat."

The housekeeper nodded in sympathy. "Not truly civilized, these people, whether they've acquired new money or not. Our Molly is a wonder with the laundry, though, and she'll get your skirt clean. Anyway, as I was saying, the master's not a great one for close friendships, but then, he's had his disappointments in life, poor man, so he keeps to himself. However, there are several suitable families within thirty miles who would jump at the chance to attend a ball here. Mr. Bass—the master's agent—tells me they're interested in everything to do with the master and the house."

Given human nature, he was probably right. Twenty-five years ago it must have been the talk of the town when dray after dray arrived, lugging the stones of the abbey.

With a sigh, I glanced out the windows at the inviting morning, then turned resolutely back to my second biscuit, on which I had spread greenish preserves. Mrs. Duckworth told me they were made from scuppernong, a type of Southern grape. "All right, we'll start on the house. I hope I shan't have to be led about for many more days. This place is so enormous and all perfectly kept. I don't know how you do it."

The housekeeper's bosom visibly swelled. "Ah, well, that's as it must be. The master demands perfection, and I do my best to see that the staff delivers it." She fiddled with her chatelaine, making the many keys clink. "But I'm not as young as I used to be, although I must manage well enough, for Master Bernard says he cannot imagine what he would do without me. And it's not only the housekeeping he trusts me with." She lowered her voice. "There's so few he can confide in. He is so very happy to have *you* here now. Why, this morning he was whistling before breakfast. Can you believe that?"

I thought how M. Bernard had looked on the terrace and could well believe it. I idly tugged up the lace at my bosom. "I hope I can live up to his expectations."

"Oh, you'll do fine. Your youth is to your advantage. You're moldable and not at all like . . . some people."

We began the tour after I snatched up a fan to flutter as we walked. The humidity wrapped around me like a warm, damp cloth.

I was led through salons and hallways, a sculpture gallery full of chilly marble statues, and a library with thousands of volumes behind glass doors and an enormous Irish wolfhound snoozing on a tiger-skin rug before the hearth. We wandered up wide, stately staircases and narrow, winding ones.

We crossed acres of floors of marble or polished wood with elaborate inlaid veneers. I marveled at mahogany furnishings, heavily carved and gilded, at rich upholsteries in scarlet or sapphire, emerald or gold, at urns and vases of ormolu or porcelain, at walls with white and gold paneling or with gloriously painted scenes.

Wide-eyed, I took in all the themed chambers decorated to display treasures from my godfather's travels. I learned that it wasn't just depictions of plump, puffy bare flesh that embarrassed me. I was also disturbed by spare, skinny, carved wooden African statues with exaggerated bits of their anatomy poking out. Or perhaps they weren't exaggerated? How should I know?

Mrs. Duckworth was able to impart a good deal of information about many objects—their source, value, and history. "I ask Master Bernard about them. I like to know. It makes me care for them better somehow. He's always patient, always ready to share his knowledge."

Sometimes a housemaid would be laboring away in a room, scrubbing or dusting. When we walked in, she would glance up furtively without ever pausing in her task.

To one poor servant, Mrs. Duckworth barked out, "What are you about, girl? Are you stupid? You can't use beeswax on a gilded armoire." How different the housekeeper's voice sounded then—harsh and screeching.

The girl jumped and muttered, "I so sorry, Miz Duckworth."

The only other time the housekeeper paid attention to a servant was when she introduced me to a woman named Daphne, who was putting the last touches on a vast, billowing flower arrangement on a hall table. Daphne was squat and toadlike and bright of eye, and she walked with the use of a knobby cane. She made me think of a homely fairy working her magic with blooms. She beamed at us and we beamed back. Later I learned she was the single slave the housekeeper entertained in her private apartments for tea. "Isn't it peculiar to have people always about but to act as if they don't exist?" I asked.

"It's the true order of the world," Mrs. Duckworth said complacently. "Don't worry," she added, patting my arm, "you'll soon become used to the ways of the very genteel."

In my family home we always spoke with friendly civility to Bridget and felt a mutual fondness between us. She took care of us and we took care of her. The world at Wyndriven Abbey was exalted far above my old life. Would I ever learn to practice the snobbery that would be expected of me here? I wouldn't. I simply couldn't. I was too interested in everyone and their stories to discount them as people.

"Don't you wonder, though," I asked Mrs. Duckworth, "what the servants are thinking?"

"Oh, they're not thinking. They're simple creatures. Not like us. But one can't help knowing a few things. Charles is wooing Talitha, for instance. I'm forever finding them together and having to chase him off. If it keeps up much longer, I shall have to speak to Master Bernard about it."

"Can't they marry? They're old enough, surely."

"Oh, they could jump the broom at Christmastime, if the master approves. That's a slave custom they pretend means they're husband and wife. Foolishness."

From what I had seen of Charles and Talitha, they seemed a perfect match, both of them with natural grace and beauty. They would have such darling children. But who knew what heartaches and rebellious thoughts brooded inside them when confronted with such attitudes as Mrs. Duckworth's? If I could, I would help Charles and Talitha.

"Is there a Mr. Duckworth?" I asked suddenly.

The housekeeper turned flustered, rattling her keys. "Why—why I never thought of marriage for myself. Too busy with more important things. The 'Mrs.' is an honorary title customarily given to housekeepers."

As she spoke, we entered the section of the house that comprised the former abbey. An ancient, unclean smell met us as soon as we crossed the threshold, which was seven feet wide—the width of the medieval retaining walls. It reeked of dark, secret crevices—a mixture of mildew and fungus, rot and decay.

"I do my best," Mrs. Duckworth complained when she saw my expression, "but try as I might, I can't get rid of that stink. I've tried carbolic soap and turpentine and pomanders everywhere."

"The cloves and cinnamon smell lovely," I said, although they couldn't hide the stench underneath.

The stone walls might be covered with rich paneling, but drops of moisture collected on surfaces, and in places a faint, fuzzy gray film grew. I shrugged. All part of the fascinating Gothic charm.

"My greatest fear is mushrooms sprouting in hidden corners," Mrs. Duckworth confided.

I nodded sympathetically. Indoor fungus was truly fearsome.

Once there had been dormitories and cloisters, but long ago those areas had been converted to the usage of a secular household. Once this had been a sacred place, but it had long since been desecrated.

I remembered the heroine Catherine, in *Northanger Abbey,* questioning George about supernatural phenomena. I had always thought Catherine and I would have been good friends, and now we even had abbeys in common. I decided to try similar questions with the housekeeper.

"Does the house have a ghost, Mrs. Duckworth?" I asked.

"Certainly not!" she said.

"A vampire?" I couldn't resist.

"Neither I nor the master would stand for such a thing." She briskly swished her alpaca skirt as she entered the next room. I had offended her. I wondered, though; the stage here was clearly set for phantoms. How could there possibly not be one?

She began to puff and wheeze as she walked.

"Would you like to stop and rest?" I asked.

"No, Miss," she said. "We'd never get through if I gave out when I felt a bit winded."

Eventually she was too breathless to speak much.

On and on we explored. At first I had tried to mentally map out

the rooms in relation to one another, but I was soon hopelessly confused and gave up. The housekeeper pointed out various locked
doors that she did not open. How was it that among all the glories
of this place, those forbidden spaces interested me most? I was a
goose.

She indicated the double doors closing off the east wing. "You'll
hear workmen hammering and sawing in there, but the connecting
doors are kept locked."

As we passed a door in an upstairs hall she said, "That leads to
the attics." She leaned in toward me. "They're full of items that the
master desired me to burn, but I can't bear the waste. I have them
taken up there and he's no more the wiser."

So, the faithful housekeeper had her secrets, and there were corners of Wyndriven Abbey of which its master was unaware.

The portrait gallery was lined with three hundred years' worth of
paintings of the abbey's former owners. My godfather had "bor-
rowed" all these ancestors. Next to M. Bernard's portrait, however,
a rectangular, faded patch gaped on the wall.

"Was that where Monsieur Bernard's wife's portrait hung?" I
asked.

"Various ladies' pictures have hung there," Mrs. Duckworth said
stiffly. "The master has been married more than once. He does not
care to have painful memories thrust upon him, however, so the
paintings have been removed."

I would have asked more, but I saw from Mrs. Duckworth's
compressed lips that there would come no more information at this
time. *More than once,* she had said. How many marriages? And if there
were no ghosts, perhaps there was a mad wife shut up in one of the

locked places? Maybe in the east wing, allegedly under renovation? It would be amusing (albeit tragic) to imagine a suitably mad wife for M. Bernard. Hah! Secrets waiting to be uncovered. This house lent itself to mysteries. Eventually I hoped to poke about without Mrs. Duckworth.

It took us two hours to tour the house, moving constantly. By the end I was numb, except for my feet, which hurt from treading in tight slippers. I could no longer think up admiring comments.

There was such a thing as too many paintings composed of graphic scenes from the Old Testament and mythology. There was such a thing as too much grandeur, too much opulence and curlicues and gold leaf. Too many rooms to be the dwelling of one man and, now, one girl.

CHAPTER 5

FASHIONS

A swarthy, capable-looking woman with a surprisingly dark mustache burst through the doorway of my bedchamber in the late afternoon. Behind her staggered the footmen, bearing bolts of fabric, beading, ribbons, and laces, which they deposited on the wide ottoman.

The dressmaker nodded with satisfaction as she looked me up and down. "It will be a pleasure," she said, "to create for a *demoiselle* such as Mademoiselle Petheram."

Mme. Duclos spread out fashion plates from *Le Petit Courrier des Dames* and proceeded to make my head swim with all her plans for my wardrobe. I ran my fingers over the bolts of muslin, cambric, tarlatan, brocade, and silk.

There were to be day dresses and evening dresses in tulle and grenadine, trimmed with ribbons, an outdoor frock in gooseberry green and black taffeta with wide stripes, a riding habit in russet surah. Madame rattled off descriptions of pagoda sleeves and engageantes. There were to be Norwich shawls and paisley shawls and lace shawls and jackets and mantelets and cloaks. If Mademoiselle would permit, Mme. Duclos would arrange with a milliner she knew, of wonderful taste and artistry, to create for Mademoiselle such bonnets and hats that would set off her coloring *extraordinaire.*

She took my measurements, and I held up this fabric to see how it hung and ran my hand over that one to see how it felt. So many options. I did request an emerald green silk evening gown with jet beads stitched in the skirt, but other than that, I mostly let Madame do the choosing. Who would have thought that I, Sophia Petheram, could feel almost ill at the thought of so many dresses, as from a surfeit of sweets? I was sure to recover quickly, however, and be sorry later that I hadn't expressed more opinions.

After the dressmaker left, I sat on the ottoman and brushed the crushed white velvet with my hand. Without the pearls stitched in, it would have felt so soft—like a pet to stroke. Pure, pure white. My pet polar bear ottoman. I grinned, but stopped smiling as I peered closer.

Something was wound around the base of a pearl. A thread from one of the bolts of cloth? I worked at it with my fingernails, then drew out the small scissors I always carried in a sewing kit in my pocket. I managed to snip an end. Carefully I unwound a two-foot length of hair. Because that's what it was—a fine, thin strand of reddish hair. Not my shade. I lay the strand on the white velvet. It was more of a strawberry blond, the pale pinky gold of this morning's sunrise. Tatiana?

Or Adèle?

Now, why did that name spring to mind?

I opened and closed the scissors in my hand. The strand could not, of course, belong to a Negro maid. And besides, a maid wouldn't have dared to scrape her name into the paint of the bed. Could Adele have been one of my godfather's wives—the French one my father had mentioned—and she had scratched her name in order to leave her mark? But no, the timing was wrong. For Adele to have etched her name there, she would have had to have been here *after* Tatiana decorated the room, eleven years ago. My father had mentioned M. Bernard having a French wife back when he met him twenty years earlier. How many wives had my godfather outlived?

If I were to jump to conclusions, as I often dared to do, it seemed at least three. M. Bernard indeed was unlucky in his marriages. Sadly, early deaths happened all too often. Why, in Boston my father knew a man who lost four wives one after the other, all in childbirth, and another whose five children were all taken with cholera in a single month's time.

Of course, the hair might have been left by a guest. Adele might also have been a guest. I didn't actually have a smidgen of knowledge of any facts. But naturally that didn't stop me.

The hair might have circled around the pearl accidentally, in some odd fluke of a way. Or had someone—this mysterious red-headed lady—absentmindedly wound the strand around the button with her fingers? Or she might have done it on purpose, winding it round and round, so that, like the person who had scratched her name into the bedpost, something of herself would be left behind.

Without knowing why, except that I had always felt a sense of kinship with other redheaded people, I placed the single hair into an envelope and tucked it beneath the blotter on the desk.

Although it was not yet five o'clock, I unfastened and removed my hoop and my dress, sponged myself with cool water, dragged back the coverlet on the bed, and slipped inside, pulling the sheets over my head.

How strange that I should feel so . . . strange. It was silly to be disturbed by finding the hair. After all, generations of women had lived and died in Wyndriven Abbey in its various phases of existence. I knew that, of course. What bothered me was the fact that my godfather's wives were so recent—and the strand was a shade of red.

However, the hair wasn't the only reason for my disquiet. Knowing my past predilection for luxury, I should be in raptures to reside in such surroundings, showered with lovely things. But everything was too much. It was as if the world here were coated with glamour, as in some fairy tales, with nothing really as it seemed.

I mentally shook myself and stretched out my arms. Whoever those women were, their fate would not be mine. I was very much alive and well and intended to stay that way. I had been offered this opportunity and was not going to mope. M. Bernard's philosophy was a good one for my present circumstances. *Carpe diem!* I would pluck the day, whatever that meant.

"Miss Sophia!"

Mrs. Duckworth sounded surprised to find me huddled in bed. "Are you feeling ill?"

"No, ma'am." I poked my head out.

"You *will* go down to supper with the master, won't you?" Her hands wrung the hem of her apron.

"Of course."

She relaxed and bobbed her head. "Good. I'd hate to tell him you weren't coming. He has a treat planned, and it's time you dressed for it. He has made a special request for your outfit."

"For my outfit?"

"Yes, indeed." She gave a little chuckle. "You'll be a trifle surprised. Master has always had particular tastes and is *that* determined about them."

I followed her to the wardrobe now, curious.

Mrs. Duckworth brought forth an odd foreign costume.

It consisted of pieces much too small or too sheer to cover me properly. There was a skirt of gossamer silk, the color of bluebells and heavily embroidered, a short blouse embellished with silver beads, and a gauzy shawl or veil.

I eyed the garments doubtfully. "They're pretty, but I've never worn anything like them. They're a bit . . . sparse of material."

From the way Mrs. Duckworth clicked her tongue, I knew she was displeased. "You can't believe the master would *ever* require anything that was improper. He has prepared several foreign outfits for you that are different from what you are accustomed to, but not ill judged, and surely you'll humor him by wearing them. He's a man of fancies—it comes of having traveled so much. They remind him of places he's been and times he remembers fondly."

Did I have a choice? One always has a choice. I could snatch an evening gown from the wardrobe and put it on myself. I could announce that I wouldn't go down to dinner and then sit sulking in my bedchamber all night.

Some mischievous spirit entered me. *Carpe diem!* Monsieur's fancies were simply part of his quest for the picturesque and unusual. Unlike other garments in the wardrobe, the costume would certainly fit and be comfortable. One could not don a corset or hoop with it, after all. And I would like to see myself as an Indian girl. Besides, except for the bare stomach, this outfit was not unlike the costume Mrs. Amelia Bloomer, the dress reformer, was currently promoting. I insisted on wearing my camisole beneath the midriff-baring top, however.

"Now," Mrs. Duckworth said, "I do believe—yes, there it is—here is a box of accessories meant to adorn it."

Silver bangles, a gem-set tiara representing the sun, moon-shaped earrings, and a starry pendant were nestled in the crinkly tissue paper of the jewelry case she handed me. There was also a single hoop that might be a nose ring. It I left in the tissue.

Surveyed in the eight-foot pier-glass mirror, my outfit was both interesting and quaint, although it would have had smoother lines without the camisole. My godfather would tease me about it, of course.

I studied my reflection, partly wanting the reassurance that I still looked like me and partly hoping I would have changed at least a little in this setting.

I was only Sophie turned out in foreign clothes.

As I entered the banquet hall, my godfather's eyes twinkled when he took in the camisole, but to my surprise, he made no comment. Instead, he called me his lovely Morgiana. He told me that Indian dancing girls wore this clothing, their jewelry jangling as they twirled, and that the blouse was known as a *choli*.

"English missionaries introduced it to the women of India," he said. "The parsons were too distracted from their good work by bare breasts. Evidently they did not mind the bare belly."

Men in Boston did not discuss bosoms in mixed company. And hopefully not in masculine company either. At least my brothers didn't. I tried not to register discomfiture at his allusion to them. Instead, I said, "It's very comfortable." Then the silly, naughty spirit reared itself again, urging me to say something scandalous myself. "Of course, anything would be comfortable beside whalebone corsets that one can hardly cough in—or even *breathe* in—and petticoats and crinolines that one can hardly sit in. Why, I have nearly fallen countless times because I can't see where my feet are stepping." I watched his face to see what he thought of my mentioning unmentionables.

He lowered his eyes lazily to the area of my skirt. "Are you wearing underdrawers with this *ensemble*? The Indian maidens would not, you know."

"They *what*?" I was thrown into confusion. "Of course I am—of course I'm wearing them," I said, almost spluttering.

"Oh, Sophia, *ma belle*," he said as he adjusted my tiara before sweeping one hand through my hair, "how long has it been since I told you that you were a delight? A whole day? I am remiss! An hour should not go by."

I began to sit down at the table, although it wasn't set for dinner. M. Bernard stopped me.

"No, we are not eating here. I have prepared a little surprise for you. Come."

He took my arm and led me down a corridor to glass doors opening onto the veranda. Outside, dusk had fallen and mellow violet air enfolded us. Lighted Moroccan lanterns lined a path leading down the veranda steps. We stepped upon the golden glow.

M. Bernard didn't speak and neither did I. Speech would have spoiled the expectant hush. We rounded a thick stand of towering evergreen trees.

I gasped. What I beheld was a dazzling sight. A building rose ahead—a building of light.

"It is the orangery," M. Bernard whispered. "We dine there tonight."

A thousand candles blazed behind glass walls.

CHAPTER 6

THE GHOST GIRL

"I used to plague my father to tell me all he knew of you," I said, leaning back against the cushions (so much easier to sprawl when one wore dancing-girl clothes).

"Poor Martin. He knew little of me beyond our business together. Was he driven to make up tales to satisfy you?"

"No. I did that for myself."

"Tell me some, Morgiana. Or should I call you Scheherazade?"

And so I did. I told of how I imagined him fighting rebellious Mongol tribesmen and living among the Bedouins. How, to me, he had found lost Atlantis and studied with Tibetan monks.

He laughed, but I could tell he was pleased. "You fancied me quite the hero."

"I wasn't disappointed when I met you yesterday. I still fancy you quite the hero. Of course, I often put myself in your stories as well."

"I am glad. Since I fancy you quite the heroine. That is why I created this fairyland for you tonight."

I basked in our surroundings. My heart swelled so at the beauty that it was almost painful. Slender tapers were wired in all the orange and lemon and lime trees planted in great earthen pots lining the room, and the brilliant skins of the citrus fruits as well as the glass walls reflected the flames. Splendid silken cushions filled our dining bower, bordered with scarlet flowering vines twined over lattice.

We reclined upon the pillows and supped from foods spread on an enormous brass tray. Even the meal was magical. Cakes, so light and airy it seemed they might float away; cubes of pale, creamy cheeses that melted in my mouth; vegetables dipped in spicy sauce; pastel fruit that tasted of sunlight in far lands.

"I wanted you to be able to try new dishes without trepidation tonight," he said. "No unexpected meats. No squid intestines. Not tonight anyway."

"Thank you."

"And here, drink this." He tilted a metal pitcher enameled with bright flowers and poured golden liquid into a matching goblet. "It is called metheglin—honey mead flavored with lavender. A beverage favored by fairies."

As I sipped, I idly wondered if it were alcoholic, but I was so enraptured I didn't care.

Achal, M. Bernard's valet, sat cross-legged behind a carved and pierced screen, playing a queer stringed instrument. It was a sitar, M. Bernard told me. Achal was an Indian man, probably older than middle-aged, but as slender and slight as a young boy, wearing a long tunic and pale, tight trousers. His music was haunting.

The very air sparkled. At least it did to me.

As I reached for another cake, a movement in the glass wall halted me. I peered closer. It was my own reflection—a ghostly Sophia, pale and insubstantial, watching us with the darkness pooling behind her eyes.

"I toured the house today," I told M. Bernard quickly, so I would stop looking at the ghost girl.

"And what did you think of it?"

"It's incredible, fascinating, beautiful. Also mysterious. I don't have enough words to tell you all I thought of it."

"That was why I needed to own it."

He told me how, years earlier, when he first laid eyes on Wyndriven Abbey over in England, he knew it must be his. And then when he traveled to Mississippi for the first time, and saw this land, he determined to live in it here. He had recently returned from Persia, and the lush green of the American South, he said, enchanted him after the desert, like drinking water after a long thirst. He bought the land from a Choctaw Indian and then brought Wyndriven Abbey over. Most men would have believed such a thing impossible, but not my godfather.

I wondered about the noble family who had once inhabited the abbey. Perhaps it had become a burden to them and they were happy to be out from under it. Still, had it been painful to lose it first to M. Bernard and then to see it ripped from its original location? But then, they had wrested it from the Church, so it was turnabout. It must be the way of things throughout history—wins and losses.

"Did you bring over the furnishings as well?" I asked.

"I did. Every bit of it just as the former owners had left it. They wanted nothing from the place. For weeks after everything was finally here, I explored what I owned. China in the cupboards and boxes of yellowed papers in the muniment room and linens in chests and presses. I even found a parcel no one had ever bothered to unwrap."

"What was in it?"

"In what?"

"The parcel."

"Shaving supplies. Nothing thrilling."

"What a shame. It should have been jewels." I took a bite of cake. "Do you ever wonder how the stones felt to find themselves in Mississippi instead of the English countryside? It must have been a shock."

M. Bernard nodded. "I am hoping it was a pleasant surprise. I hope they are still reveling in their good, stony fortune. English winters can be most unpleasant. Do you know I actually did live for several months among Bedouin tribesmen in Araby?"

He told me of that then, and of the mad duke he met in a castle in Bohemia and of the old Comanche he had discovered wandering in the western American desert who had been turned out of her tepee by her own people, to die alone. His enchanting voice painted enchanting pictures.

"What did you do with her?"

"I took her to the nearest fort and paid someone an exorbitant sum to care for her till she died. The poor old thing was terrified of white people, but I could not leave her wandering once I had found her."

"Certainly you couldn't. You had to do what you did, like the Good Samaritan. It amazes me that you're so familiar with such far places and such people."

"Well, American citizens and surroundings can seem nearly as alien. Wait until you hear of some of the characters I have met in the teeming jungles of New York City."

"Have you considered writing a book?"

"I prefer to live my life in the present rather than mulling over what is long gone. Remember—*carpe diem*. It is my desire to live shining new adventures. I am hoping you will join me in my travels someday. But not for a while. I want you to become very familiar with the abbey so you will think of it as your home."

I studied him as he spoke. I could see how he would be a great sportsman and explorer. He had a devil-may-care quality that would lead him always on to the next test, the next setting, the next adventure. But I thought I could also detect a sensitivity in him; after all, he was so good to me and had been kind to the servant boys and the poor Comanche woman.

Gradually longer pauses stretched between stories. M. Bernard signaled subtly to Charles, who waited behind a palm tree, and gestured for him to remove the tray. My godfather quenched all but one of the candles himself, pinching the flames between his fingers.

In the dusky light his shadowy figure returned to my side.

"Now," he said, "lie back with me and watch the stars. The breeze today blew away the haze of humidity, so we should see them clearly."

I lay back and peered through the glass roof at glimmering pinpoints until I felt dizzy. Achal's music was a lullaby. I drifted off to sleep.

I dreamed as I slept. At first it started pleasantly: I stood alone in my bedroom at the abbey, fingering a necklace of blood-red rubies, enjoying my pretty surroundings. However, the atmosphere changed slowly for no reason I could fathom. Sluggishly a nameless terror seeped into me. Something ghastly was about to happen. I sprang toward the door to call out frantically, "Anne, sister Anne, do you see my brothers?" And she answered from a distance, "Not yet." That was all.

I awoke with a jolt. My face was burrowed into something silky—M. Bernard's silver satin waistcoat.

I sat up abruptly, sweating, my heart racing.

"What is it, *mon bébé?*" he asked, concerned.

"I had—I had a bad dream."

"Tell me about it, and I will make you see that all is well and that no terror may touch you when I am here."

And so I told him.

He nodded. "Those nightmares, where you do not actually know what you fear, are horrifying. I have them quite often, strangely. I have been through true danger, but that unknown dread is far worse. From the corner of my eye, I will glimpse something shapeless and shadowy struggling to take form just behind me. And I run because I cannot bear to see what it truly is, once the darkness has writhed into a shape."

I shuddered and rose shakily. "I'd better go to bed."

"I will walk you to your door." He took my elbow. "But I assure you, you need not depend on your brothers for rescue. If ever you are in trouble, I will do the rescuing."

CHAPTER 7

LOCKED AND ABANDONED

No worries over nightmares plagued me on my second morning at the abbey.

It was a "misty moisty morning," in the words of the nursery rhyme. The fog softened all lines and lent a dreamlike quality to my meanderings. It didn't seem quite day or quite night. With no sun, I allowed my hat to hang by its ribbons from my neck.

The grounds were magnificent and very European-looking. With their crisply carved hedges, statues, and fountains, they resembled illustrations I had seen in books. It was hard to believe we were here in Mississippi. The gardens had been laid out with an artist's eye, which I assumed was my godfather's, so each vista seemed more lovely, inviting me on and on to the Italian garden and shrubbery, the rose garden and knot garden and herb garden.

I met Willie, the head gardener, out clipping away with his shears at the legs of the elephant topiary. He was small and very dark, with a grayish tinge to the wrinkles in his face and with white, cottony hair. He was the husband of Daphne, the flower fairy. Particularly fitting, since he made me think of a gardening gnome.

"They're spectacular," I told him, gesturing at the sculpted shapes. "And do you clip them all yourself?"

He grinned and looked down at his boots (which were large for his small frame, making his shape resemble a capital letter *L*). "Yes, Miss," he said shyly. "I does."

"How do you think of the forms? Do you have a book?"

"No, Miss. When I was a young'un, back in the old place, before I come here, I saw them beasts. Them I cuts from memory. Them others"—here he indicated the geometric or fantastical shapes—"I cuts how my eyes likes them to be."

His voice was soft.

As I continued my exploration, I wondered at the work it must take to fight the quick-springing Southern weeds and many insects. Even the outbuildings appeared charming and immaculate. Pear and plum trees were trained against the walls of the carriage house, and a profusion of yellow roses clambered over the stables. I thought of the words of the noted author Hannah More, when she wrote of Hampton, "So clean, so green, so flowery, so bowery."

Only two details seemed neglected. One was the misshapen oak tree in the front. It was so ugly and out of place; why did M. Bernard not have it removed? The other unkempt spot lay past the orangery, where a brick wall surrounded what appeared to be a crumbling medieval chapel.

Above the top of the wall I could see that vines rambled, the roof sagged, and the upper windows were boarded over. Exuberant ivy and wisteria and the cruelly thorny vines I later heard Willie call "devil's gut" shrouded the walls. It took me some time to discover the entrance. When I did lift choking vines to find the gate, it was firmly locked and barred.

A stone angel atop a pillar stood guard nearby. She was covered with splotchy lichen and moss, but that didn't change her graceful beauty. For a moment I could only stand motionless, spellbound by her expression—infinitely sorrowful and wise and compassionate. I touched her stone foot just as a groundsman passed by.

"Why is this place locked?" I asked him.

He squinted down from beneath his straw hat. "Master, he say it be unsafe. He don't want no one getting hurt in there."

Why had M. Bernard brought the chapel here to begin with, if he was only going to let it fall into ruin? Maybe even my energetic and wealthy godfather couldn't make all renovations at once. It must cost a fortune each month simply to keep this place running, and the expense of the east wing renovation was surely immense.

I headed out across the lawn, and soon my boots and the stockings inside were wet with dew. I roamed through the peach orchard and pecan grove and on to a little hill where rose an odd structure. It was built of some sort of pinkish sandstone mixed with blue-gray seams that lent an ethereal look, as if it were floating enchanted in the pearly mist. As I drew closer, I guessed the building mimicked foreign ruins. Or maybe it was authentic foreign ruins since one couldn't be sure with my godfather. Great blocks of stone covered with a filigree of vines lay tumbled around, and sculpted, grotesque figures, meant to be monkeys, leered and grimaced from above.

I poked about, searching for the entrance, which seemed to be concealed. Of course, if I found it, it would probably be locked anyway. This building, like the chapel, certainly appeared to be in dangerous condition.

I had just detected a hairline crack, which might be part of a secret door, when a snort sounded from behind me. I whirled around.

M. Bernard loomed above me on a sleek gray Thoroughbred (the source of the snort). The Irish wolfhound who had snoozed in the library the day before came loping up. The horse tossed its head and pranced.

"Heel, Finnegan," M. Bernard ordered. The dog immediately obeyed.

I shrunk against the stone wall. The horse's eyes looked wild.

"Aramis will not get too close," my godfather said. Surrounded by gray mist, the bluish sheen of his beard was more pronounced. He might have been some spectral knight in an Arthurian tale. "He obeys me absolutely. He is a handsome brute, is he not?"

"Indeed, sir, he is." I forced myself to reach up and stroke Aramis's velvety shoulder. I withdrew quickly when the beast flared its nostrils and blew.

"He came to me a wild creature," M. Bernard said. "But I worked with him and cowed him into submission until he is as you see him, gentle as a dove."

"You have him under control, but I shouldn't like to meet him without you holding the reins."

"And I would never allow that to happen. I am too careful for your welfare." He patted Aramis's neck. "I have purchased a mare for you—pure white; her name is Lily. You may have her saddled whenever you like."

"Do you mean it? I can ride now? Today?" My eyes widened at the prospect of a horse of my own.

"You know it is my pleasure to make you happy. My only stipulation is that a groom must accompany you on all jaunts. There is wild country here. I wish I could attend you myself, but duty calls. Do you admire my folly?" He cast his eyes over the ruin.

"Folly? Is that what it is?" I had heard of these buildings, constructed purely for decoration by the wealthy to represent Egyptian pyramids or Tatar tents or other interesting edifices. Perhaps ruins created deliberately explained in part the ruined chapel left in disrepair. To my godfather, maybe, they were quaintly scenic—even the horrid monkeys.

He nodded. "I patterned it after the remains of a temple I visited in northern India and filled it with rare and intriguing statuary and art similar to the original."

"May I go inside? I thought I found a concealed door."

"You are astute. There is indeed a concealed door, and the interior would interest you a good deal, but you must not enter without me."

"Will you come now?"

"No, I am afraid that pleasure must wait. Someday I will show it to you, but I have other things to attend to. Later we shall have all the time in the world for such adventures together."

I opened my mouth to say I wished he could put off his business and spend the day with me, but I closed it again. He was a busy man with "solemn duties," and I would sound selfish and childish. "Then I'll go introduce myself to Lily," I said instead.

"And I will see you tonight."

He lifted his top hat and cantered away. I had to agree with Mrs. Duckworth that he did indeed have an excellent seat on a horse, and the sight made me draw in my breath a little, he appeared so distinguished. How well we'd look riding together.

I hastened to the house. Without a maid's assistance, I dressed in a riding habit from my wardrobe and headed out to the stables.

The chief groom, a man named Garvey, sauntered out to meet me. He was a tall, well-built, good-looking black man. I might have been inexperienced in a broad range of real, live people, but "the rake" was a stock character in the romance novels I had devoured. From his manner, I assumed he wreaked havoc among the housemaids. When he spoke, I could smell whiskey on his breath. Perhaps it was the whiskey that gave him his oozing confidence. I wouldn't have thought slaves would have access to alcohol, but then, I didn't know much about such things.

He tipped his hat and smiled ingratiatingly. "So, little Miss, you come for a look at your mare? She's a right pretty thing."

"More than a look, I hope," I said, speaking coolly, for I didn't like this man's demeanor. "I should like to take her out right now, if there's a groom to accompany me."

He tossed the harness he was holding to a young boy. "Oh, I'm fixing to go with you, Miss. It be my pleasure."

"Very well."

He went to fetch Lily.

My horse had great, limpid eyes and a gentle manner that caused me to wrap my arms around her head. "You darling thing," I whispered. She rubbed herself against me.

Garvey helped me climb up before mounting another steed.

I hooked my knee around the pommel, spread my skirts, and was off.

We left the tended gardens behind and soon were trotting over uneven ground, with swampy patches and clumps of trees. I could sense Garvey's hot brown eyes on my figure as I rode.

I urged Lily into a gallop across the parkland. I had never before ridden in such a place—so open, so free. The steamy heat of the horse added to the sticky, cloying heat of the air. Still I loved this, with the wind whipping my cheeks and hair and the feel of Lily's long stride beneath me. I hoped Garvey was left behind, but he overtook me in only a moment.

He pulled in his reins and looked me up and down. "You quite the rider, Miss. The master be glad of that. He likes a quick gallop hisself."

We stood upon the fringe of the woods. "I'm going in there," I said, pointing into the trees.

"Better not, Miss. There be low-hanging branches and roots to trip up your mount. We wouldn't want a pretty lady like you to take a tumble, now would we? Not to mention the steel traps the master has set out for poachers. But there's a right fine view up on top of that hill. It goes on for miles."

For a moment I considered ignoring Garvey and plunging into the forest anyway—he had that effect on me—but the fact that his words actually made sense stopped me. I would never purposely do anything that might hurt Lily.

We rode to the glorious outlook he had indicated. The fog had burned itself away, so now I could make out the church steeples of Chicataw above the distant treetops. I recognized my favorite church from when I had driven through town. It had been of yellow brick, with a sunny, peaceful, daisy-dotted churchyard, where, it had seemed to me, only the contented might sleep.

For some reason I was glad to know where the town lay.

Garvey returned to the stables and I returned to the house an hour before time to dress for dinner.

A voice said from behind me, "Did you enjoy your ride, Miss Sophia?"

I jumped. Ling certainly moved silently. "You startled me!" I cried, twirling around. "Yes, sir, it was a pretty day and a pretty place and a pretty horse."

He bowed and withdrew.

I stood still, watching him melt into the shadows. I wondered what he thought of me. Usually I could tell if people liked me or were indifferent or found me annoying, but I couldn't read Ling's face. I was anxious to know—his good opinion would be valuable.

I shrugged and ran up the stairs, two steps at a time, swinging my hat by its ties.

Before I reached my bedroom, I paused in front of a marble-topped credenza in the upstairs hall. On it stood a framed daguerre-otype of M. Bernard that I looked at every time I passed by. He sat in a velvet armchair, his head slightly bowed and his eyes half closed, as if lost in thought. Probably it was the only stance he could maintain for the long time required to take the picture, but he appeared to be meditating deeply. I picked it up and carried it into my bedchamber, placing it beside my mother's miniature. When I got up the nerve, I would ask my godfather if I might keep it there.

CHAPTER 8

LETTERS WRITTEN ON FINE PAPER

June 15, 1855

Darling Junius and Anne and Harry,

Are you impressed to receive a letter from me on this thick, creamy paper? With the de Cressac crest on it, please note, just like the letters that used to arrive at our house. And you should see my bedroom and the pretty little desk I'm writing on. I'm hoping you will see them soon. When you come, you'll find me blooming—and considerably better dressed.

You cannot imagine how I miss you all! Every other moment I think of something I want to say to you, but can't. Yes, I arrived safely. I'll describe the trip in a later letter. I didn't write immediately because I wanted to be able to tell you more about Wyndriven Abbey and M. Bernard (which is what my godfather asks me to call him).

I'm learning my way around the house/castle/walled city. I will venture out to the conservatory and back tomorrow and shall count myself lucky if I'm not lost, to be found wandering white-haired and witless many years hence. By the time of your first visit, I shall be able to give you The Tour myself. Junius and Harry, wait until you see the armory! Such long swords. Very pointy.

The household is fascinating. There is an army of African slaves, as I worried there might be, but there are also other kinds of foreign servants. The housekeeper, Mrs. Duckworth (whom, to myself, I usually call Ducky—since M. Bernard called her that once, and it fits), is British; Achal, M. Bernard's valet, is Indian, and his main job appears to be gliding about on the dusky fringes, handing M. Bernard canes and things; the cook is French; and Ling, the butler, is a Chinese man. He's very old, with long, straggly whiskers that look as if he might chew upon the ends.

As for the Negro servants—there's so many it's a challenge to learn all their names. Why, there are two men simply to care for the candles and lamps (David and Clovis—there! I remembered). Our coachman reminds me of that client of Papa's, Mr. McTavish. Except that Samuel Coachman is not fat or white or Scottish. I try to help Willie the gardener sometimes. I don't think he's too terribly bothered by it, but this is the sort of thing he says when I'm snipping away at shrubbery: "Miss Sophia, you gotta be more careful. You just gouged a big hole in that there bush." You'll agree that being more cautious is good advice for the likes of me. I wish I could be friends with all the servants, but they won't let me, so instead, I try to be dignified. That doesn't work either.

My godfather is all that is generous and welcoming. He's a fine gentleman, and quite young, really, compared to how we thought he would be. He looks piratical. Did you ever suspect how fond I am of brigands? I'm anxious for you to meet him, as I've never met anyone like him before. It's hard to imagine there could be anyone else like him. He treats me with great kindness. He is a widower a few times over, poor man. He is so good to me that it's now my Goal in Life to help him be happy.

I tell him stories in the evenings, as I often told to you, as well as other amusing and useful things I learned from my vast reading of ladies' periodicals. The other day I informed M. Bernard how The Girls' Book of Diversions *described the best methods of swooning. Do you remember when I read it aloud to you? It said, "The modes of fainting should all be as different as possible and may be very* diverting." Anyway, I demonstrated some of the modes of fainting we all (except Junius) devised, and he laughed and laughed. No, Anne, I was not being a romp—or at least not much—and he liked it. By the way, he doesn't approve of corsets and tight lacing any more than Papa did. He compares them to the bound feet of women in China or the neck rings worn by some Asian and African tribes. Not that we talk of corsets or undergarments often.

He loves to tease. He's a great one for laughing. I like him so much, I would follow him around constantly like a puppy dog if he (or I) would let me, but he spends the days either shut up in his office with his agent (Mr. Bass—a thin, nervous fellow with a prominent Adam's apple) or riding around to supervise his holdings, so I don't usually see him till I'm dressed for the evening. It's all so different from what I'm used to. From the time I get up until suppertime, no one tells me what to do, so I must tell myself what to do.

Here is my daily schedule I have just now planned:

> After breakfast I will:
> * walk or ride (yes, I have my own horse—her name is Lily)
> * read
> * write letters
>
> After luncheon I will:
> * do needlework
> * play the piano
> * study history and geography so M. Bernard will not find me too
>   shockingly ignorant

Ducky says perhaps M. Bernard will give a ball in my honor. How many times, Anne, did we imagine such a thing, and now it may come true. And I am to have a French maid. Probably she's to help me learn French. Are you snickering? True, it was not my best subject. . . .

Anne, what happened in the last installment of "The Bride of Lord Blackwood" from the Ladies' Repository? I never did get to finish it. Remember how they kept referring to the heroine as "the laughing fair"?

M. Bernard has given me so many lovely things, and I feel selfish to have so much now, and you so little, but I can't ask him for gifts to send you just yet, although I want to badly. I'm guessing it would sound rude to say, "Give me some presents so I can pass them on to my family." I will send things just as soon as it wouldn't seem awkward.

Have you found employment yet, Anne?

Please, please, all of you, write me—in care of M. Bernard de Cressac, Wyndriven Abbey, Chicataw, Mississippi. After all, you do want to receive correspondence from me, don't you? Interesting letters where I tell you details about the Mysterious Locked Folly or the Locked Chapel Gate or the Locked East Wing. I shan't write them if you don't also write to me.

Yr. affectionate sister
(and Laughing Fair),
Sophie

July 10, 1855

Dear Family,

I was so happy to receive your letters a few days ago, but I'm a little sad to hear how things are changing at home. Somehow I want everything to remain exactly the same forever. It breaks a bit of my heart that you must let Bridget go and sell the house. Anne, I'm proud of you that you've found a position. I wish it were something better, though. How annoying that women are so limited in their occupations. You write bravely, but from reading between the lines, the children you're teaching must be little beasts. I won't consider you a whiner if you complain about them in your letters. Go ahead—tell Sophie all the ghastly details. And, Junius, you know I have always been proud of you for going into the office every day doing a job you hate because you are Responsible. Responsible people are valuable. Not, of course, Harry, that you are NOT valuable. Do remember, though, that Papa let you sit out of school these months because you're supposed to be preparing yourself for exams next year.

You mustn't fear that my time here will turn my head. Yes, I have a horse and a maid and jewels and heaps of lovely dresses and so on and so forth, but I'm still myself.

I do worry over the debt I'm incurring. There's no way I can ever repay my godfather. The tapestry I intend to stitch and the slippers I've beaded for him are of as much worth as the pictures I used to scribble for Papa when I was little. But how can I refuse Monsieur's presents? Can I turn away a coquettish cap of bronze-green velvet topped by a pheasant feather? (You would love it, Anne.) How can I say, when M. Bernard clasps a velvet ribbon with an agate cameo centered on it around my neck, that I would really rather not have it? I cannot. It would be rude, and Monsieur delights in my looking nice, and besides, I really love the gifts. Do you understand my predicament? I know. You're wishing you had such a problem.

At least I do some useful things other than frolic about. I am becoming Well Educated. M. Bernard is widely read and sophisticated about so many different subjects, and he is teaching me all the time. Not in a pompous, annoying way, but in an interesting, enlightening way. I have had to practice subtlety since I don't want him to know exactly how naïve and ignorant I am. I left normal school so early, and I'll admit now to whoever-it-was that used to lecture me——yes, Junius, it was you——that I read too many romances and too little else. Therefore, I keep still when M. Bernard speaks of unfamiliar subjects, and then I look them up later. Most of the books in the library are behind locked doors because of their value and rarity (although some of them must be quite naughty——those Monsieur says he locks up so the servants won't be shocked or "titillated"), but the volumes of the Encyclopedia are out on a table. M. Bernard occasionally assigns me reading. Currently it's La Comédie Humaine by Honoré de Balzac. Fascinating and disturbing. M. Bernard says, "Balzac writes of real life," but I argue, "Real life isn't always squalid, which M. Balzac seems to think it is." I enjoy arguing with my godfather. Don't worry, I'm still polite. I know you thought Balzac inappropriate for young ladies, Anne, but my godfather says it will widen my understanding of the world, and I trust his judgment.

Oh dear. I'm sorry about that splotch. I'm training myself not to drip perspiration on the paper as I write (I am most careful to keep my arm from resting on it), but sometimes the drops fall before I can catch them. Sorry for being disgusting.

Now, would you like to hear about the good works I'm doing? I bravely told my godfather our family's problems with the institution of slavery. He was patient with me. He explained how generally slavery would not be a worthy thing, but how at various times in world history it's been necessary and it's necessary now, because of the economy and in order to care for the people who have already been brought over. He also pointed out that the slaves are not often cruelly treated. He says, "If a man has an expensive horse, would he beat it and injure it so it would be of no use to him?" He made sense at the time, but then, when Monsieur is speaking, he could say two plus two equals ten and I would believe him, although later I have questions. For instance, how can he possibly consider a person in the same category as an animal? (Although we do love horses.) I'm getting used to it, but *still, each thing an African does for me makes me uncomfortable. As if I should constantly apologize.*

Last week my godfather let me visit, along with Ling, the field workers at the plantation who are ill, so I could see how well his people are cared for. Ling administered Oriental herbs, and I administered soup and sympathy, but they wouldn't say anything except, "Thank you, Miss," without ever really looking at me. The Negroes' cabins are small and suffocatingly hot and dark and, when they're stewing chitlins (spelling?), foul-smelling. However, they're in good repair and clean. (Chitlins, if you don't know, are pig intestines.)

Monsieur also took me to the gospel meeting out there last Sunday night. He allows the slaves to hold meetings, but he himself is not a churchgoer. He went because he was the guest preacher. The regular minister is Willie the gardener. I heard Willie preach once during a Wednesday-night meeting out in the abbey's pecan grove. In everyday life he is a gentle, quiet little man, but when he's behind the pulpit, he becomes a Roaring Lion! (Not to be confused with a Ravening Wolf, such as mentioned in the Bible.) He bangs the pulpit, which is a log, and shouts and keeps everyone on the edge of their plank seats and has this mantle of authority I would never have imagined he could have. When I heard Monsieur's text on the Sunday I went, I stopped wondering why he wished to preach. He spoke about obedience to masters and contentment with your place in life. Most fervent and convincing.

The music moved me more than any I've ever before heard in church. Lots of swaying and clapping, with the sun setting brilliantly in the background. I swayed and clapped too, much to M. Bernard's amusement. One song is still in my head. It went: "Oh, scoff, you scoffers, scoff! Them sinners who are scoffing can't hear sweet Jordan roll." When I first heard it, I looked at my godfather pointedly. He's definitely a scoffer.

Please write again soon. I adore my M. Bernard, but I adored all of you for the first seventeen years of my life. I am very happy here, but would be happier if you were with me. That is the one thing that makes me less than content.

Yr. loving sister,
Sophie

August 3, 1855

Dearest Sister,

~~*I hope this letter finds you*~~
~~*I take pen in hand to*~~
Please don't show this to my brothers, Anne. If you were here, we would escape to some secret place—far out in the gardens or into one of dozens of rooms where we wouldn't be overheard—and I would tell you Things.

I dropped my pen and crumpled up the paper. How could I admit even to Anne the ridiculous feelings that stirred in my heart these days? I wandered over to the window. There was M. Bernard, striding vigorously across the lawn. My chest constricted in a way that was both pleasant and painful. I so loved his walk.

He looked up and saw me. He waved and I fluttered my fingers back. I watched until he disappeared into the stables.

It was nearly time to dress for supper. What should I wear? Last night he told me he liked me in white ("so pure and innocent"). Something white, then . . .

I couldn't possibly be in love with him. Or could I? I pressed around my feelings as one might press around a tender spot to see how sore it was. When I used to make lists of the qualifications necessary for my True Love, I would never have put "Godfather," "Oldish," or "Married three (I think) times" on the notepaper I decorated with cherubs and hearts.

Talitha entered with a large parcel.

It contained a rectangle of canvas and a basket brimming with embroidery silks.

How thoughtful of M. Bernard to have remembered and to have acquired them. That was part of his allure—he was so interested in everything I said or did. He made *me* feel captivating.

Resolutely I sat down at my desk to sketch out a plan for M. Bernard's small tapestry. Maybe a forest scene, since that would encompass so many pleasing colors. I would have brightly garbed figures making merry about a fire, surrounded by brilliant wildflowers and bending trees in all shades of green.

I sketched quickly, excited to begin a beautiful piece of work for him. I ceased for a moment, tapping my pencil against my chin. How many figures?

As I paused, I spied the tiniest tip of a sheet of paper peeking out from a crack at the base of the desk's pigeonholes. It would be visible only in this light and only from my exact angle. Something had slipped back there, unnoticed. I snagged the edge with the letter opener.

It was a sheet of thin notepaper, evidently the final page of a letter, since there was a signature following the paragraph.

I read:

You know that your temper ever has been as fiery as your tresses. As your only kin, and one who has your best interests in heart, I remind you of your duty to your husband. He loves you dearly and would give you anything you wanted. Tara, you must remember that gentlemen may have tastes that you, as a lady, find difficult to share. However, school your tongue and your high spirits, and be a more accommodating and pleasant companion to him, and I am certain to hear a more favorable report in your next correspondence.

> *Sincerely,*
> *Aunt Lavinia*

I read it through a second time. Another bride for M. Bernard. Tara. With fiery tresses. I carefully folded the paper and placed it in the envelope with the strand of hair I had found that might well have been hers, and slipped it back under the desk blotter.

That evening I wore white organdy. When I sat waiting at the banquet table, Charles brought a note saying, *Forgive my absence, chérie. I am called away for a few days——B.* I pushed aside my plate and retired to my room, too disappointed to eat.

CHAPTER 9

REVELATIONS

"Do you think we might ever expect callers?" I asked Ducky the next morning when I spied her passing in the hall. She paused and a closed look shadowed her features. She was going to be careful with her answer.

"Master Bernard doesn't bother with such goings-on. I told you he considers Southerners terribly common. He discouraged them long ago."

I sighed and looked down at the marble tiles. My wonderful new clothes had arrived from Mme. Duclos. They had given me much pleasure at first, but what was the use in trying to dress prettily if no one ever saw them? "Might I·call on the neighbors, then? I really . . . I really would like—"

Ducky shook her head violently. "Oh no, Miss Sophia. That wouldn't do at all. It would appear as if you didn't trust the master's judgment. Besides, a newcomer should never be the first to pay calls. Even the locals know that." She beamed brightly, comfortingly now. "But don't forget there might be a ball someday."

Oh yes. The alleged ball.

"When do you expect Monsieur Bernard back?" I blurted out behind her as she started on her way again.

"He never lets us know his plans," she said over her shoulder. "Keeps us on our toes." She continued on down the hall, too busy today to exchange chitchat.

Charles and Talitha, talking together earnestly, rounded a corner just then and nearly ran into the housekeeper. Guilt swept over their faces. Mrs. Duckworth tutted with annoyance and shooed them apart. Charles immediately sped ahead, and Talitha changed direction. I watched after them.

I did love a good romance, and those two offered material for study. They were careful to never purposefully draw attention to the fact that they were courting, but I prided myself that I could detect the signs of their attachment. When Talitha was in Charles's presence, a softness and warmth came over her features that were never there normally. She smiled often and even laughed, while Charles was more animated around her, more intense, with bright color in his cheeks. When they were in the same room, even when they made no move to draw closer or speak, I would note how often they would look toward the other, with silent communication flashing between them.

Perhaps when I had been here longer, I could arrange meetings between them, supposedly to help me with something or other, but really to give them time together.

I gave a little sigh and continued down the corridor without being entirely sure where I was going. If M. Bernard was to be gone often,

I would die from loneliness. It was as if I were only truly alive when I was with him.

Sometimes the housemaids talked and laughed as they worked in nearby rooms. If I entered, they would immediately hush and meet my attempts at conversation with mumbled answers and averted eyes. They probably deemed me an inane, silly, smiling creature. Sometimes they broke into song. When they did that, I hid outside the door to listen. I loved their rich, throaty voices and mournful tunes. In my first days here they had been only a sea of dark faces. Now I recognized them. I knew names. But that didn't matter, because to them *I* was the faceless one. The Spoiled White Girl. Maybe I was wrong, but that was how it seemed. They had each other and I had no one. Not even my family anymore. No letters had arrived since the first flurry.

The hours stretched before me, and I struggled to fill each day. Like a phantom girl, I began to glide about behind the scenes, exploring. Sometimes as I slipped down unused passages, I would feel suddenly lost and disoriented, wondering, *Where am I?* Then I would have to remind myself, *This is Wyndriven Abbey. Your home. You belong here.*

I did belong more as I became familiar with the unused floors and interesting crannies of the place. Since the abbey had been brought over lock, stock, and barrel, there were many ancient treasures to poke my nose into. Chests held brittle, yellowed linens featuring embroidery with unusual antique patterns that I sketched in order to stitch later. Cabinets contained three hundred years' worth of odds and ends. I spirited away a small bronze statue of an angel to place in my bedchamber. I didn't ask anyone. M. Bernard didn't even know he owned it. Less guilt about my nosiness troubled me here than when I used to riffle through Anne's things when she was out.

One afternoon, more phantom-like than ever, since I flitted about in an overskirt of pale, silvery, shimmering gauze, looking insubstantial as mist, I entered a room on the top floor I had only glanced in before.

This chamber held no furniture, but the ceiling was painted cerulean, with gilt moon and stars, and all around the fireplace were depicted Mother Goose characters—Humpty Dumpty and Little Miss Muffet and Jack Be Nimble. Iron bars spanned the windows. Obviously it had been a nursery once, now emptied of its furnishings. On a window seat, nearly behind the curtain and looking dusty and forlorn, lay a small pile of books.

What a novelty in this house—books lying free. I picked up one. The title on the marbled cover was *Histoires ou Contes du Temps Passé*, by Charles Perrault. The writing was in French, but from the illustrations I could tell it was a book of fairy tales. I turned to the fly-leaf. The name "Victoire" and the year "1814" were written in a childish hand, with the cross on the letter *t* carried over the other letters in a long line. Beneath this appeared the name "Anton" and the year "1830." Although the writing in the second name was more mature, still the letter *t* was crossed in the same way, making me believe the same hand wrote both. Perhaps Anton was Victoire's child.

It was silly to think every female name I saw here must be a wife.

Too much solitude made me dwell overly on these things. But if Victoire were indeed another former spouse, their number was four now. Then what of Anton? M. Bernard's son? If so, he was most likely long dead, as I had never heard of him.

This must have been his nursery.

Tatiana's baby would probably also have slept here had it lived. Tatiana, who died in childbirth eleven years ago.

A chill oozed into my bones. What a sad room. Decorated for one child who evidently didn't live to grow up and for a baby who would never sleep here because it slept forever with its mother. I didn't blame my godfather for emptying the chamber. The volumes must have escaped notice. I took them down to my room and placed them on my desk.

Late that afternoon Mrs. Duckworth popped in to bring a tray.

"Let's eat cozily here together," she said, "it being such a damp, nasty day. Unseasonably cool for August."

She laid the tray on the ottoman, and we pulled two chairs up to it. Twilight had come early. Candles blazed in the crystal chandelier shaped like waving seaweed, and a fire snapped in the hearth—the first we had needed since my arrival. The flames, however, couldn't compete with the underwater gloom of my chamber. It was certainly beautiful—fantastical, even—but right now it made me feel cold, cold, cold inside. Ducky's company was welcome.

The tray held a pot of warm, creamy cocoa, thinly sliced pears, and shortbread cookies. All rich and sweet, just as I liked them.

As always, Ducky was amiable and full of prattle about the coal black, two-headed calf born on the plantation and the funny mistakes made by one of the kitchen maids.

I listened and nodded as I ate, but I could think of little to say in response.

"Why, when Alphonse told her to—" Ducky ceased speaking. The spots of color drained from her face. "Where did you find those?"

I followed her gaze. She was staring at the books I had brought downstairs.

"They were in a room on the top floor," I said. "Was I wrong to bring them here? Whose were they?"

"I must have overlooked those when—" Ducky took a long sip of chocolate, then sighed. "'Twas Master Anton's nursery. Master Bernard's son, who has been dead and buried these twenty years." She dabbed her eyes with her apron. "A fine boy—full of life, only five, but . . . the spitting image of his father. You know, when they die as children, they remain dear little ones in your memory forever."

"What happened to him?"

"He—" She closed her eyes and swallowed. "He wandered too close to the grate, and his nightgown took ablaze. His mother rolled him in the rug quick as she could, but he was burned too badly. He lingered two weeks before passing away. 'Twas something so horrible . . . so horrible none of us who saw it have ever been the same again."

No wonder the many hearths in the abbey were guarded by unusually massive screens. I automatically pulled my skirt farther from the flames and clasped my hands carefully together in my lap.

Now or never. "Du—Mrs. Duckworth, there are things I need to know if I am to live here."

She bobbed her head and sighed again, long and wheezy. "Yes, of course, of course. You want to know about Master Bernard's wives. I told him you ought to be told his history, but he wouldn't hear of it. He can't bear to have their names mentioned. But you have a right to know if— Yes, I'll tell you, but please don't let on to the master."

"I won't say a word." I made a motion as though sealing my lips and watched her with bated breath.

She crossed her arms under her ample bosom, eager to talk now that she was allowing herself to do so.

"The first was Madame Victoire. She and the master met in Paris, and a more beautiful girl you could not imagine. All that abundant red hair—Master Bernard has a weakness for redheads, you know."

She looked at me significantly, and I could only nod.

"The master was just twenty when they married, and they were happy for a long while. That was when he began his travels, and Madame Victoire would accompany him, for she was an adventurous lady. Two years later Master Anton was born, and the master could hardly contain himself for joy. You know he's fond of little ones, don't you?"

I nodded. I had often seen him teasing the servant children and giving them sweets from his pockets.

"Well, when he was home (for he wasn't often, though Madame no longer went with him after the baby arrived), he would pop into the nursery every day to frolic with his dear little son.

"When Anton was born, Master Bernard bought the land here

and brought Wyndriven Abbey over. All was well until the . . . the accident happened. Then everything changed." Ducky became agitated, fiddling with her keys till they jangled. "Master Bernard blamed Madame, you see. Mammy was laid low with a fever, and Madame Victoire had charge of the child. It could have happened when anyone was watching him—that sort of tragedy does sometimes, no matter how much care is taken—but it happened when the mistress was there. After that, she and the master hardly spoke to one another.

"I know it's no excuse for what she did, but she was terribly unhappy. The master hired a new secretary, and he was an attractive young man. A Yankee, younger than the mistress, but then, she was still a beautiful lady. They began to spend time together, and one thing led to another. The master has always been away so much." She shook her head sadly. "I've told him and told him he ought to stay home more. That young wives get lonely, but . . . Anyway, I had an inkling of what was going on, and I worried myself sick, but I thought it all ended when the secretary—Mr. Gregg, his name was—found another position near New Orleans. He only went there, though, to prepare for Madame to join him. Somehow they arranged for her to run away to him—through the mistress's maid, probably, as she too disappeared with the mistress." Her voice lowered. "I've never told anyone else this, but I saw Madame Victoire once, a few years later. Somehow she'd gotten into the house, and I spied her from far down the corridor, entering her old bedroom. It gave me palpitations, it did, but then I realized perhaps she had come to fetch something precious to her that she'd forgotten, and I didn't sound any alarms. She wouldn't harm anything, and it would only hurt the master to be told. I hurried off so I wouldn't have to confront her."

"I think you did right."

She paused for another long sip of cocoa.

"And so Tatiana came next?" I urged.

She shot me a sharp look. "How do you know that?"

"Because you told me on that first day that she decorated my room."

"Oh, yes, so I did. Well, the master met her during his travels in Russia after his divorce was final. She had the prettiest accent and the prettiest little ways." She smiled fondly at the recollection. "She was lonely, of course, so far from home and with the master gone so much, but she never complained. And then she became with child. It wasn't a happy time for the master, though, because it all reminded him of little Anton. And then the baby died and the mother as well. I was gone when it happened—the master kindly had sent me for my one-and-only visit to family in England." She snorted and blew her nose into a much-beruffled handkerchief. "Oh, it does bring it all back. This has not been a happy household. Not happy at all."

"How awful for poor Monsieur Bernard." I couldn't let her stop now in spite of her distress. "And he's been alone all this time?"

"No," she said reluctantly. "Next came Madame Tara. She was Irish—and they never had a happy day after she arrived here. Always provoking Master Bernard about this or that. There were terrible rows. I'd hear them shouting in the library. Sometimes she'd even smash things, vases and things. Oh my. She wasn't much of a lady. They hadn't been married long—only a year—when she . . . died."

"How did she die?"

Ducky shook her head and drew her fingers through her hair until it was pulled wildly from its bun. "I shouldn't tell you. Really, I shouldn't."

I patted her shoulder and said nothing for a moment to allow her to gather her composure. Then, "Please, I need to know," I said softly.

Ducky glanced toward the door. "She . . . she committed suicide. One of the servants found her. She stabbed herself."

"Not in my room?" I cried in horror.

"Good heavens, no! No. 'Twas in the yellow salon. She liked it best of all the public rooms. She used one of the fancy jeweled knives from the armory, though how she got it I don't know, as Master Bernard has always kept it locked. She was a sly thing, though; she would have found a way. He had her body interred at night, even though the law now says you may bury suicides during the day."

"Is she buried in the churchyard, since they also allow that now?"

"Not in the Chicataw churchyard, if that's what you mean. All of Master Bernard's beloved dead lie in the walled churchyard on the property."

"The one that's so overgrown?"

"Yes. He can't bear to— It's so full of terrible memories, you see. He can't stand to have anyone go in there to trim or clean or restore it."

So that explained the mystery of the tumbledown chapel. "And there is another wife?"

"Yes," she sighed, "one more. Madame Adele. He married her over in France just a few months after Madame Tara died. I advised him not to wed another foreigner, though for him, I don't suppose a Frenchwoman *is* a foreigner. But they have such difficulty adjusting to life here, and a person simply can't understand their thoughts and ways. So inconstant and unnatural. She lived here for a few years, but was always unhappy. Never would learn English, so she could speak only to the master and to a few of us servants. Nothing her husband gave her was what she wanted; nothing he did for her was enough. His only fault ever has been his choice of women. Such a fine, intelligent man, but he never could pick women. She used constantly to write letters to her friends across the water. Her constitution was delicate and she looked consumptive. Her health took a turn for the worse, and about eighteen months ago Master Bernard whisked her off to some healing springs in Arkansas. It happened so fast, they left before I even knew it. She died while they were gone. He brought her body back to be buried here."

My godfather had indeed been unfortunate in his relationships. All those tragedies lying behind his handsome face. I wondered he could still smile, let alone laugh and tease. I would be a comfort to him. Of course he could never forget his beloved little boy and these women who had been dear to him, but I would help him know there could still be healing and happiness in this world.

Ducky busied herself sweeping up crumbs and stacking plates on the tray. "So you see," she said, not looking at me, "why sometimes he might be moody and sometimes he might have troubled days."

"I've never noticed any moodiness. Perhaps he puts on a good show for me."

"Yes, well, he's much more like himself now, since you've come. You're helping so much, my dear." She patted my shoulder.

"Eventually, though, you're bound to experience his melancholy. He can't help it, my poor master. He has always had a passionate temper, but since Anton passed away, he often becomes despondent as well. When he does, remember what he has been through and what a fine man he really is."

She picked up the tray and plodded toward the door before hesitating and turning. "You do . . . you do *like* Master Bernard, don't you?" Her eyes were intense and anxious.

"Of course I do. He's wonderful."

She bobbed her head, satisfied, and left the room.

CHAPTER 10

IN THE PECAN GROVE

The man came to work on the paneling in the east wing the day after Ducky disclosed M. Bernard's history. She told me he was called Peg Leg Joe due, obviously, to the fact that he wore a wooden leg. He was a free black man who once was a sailor and who now traveled from plantation to plantation offering his services as a master carpenter.

I caught a glimpse or two of him as he came and went. He was an odd-looking fellow, extremely tall and thin, with hollow cheeks and one squinting eye. He added to his height by sporting a rusty black silk stovepipe hat along with his shabby workman's clothing. There was something about the man that made me curious. He had a certain dignity and erectness in his bearing that invited attention.

After his arrival a new feeling sprang from the African servants. They seemed as stirred and shaken as if they were just now waking from a hundred-year sleep in an enchanted castle. Their movements quickened, and whispers and darting glances shot back and forth. An underlying excitement vibrated. No outsider but me would have noticed. I noticed because I had no other occupation to distract me. Even Talitha, usually so calm, became absentminded and inattentive.

A few evenings after Peg Leg Joe came, I attempted, as usual, to chat with Talitha as she dressed me for dinner. At first she acted as if she didn't hear me. When I persisted, she gave a sigh and said, "Please, Miss Sophia, you ain't used to the way it be down here. Don't try to be friends. I can't be no friend to you. I'd pay the price if I tried. So please don't talk to me that way no more."

I felt as if I'd been slapped. Why should I not treat her normally? But if it would get her in trouble, I would stop trying.

When she fumbled in clasping my necklace, I asked hesitantly, "Will you at least tell me if something unusual is going on with the servants? Everyone's acting so odd. Does it have something to do with Peg Leg Joe?"

She didn't answer, and I gave her a feeble smile. "Never mind. I understand. Here, I'll do that." I took the necklace and tried to clasp it myself, but I could hardly make my fingers work, I was so busy blinking back tears. No wonder M. Bernard's wives had been miserable, with my godfather gone all the time and no one willing to talk to them.

Talitha looked at me for a moment. Then she took back the necklace and fastened it firmly. "No, Miss, really, it ain't nothing you'd be interested in. It's only—there be a hallelujah meeting tonight. Peg Leg Joe, he a preacher, and everyone say he deliver a rip-roaring sermon. We excited about that. That's all."

"What's a hallelujah meeting?"

She licked her lips. "One without white people. Where we can sing loud and worship as we see fit without bothering no one."

I had thought they already sang loudly at the meeting I attended. "I hope you enjoy yourselves," I said.

During supper I pondered the hallelujah meeting. It was not a coincidence that it was to be held when the master and Garvey were both gone. The head groom was not well liked among the servants. No, something more than a church meeting was in the air.

After Talitha thought I was in bed, I dressed in a dark gown and slipped out into the ink black night. The air smelled of secrets. A rumble of singing flowed from the pecan grove. I went toward it slowly, feeling my way, as I had brought no lantern and the sky was overcast. The second time I stumbled and barked my shin, I nearly turned back—I could have been in my soft bed right then instead of maiming myself in the woods. But no, even if all they did was sing, listening to their lifted voices would be worth a few scrapes.

I hid behind a tree close enough to hear and view the gathering, just as the music ceased. As far as I could tell, all the African house servants and yard workers were present, seated on logs or planks stretched over barrels. The congregation was in the gloom, but I could make out Charles and Talitha, seated so close together they seemed one wide figure. Something prickled down the back of my neck as I watched them. It took a moment to recognize the emotion: envy. I wanted what they had.

Peg Leg Joe, standing in the front, shone in the light from a single lantern. The glow defined the deeply grooved lines in his face and cast looming shadows on the trees behind.

"And what do Moses say to Pharaoh?" Peg Leg Joe demanded.

"Let my people go!" the audience shouted.

"But Pharaoh's hard ole heart wouldn't have none of that. What he say?"

"He say no!"

"Again and again Moses ask, and always that fool Pharaoh say no. So, what do them children of Israel do? They flee from the house of bondage to the Promised Land, a land flowing with milk and honey." Peg Leg Joe's voice was deep and gravelly, his gaze as he peered out over the congregation intense. "There be a preacher yonder, who help you find your paradise. When you seek him, remember how Jesus call Peter his rock.

"And the Lord and His helpers went before them children of Israel in the wilderness to see they come to no scatterment, to dash their enemies in pieces, to give them places to rest their heads and food to eat and sweet water to drink. So, y'all's eyes, watch to see your chance. Y'all's hands, prepare with this and that tucked away. Y'all's feets, get ready for some powerful walking."

He began singing, rich and rumbling:

When the sun come back,
When the first quail call,
Then the time is come.
Foller the drinking gourd.

Foller the drinking gourd,
Foller the drinking gourd;
For the ole man say,
"Foller the drinking gourd."

The river's bank am a very good road,
The dead trees show the way,
Left foot, peg foot going on,
Foller the drinking gourd.

When the little river
Meet the great big one,
The ole man waits——
Foller the drinking gourd.

Soon they were all singing, swaying and clapping. I turned into the night and crept back to the house.

My godfather must not learn of this.

CHAPTER 11
EN RAPPORT

He was at supper two nights later. I paused in the doorway, feeling almost tremulous at the sight of him. So, I told myself, I could go on living. He had been gone only a week, but it had seemed ages.

"I'm so glad you're back," I said.

M. Bernard reached out his hand, and I flew across the expanse between us to take it. The warmth of his smile washed over me. "You must excuse my absence," he said. "It was unavoidable, but the silver lining is that being parted ensures you will be particularly happy to see me when I return." He squeezed my hand, dropped it, and turned with gusto to his heaping plate of "specially fattened" greenish oysters.

I sat in my chair and pulled my ring on and off, gazing upon my godfather's splendid profile.

He held out a drooping shellfish speared on his fork. "Oysters, *oui?*"

"Oysters, *non!*" I said, turning my head away.

He rolled his eyes and laughed good-naturedly.

"Did your business turn out well?" I asked.

"It did," he said. "I made a great deal of money this week. Enough to buy you many pretties."

We ate in silence for a few minutes. I wanted to keep him talking, but the only subjects I could think of were his dead wives and Peg Leg Joe. I kept still.

"So," M. Bernard said abruptly, "you have moved my photograph to your bedside table." ·

Warmth rushed to my cheeks. "Yes. You don't mind, do you? I—" What reason could I come up with other than the truth: that I wanted his face to be the last thing I saw before falling asleep?

He paused to allow me to finish my sentence, but when I did not, he said, "It was taken by an acquaintance of mine in France, André Disdéri. Perhaps you have heard of him? I am happy you like it. Happy you care enough to want me to watch over you in your bed."

My cheeks grew hotter still. He knew. He knew how I felt.

"There must be something wrong with the frame," I blurted out to cover the awkwardness. "Every morning I wake to find it lying facedown. Something must be off balance."

M. Bernard shrugged. "*Mais oui.* It is a frame of not much quality. Sometime I will acquire a better one if you like the picture so."

I took a sip of water and lowered my eyes because he was watching me intently.

"You are even more beautiful than when I left, Sophia."

"Thank you. So are you." Had I actually said that out loud?

I shifted in my seat and glanced up at him through my lashes. A look of amusement and smug self-satisfaction flashed across his face so quickly that I would have missed it had I been a second later. Yes, he knew. And he thought it funny. Something squeezed my chest, and it was not the half-pleasurable emotion that had confined my breathing in the past weeks.

As Ling left the room after serving the sherry, M. Bernard said, "Now that you have been here awhile, what do you think of our Ling? Do you find him a treasure as do I?"

"He certainly appears wise. He's fascinating."

"Do you think perhaps I should grow my whiskers like his?" He cast me a sidelong look, his eyes brimming with laughter. "Would you find that style enticing on me as well?"

I lifted my chin. "I said 'fascinating,' not 'enticing.' But why not? Ancient-Chinese-man facial hair might suit you, sir."

"Oh, you think so, eh? Do you suppose he chews upon the ends to make the tips so scrawny and pointed?"

"Why—why that's exactly what I wondered!"

"Indeed? We are *en rapport*, then, you and I."

"I've been wondering: How did Ling and Achal come into your service? Where do you find such loyal servants who would leave everything to follow you across the world? Don't they miss their families?"

M. Bernard lightly touched my cheek to turn my face toward the light. "You are so curious about everyone and everything. It can be an attractive feminine trait"—he dropped his hand and turned back to his plate, which now held cold beef tongue—"but more often a nuisance. You must curb this interest in things that do not concern you. Especially about the lower classes. Bah! What do they matter? They are simply servants. They exist to labor for their betters, that is all."

I felt rebuked. It was also distressing for my M. Bernard to speak so arrogantly. Yet, who could blame him? Since he was a baby, everyone had scurried around simply to please him. It was not his fault.

There was something I needed to bring up, though, and it had to do with servants whether he liked it or not. "Sir, Mrs. Duckworth said you plan to hire a French maid for me."

He nodded, waiting. When I didn't continue for a moment, he said, "Well, out with it!"

"Is that still the plan? Perhaps since I've managed without her, you've changed your mind?"

"No," he said. "I rarely change my mind."

"But must my maid be French? Talitha usually helps me, but if she won't do, couldn't I have some other English-speaking servant? Pray don't put yourself to the bother of importing someone."

"No bother at all. Every lady wishes for a French maid. And if you think you can get out of this, you are very much mistaken." He wagged his finger playfully.

"You see, I've no head for languages and speak very little French. I would be more comfortable with someone I could talk to easily."

"In this you must be guided by me. You shall have Odette. She comes highly recommended. She is an impoverished gentlewoman and therefore much more suited than the locals to serve the needs of a fashionable lady. The delays have been preposterous, but she should arrive within the month." He gestured dismissively. "Let us speak no more of the matter."

Arguing would be useless.

M. Bernard launched his plans for our first trip together. "I am picturing you mounted jauntily on a camel. It is not much different from riding a horse once you get used to the swaying. The hump, you know. You will have to wear trousers—Sophia, am I boring you?"

He said this last because I was staring sightlessly over his head, thinking how my godfather's adventures abroad had certainly been exciting for him, but that at home he had left behind solitary women cut off from everything they knew. "Oh!" I said, startled. "Did you say something about humps?"

He arched one black brow. All through the dessert course he was at his most charismatic and I was once more under his spell, which had frayed ever so slightly about the edges during dinner.

Later I stood by the balustrade of the veranda, waiting for M. Bernard to join me after his solitary gentleman's cigar and port. There was a soul-stirring vibrancy in Mississippi summer nights. The air was perfumed with late roses and crushed flower petals. Fireflies glimmered in the dusk and bats swooped black across a purple-edged sky.

It wasn't long before M. Bernard appeared, followed by his gigantic Irish wolfhound. He removed his richly colored dressing gown and draped it on the back of a woven-wicker chair. The collar of his loose shirt was open, and he wore a smoking cap embellished with a beaded design. He stood silently at my side, following my gaze into the twilight.

A mosquito buzzed between us. At first we ignored it, not wanting to disturb the magical moment, but it was persistent. M. Bernard swatted at it and nearly hit me.

"It's just a simple country mosquito," I said. "It doesn't know that it's bad manners to buzz in our ears."

My godfather chuckled and squeezed my waist. "Simple country mosquito, indeed," he murmured.

Normally Finnegan ignored me, but now he raised his head, bared his teeth, and growled, low in his throat. I drew away.

M. Bernard dropped his arm from my waist. Placing his knee on the dog's back, he gave a vicious twist to Finnegan's ear until the dog yelped. "Never, never snarl at Sophia, sir."

"Please, Monsieur," I whispered. "I wasn't frightened. Please don't hurt him."

Foolish Finnegan growled again, and M. Bernard twisted harder. "It is how he learns what is expected of him. Sometimes it hurts to learn."

"Well, it won't be necessary after this," I said, reaching out a tentative hand to stroke the dog. "I shall make Finnegan my friend."

My godfather let go of the dog's ear, gave him a brisk pat, and seated himself. "Now, let me tell you how entertaining Finnegan was a few months ago when one of the local preachers made a visit."

The hound laid his great head on his paws, ignoring me now for his own good.

M. Bernard related how Finnegan bounded up to the man ("friendly as you please"), and the parson skedaddled up on his horse with his long legs flailing. "And there was our Finnegan, entirely blameless. I called after the fellow, 'He merely wanted to gnaw at your face, sir, and perhaps eat one hand. What do you care, when you have two?'" His laughter at the memory was as deep and rich as the plum cake we'd had for dessert. "Oh, if you could have seen the man, fleeing down the drive, hardly seated upon his horse."

I managed a faint smile. Poor minister. Who wouldn't be frightened of a dog that size charging toward him?

"You are too far away," my godfather said. He patted the wicker footstool next to his chair. "I nearly must shout to speak to you. Come, sit here."

It was awkward to seat myself on so low a stool in my crinoline. M. Bernard smiled at my difficulty and reached out a hand to help. I laughed a little as well, although I was still shaken by the dog incident.

He set about putting me at my ease once more. "Now, I need a story, Scheherazade. I have missed your tales these nights."

"What sort do you want?"

"Tell me about your family. Of all things, I should like to hear more of them."

"I'm worried about them right now. I haven't gotten a letter in ages."

"Oh, you know they are busy. You have related how the good Junius must work long hours and Anne must teach children. You have said that Harry cavorts with his friends. You have written to them. They know you are safe. You are off their hands. Now they need concern themselves about you no longer."

Was it true? Were they simply glad to be rid of me? No, I would not believe it. There was nothing in our past to suggest such a thing. They wanted my success and happiness and eventually hoped to share at least a little in it.

If M. Bernard felt he knew my siblings, he might aid them. I now related funny stories of how we would tease Junius for his pompous ways and Harry for being such a dandy. "When Harry came home wearing cherry-red striped trousers, Papa told him, 'If you must walk around on peppermint sticks, kindly do so in the privacy of your own room.'" I described how sweet and lovely Anne was, with her cloud of soft blond hair, and how she worried she would be left an old maid. "She's now four-and-twenty, but if she only has the chance to go out in society, not a man could help but fall in love with her."

M. Bernard snorted. "Well, perhaps there might be one or two." He leaned down and said, close to my ear, "Some prefer a ruddier glow to a lady's head." He pulled one pin from my hair and then another and another, until my curls tumbled about my face. "There! That's better. I have wanted to do that since you first came. From now on, always wear your hair down in the evenings. It is a particular desire of mine to see it long and rippling, like silken embers."

The weight of hair clung clammily to my neck. I had put it up for over two years; my hair fell past my hips, and it was inappropriate to let it hang wildly. I wondered: Did he want it loose because he still thought of me as a little girl or because he considered me a woman to admire? From the way he was looking at me now, it was the latter.

I pretended to be engrossed in petting Finnegan.

Once I had collected myself, I tried again to interest him in my siblings. He had said that "of all things," he wanted to hear about them most. "You would like my family, sir. Maybe soon they might come for a visit? I can't wait for you to get to know each other."

"Why?" His voice was hard-edged. "Do they wish to meet the Midas in his palace?"

I stared. How did he know that my brothers thought of him only in terms of his wealth? "No," I said quietly. "They wish to meet the man who gives me such happiness."

He seemed to consider his long hands. "Perhaps someday they might come," he said slowly, "if their absence makes you less than content here. It would be good for them to see how well you are cared for. But first you and I must become closer. I am a lonely man, Sophia. Unlike King Midas, people I touch do not turn to gold." He paused and looked out into the darkness. "Instead, they shrivel away—poof!—to dross. My tender feelings have been betrayed more than once. I have been unhappy in my connections."

That a person so confident should show this gap in his armor touched me. I would not disclose Ducky's confidences, but I had to say something. "I know you've had your trials, sir. I hope I can bring you some comfort."

He smiled. "You, *chérie,* will be the saving of me. Of this I am certain now."

We were leaning in close. He shook himself and stood. "It is late. I have kept you talking too long."

He walked me to my bedroom door and bid me good night.

When I entered my room, I nearly stepped on the shattered glass from M. Bernard's photograph where it lay, as if flung, facedown near the door.

Who had dared do this?

Gingerly I cleaned up the pieces, wrapped them in a scarf, and hid them beneath some linens in a chest in the hall until I could think what else to do with them.

Someone in this household hated my godfather.

CHAPTER 12

A MUSICAL INTERLUDE

Peg Leg Joe's sermon and song had given me a great deal to think about. From my reading of articles and advertisements for runaway slaves in Boston newspapers, it had been clear that a steady trickle made their way northward. They would sneak off in the dead of night, stumbling along as I had when I went out in the pitch dark to hear Peg Leg Joe preach. There were no mass exoduses. Most never dared to leave, but there were safe houses—stations, they were called—for those who did make their way through the Underground Railroad. Peg Leg Joe had mentioned a minister nearby who might guide them on the first stage of their journey.

They would puzzle out the clues in the "Drinking Gourd" song and follow them. I had written the song out so far as I could remember it and kept the paper beneath the desk blotter with my other secrets. It mentioned rivers—the nearest were the Tennessee and the Tombigbee, so perhaps those were the ones alluded to—as well as signposts, such as dead trees marked by Peg Leg Joe. My mouth grew dry as I pictured the route's hardship, terror, and weariness, at best, and the bullets, whips, chains, and sharp-toothed dogs, at worst. In icy winter the difficulty would be greater.

I suddenly comprehended the opening lines of the song: *When the sun come back, when the first quail call, then the time is come.* The slaves would not venture out until springtime. I admired and feared for anyone who dared try it, and wondered if I would take the risk were I in their place. My godfather would show no compassion to runaways returned by patrollers.

The nights grew cooler although the days still sizzled. The excitement among the servants flickered out as their lives and unrelenting chores dragged on in the familiar pattern. Peg Leg Joe remained at Wyndriven Abbey. I saw him behind the east wing occasionally, sawing or sanding boards or carrying materials to and fro. Our paths crossed once, and he tipped his hat and eyed me shrewdly.

"Mr.—" I wanted to be respectful, but I didn't know what to call him. "Peg Leg—"

He smiled and his face suddenly wasn't so scary. "Plain ole Joe will do, Missy. What I be doing for you?"

I lowered my voice. "I want to help. Is there some way I can help?"

His expression did not change. "You got a hankering to do a little carpentry, Missy?"

"No, of course not. I mean—" There must be code words for my desire to work with the Underground Railroad, but I knew none. How did anyone ever begin to help? How did anyone ever trust anyone?

He raised his eyebrows, waiting. "I keeps you in mind, Missy," he said softly when I said nothing more, and strode on.

I watched after him, feeling foolish.

Even if Joe chose to trust me, what could I possibly do? I had no more freedom to leave the place than the slaves themselves. More than ever, I realized how isolated I was to be kept.

During the daytime I was surrounded by others, yet I might as well have been alone. It was like the line from the poem "The Rime of the Ancient Mariner": *Water, water every where, nor any drop to drink.* People were everywhere, but my only daylight friend was my horse, Lily, until one morning when I sat reading on the veranda.

A yellow-striped cat sauntered up, rubbed himself against my skirt, and immediately took his place in my heart. He truly was a ragbag of an animal, with a torn ear, one eye swollen shut, and splotchy, mangy-looking fur, but he purred loudly and arched his back in the sweetest way and jumped onto my lap to be stroked. I ignored the fleas he was certain to carry and the hairs he left all over my skirt.

Charles and George were across the lawn, bending over something. I carried Buttercup—for that was clearly to be his name— over to them and laughed when I saw they were racing box turtles. They looked sheepish to have been discovered so, but when they saw my pet, their eyes widened.

"This is Buttercup," I said. "When the exciting race ends, would one of you please bring a saucer of milk and a sardine or something of that sort out to the veranda?"

Charles's eyes twinkled as he nodded. He joined me by my bench a short time later, with a smelly, fishy snack.

"I would like to bring Buttercup inside and give him a bath," I told him, "and let him sleep in my bedchamber, but something tells me my godfather wouldn't like this dear little fellow."

"No, Miss Sophia, I don't guess he would. That cat belongs in the stables, you know."

"I'm sure Monsieur would buy me a monkey or a—a puma or some such thing if I told him I wanted a pet, but I prefer Buttercup."

Charles paused a moment, wondering, I suppose, if he should allow himself to ask the question. Finally he gave in and asked, "What exactly is a puma?"

"One of those big wildcats. Like a lion, only skinnier, I think."

He grinned. "Yes, Miss Sophia. I can see the master giving you a puma with a diamond collar. No diamond collars for this poor beast, but I can bring him something to eat every morning right after breakfast—if he sticks around, that is."

"Oh, thank you," I said, from the heart. "How good you are."

And so every morning Buttercup would meet me to receive his milk and meat, and he was a joy and a comfort. My cat and my horse reminded me that I existed during the daytime. From the moment I awoke, I anticipated sunset. As the sultry days cooled into hints of autumn, M. Bernard and I usually spent our evenings by the library hearth, with the dancing flames reflected in his sherry. The glow of the fire lent an intimacy that seemed to give every word we spoke importance, although we never talked deeply upon any significant subject. Monsieur's easy elegance in his russet velvet jacket and the mellow leather of the book bindings added to the warmth of the atmosphere.

Sometimes I would use a long fork to toast bread and we would discuss our day as we nibbled. Other times I would read to my godfather while he smoked his pipe, or he would read to me as I embroidered, or we would play chess or backgammon or piquet (with me never winning, but I didn't care a pin for that since I so enjoyed watching Monsieur enjoy winning).

Often I told stories that I spun from tales I had read, interwoven with my own fancies. I reeled them out in serial form, usually leaving the hero or heroine in dire peril to be resolved the next night. During the day I would jot down ideas for later use so my mind would not be blank when Monsieur requested a story. As part of my goal to cheer my godfather, it seemed vitally important to continually pique his interest. This could be tiring as well as stimulating. I understood Scheherazade's frame of mind as I wondered how long I could last before my powers of invention drained dry.

I allowed my godfather to stroke my hand or bring it up to his lips or his cheek, labeling his caresses his "Frenchities." Besides being smitten by him, I genuinely liked him, although sometimes there was a look in his eye that made me uneasy. He could be . . . dangerous. Now, why did that adjective leap to mind? Perhaps because it fit. M. Bernard resembled a tiger—sleek, velvety, smiling, dangerous. And very attractive.

"Tonight," he said one evening, "we will have some music. You ride well and play chess tolerably, and now I shall hear how you handle the piano."

I seated myself at the instrument in the music room.

"Have I told you, sir," I said to him, "that the piano was one of my favorites of all your generous gifts?"

"And what," he said, from across the room in his chair of straw-colored satin, "were your other favorites?"

"Don't laugh," I said, "but I still love the rocking horse and the big doll. I named them Araby and Elodie. I haven't played with them since I was a child, of course, but I still feel a lingering fondness for them. One does, you know."

M. Bernard's lip twitched. "Oh, *oui,* one does."

I performed some Beethoven, followed by Schubert.

He applauded. "Brava. My money was well spent on your lessons." He rose and picked up the cello that rested on its stand in the corner. "Let us attempt a duet. You play well enough to follow me."

He held the instrument between his knees, its graceful curved neck beside his head. He raised the bow, paused, and then brought it down on the strings.

The deep tones sent a thrill through me that was almost a heartbreak. For a moment I couldn't move. Then my fingers began flying over the keys, either harmonizing or else joining in his wandering strains. We played faster and faster, the notes moving through my entire body.

A lock of hair fell over M. Bernard's forehead and his brow furrowed as he concentrated, his broad shoulders and upper torso moving with each passionate stroke of the bow.

Sometimes I played lightly, trilling, in contrast to the rich throbbing of the strings. Sometimes he would be playful and I would follow suit.

As our music filled the room, it seemed as though our souls were caught up together in rapture, breathless. He let the last note fade away, and I rested my fingers upon the keys, spent but exhilarated.

He rose, laid down his bow, and leaned the cello against the chair. He strode toward me, full of purpose. He took me by my shoulders, raised me up, and leaned my head back. He lowered his face to mine, and his mouth came down on my lips, hard, ardent, deep, his hands buried in my hair.

All my body responded, pulled into him, even as I had been pulled in by the music. Swallowed.

I couldn't breathe. This wasn't right. What was I doing? I raised my arms and gave a shove against his chest. He staggered backward, and I fled, unseeing, from the room.

His laughter followed me.

I slumped at my dressing table after Talitha left, unsure of everything—even if I had liked or disliked the kiss. It had roused powerful emotions, that was certain, but then, so had the music.

I was M. Bernard's ward, under his protection. Even though, in my daydreams, I had imagined my godfather returning my affection, his actual embrace was surely inappropriate and it worried me. Did all girls feel this way when romance moved from imagination to reality? As for M. Bernard, could he possibly be . . . *in love with me?* He had laughed afterward. Probably he had simply been carried away by the music.

I had to ask myself the question: *Why*, exactly, had he invited me to live at the abbey in the first place? In all the years of letters and gifts from my godfather, I had never wondered why he cared for me as he did; I took it as my due. Was it all owing to my mother? Perhaps he had loved her and therefore brought me here hoping I would resemble her. In order to seduce me as he had not been able to seduce her. At least, I hoped he had not.

No, that was ridiculous.

A memory echoed and rose to the surface, long forgotten, but stored away in detail.

I am very young, no more than five or six. I am lying on a sofa, my eyes closed, swathed in a scarf of Indian silk and nursing an aching ear in which someone has stuffed a bit of roasted onion.

My father and someone else, I don't know who, enter the room. My father says, "De Cressac has suggested he be legally named Sophie's guardian should she be underage at my death."

I lie perfectly still, perfectly silent.

"Shall you do it?" asks the unknown voice.

"I must," my father says, "so she, at least, will be provided for. I wish he'd be mindful of the others as well; if he isn't, they'll be left nearly destitute. He's always taken an unusual interest in Sophie, and I don't know why. . . . Well, we all adore her, but he's not the sort of man who would saddle himself with someone else's child out of tenderness of heart." He sighed. "In the end I have no choice but to agree, whether for good or ill."

It suddenly occurs to me that the onion might edge its way into my brain. I gasp. The interesting conversation ceases.

CHAPTER 13

DISENCHANTMENT

A tune played over and over again in my head—strains of our music from last night. Beautiful, really. We were very good together.

Talitha brought a breakfast tray with a lopsided bouquet and an envelope upon it. I eyed the note with trepidation. I'm not sure what I expected—either passion or apology. It was neither.

Ma très chère Sophia, it read, *I am sorry the flowers are not more gracefully displayed. Obviously I arranged them myself. I tried. What shall we name our musical composition? Perhaps "Meanderings on a Mellow Evening in the South"—what do you think? Please don't be missish about the kiss. I wanted to do it and I enjoyed it. That's all. You need not fear it will be repeated—for a while, anyway. B.*

He had kissed me on impulse because we had bonded through stirring music. I had read too many romances. He had become my guardian because he was my godfather. His actions had been improper, of course, but I must remember M. Bernard did not look at such things as I did—the free-spirited French and all. . . . I squirmed inwardly. *Possibly in love with me,* indeed.

M. Bernard would have worn a comical expression as his large hands poked the flowers into the vase and the daisy kept flopping down.

It would be hard to forget such a kiss. It had been exciting— *Admit it.* Not enjoyable precisely, but exciting. I smiled a little and touched my lips.

What did he mean by "for a while"?

I started to tuck the note beneath the few letters from my family in my jewelry chest, then pulled them all out. I carefully reread each one, seeking clues as to why no one had written again in so long, but could find none. Perhaps there was trouble somewhere with the mail delivery; Chicataw was far off the beaten track. But what if some illness or misfortune had befallen my brothers and sister? Anxiety gnawed at me as I wrote them another letter, pleading for a response.

That afternoon, when I went out for my ride on Lily, a new saddle awaited me. It was of tooled leather in a pattern of twisting vines and flowers, embedded with mother-of-pearl and silver and glowing bits of amber and garnet. With such a saddle, Lily resembled the steed of a fairy princess. I rode her to a meadow, followed by Garvey, naturally, and stopped there, where I braided Lily's mane and twined it with a wildflower chain. Garvey eyed me sardonically, but I was used to ignoring him.

I took my horse now to the veranda just outside of M. Bernard's open office window and looped her reins around a post in the balustrade. I ran inside to ask him to look out at Lily. My godfather would know how pleased I was with his gift if he saw I fussed over her so. Also, I thought, he would see that I had recovered from last night's awkwardness.

The office was unlocked and empty. Always before, if M. Bernard or Mr. Bass was not present, it was bolted. A massive desk hulked in the center.

The top drawer gaped open. Not knowing why I did so, I peeked inside. Only one item lay in the exact center: an envelope slightly yellowed about the edges with the name "Victoire" written upon it. I picked it up and took a quick look around.

It was shameful to read letters addressed to others.

Go ahead. Open it. The owner is long gone.

Slowly I drew the notepaper out of the envelope. A faint perfume clung to it. The paper was tissue thin, with scalloped edges.

Dearest Victoire,

How thankful I am there is a Trustworthy One to bring this epistle to your fair hand. One by one, the brown leaves fall. Golden summer ends. But how sweetly our pathway was strewn with roses when we walked it together.

(At last! A love letter written upon good paper!)

I was able to find another position quickly after de C. sent me packing. I now have lodgings that are not so fine as what you are used to, but that you will be happy in, I hope.

Dearest, I cannot rest until I rest with you. You MUST leave that Person who is your husband in legal terms only. I am the husband of your soul. I love you. I adore you.

Send instructions to me by way of that same Trustworthy One. Tell me when it is safe to whisk you away. I breathlessly await your answer.

I bid you adieu.

Your adoring,
C. G.

The last name was Gregg, Ducky had said. He certainly could write a lyrical love letter. I wondered if he had copied bits from a book.

So . . . Victoire had left. She had abandoned M. Bernard. Ducky had seen her only the one time afterward. Perhaps Victoire bore children to Mr. Gregg that would ease, somewhat, the sorrow over little Anton. She might now live happily in a cozy, bustling household. Somehow, though, I doubted it. Fragile threads of tragedy seemed to cling to the letter.

Of course it had been a tragedy for my godfather. Poor, poor man. How terrible for M. Bernard to have kept this note so close. To read over and over again. Why? Why would he inflict such pain on himself?

I was puzzling over this when voices sounded nearby. Frantically I stuffed the paper in the envelope and replaced it in the drawer. How would I explain—

"How dare they?" It was M. Bernard's voice, tight with anger, speaking from outside the open window. "Right here at the abbey."

"It may not be the fellow I heard about in town," Mr. Bass said hesitantly.

"Hah," scoffed M. Bernard. "You think there is another one-legged former sailor carpenter hiring himself out to plantations, do you?" There was a pause. "Hmm, here is Sophia's horse—where is the rider?"

I dashed from the room and flew down the corridor.

My breath came ragged as I sped to the door into the east wing. As always, it was locked. I raced outside to peek through one east wing window after another, glancing wildly about, terrified that someone had followed me. No Joe. Even now M. Bernard was probably sending for the marshal—or worse, for Garvey, with a weapon to apprehend the carpenter.

I finally found an unlocked outer door and burst inside, nearly knocking Joe's wooden leg from beneath him as he stood attaching molding. Thankfully he was alone. He righted himself and raised his eyebrows, mildly inquiring, as if it were no great surprise to find a young lady panting and panic-stricken in the empty wing.

"You've got to leave right now," I whispered. "Monsieur de Cressac knows who you are."

Joe said nothing, simply nodded and turned to depart.

"Be careful," I said. "And good luck."

Without pausing, from over his shoulder, he said, "Thank you, Missy. I is gone 'fore you knows it. Done it many a time before."

My heart still racing, I went to lead Lily back to the stables.

After a silent meal with a brooding M. Bernard, a meeting was called with all the servants. The Negroes gathered, old and young, in a half circle at the bottom of the veranda steps. Ling and Mrs. Duckworth, Achal and Alphonse stood beside the master at the top. Garvey stood slightly behind, clutching a cruel-looking cat-o'-nine-tails whip. I cowered just outside the morning room doorway. My godfather had indicated I should attend. Part of me could not bear to, and yet I dared not defy him and stay away altogether.

M. Bernard stood scanning the group for several moments. His grip was so tight on the walking stick he held that his knuckles were white. A muscle beside his eye twitched. Most of the servants bowed their heads. Some shuffled their feet. Tension was palpable in the air.

"My people," M. Bernard said finally, in ringing tones, "as you all well know, a person has been here. A liar come to stir up trouble. The patrollers are now on the heels of the rogue, and he will be caught and jailed. But you—all of you—I have housed you, fed you, cared for you, and yet you have harbored this snake. What should be done to such disloyal slaves?" Here he hit his stick in his other palm with such a crack that everyone jumped. "You agree you deserve punishment, do you not?"

The servants made no response, still looking at the ground, wisely drawing no individual attention. Had I been the object of Monsieur's wrath, I believed I would have withered away.

"But"—M. Bernard's features contorted a little as he brought himself under rigid control—"I choose to be merciful. Your food rations shall be cut only for this month. However, you must reveal the identity of the person who warned this scoundrel to leave before I could confront him. Who was it? Tell me now."

I grasped the doorframe. I had never thought of this. It hadn't occurred to me that M. Bernard would realize someone had alerted Joe to flee. The moment stretched on. No one spoke. Even the little ones stood still, huddling behind their mothers. A crow cawed hoarsely from the forest.

"Very well," my godfather said. "Children, go back to the quarters. The others will be there shortly." He waited until they were gone. "Now, if no one will speak, then someone innocent must suffer. You, Willie, come up here."

The poor old gardener shuffled up. He seemed to shrivel smaller as he approached my godfather's powerful frame. M. Bernard removed his coat and handed it to Ducky.

"Take off your jacket and shirt, Willie," M. Bernard commanded. "Bend over the rail. Garvey, the whip."

Garvey stepped forward and handed his master the whip.

Willie, who always was dressed neatly, looked exposed and skinny, naked from the waist up.

I darted up to M. Bernard and grabbed his arm. "Please," I begged, "don't do this. Perhaps no one warned the man. Perhaps he left of his own accord."

"Go inside, Sophia," M. Bernard said coldly, shaking his arm free, "if you cannot watch quietly." Then, hissing so softly that no one else could hear, "And never presume to tell me how to manage my own people."

I retired to the morning room, despising myself for not confessing it had been me who had warned Joe. I simply could not do it. As penance I leaned my cheek against the door and watched M. Bernard bring the lash down on Willie's bare back, wincing each time as if the sting were against my own flesh. Again and again and again.

As the lash dropped down in between strokes, it left lines of crimson on the flagstones. The sounds of Willie's suppressed agony would be forever in my ears.

Each lash was a deathblow to the infatuation I had carried for my godfather. Eventually M. Bernard grew tired and ceased, his breath heaving. I dragged myself up to my room.

After a while Talitha entered. "Master say come out on the veranda."

I shook my head. "I can't face him after what he just did."

"Yes, you can. You got to." She straightened the sash of my gown.

"How could he do that to Willie?"

"Easy. He got an arm on him, the master do." As she was briskly brushing through my hair, she said, "It's a good thing Peg Leg Joe got a head start. It's a good thing someone warned him. They would've strung him up."

"Yes, but will Willie be all right?"

"He been beat before. He tougher'n he looks." She hesitated, rubbing her wrists, before saying, "The best way you can help us is to butter Master up and smooth him out so he ain't angry no more."

After pondering her words, I nodded slowly and rose. She was leaving ahead of me when I stopped her. "Talitha?"

She turned and waited.

"Charles is always good-humored with you, isn't he?" I asked.

Her brow wrinkled. After a moment she nodded.

I wound and unwound one of my curls around my finger. "I'm sure you can say anything you want around him and he'll still care for you."

"Yes."

"You're very lucky."

Compassion flashed across her usually cool expression. I gave her a bleak smile and passed by her to join M. Bernard on the veranda, where he was pacing.

I apologized for interfering in his treatment of the servants.

He shrugged. "You do not understand how these people must be dealt with. They cannot be allowed to get out of hand. There are too many of them. Have you heard of the carnage of the 1791 slave rebellion in Haiti? My great-uncle's entire family—with all six of his children—was slaughtered there. As the standard of their uprising, the Negroes carried a pike with the carcass of an impaled white baby."

Such a thing could never happen in our country. Not among the people I knew, black or white.

He brushed his hands together as if washing them of the consequences. "I have no choice but to keep my people subdued. Did you think I enjoyed the whipping?"

I shook my head, although I wasn't sure; if he didn't want to do it, why did he carry it out himself? Why not have Garvey wield the lash?

A sharp little silence followed as M. Bernard sank down on a bench. I sat beside him.

Buttercup wandered up to rub against me. I scooped him into my arms.

"What is that animal doing here?" my godfather demanded.

"Isn't he a darling?" I said, my hot cheek against Buttercup's fur. He was hot also, but in a comforting, fuzzy way. "He visits now and again. I've named him Buttercup."

"He belongs in the stables. I will give you a suitable pet if you desire one."

"A puma?" I whispered.

"I beg your pardon?" he said sharply.

I shook my head. "Nothing. I don't want a pet. I just like to play with this cat once in a while."

"No playing with him in the future. I cannot abide felines."

Without responding, I tossed Buttercup down and shooed him away. I would feed and cuddle my cat whenever I wanted. I had no intention of giving him up.

M. Bernard glanced over and raised his brows, questioningly. There were shadows under his eyes and he looked drained. Maybe all this was harder on him than I realized.

I searched for words to say. "Shall I tell you about the time when I was small and thought I was sprouting wings?"

"Tell on," he said wearily.

I worked to win him from his ill humor, and soon I was succeeding. He relaxed and slowly grew languid and affectionate in the heavy air. He leaned in to me and chuckled once.

"You have a gift, Sophia," he said. "It is a joyfulness of spirit that can turn darkness into light. When you smile, it makes others want to smile."

"Like a clown," I said, laughing, but his comment gratified me. There was something pleasing in my power to sway M. Bernard's mood. Perhaps it had to do with the age-old tricks employed by women. Helen of Troy and Delilah and so on. Interesting company. He was so strong, so sophisticated, so powerful, and yet Talitha was right—I could influence him.

CHAPTER 14

ODETTE

"Bonjour, Mademoiselle," the maid said, curtsying.

"You must be Odette," I said.

Talitha had brought her to my room and ducked away as quickly as possible. The Frenchwoman was pretty, perhaps still in her twenties. She had sleek black hair and bright, malicious black eyes. Before we spoke, they flicked up and down over me, obviously finding my person lacking. Her gray dress and white apron were crisp and immaculate, tightly fitted to her swelling bosom and drawn in to a tiny waist, with a perky bow behind.

"Je ne parle pas français." That was nearly the limit to my French.

"Oui, Mademoiselle."

What was I to do with her now? I gestured to indicate the powder closet and wardrobes. She opened them and, with a contemptuous little smile, ran her hand through the hanging garments. M. Bernard had said she was an impoverished gentlewoman—which must explain her manner, as if she were much too good for the job she was compelled by circumstances to do.

Already I missed Talitha.

In the next days it grew ever harder. Odette followed whenever I roamed outside, despite my insistent gestures for her to depart. On the third day after she had shadowed me about the gardens, a surge of defiance sent me to confront M. Bernard as he worked in his office.

He turned his brilliant gaze my way when I entered. "What a pleasant surprise. To what—" He ceased speaking at sight of my expression. His countenance changed to one of patience and long-suffering. "You have something to say. All right, out with it. What is it that mars your so-lovely face with . . . righteous indignation, is it?"

I strode briskly up, starting out strong, but then sputtering. "You can't—she can't— Sir, I can't continue to have Odette descend the second I step down from the veranda. It's intolerable to have her there every moment I'm outside."

"Sit down, Sophia. You need not continue to loom."

I sunk to a chair, his tone rapidly deflating me.

"Odette attends you on my orders," he stated firmly. "You are under my protection, and you are too precious to allow the possibility of mishaps. There are poachers in the woods, sometimes slaves eluding the patrollers. Perhaps even that one-legged scoundrel who escaped."

"But—"

He held up his hand. "Be so kind as to let me speak without interruption. It is not only that. As a man of means, and as a businessman of consequence, I have naturally incurred enemies. My traps are not intended only for poachers. Then too, you are so delicate, such a lady, that Odette watches to ensure no tumble or accident befalls you."

"Sir, I am not so helpless or dainty or—or—stupid as you insinuate." I tried to speak with dignity.

"Oh, but you are very breakable." He spanned the fine bones of my wrist with his thumb and little finger. "Now, do not embarrass Odette by trying to make her disobey my orders. And no more on this subject. It bores me."

Anything else I might say would only make me sound foolish, so I curbed the hot words that sprang to my tongue. Ducky's comment about Adele came back to me: *Nothing her husband gave her was what she wanted.* Could it be that he only gave her what he had already decided she must have? I turned to go.

He stopped me. "There is something I needed to ask of you before you leave me to my accounts."

I waited.

"I must travel on some distant business soon. Will you take charge of my keys in my absence? It is a dire responsibility. I shall entrust you with keys that even our good Ducky does not have. They must be guarded and never used."

My mouth went dry. "I would be happy to do that, sir." His keys!

I tried to be considerate of Odette. After all, she was a foreigner alone and out of place, yet her attitude toward me was baffling. She seemed to resent me so much more than could be accounted for by the fact that she had been wellborn and come down in the world. It was as if she had arrived at the abbey prepared to hate me.

Perhaps I could win her over by kindness. When she finished my hair one morning, I presented her with the gift of a crimson scarf that would set off her coloring beautifully.

"Merci, Mademoiselle," she said in a flat voice, and turned to leave, pinching the scarf between her fingers.

"And will you please mend the cranberry silk? I stepped on the lace last time I wore it."

She turned around slowly.

"It's torn," I said. "Torn. The cranberry silk."

She watched me with a faint, mocking curl of the lips as I gesticulated awkwardly to make her understand. I dropped my hands. "I know you can speak at least a little English, Odette. I know it."

An absolute blankness came over her face.

I snatched the gown out of the wardrobe and shoved it in her arms. As usual, she eventually tired of her game and did what I had been trying to make her do for the past several minutes.

"I know it!" I called again after her as she left the room. "And here's your scarf!"

She swept on toward the service stairs without a backward glance as I dangled her gift out the doorway.

The scarf was too good for her anyway.

She seemed to take pleasure in cinching my corset too tightly, which was daily torture, but she never made mistakes I could complain about to my godfather. Instead, she kept my things perfectly. She had a wonderful way with my hair. For the daytime she would coil and twine it, allowing a few curling tendrils to escape. In the evenings, since M. Bernard wanted it left down, she would tuck in a jade comb or a silver pin or a posy at the most becoming angle.

A few times a week she dressed me in the exotic foreign costumes my godfather demanded. She even added to their allure. For my Indian outfit she procured kohl to outline my eyes. For my *ensemble* from Istanbul she chose a pale sapphire sash to set off the soft white trousers and deep blue silk outer robe.

Once, when she clothed me as a Manchu woman, she murmured something that included the word *poupée,* which I knew meant "doll." I set my jaw and looked her straight in the eye. Yes, perhaps I *was* the master's doll. What of it? I didn't mind humoring Monsieur's whims in my dress and hair. There was little enough I could do to cheer him and repay his generosity.

CHAPTER 15

TIGER, TIGER

I preened in front of the mirror late one day not long afterward. Odette had just finished helping me into an evening gown of white grounded silk. The bodice and tiny sleeves were finished with broad bands of sapphire-embossed velvet. Opals dangled at my ears and on my wrist, and Odette had inserted lappets of blue and gold ribbon, intermingled with golden leaves, into my rippling hair.

"*Vous etes jolie,*" Odette said.

She had never complimented me before. Was she softening toward me? Come to think of it, she had acted odd all afternoon, seeming to hurry through my dressing, as though she were expecting something.

A quick knock sounded at the door, and Talitha poked her head in. "Miss, Master say you're to go to him in the crimson salon. Right now."

I nodded, immediately on edge. This had never before happened.

When I entered the salon, I drew back at the sight of M. Bernard's expression. His mouth was hard and his nostrils white and pinched, his eyes ablaze. In his hand he held crushed papers. He waved them so close they touched my nose.

"I do not know what to say, Sophia. That you, at your tender age, should already be an experienced trollop. What am I to think?"

"What—I don't—what are they?" I faltered.

"You pretend you do not know?"

His hot breath shot into my face.

"I don't know what they are," I said.

He grabbed my upper arm and squeezed painfully. "You do not recognize these missives, which you saved carefully in your jewelry chest? Letters from some man describing your lovely eyes, your lovely skin. Are such personal compliments from gentlemen so frequent that their presumptuousness is not memorable? What other liberties did you allow this *cochon*?"

The letters from Felix out of my jewelry chest. Those innocent, sweet love letters. M. Bernard was insinuating something vile. I glared at him. "Sir, is it the act of a gentleman to read correspondence addressed to me? They are private notes, written years ago for my viewing only. The young man who sent them was always respectful. I saved them because I had never before and have never since received such kind words."

I snatched the papers from his hand, broke from his grasp, and fled, scorching heat flaming my cheeks. I passed Odette in the corridor. She averted guilty, beady black eyes. *She* had given them to my godfather.

I flung the poor notepapers into the low blaze of my fireplace and threw myself on the bed, weeping bitterly. He had spoiled everything with his ugly, unjust, and untrue insinuations. I wept until I could weep no more.

I was staring bleakly at the underside of the bed's quilted canopy, thinking it resembled the lid to a coffin, when Talitha entered. "Master asks, do you be coming to supper?"

"Tell him that no, I'm not."

She didn't withdraw. "Please, Miss Sophia."

I said nothing.

"Please, he be angry."

"Then let him be angry. This time I'm not coming down."

I rolled over and buried my face into my pillow, but I could still feel Talitha's presence. I heard her cross the room. She gave my back an awkward little pat.

"Thank you," I whispered, "but I'm still not coming down."

She sighed and left the room.

When my bedchamber was darkening, I wriggled out of my gown and into a nightdress. I ripped the ribbons and golden leaves from my hair and hurled them toward the dressing table. When Odette entered, I feigned sleep. At the sound of her footsteps, suffocating red fury flooded me. I wondered if she could feel it.

"*Je suis désolé,*" she murmured. Her fingers brushed the place on my arm marked by M. Bernard's fingers. I recoiled.

She was sorry. If she was sorry, then why had she done it? I kept my eyes tightly shut. I heard her pick up and shake out the dress, hang it, and leave the room.

M. Bernard commanded her presence, so Odette I must have. She could pry into my drawers, my trinket boxes. What if she were to find the secrets I'd hidden beneath the blotter? I slipped out of bed to remove the paper on which I'd written the lyrics to the "Drinking Gourd" song, as well as the envelope containing the red hair and the note to Tara. I had memorized the words to the song, so I burned that page in the fireplace. The envelope I placed casually in the desk drawer. If Odette found it there amid the jumble of odds and ends, she would attach no significance to it.

Off and on all night long I awakened and replayed the scene with M. Bernard, thinking of what I should have said. When I slept, my dreams were ill.

Cool air tickled my legs. The bedclothes were down at my feet. Slowly, stealthily, my nightgown was moving up my body, inch by inch. Now it was just below my knees, now just above. I gave a short, strangled scream, bolted straight up to snatch the blankets from the foot of the bed, and awoke completely.

I peered into the shadowy corners of the moonlit room. No one. The door was locked. *Or did I forget to lock it?* I tiptoed to the door and found it gaping open. I shut it and turned the key.

No one was in the room. It had been a nightmare.

"Charles," I said the next morning, "would you please bring my trunk down from the attic and put it in my bedroom?"

He raised his eyebrows, but said only, "Yes, Miss."

Out on the veranda I cuddled Buttercup.

"I'm leaving," I whispered. "I'll never return to this place."

I set him gently on the bench with one last stroke down his long tail and stepped into the garden for a final stroll and to make my plans. Buttercup lightly leaped down to follow me.

"Come along, then," I said.

We made our way down the sinuous paths between the beds, Buttercup nosing under my skirts and twisting between my legs to nearly trip me. I would miss him so much. "I'll ask Charles to keep feeding you," I told him.

Today I would inform M. Bernard I was leaving. Surely he would loan me traveling money in order to be rid of a person he so despised. My family would be disappointed to see me back already and all their hopes dashed, but I had no choice. I would finally learn why their letters had ceased. I would find some sort of job. Perhaps as a seamstress. It would be terrible, but I could help out family finances a little.

An hour later, as I was placing into the trunk the few possessions I considered mine, my godfather breezed into the room.

"They told me you had ordered your baggage brought down, but I did not expect—this." He captured my hands and held them tightly in his own.

I turned my head away. "I'm leaving, sir. If you'd be so good as to loan the money for the train, I'll pay you back as soon as I can." I had to speak carefully so my voice wouldn't break.

"Your stay here is not a visit," he said, his tone gentle. "This is your home and I am your legal guardian. Will it help if I apologize? Here, I am doing it. I do beg your pardon. The letters came as a shock; at your age I had thought you completely inexperienced in matters of the heart. But upon consideration I should not have spoken so. I am sorry I was abrupt."

Abrupt? Was that how he chose to describe his speech and actions of yesterday? Had he forgotten how his words had lashed me like a whip? Should I show him the bruises on my arm? I snatched my hands from his. "I can't possibly stay here when you called me—when you called me a . . . *trollop*."

"I was wrong. It was unforgivable, but—will you forgive me anyway?" His tone was soft and pleading. "I will do all in my power to make it up to you. You see, I was worried you had given the young man encouragement, to have those many epistles from him. I have been—I have been betrayed before, so I am perhaps oversensitive to these things."

At this moment I couldn't blame Victoire for leaving her husband.

I was so weary from lack of sleep and the difficulty of holding up through the morning that I swayed on my feet.

He pulled me against his chest and put his arms around me, and I didn't pull away, though I remained stiff.

"I'll try," I said at last.

With one hand, he brushed the hair from my face. "Oh, *ma fifille*, were you crying all night?"

"Not all," I said shakily.

"'Not all.' *Pauvre petite!* No wonder you were not thinking clearly. No wonder you thought I might let you go. Here, sit down on the ottoman and I will go myself to fetch you a nice, warm posset."

I sank down and waited.

When he brought a steaming cup, I sipped it carefully, grateful for the comforting cream and potent nutmeg warming my throat. M. Bernard sat beside me.

"Sir, I will stay," I said grudgingly, "but—but I truly am

concerned about my family. That's part of the reason I wanted to leave. *Something* must be wrong."

"Still fretting about the lack of letters?"

"I have received no mail since early July. Are you certain nothing has come for me during these weeks?"

"Of course I cannot be certain. All the post is brought to my office to await my sorting. Perhaps I missed something in the mountain of business correspondence. I will check again today."

"And please, please may I invite my brothers and sister for a visit?"

"I told you they might come," he said, stroking his beard, "once we knew each other better. Perhaps November. What do you think of November?"

He held all power in his hand. He could bring my family or he could refuse to let them come. I mustn't show I was still upset. "Yes, please, Monsieur. If it—if that's the soonest that can be contrived."

"So," he said, "may I return to my pressing duties without fear you will try to rush off and leave me?" His voice was caressing, his expression droll.

I turned from him so he couldn't see my face. "I think you're now safe."

That afternoon Talitha brought me five letters from my family. They ranged in dates throughout the past six weeks. In one Junius complained of numerous matters, while pretending to be stoic and long-suffering. Three were from Anne, who wrote a lot of fripper-ies and teased about the whirl of gaiety she supposed I must be experiencing. The one from Harry jabbered on about his escapades.

All three of my siblings gave cause for concern, although Harry was the only correspondent who wasn't trying to hide anything. He blatantly related his scrapes. He was taking fancy dance lessons and bragged about the horse he had "invested" in. Someone with as few means as my brother had ought not to invest in something that must eat and could easily die. But Harry had always despised prudence.

My godfather had withheld these letters from me for weeks while I worried myself sick over my family. He wanted me to have only him.

CHAPTER 16

THE FOREST

The scene in M. Bernard's tapestry simply would not cooperate. I had intended a landscape of revelry, full of bright, pleasing color. I bit my lip as I stitched. Instead, the embroidery silks my godfather had bought for me were darker and duller than I had wished. The background was a green so murky as to be nearly black, and the dim wildflowers were absorbed into the setting.

I stabbed my needle into the canvas and turned to gaze at the flames of the library fireplace. Occasionally they whipped sideways when especially violent gusts of wind made their way helter-skelter down the chimney.

Ducky had mentioned my godfather could be moody. At the time I had not yet experienced it, but I had since. When he was irritated or bored or frustrated, his mouth would become thin and his eyes would narrow and glitter in a thoroughly unappealing fashion. No one had ever treated me as harshly as he had the day before. I understood he had a painful past and that some of his words and actions must be excused by that, but still. . . .

He had purposely withheld my letters. Separating me from everyone I cared for was not an accidental oversight. I shivered.

He was instantly solicitous. "What is it, *ma caille?*"

I must find a way to meet other people.

I moved to the chair across from him. "It's only that I wondered if I could attend church on Sundays."

He turned his goblet of claret round and round so the firelight winked in the crystal facets, studying it. He did it for so long I wondered if he'd heard me.

I was about to repeat my question when he said, "I think not."

"I understand you don't care for religion, but I could go by myself."

"I said no." His voice and expression were lifeless with disinterest.

I gritted my teeth to keep from speaking so sharply that he would be shocked out of his boredom. It disturbed me how often I had to reign in my temper with M. Bernard. I had never even known I could be angry back home in Boston.

He shook himself. "Listen! Hear how the thunder rumbles in the distance. It will storm before morning."

The tempest broke around midnight. A great boom awoke me. Panes rattled in my windows and branches crashed into the walls. Wind-ripped leaves plastered themselves against the glass and rain poured down like a million fists pounding. I snuggled deep beneath my covers. Wild storms were delightful as long as I was safe inside.

But then came other sounds: footsteps pausing outside my door and the knob being tried. My godfather's voice calling—soft, insistent—"Sophia, Sophia." And then louder: "Sophia!"

I clutched the bedclothes up to my chin, afraid he would hear my heart banging in my chest.

He tried the knob again, paused, then gave a grunt, and his footsteps receded.

Did he intend to make me his mistress? So no one else would ever want me? So I'd be forced to stay at Wyndriven Abbey forever? The writings of Balzac were full of mistresses, and I knew their qualifications involved sumptuous bedrooms and gifts of jewelry. If certain aspects of my life had come from the pages of a fairy tale, I had now entered between the covers of some lurid novel.

The next morning my godfather burst outside to find me on the veranda with Buttercup curled up like a round cat cushion in my lap, surrounded by a soggy world.

I dumped off Buttercup, nudging him away with a foot, cursing myself for letting M. Bernard see my pet once again. I shook out my skirts and looked up with quick-gathered self-possession.

"You have cat hair on your face," he said as he wiped off the bench next to me with his handkerchief and seated himself.

"Oh. Sorry." I brushed my cheeks quickly with both hands. He always knew how to rattle my composure.

"It was a violent storm we had during the night."

"Yes, sir, it was."

"Were you frightened?"

"No, sir. I enjoy storms."

"I worried you might be huddled in your bed terrified. I tried to come reassure you."

"Did you?"

"I did, but your door was locked. Do you lock it every night?"

"I do."

"Do you think someone is plotting against your virtue?" A gleam of amusement twinkled in his honey brown eyes.

"No, sir. I simply feel more secure with the big, dark house shut out."

"You know I have all the keys, don't you? I could enter at any time I wanted."

"Yes, sir, I know that. But I'm also aware you have respect for my honor."

He shrugged and rose. A great pressure eased from my shoulders when he said, "I do, you know. I do indeed have respect for your honor, and I give you my promise I will always guard it. And next week, when I am away on business, you shall have my keys to keep. Good day, *ma chérie.*"

He strode away, whistling. I had made a narrow escape.

I passed Odette coming out of the stables with Garvey that afternoon. He sweated and swaggered; her expression was self-satisfied as she straightened her skirts. Whatever they had been doing evidently did not need a command of each other's language.

She saw me, arched her thin black eyebrows, and swept up behind to follow wherever I went.

I said nothing but, filled with a trembling determination, headed off across the parkland. I skirted downed limbs and picked my way through puddles. I led her over the most uneven ground, scrambling through brambles and squelching over soggy hollows where I had to pull my feet out with sucking slurps. As she tagged along, she kept emitting exasperated sighs and phrases that sounded like French oaths under her breath.

"Why don't you turn back?" I called over my shoulder, not expecting an answer. I often asked this during our rambles and, of course, never received an answer. We tromped through goldenrod that made her sneeze and up hills so briskly her breath came in labored pants.

And my godfather thought *I* was delicate. Her discomfiture lent a certain pleasure to my walks.

My half boots were clotted with black mud. More mud splashed on my dress. The hem of Odette's skimpy gray twill maid's uniform was filthy and soaking wet. She must clean and repair her own garb as well as mine. Hah!

Suddenly a little cry sounded from behind. I whirled around. Odette had tripped over a clump of tall weeds. Once I ascertained she wasn't truly hurt, I picked up my skirts and was off, dashing for all I was worth into the woods.

I crashed through a thicket of brambles and found myself surrounded by corrugated trunks of trees so dense that only the merest speckling of pale light filtered through from above.

I was alone. I was alone outside!

Odette called my name and I waded in deeper. I wasn't a fool; I did watch for the traps Garvey had said were planted here, as well as for poison ivy. I simply didn't let them worry me unduly.

What was this unaccustomed feeling? Serenity. It was serenity and well-being. As if I had come home after a long absence. I plucked a lacy fern frond to tuck into my pocket. Later I would press it between the pages of a book.

By stepping carefully from stone to stone, I crossed a wide brook. There seemed a clean, pure goodness in the gurgling, laughing sound it made. No wonder in the old tales crossing running water left one safe from evil. The smell of the forest was earthy and mossy and rotting, but in a clean, natural way. Birds warbled and squirrels scrambled.

Here I could think. Here I could consider the happenings of the past months.

I had been losing myself. I had to strive to remain Sophie-like. Thank goodness I was no longer besotted with my godfather. Thank heavens my self-esteem had been fostered by a loving family or his powerful personality might have eroded mine away completely. As it was, I was ashamed to realize that during this time I had spent with him, I had relaxed some of my principles.

"Oh, Anne," I whispered, "what should I do?"

There was no question I shouldn't be living unchaperoned with M. Bernard. My family would never have allowed me to come here had they known he was a widower. Panic skittered in my stomach when I remembered the rattling of my bedchamber door.

And yet, I had glimpsed his vulnerability, his pain. He had survived many blows in life. Everyone he had cared for had left him, one way or another. I couldn't abandon him now. He had said he had regard for my honor. He had given me his word. I still enjoyed most of our time together. He was intelligent and interesting and generous and could be sensitive and kind. He had the power to be a great man if his noble side were nurtured. I could help him become the gentleman he should be.

And there was such a thing as a chair thrust under the doorknob if I needed that security.

The shadows lengthened. I must go back.

I had no trouble finding my way out of the forest. Some sort of sixth sense guided me through the trees.

Odette slumped miserably beside a low brick wall not far from the edge of the woods. I almost felt sorry for her.

She raised her head when I approached.

"Listen," I said. "You can understand what I'm saying, so drop the pretense. You may tattle to my godfather, but if you do, I'll only make your life harder. Every once in a while I must get away to the woods by myself. If you'll stay here by this wall with your sewing or whatever, I'll promise to be back within two hours and to keep my clothes clean. A break for me, less work for you. What do you say? A truce?"

She studied me, taking in my disheveled aspect, then savagely kicked against the wall to knock loose a clump of mud from her heavy boot. *"Très bien, Mademoiselle."*

CHAPTER 17

COME OUT NOW

"I am leaving today," M. Bernard announced a few mornings later. "I must be gone a few weeks. As promised, you shall safeguard my keys."

He held out the iron ring and I took it, trying to hide my excitement. It was weightier than I had expected.

"Are you ready for such a 'heavy' responsibility?" he asked with laughter, but also with a certain consideration.

"I hope so."

"You may use all except three. This one"—he showed a plain black key with scratches on the shaft—"goes to the churchyard gate. And this one"—he held up an enormous key with a cross shape piercing the head—"opens the chapel. This last unlocks the folly. Those places are unsafe and I must forbid them. All the rest I make you free with, including this brass one, which goes to the tantalizing bookshelves. See how I trust you?"

"Thank you, Monsieur."

He kissed the top of my head and left.

I had M. Bernard's keys. At last.

I inspected the east wing, which was still allegedly under renovation. It was indeed still under renovation.

Next I tried the muniment room. Dust motes danced in the light streaming through windows and the walls were lined with cabinets. Halfheartedly I opened drawers and doors, revealing stacks of brittle yellowed papers. There were lists of all the purchases of this great household for several hundred years. At another time it might have been interesting, but it wasn't what I was looking for today.

What *was* I looking for? Something intriguing—something to do with my godfather's brides. They had walked these same floors I walked. Three of them had slept in my bed. I wanted to know their thoughts. I wanted to know if M. Bernard was as demanding of them as he was of me, and if they had loved him.

The fluid, serpentine wriggle of a centipede as it squirmed along the edge of the sheaf of papers I held made me drop it with a strangled squeal.

The door flew open and I jumped. Charles jumped as well. We both grinned sheepishly.

"Sorry, Miss," he said. "Thought I heard a mouse."

"That was me. Squeaking mousily because of a centipede."

He stooped to help me gather up the scattered papers.

"I have permission to be in here," I said. "Monsieur Bernard gave me his keys."

"Congratulations, Miss," he said.

I laughed. He didn't go so far as to laugh, but his eyes danced as he bowed himself out.

Thank goodness it had been Charles and not someone else. It

had looked as if I were poking my inquisitive nose into everything. How shameful that that actually was what I was doing.

If there were any traces of the wives in here, it would be like trying to find a needle in a haystack. I stuck my head out the door to make sure no one lurked nearby before slipping out and tiptoeing down the corridor.

I scurried up two flights of stairs to the attics. My heart lurched when one of the doors along the third-floor corridor slowly opened. I froze. No one but me ever came up here. Out glided Odette. I was gratified that she started at the sight of me. We stood looking at each other for a moment. I couldn't imagine what call there could be for my lady's maid to be in this rabbit warren of cramped bedrooms. Naturally no babbled excuses came from Odette. She flicked her bright black glance my way, then twitched away her stiff skirt so it wouldn't touch my flounces as she swished off down the hall.

I watched her back, wondering if she were a thief, scouring the house for objects to steal. In the chamber she had exited was a delicate, mother-of-pearl inlaid writing desk with one narrow drawer jutting open. Other than that, nothing seemed out of place. I checked inside the drawer—empty. Except . . . scratched into the wooden side was "Adele" again. My godfather's fourth wife must have had a habit of labeling things. And yes, the desk might well have come from my bedchamber. There was nothing else of note in the room. If Odette had taken something, it had been small.

I shrugged. Maybe later I would care if my maid were a thief. Maybe later I would tell Monsieur what I suspected and be rid of her. But at this moment I couldn't do it. I was feeling a grudging complicity with Odette because she had not betrayed my woodland rambles.

As I climbed the narrow attic stairs, the stench of mice met me, along with some other smell I didn't recognize.

The attics were dim and dingy, with pale light filtered through grimy dormer windows. What looked like shredded black rags hung from the lowest beams, where the roof nearly met the floor. Bats. That was the other smell. They hung quietly, minding their own bat business.

I wove my way between tarnished birdcages, sofas with stuffing billowing out, antiquated tallboys and washstands. What fun Anne and I would have had up here when we were younger, setting up houses and playing dress-up.

I moved around a dust sheet—covered mound and nearly stepped on a portrait lying face-up on the floor. A red-haired woman laughed up at me. Evidently it had been leaning against the wall but had fallen. The frame was cracked. After a second to slow the rapid beating of my heart, I set the painting up against a crate and studied it.

Which one was she? Which bride? She wore the style of the past decade. She had to be one of them. She stood beside a horse, and her expression was one of mischief, as though all the world were a joke. I could guess. I would guess it was Tara, of the fiery temper and the vase-smashing fights with her husband. Yes, somehow I was certain of it. The suicide.

So . . . were the other wives' portraits up here as well? I began peeking behind paintings propped against walls. Most were

landscapes and still lifes consigned to the attic for one reason or
another—discoloration, a tear in the canvas, a broken frame. Ducky,
who couldn't abide "waste," had everything brought upstairs. But
three more of these paintings had been banished here because
M. Bernard couldn't bear the sight of them, had ordered all traces
of his departed wives destroyed. The heartsick people I had known
had done just the opposite—they had carefully preserved their
memories.

I found what I was looking for.

Ravishingly beautiful Victoire held a slender, dark-haired child,
who must be Anton, on her lap. Here stood Tatiana in the orchard.
A Russian family who attended our church in Boston had had the
same high cheekbones and slightly slanting eyes. And here must be
Adele, pale and hollow-cheeked, with eyes that were pools of melancholy.

Each of them had hair that could be described as "red." All were
different shades, however, from the pastel blushing gold of apricots
to rich, deep auburn to pale strawberry to the intense glow that
edged smoldering coals.

Seeing their faces only whet my desire to know more of these
women who, at this moment, I thought of as my "Sisters." Victoire,
Tatiana, Tara, and Adele.

I riffled through trunks, slamming down lids if the contents were
too antique. Twenty-five or so years ago—that would be Victoire's
time period. I found three trunks I guessed were hers. The gowns
inside had the wide shoulders and collars of the 1830s. As I held
them up, they released a musky, exotic scent. Here was a small

portrait in a silver frame of a woman from the early years of the century—Victoire's mother? I cherished my own mother's miniature. Never would I have left without it. Victoire had stolen away the first chance she got and couldn't take many things with her. Perhaps this was what she had returned for when Ducky saw her, but all her possessions had been up here by then.

One chest contained a boy's clothing and playthings—a small boy barely out of leading strings. Anton. There was something particularly tragic about the plush dog tucked carefully among the garments, with its fur nearly rubbed away from loving. How lonely for it to remain when Anton did not.

It was wrong of Victoire to leave her husband for another man—there was no doubt of that—but who knew what hole had opened in her soul at the ghastly death of her son? And who knew what had gaped in M. Bernard's at the same time?

Tara's trunks had her name engraved on brass plates. I fingered her possessions gingerly. She had stabbed herself. Some agony had possessed her so powerfully that she ended her own life. Maybe something of the emotions clung to her things.

Tatiana's chests contained a baby's layette among the larger items, the seams and trimmings beautifully stitched, probably by the expectant mother.

Adele's baggage, naturally, had her name scratched into the wooden bands.

I handled gowns in rich fabrics and underclothing edged with exquisite lace from the past three decades, books and memorabilia, scrapbooks and toilette sets in silver and marble, ivory and tortoiseshell. There were dancing slippers that had danced their last, beaded reticules and plumy fans, ribbons and bonnets, dried flowers that fell to pieces when I touched them. I found no jewelry. My godfather didn't order *that* destroyed. Was it possible I had been the recipient of some of these ladies' jewels? There were no journals or correspondence either. He might have carried out the burning of those himself. He might have discovered Victoire's illicit love letter that way.

All the brides were fairly young, all spoiled with stylish (for their time) clothing, all red-haired, but all showed signs of individuality in their possessions. Tatiana fancied cats. She had some little flowered china figurines of tabbies and a picture of kittens playing with yarn. I hoped she'd rebelled against her husband and adopted some predecessor of Buttercup's. Adele, who was only eighteen months gone, was fond of poetry; there were several books of French verse among her things. From one of the volumes drifted the dried frond of a fern. A good many foreign souvenirs nestled in Victoire's belongings—she had traveled with M. Bernard. Tara, meanwhile, had been quite the equestrian; no less than four riding habits lay among her effects.

As I smelled their perfumes, touched the objects they had touched, I felt no morbidity because they were deceased, or at least all deceased but Victoire; what I felt was a growing fondness. I would have liked these women. Maybe I was so lonely I needed dead people to be my friends.

Four women's lives were shut up in these trunks.

"You can come out now," I said aloud, and the dusty air stirred with my voice.

Look, they would say, if they woke and watched me, *she's found my picture. She knows what I look like. She's reading my book. Now she's touching my green dress. She cares.*

I scrambled to my feet when a shadow flickered and a sharp tap sounded at a window. Only a cardinal flying into the glass. I peered out to see if I might look down into the churchyard, but the garden walls and the roof rose too far off to overlook. I should like to place flowers on their graves. I had the key. . . . But no, it was forbidden to enter that place.

It was in Adele's trunk that I found the hair receiver—a rosy porcelain box with a round hole in the lid, filled with her deep auburn hair. An idea began to take shape. *I* would remember them, with substance and flame. Hair from their brushes and combs, strands clinging to their clothing and bonnets and hats could be shaped into a bracelet or a brooch. Or—no. It could be woven into the tapestry I was stitching for M. Bernard. The combined hair of myself and his departed wives would form the fire blazing in the forest setting.

A while later, with a small packet stuffed with the tresses I had painstakingly collected, and with the trunks neatly repacked, I descended to my bedroom to begin plaiting. I added the strand from the envelope to the others so it wouldn't feel left out.

I used a makeshift loom formed of straight pins poked into the lid of a hatbox to braid several strands into one fiber thick enough for embroidery silk. Shimmering, glowing shades emerged from the mingled colors. There should be enough strands to weave into a bracelet as well as the tapestry.

As I plaited, the names of M. Bernard's wives repeated

themselves in a litany in my head: *Victoire and Tatiana, Tara and Adele. Victoire and Tatiana, Tara and Adele.*

It continued as I sat down at my embroidery frame beside the library hearth and began to work on the tapestry, delicately knotting. I wondered: What would M. Bernard see when he gazed into this particular fire?

CHAPTER 18

DISCORDANT NOTES

"Did you enjoy the freedom of the house?" my godfather asked upon his return. He had sought me out and watched quizzically as I handed him his keys. "Did you sample wine in the cellar and wield swords from the armory to fence with footmen?"

I snapped my fingers. "Oh, if only I had thought of those things. Next time . . ." I shrugged then. "In reality, I didn't do much with the keys. Only chose a book from the locked cases and peeked into your office. Of course you work hard there, but to me it was simply a lot of fusty old papers."

" 'Fusty old papers.' Should I be insulted that thus you dismiss the place where I deal with fortunes?"

I glanced up at him sharply. Had I made a mistake?

He rumpled my hair. He was being playful.

"No, *mon bébé*," he said. "I do not want you to trouble your pretty head with my business dealings. I want you simply to enjoy yourself all the day long and then dress yourself beautifully at night to please me. What book did you take from my collection?"

"*Arabian Nights.*"

"Entertaining literature, although not for the fainthearted."

"There are some awfully bloody bits in many of the stories. Scheherazade had a ghoulish imagination."

"Indeed—although perhaps it wasn't all imagination. Terrible actions sometimes bring about terrible retribution. Will you wear your Arabian costume tonight in keeping with your reading material?"

"Of course! How did you know?"

"Nothing escapes me."

"I wanted to put it on and invite forty thieves for guests. I was foiled, though, because we lack convenient thieves." For a second I felt uncomfortable, remembering my suspicions of Odette.

M. Bernard gave a wry smile. "You might be surprised at how easy they'd be to find, if they'd admit to it. Now"—he patted his pocket—"guess what present I have brought you."

I clasped my hands together. "Let me see . . . Is it a gilded boat to be pulled by swans on the lake?"

I expected him to laugh, but instead, the light in his eyes was quenched. He frowned. "Is that what you wanted? You wanted a boat?"

My mouth trembled, unsure what to say now as he glared at me. This time I *had* made a mistake. "No," I said carefully. "I was jesting. I didn't want a boat. I—I—"

"Here, take the things." He thrust out a small package. "Give them to Odette for all I care." He stormed away.

I opened the lid of the box and looked sadly down at a pearly collar and cuff set. It was true I didn't want them. Not now.

Such lightning-quick changes of mood in M. Bernard sent my nerves twining and tangling like knotted sewing silks. I must learn to think faster on my feet. The entire household and the very walls of the abbey reflected Monsieur's temper. When I could pacify him, I performed a service to All Mankind. In my old home, people had always taken care of me. Since coming here, for the first time, I felt the responsibility to watch out for the welfare of many others. I knew I was doing satisfactorily because Ducky constantly told me how much better the master was since my arrival.

My godfather's wives had had to deal with him. Since finding their possessions, their personalities had become ever more vivid in my imagination. I could guess how they would have reacted to M. Bernard's abrupt fits of temper. Tara would have flown into a rage, Victoire would likely have withdrawn, Tatiana would have abased herself, and Adele would have fallen into melancholy. I would handle him better than they had.

Victoire and Tatiana, Tara and Adele. Did they stir ever so slightly when I sat in a chair they once occupied? Did they sense it when I stood before a mirror that had reflected their image? Had they sometimes used this fork or drunk from this cup?

By the time I saw my godfather again, he was restored to good spirits and we spent the evening in the library playing piquet. I adjusted my sleeve so it would better cover the bracelet I wore. I didn't want M. Bernard to notice it, even though the strands of hair were twisted so cunningly it might have been a copper chain. I glanced at my tapestry stretched on its frame. The flames I had begun stitching were so bright against the dark background as to seem almost garish. In spite of my apprehension, I rather enjoyed my heightened senses from having him so near these interesting creations.

He appeared to be absorbed in his cards when he said casually, "By the way, I visited your old home while I was away."

I dropped my cards. "You were in Boston?"

"Obviously I was," M. Bernard said as he bent to pick them up, "since I have just told you I visited your old home. I extended our invitation to your family in person. Both Junius and Anne were there, and they entertained me with the best their house offered." He chuckled briefly, as if the best their house offered was paltry indeed.

I swallowed back my annoyance as he continued. "Your former surroundings fascinated me. You see how I want to know everything about you?"

My godfather would have filled the shabby, familiar parlor with his presence. He would have easily captivated Junius and Anne.

"And was everyone well?" I asked, eager for news of them.

"Tolerably. Junius had a cold. At least, he blew his nose frequently. I enjoyed a long talk with Anne in which she admitted her relief to have no worries for your future. They seemed delighted to accept my invitation for our house party. So it is certain—we shall see them at Wyndriven Abbey in the second week of December."

"December? I had thought they'd come sooner." I quickly added, "But it's not so long to wait, and it'll be lovely having them for Christmas. They will stay several weeks, won't they?"

"Coming from such a distance, I expect so."

"You'll enjoy them."

"Yes, I hope to, although you must take care not to neglect me while they are here." He placed the cards back in the box, showing our game was at an end. "And there is something else I should like to do, but it would be better received coming from you."

"What is it?"

"I wish to give money to your family, although I do not want to hurt Junius's pride, since he is the main breadwinner. Do you think we can contrive to send, oh, a few hundred dollars without embarrassing them?"

I threw my arms around M. Bernard's neck.

One morning not long after my godfather's return, he sought me out, grabbed me by the hand, and led me down to the lake. He used his walking stick to point ahead at what was tied to the little dock. There bobbed a small rowboat, looking more like a child's toy than a real vessel, just the size to fit two adults on its polished seats if one of the adults was small. Its gilded prow was carved into the curving neck and head of a swan.

"Perhaps," he said, "our living fowl would not agree to pull it, but I thought it would still please you. I sent Bass scouring the coast to find such a pretty plaything for my Sophia."

He watched with pleasure as I dashed up to the boat and ran my hand along its smooth side. "How clever you were to find this! I was jesting about the boat because I never dreamed such a thing was possible, but you've made it a reality."

He held me about the waist until I could sit down. He climbed in as well and then rowed into the middle of the lake. We cut through a dusting of golden leaves that floated on the surface while the swans glided out of our way. Once in the center, he let the boat rest in the still, green water.

I pointed to a silver streak darting by. "Look. A fish!"

"Nothing but trash," M. Bernard said. "Before your brothers come, I shall have it stocked with catfish so they can take in some fine Southern fishing."

The world glowed idyllically in the autumn sunshine. M. Bernard lay in the bottom of the boat with his head against the prow, watching me sleepily. His legs straddled my fawn-colored half boots. I leaned back and closed my eyes, enjoying the sunlight through my eyelids and the faint motion of the water. I could spend hours like this.

Eventually M. Bernard roused both of us and taught me to row by leaning around me and wrapping his hands over mine on the oars. His warm breath tickled my neck when he gave instructions. At one point he might have kissed the tip of my ear or his lips might have accidentally brushed it, I couldn't decide which. At the thought that it might be an embrace, my breath quickened. This was the right setting for a kiss, and a month ago I might have welcomed it.

I rowed frantically toward a dense stand of cattails. "Will you pick me one?" I asked.

"Of course," he said, amused.

He stood up in the boat, gave the silver skull knob of his walking stick a twist, and pulled a long, thin blade from the wooden shaft. I turned cold. I hadn't realized it was a sword stick. He cut an armful of cattails.

I stroked their velvety brown heads. "I'll put them in a vase in my room. There's something endearing about them. They really do feel like a cat's tail. I love it when I stroke—" I bit my tongue and let the sentence hang.

M. Bernard raised his eyebrows. Suddenly one of the cattails burst open and the fluff shot straight at him, the down clinging to his hair. I tried to keep a straight face, but my godfather looked so surprised and so comical that laughter burst from me.

I clapped my hand over my mouth and sobered instantly. "I'm so sorry. May I help you pick them out?"

He grinned. "Please do."

I sat close to clean the seeds from his skin and hair and beard. I flicked them off to float on the water like fairy boats themselves. My godfather seemed to be enjoying it. He called me a bewitching rogue.

We rowed back to shore immediately afterward.

That afternoon my heart sank when I heard M. Bernard's raised voice coming from his office. The pleasant mood hadn't lasted even a day. The door burst open and he stalked out with a face like a thundercloud. Poor Mr. Bass. Poor me. This boded ill for the evening.

The atmosphere of his ugly humor hit me the moment I entered the banquet hall. All through the meal M. Bernard rebuffed every attempt at conversation. He seemed absorbed in staring down at his food. A particularly bloody sirloin oozed on his plate.

"Ling!" he bellowed. Revulsion distorted his features.

The butler had been waiting to pour the spirits. He scurried up without his usual dignity.

"Yes, sir?"

"Take this away. I cannot abide the sight."

Normally M. Bernard was fond of rare meat. As Ling picked up the platter, his gaze met mine and held for just a moment. And in it I read a strange thing. I read pity.

Surely I must have been mistaken. I twisted off my ring, and it clinked loudly on the china. M. Bernard directed a sharp glance my way. He said nothing, however, simply turned to his wineglass.

After emptying it, he shouted at Ling, "More wine! Leave the bottle."

He ate no food, but drank glass after glass, his face flushed, glaring straight ahead at the candelabra, the reflected flames glittering in his silver earrings and his eyes.

As I rose thankfully to leave the room, he mentioned no plans for the evening. I supposed we would meet in the library eventually.

Forty minutes later, however, I descended to the rich notes of the cello. The throbbing strains led me down the spreading staircase, along the cold marble hall lit by glowing sconces, past dark gaping doorways, toward sounds and light streaming from the music room.

M. Bernard made no comment when I entered—perhaps didn't even see me—but seemed enthralled by his own playing.

Seated at the piano, I listened for a moment, then attempted to follow, but I could not keep pace with him. His notes were discordant; I couldn't harmonize.

I ceased playing and listened, spellbound and disquieted. At first his strident bowing conjured up visions of tempest and storm, passion and fury. Then his bow slowed, and its moaning wrought images of bleakness and decay and ancient, secret chasms. The chords ebbed and flowed, now swelled, shrieking. Through this strange spyglass of music, I saw writhing bodies with tortured arms outflung. I glimpsed hell.

Agony engulfed me. I could bear it no longer and fled, the sounds reaching after, taunting. I stumbled to my bedchamber and slammed the door shut, leaning against it, breathing heavily.

What had happened down there? When we made music together the first time, he had kissed me at the end. What would have been the aftermath had I stayed tonight?

After Odette left, I heard a sound from outside. Softly I opened my balcony door and peeked down at the veranda.

M. Bernard hunched there on his hands and knees, retching, vomiting wine.

Much later, probably after midnight, I was jerked awake by another noise that ceased before I could identify it. Whatever it was turned the very marrow of my bones to ice. I rose, wrapped my coverlet around me, and stepped outside.

A lopsided, gibbous moon, striped with shredded black clouds, bathed the gardens in pale light. The distant lake reflected it, and the Palladian bridge and my swan boat created a haunting scene from fairy tales. Perfectly peaceful. Nothing amiss.

A movement among the shadows near the water caught my gaze. Two tall, lithe figures, hand in hand, moved into the silver light. I recognized the silhouettes of Charles and Talitha. He pulled her close. I abruptly dragged the curtains across the vista and turned away. It had been too beautiful to watch.

CHAPTER 19

THE REVEREND
MR. STONE

M. Bernard came up behind me in the morning room and put his hand briefly on my shoulder as he jauntily swung his leg over a chair.

"I am famished."

I wasn't surprised he was hungry, but I *was* surprised by his unclouded brow and unshadowed eyes. He cheerfully gobbled down eggs, sausage, ham, an orange, and a scone, all during the time it took me to finish one slice of jam-smeared toast.

Evidently my godfather's wild music and stomach purging suited him.

"*La vie est belle,*" he said, rising. "I am now ready to take on Bass and the overseer who caused me afflictions yesterday. By the way, I am sorry if I was not sociable last night. It is their fault. I cannot tell you how frustrating they were, but I will soon have them sorted out. Have a glorious day, *mon cœur en sucre*—which, if you are wondering, means 'heart of sugar.'" He flipped my curls with one hand as he sailed from the room.

Odette was hovering outside on the veranda. She followed as I headed out across the gardens and through the parkland.

It was a brilliant blue October morning with sharp gusts of wind skittering around corners. Whereas not long ago the leaves had been the dulled green of fading summer, now autumn spattered the scene. Odette seated herself at her usual station beside the brick wall.

As the trees closed around me, I breathed in the clean, fresh air, tangy with pine, so different from the cloying perfumes and underlying odors of Wyndriven Abbey. Deep within the forest, I loitered beneath a great oak flushed with scarlet and gold.

From somewhere—above me?—someone cleared his throat. I leaned my head back and was startled to see a pair of black-clad limbs dangling directly over my head.

"I warn you," said a voice, "I can hold on no longer."

The man came crashing down just as I scuttled out of the way. I stood transfixed, watching him untangle his long legs and stand, brushing himself off. He was a tall, loose-limbed young gentleman, wearing a black frock coat and a sheepish expression.

"I don't quite know what to say," he said, reaching for a shovel hat that hung on a twig near where I stood. "I must recover my dignity. Do you see it lying around here somewhere?" He glanced absurdly about. "There was a fascinating patch of lichen on that oak, and I managed to shinny up to fetch a sample. I was just going to drop down when you came along. I didn't wish to frighten you, but you simply *would not* leave, until I was ready to lose my grip. I do apologize."

"And I apologize for not departing quickly when you were in such a precarious state."

He grinned down at me. He had a wide, humorous mouth beneath his large nose and a thatch of unruly brown hair. There was something droll about his appearance, and I couldn't help smiling.

"No fault on either side," he said. "And obviously no one is near to do proper introductions, so may I introduce myself? I am the Reverend Mr. Gideon Stone." He sounded solemn when he said this, but then his grin returned. "I'm sorry. I've only been out of seminary eight months, so being a pastor is still new. Sometimes it feels as if I'm pretending. My church is the yellow brick one in Chicataw. And you are?"

"I am Miss Sophia Petheram, from Wyndriven Abbey."

An almost imperceptible change came over his friendly expression, and there was a tinge of coolness in his voice when he bowed slightly and said, "Pleased to make your acquaintance, Miss Petheram. I take it you are the—companion—of Mr. Bernard de Cressac?"

"Why, yes—yes, I am," I stammered, confused by his change in attitude. "How had you heard of me, sir? I thought my godfather had no dealings in the town."

"Your godfather? Oh, I didn't know that was the relationship." He nodded his head as if something were explained, and the warmth came back into his tone.

"What did you think was the relationship?" I demanded.

It was his turn to redden and stammer. He fiddled with a loose button on his coat. "I—I—the word around Chicataw—you see, a few people saw a pretty young lady traveling in de Cressac's carriage last summer, and they assumed—the word spread—it's known that his wife had died a while back, so—"

"They assumed something very wrong," I said severely.

"Yes, I realize that now I've spoken to you. Gossip is foolish and hurtful. I shall deliver a sermon on the subject in the not-so-distant future."

"You may—if anyone wonders—you may tell them that Monsieur de Cressac took pity on me when my father died, and—and acts as a father toward me." This was not strictly true, of course.

"If the subject ever comes up, I shall set the matter straight. Have you no other living relations?"

"Two brothers and a sister. They're visiting here in December."

"That's good. That's good they're coming."

We stood self-consciously looking at each other now, wondering what to say next or how we should take our leave. Instead, my eye fixed on something else. "Oh dear, you've torn your coat." I pointed to a ripped seam under Mr. Stone's arm.

"Yes, well, it happens. My housekeeper will have to stitch it up, and she'll be most displeased. She lectures me regularly about the damage to my wardrobe from studying nature. I'm afraid I'm a careless fellow."

"Let me mend it. I keep a sewing kit in my pocket."

"What admirable foresight!" He hesitated. "Well . . . if you really don't mind, I'll take you up on that offer. It's kind of you to save me from Mrs. Penny's wrath."

He removed his coat, and I pulled out my sewing kit. He looked even younger in shirtsleeves. As I stitched, we shared our histories. After he had finished seminary in Memphis, he had accepted the invitation from his cousin to take on a local church. The cousin, a Mr. Vassar, owned Bella Vista Plantation.

"His property joins de Cressac's, and I have no idea where the one begins and the other leaves off," Mr. Stone said. "I confess I'm glad I don't know the boundaries, as I have leave from Cousin Richard to wander where I will on my free Mondays, and I don't like to worry about trespassing."

"I have no idea either. I hadn't even thought of property lines."

"De Cressac allows you to go about unaccompanied?"

"No, sir, actually he doesn't, but I require my maid to wait for me at the edge." I poked the needle emphatically into the next stitch. "I need *some* time away to collect my thoughts."

"Everyone does. That's one reason I'm an avid student of plant life. It's an excuse to go off alone so I may hear God's messages more clearly."

I shot him a quick glance. He didn't say this in an affected manner or to impress me; he was simply a man of faith making a statement.

"I've never thought of it that way," I said, "that the unusual clarity of my mind when I'm out here comes from God."

"Perhaps part of the ambience is also due to the abundance of witch hazel nearby. Have you noticed?"

"I wouldn't know it if I saw it."

"There, see that shrub there? If you make wands of it, you can wave them over paths to protect you from passing malevolent beings. It's also used to fashion water divining rods."

"And do you believe that, Mr. Stone?" I asked, feeling mischievous.

"Which? The malevolent beings or the protection from them or the water divining?"

"All three," I said lightly. I was funning, of course, but was curious to hear his answer.

He didn't jest in return. His face was serious when he said, "I believe in the devil, of course, and the fact that malevolent spirits reside in some men cannot be denied. Thankfully God is far more powerful. But it's also true that some plants aid folks and some harm." He refused to act at all embarrassed as he continued: "I myself have seen a man miraculously finding water with a witch hazel rod twitching and nearly pulling him along, and I have also come upon plants that exuded an aura of malignance, which was not my imagination."

"Oh, I believe you. There's a tree on the drive approaching the abbey—an oak all twisted and deformed. It's evil. I can't imagine why my godfather keeps it."

"Perhaps de Cressac finds the grotesque beautiful. There are those who do."

"Some forms of the grotesque I like, but not that tree. It sends shivers down my spine." I handed Mr. Stone his coat. "There you are. Finished."

"Thank you," he said. He dug in his pocket now and drew out first a fuzzy horehound drop, next some wadded-up fishing line, and finally a pocketknife. Deftly he sliced off a twig of witch hazel. "Here. A wand for you. Now you're magically protected whether you need it or not."

I drew my thumb and forefinger along the twig. This was a very unusual clergyman. I looked up at him, and his eyes met mine. He opened his mouth, then closed it, then opened it again, trying to decide whether or not to say something.

"Have you—Miss Petheram, are you happy living at Wyndriven Abbey?"

"Why do you ask?"

Now he did look embarrassed. "I had an encounter with your godfather six months ago that left a bad taste in my mouth."

Realization dawned. "Oh, you were not the parson who—or were you? Were you the preacher who was frightened by the dog?"

"You've heard the story. Yes, it was me. I went there to talk to de Cressac, as he's a bit of a legend in Chicataw and I consider everyone in the area my responsibility. I'm sure I looked the fool your godfather thought me when I leaped so clumsily onto my horse."

"I'm sorry," I said. "Monsieur de Cressac's sense of humor isn't always . . . kind."

Mr. Stone gave a wry grin. "I'm not normally leery of dogs. It's only that that one was so big and coming so fast, and I promise you, its jaws were slathering. Little did de Cressac know, though, I got even with him and offended a portion of my congregation in the process. I preached against all he stands for—against the evils of the frivolous and lazy lives of the Southern aristocracy. How the time they allow for service and spirituality is measured in scant tea-spoonfuls. The Nash family was so unhappy with my words, they switched over to the Episcopalians. De Cressac will never hear of it, nor would he care if he did, but it made me feel better—and it needed to be said."

"You were very brave. Have . . . have you ever preached against slavery?" I asked the question tentatively. It was a sensitive subject.

"I'm not that brave. Discretion is the better part of valor and all that. I'd be run out of town on a rail, and how would that help anyone?"

I drew with my wand in fallen leaves. Could Mr. Stone possibly be the sympathetic minister Peg Leg Joe had mentioned? I might never know; such a thing must be kept a carefully guarded secret. But I could picture this young man doing valuable work with the Underground Railroad.

I, on the other hand, led a frivolous and useless life. I vowed to be of more service in the future. And where in the world had I stashed my Testament and prayer book? Now that I had met the unfortunate preacher of M. Bernard's story, I felt worse than ever about it. No wonder callers avoided the abbey. What must the county think of its inhabitants? "What legends do they tell concerning Monsieur de Cressac?" I asked.

Mr. Stone was silent as he cut his own switch and sketched alongside my designs. Our wands touched, and I felt an almost electrical charge shoot up my arm. I looked at him, wondering if he had felt it too.

Finally he spoke. "In town he's considered a romantic figure, shrouded in mystery. Can't you imagine the rumors? It's as if he's planned for that effect—his accent, his wealth, his looks. The ladies admire him from afar, of course—or so my housekeeper tells me—the gentlemen, not so much. They call him Bluebeard." He dropped his wand and paused, removing his hat and running his fingers through his hair so that it stood up even more than it already did. "Miss Petheram, you're far from your family. Should you ever need

help, I hope you'll know I'm your friend. Every Monday you can
find me in the woods."

"I'm much obliged to you, sir, although I can't imagine ever having to take advantage of your offer. I can see you don't like my godfather, but you mustn't say such a thing in my presence. He has been
very generous to me."

He directed a considering glance my way before he replaced his
hat on his head. "I would never say any such thing. I can't dislike
him, as I don't know him. I simply wanted you to know—never
mind. It was presumptuous to say what I did."

I wished I could stay longer, but it was time to return.

"I enjoyed meeting you, Mr. Stone," I said, and rose.

"Yes. Yes, well, the pleasure is mine. May I walk you part of
the way?"

"Oh, please do. I'd like that."

He shouldered his leather sample bag, and we strolled in com-
panionable silence toward a path I often used. I could hear only the
low, mourning sigh of the treetops. Where was the usual twittering
and scrabbling of small creatures?

We rounded a curve in the path and almost ran into something
hanging directly above it.

I started back and put my hand over my mouth to stifle a cry. Mr.
Stone pulled me around to shield me from the sight, but I could
still see under his arm. I stared with horror at the dangling body of
Buttercup. He hung suspended from a branch by a thick, knotted
cord, his eyes bulging. He circled slightly, round and round, round
and round, in the breeze. It looked grotesquely playful.

I fought nausea.

Mr. Stone took me by the elbow and led me away.

After a moment he asked gently, "Was it your cat?"

I could only nod and rub my forehead. After I caught my jagged breath, I said, "He's dead of course."

"Yes." Mr. Stone's mobile features registered deep distress.

"He's Buttercup. My pet. What cruel, beastly beast of a person could have murdered him?"

Mr. Stone's mouth tightened. "Some villain. There aren't many around here, but I must suppose there are some. I'm so sorry you had to see such a thing. I could help a little—I could take poor Buttercup down. And please may I offer you my service in burying him?"

I looked up at Mr. Stone and instantly received the impression that here was a man who could be trusted. "Oh, would you? Would you do that? But where? You see, my godfather didn't like me associating with Buttercup. Because he was only a common cat." As I spoke, the picture of M. Bernard, drunken and sweating, came to mind, but I could not—would not—think of it. Later . . . there'd be time to consider such things later.

"I could lay him to rest in my garden," he said. "I have a perfect spot beneath a dogwood tree. He'll be surrounded by daffodils in the spring and tiger lilies in the summer."

"Tiger lilies? Why, that would be perfect. He looks—looked—like a little tiger."

"Then that's where I'll take him. You go on, and think of your cat sleeping peacefully among the lilies."

"Thank you so much."

I left Mr. Stone to his unpleasant chore. My limbs trembled as I made my way.

Who could have done such a thing? I remembered the yowling that had awakened me during the night; but a wild animal could not suspend a cat from a cord. Some fiendish *person* had done this. I rubbed my eyes as if to rub out Buttercup's image. I could ask Charles or Talitha if they had seen anyone, since they had been out and about during the night, but something in me was too frightened to inquire more deeply into the subject at this time.

As I lowered my hands, I thought I saw shadowy movement flicker deep in the trees. I looked closer but could make out nothing from the ordinary. Just then a squirrel spiraled down the trunk of a pine. Only a squirrel.

When I reached her, Odette fired off biting French words, probably a scolding for my long absence. She paused, then said slowly, heavily accented, "You must take care, foolish girl."

I felt no triumph that she had broken into English. "I have had a shock."

Immediately she peered closer. "What? What has happened?" she asked sharply.

"I found my cat—you know, the yellow-striped one—hanging dead back there."

She drew in her breath. "That is bad. Garvey shall cut it down."

"No need. I met . . . a man from town. He said he'd do it."

"Then now we must hurry. You are late."

We started back to the house.

"I knew you could speak English." I had to say it.

"But no one else must know. Monsieur de Cressac asked particularly in his advertisement for a French speaker only. He does not wish me to understand English. It is not my job to speak to you." She swished on ahead.

"Just tell me one thing," I called to her back. "Why did you show my letters to Monsieur de Cressac? What had I done to make you hate me so?"

She gave an exasperated sigh, glanced quickly toward the house, and waited until I came close. "I did not—do not hate you. I did it because I need Monsieur de Cressac to trust me and I just wanted to see . . . something. That is all. I am sorry it was at your expense. When I came here, I thought you were—never mind, Mademoiselle. No more. We must hurry."

I scurried after, but much as I tried to get her to explain further, she remained tight-lipped, shaking her head and glaring.

That evening I had no excuse to stay away from dinner. I couldn't tell my godfather about Buttercup. I washed my face and allowed Odette to smear rouge into my cheeks to give me some color.

As usual, M. Bernard awaited me in the banquet hall, his fingers drumming on the linen tablecloth.

While Charles pushed my chair in, it occurred to me that it might be wise to mention my meeting Mr. Stone, if, in fact, the shadow I had seen had been cast by one of my godfather's spies.

I waited until halfway through my soup, and then made my tone casual. "Today in the woods I met your parson—the one Finnegan frightened. He's a student of botany and had found some interesting lichen." Should I have said "Odette and I" had met him? But if someone had seen me, they knew I had lost Odette. I hated deceit;

in the words of Sir Walter Scott, "Oh, what a tangled web we weave, when first we practice to deceive." One must be very clever and remember many details to be a good liar.

Something in my godfather's expression told me my information wasn't a surprise, but all he said was, "Did you indeed? And what did you think of him?"

"I thought him very ugly." *(Forgive me, Mr. Stone!)*

"He has a nose like a parrot," M. Bernard said, with a faint, contemptuous smile.

"More like a peregrine falcon."

"And legs like beanpoles."

"I would have said like a grasshopper."

"And his mouth!" Thank goodness M. Bernard was laughing now as he popped a cod's eye between his lips.

"As wide as that platter." I pointed to the heaping tray of sweetbreads. "He did know the names of some of the plants I'd been wondering about, though."

M. Bernard's laughter died as his eyes narrowed. "Is that so?"

Had I made a mistake saying anything to Mr. Stone's credit? But I must pursue it on the slight chance I was ever seen with him again.

"I want to know all about every last plant on Wyndriven's grounds." I tried to look up at him earnestly. "So I can discuss them with you and maybe even help you a tiny bit. You have so many cares with this vast estate. I should like to be more useful."

He gave a good-natured laugh. "I have told you, *ma belle*, you do not need to be anything but decorative. Besides, you and Ling have your errands of mercy among the slaves."

"It's rare for them to need us. Which is good, of course, but I want other ways to help."

"You may ask Mrs. Duckworth if she has some little task to set you about the house."

"I'll do that. But also I'd like to study plants—I've always loved them, and they're so different here from those I grew up with."

"My, what an eager scholar you have become in the past few hours."

"Not so recent as that," I said playfully. "Why, even when I was little, I kept our parlor aspidistra alive and happy."

"Oh, very well, if you find it amusing." He dismissed my botany interests with a flick of his long hand in a very French gesture.

Well done, Sophie. Now if I were seen talking with Mr. Stone, I would have a reason. Sometimes I impressed even myself in my cleverness in handling my godfather.

It was interesting how, although the clergyman certainly would be considered a rather homely man, his looks pleased me. Beside him, M. Bernard's features seemed too obvious and overdone.

CHAPTER 20

DIFFERENT RULES

"Miss Sophia!" Charles swooped after me down the hall, holding out a basket. "Here's the picnic Mr. Alphonse fixed for your lunch. I suggested he tuck in extra orange blossom cakes, as I know how you like them."

It was Monday, and I stood dressed for my forest walk. To have Charles act so friendly moved me. Without thinking, I laid a hand on his arm. I meant to thank him for everything—not just the basket, but for his steadfast kindness to both me and poor Buttercup.

At that moment M. Bernard rounded the corner. His eyes went straight to where I touched Charles. His brows lifted slightly. I snatched my hand back, looking ridiculously guilty as I did so. Charles bowed and slipped away.

M. Bernard paused for a moment before saying lightly, "Oho! Going for a picnic, *ma loutre?* The clouds threaten, but of course that will not stop you. You are avid about your woodland rambles."

"Yes, sir. I enjoy the outdoors above all things." I searched his face, but it was impossible to read.

"*Oui*. Above all things," he said with an odd smile.

He was displeased. "Perhaps—perhaps you would join me?"

"Not today. Urgent business calls. Instead, I wish you *au revoir* so you may wend your way. Be sure to take a wrap."

He continued down the corridor. I watched after his powerful figure sheathed in perfectly fitting ochre brown until he turned the corner. He didn't like me to enjoy anything without him. However, I certainly wouldn't cease my forest walks; they were my only escape. And it would be nice if I were to meet Mr. Stone again—although it was unlikely to happen, I reminded myself quickly.

In spite of the brooding sky and M. Bernard's instructions, I left the house without snatching up a cloak.

Odette accepted an orange blossom cake with a frown, but by now I knew her expressions well enough to guess she was pleased with it. She was already eating when I moved on into the forest, swinging my basket. I glanced around to ensure that no one lurked. I stepped quickly and circled back on myself several times to confuse anyone who might follow.

Whereas last week the autumn leaves had been mostly flaming scarlet and orange, I now trod on a natural carpet of pure fallen gold, as if I stepped through the streets of heaven. A sudden gust sent a golden shower like a blessing down upon my head.

He was there ahead of me. Mr. Stone. He hunched on a rock in a ferny glade studded with boulders, absorbed in sketching. I hesitated. Although we had introduced ourselves, it wasn't proper to speak to a young man alone. And what if he wanted to remain alone? I couldn't help it—I *must* approach him. I strode into the clearing and said, "Why, Mr. Stone, how nice to see you again."

He looked up and warmth flooded his face. He stood awkwardly and bowed. "Miss Petheram! I confess I wondered if I might find you here since we're both fond of this wild place. Would you care to take a seat on a rock? I'd pull one out for you, but they're firmly rooted in the soil."

I chose a boulder that suited my contours and held up the picnic basket. "You see, I've brought a luncheon. Will you join me? There's plenty."

"Yes, indeed. I had no breakfast and it must be"—he glanced at his pocket watch—"yes, it is, close to two o'clock."

I spread a snowy cloth on a flat stone table and distributed the sandwiches, the pears, the sliced carrots, and the orange blossom cakes upon it. "I must thank you again for taking care of the—that task you did for me last week."

"No need for thanks, Miss Petheram. I was glad to be of service."

Alphonse had even included a flask of lemonade. "I'm afraid there's only one cup," I said.

"It's no matter. I can fashion one from the leaf of a sarsaparilla. It adds a pleasant flavor to whatever one drinks from it."

"In that case, would you make me one as well?"

As I reached for the cup he made, my hand shook a little. I wondered if Mr. Stone had any idea how shocking this would be considered by polite society—a gentleman and a lady who were not related dining together alone in an isolated spot. I doubted he thought of it. I hoped he wouldn't. He was an unworldly man, and surely he, as I, sensed that we were a pair of innocents and that the world's rules changed in the forest.

I told him about my family and my old home. "You would have liked my father. He was a quiet man, but he kept us laughing with his understated sense of the ridiculous. He was interested in every subject. He wasn't successful in a worldly sense, but he was widely read. I'm sure he would have loved discussing religion and botany with you."

"He sounds like a man after my own heart," Mr. Stone said. "You were lucky to have such a father."

I nodded and looked away.

"And what about your mother? Are you like her?"

"She died a few months after my birth, but supposedly I favor her in both appearance and personality. I wish I could have known her." I looked down at my lap for a moment. At least I would see my brothers and sister soon. "It's a shame you probably can't meet my family when they're here. We spent such agreeable times together; we didn't socialize with many people outside the family, so we depended on each other."

"I'll hope that somehow I may yet make their acquaintance."

Mr. Stone had a subtle charm of his own, not at all like my godfather's. M. Bernard was overly conscious of his own charisma—he knew exactly what he was doing when he set out to enthrall. Mr. Stone didn't scintillate like M. Bernard, but he listened to each word I uttered with interest. He stated his own opinions with firmness, but he still respected mine. He clearly stood for everything good, clean, and honest, which made him comforting to be around; I could speak freely and didn't have to be on my guard. He would never, never be unscrupulous.

He told me about his own family. He was the youngest of five sons, the offspring of a planter in Virginia. "My childhood home is named Lauri Mundi. It's a beautiful place. Not nearly on the scale of Wyndriven Abbey, of course—cozier," he said with a smile, "but impressive still. My eldest brother and his family live there now with my parents. He'll inherit it, but he assures us that we'll always be welcome, that it will always be home. My other brothers have taken up professions in trade. Only I chose the Church." He looked down at his large hands, which he had clasped together. "My father and brothers sometimes act as though they pity me, but I feel mine was a true calling. My mother understands. You'd like her. She is everything a mother should be. I'm entirely happy with my choice of profession." He laughed then and added, "Except when Mrs. Wright and Mrs. Everly are feuding."

"Mrs. Wright and Mrs. Everly?"

"Two ladies in the parish. They compete in every way. If I stay fifteen minutes longer at a luncheon with Mrs. Wright, Mrs. Everly is in a huff and will promptly invite me to dinner at her home and keep me there for hours and so forth." He looked wistfully off into the trees. "Sometimes I don't at all understand people."

"Ah . . ." I could feel myself smiling mischievously. "I suspect it's women you don't understand. Do Mrs. Wright and Mrs. Everly have unmarried daughters?"

"Why, yes, they do."

"Then that explains it."

"Oh? Ohhhh . . ." He laughed a little and reddened.

We talked as if we'd known each other for years and spoke on every subject—flowers and birds, the people of his parish, rich and poor. I questioned him further on his opinion of the institution of slavery. Already I valued his judgments.

Mr. Stone nodded. "You might well wonder, since I'm a child of the South and my father is a planter. He knows my beliefs—that no man should have such power over others. In the Bible we're urged to let the oppressed go free and to break every yoke. Our Constitution grants rights that all people, regardless of their race, should have. The day will come when all black people will be freed, I'm certain. I can only hope it will be without the shedding of much blood. I fear a terrible retribution may come upon the South because of the practice." He had begun by speaking quietly, but as he continued, his voice gained an intensity that made it obvious he was passionate about the subject.

It had to be him. He had to be the preacher Peg Leg Joe mentioned. And then I remembered what Joe had said about recognizing the man—how the apostle Peter was a "rock." Mr. *Stone*! Yes!

I hesitated only a second before asking a question to help me be certain. "I've sometimes heard the servants singing a song about a drinking gourd—do you know what they mean by the 'gourd'?"

"A gourd to drink from, of course," he said, not meeting my eye.

"No! Really. Like in the song. It's something more."

He rubbed his chin and looked so uncomfortable I almost wished I hadn't asked. Me and my cat-killing curiosity. Oh dear, how could I have thought of that awful idiom? I shuddered.

Finally he said reluctantly, "They call the Big Dipper the drinking gourd."

"Yes, it does look like one, doesn't it? And how would you go about following it?"

"The North Star is in the constellation." His voice was very low.

I wanted to subtly offer my aid, if only I had something to give. "I would help them follow their star if I could. Please know that."

"Of course you would."

"I've tried to make friends with some of the African servants, but it's as if I can go only so far and then there's a wall between us. They don't trust me."

"And why should they?"

"Because I'm me."

"Well, they may actually like you, but their history in this country won't allow them to place much faith in any white person."

I sighed. "If I were queen of the world, I would change everything."

"Everything? Surely you'd leave the orange blossom cakes as they are." He took the last cake, broke it, and held out half to me.

"Well, yes," I said, taking it. "Maybe the cakes . . . but only if there were enough for everyone everywhere."

I didn't eat my piece, however. Instead, I told Mr. Stone more about my life at the abbey, touching upon my godfather's difficult moods. Mr. Stone was a man of God and people must often confide in him, so I didn't feel I was being disloyal. "He is unused to ever having his will crossed. No one dare oppose him. Mrs. Duckworth, the housekeeper, told me once that her master would never desire that which was improper; they both consider that they can arbitrate what's right simply because it's what he wants."

"A dangerous way to think," Mr. Stone said. His tone and expression were grave. "Tread carefully, Miss Petheram."

"Oh, I keep my wits about me," I said blithely. "I'm all the time learning better how to deal with him." I felt lighter simply from sharing my concerns. I stood and stretched, then wandered over to pick up the sketchbook Mr. Stone had left lying open. "May I?"

He nodded. "I'm putting together a book about plants in this area. Only for myself, of course. Other volumes on the subject have already been published with fine illustrations, but I enjoy creating my own."

I glanced through the pages at beautifully drawn flowers, trees, details of leaves and grasses. "These are wonderful. You were sketching when I interrupted you. Would it bother you if I were to watch you take up your pencil again? So I could see how you go about drawing."

Enthusiasm lit his face. "I've counted six different types of ferns in this glade alone. I'm working on these right now," he said, pointing. "They're Eastern Bracken. See how the small stems branch out from the center stem and how each stem has many leaves? That's a decompound frond."

"Decompound. It's so delicate—like lace. I wonder if I could crochet ferns to adorn a skirt."

I perched myself nearby and tried to sit absolutely still with my chin propped on my hands so I wouldn't be a nuisance. However, after only a few minutes his eyes weren't on his sketching pad; they were on me.

When he noticed that I noticed, he smiled. "I was just thinking that in this setting, in that gown, you look like a wildflower yourself. 'Consider the lilies of the field.'"

I glanced down at my dress of lavender poplin with apple green ribbons appliquéd about the hem, and I beamed up at him. I was glad he compared me to a wildflower rather than a rose. Roses were so common. "That's from the Bible, isn't it? Not Shakespeare? 'They toil not, neither do they spin.' I'm not much of a scriptural scholar, but I remember that verse because it read like poetry."

"A great many of the verses in the Bible read like poetry. I've tried to write psalms myself. King David is much better at it. The rest of that verse—it's from Matthew six, by the way—says that 'even Solomon in all his glory was not arrayed like one of these.' Of course," he added, with a significant grin, "the beginning of the verse instructs us to take no thought for our raiment."

"There's nothing wrong with pretty clothes," I said as I smoothed out my skirt demurely, "as long as one doesn't dwell upon one's appearance constantly. But the rest of the scripture fits me well. I certainly toil not, although I asked Mrs. Duckworth for some tasks about the house, and the only one she set me was helping Daphne with the flower arranging, which Daphne resented. And neither do I spin—except for my bracelet, of course. I did more or less spin this." I held out my hair bracelet, mostly so Mr. Stone would notice what a slender, dainty wrist I had.

He walked over to examine it more closely. "It's an unusual piece of jewelry. Is it human hair?"

"It is. You'll think me gruesome, but it's strands from myself and from my godfather's four wives." I then told him about my investigations into my godfather's past relationships. "And that day when I found their portraits and all their possessions—things they'd loved—consigned to the attic, it made me so sad that I wanted to bring a piece of them downstairs." I laughed a little self-consciously. "When I speak like that, it sounds as if I meant to prop one of their limbs in the corner of the drawing room, doesn't it? But I promise it was with positive thoughts toward the ladies that I spun the bracelet. I didn't want all traces of them to disappear."

Mr. Stone had been listening in attentive silence, a furrow between his brows, but now he said slowly, "De Cressac has been married four times?"

"Yes, he was divorced from the first; the other three are dead."

"And you tell me they all had red hair?"

"Well, redd*ish*. According to Mrs. Duckworth, he's always been attracted to ladies with that coloring."

"Miss Petheram, forgive me for asking, but am I right in assuming your siblings' hair is of a different shade? He took no interest in them?"

"No. No, I'm the only redhead among us. But then, he's my godfather and not theirs, so naturally he'd notice me rather than them. And he was fond of my mother and I resemble her." By now I was feeling distinctly uncomfortable. He was voicing my earlier concerns, which I didn't like to think about.

"My dear girl, thank heavens your family is coming soon. And by the way, you have very tiny wrists."

He called me his dear girl. And he noticed my wrists.

Thunder had been rumbling for the last few minutes. Now a great crack boomed, making us start, and it was as if the bottom had been let out of the sky.

We both leaped to our feet.

"I must go!" I cried over the pounding rain. "Don't worry—I'll be fine."

He reached out to me, but I didn't realize it until I was already darting through the trees.

Odette had been wiser than I. She had worn a hooded cloak. I lowered my head and sloshed through the driving downpour. The moment we entered a side door, she muttered something and raced on ahead, presumably to prepare a bath and dry clothing. I followed behind, wringing out my hair and shivering.

That night at supper only George served us. It didn't seem right, with only half the bookends. I missed Charles and longed to ask where he was, but I didn't dare.

However, something happened at that meal that made me think perhaps I had another friend in the household.

"You are tense, *chérie*," M. Bernard said. "Have you had a stressful day? It rained, as I told you it would. Don't tell me it caught you unprepared."

"No, sir," I said, happy that I'd shaken out and dried my hair. "I lost track of the time, though, and had to hurry to dress. Perhaps that's why I seem stiff."

He put down his fork on his plateful of eels, rose, and stood behind me. He lifted my hair, bundling it in one hand, and with the other began to massage my back above my dropped-shoulder collar of Chantilly lace. This, of course, made me even more tense. "Ling tells me you did not go on your picnic today," he said.

Before I could act surprised, I saw Ling, from across the room, almost imperceptibly shake his head.

I had learned something of Ling during my four months at Wyndriven Abbey. Once I wouldn't have caught his gesture, let alone deciphered it quickly enough to act upon it. Now I said without pause, "As you pointed out, the weather appeared threatening." For some reason Ling thought it best my godfather not know I had been in the forest that day.

"Then perhaps, since you are fond of picnics, you will not object to dining with me *alfresco* at luncheon tomorrow. In the orchard, I think."

"I'd like that." I managed a smile and an upward glance, then added: "I can't wait! I don't see enough of you."

He drew one finger across my upper back, raising goose bumps, and once again sat down to his eels.

Thank heavens for Ling. I only hoped no other of my godfather's henchmen had seen me outside, revealing the lie.

I caught Talitha in the hall on my way up to bed.

"I missed Charles at supper," I said. "Is he ill?"

She looked furtively around. "No, Miss Sophia. He ain't sick. He been sent away. He—he made the master mad, so he sent Charles out to the cotton fields."

My stomach turned over. Charles's only fault had been kindness to me.

Talitha continued to stand before me, some great emotion working in her beautiful features. Finally she spoke, low and fierce. "I told him and told him he acted too friendly with you. But he say, 'Oh, the poor girl don't got nobody. Oh, the poor girl need someone be nice to her.' Well, you see what being nice to you done to him?"

"I do see. I'm so sorry," I said. "I had no idea . . . I just—"

She flinched away as though I were poison when I reached toward her, and she was gone before I could finish. I didn't know what I would have said anyway.

I was constantly making careless mistakes, but this was no left-the-silk-gloves-out-in-the-rain sort of a mistake. This was a ruined-a-man's-life mistake. Pleading with my godfather wouldn't restore Charles to his position. Sick at heart, I knew that if I showed any further interest, it would only make matters worse.

During the past months of watching the tall footman, with his dignity and humor, and Talitha, with her strength and elegance, I had grown to admire them and to long for what they had. Their bond was so strong that when I stepped between them, I imagined I could feel it tangibly. How could I have been so careless as to have caused this separation?

I vowed to be more cautious until I could help them escape to freedom.

CHAPTER 21

ENTERTAINING

M. Bernard awaited me, seated at a table beneath the still-laden branches of the orchard. The sky was a bright autumn blue and the temperature balmy. Silver-covered dishes lay on a damask cloth, and George stood discreetly at a small distance to serve as needed.

"So elegant," I said, seating myself. How different this picnic was from my last one.

"I can seldom shirk my duties, but I wished particularly to please you today."

I made myself smile. "You're so thoughtful."

For the next hour I had the pleasure of basking in M. Bernard's fascination. And in return I simpered and blushed, looked up at him through my eyelashes, shyly admiring, and ate a sampling of each delicacy George uncovered. I dared not refuse to play this game.

A green and gold beetle crawled on the tabletop toward the

asparagus. It became a diversion to see if it would reach its destination unnoticed. I hoped it would. I had already eaten my asparagus
anyway.

M. Bernard's gaze followed mine and fixed on my little beetle
friend. His jaw tightened. When it was just about to reach the platter, he brought his palm down hard. I winced. He wiped his hand
on a napkin and gestured for George to clean up the squashed
remains.

He stood. "And here is a pear for dessert." He drew the blade
from the shaft of his walking stick. The sight of the wicked steel for
the second time made my mouth go cotton dry. He cut a golden
pear from a high branch and let it drop into his hand. He tossed it
to me, and I reacted quickly enough to catch it.

My godfather didn't obtain fruit for himself. Instead, he watched
while I ate, as if it gave him pleasure to see me bite and chew.

"It's delicious, but I can't finish it," I said finally, laying the half-
eaten pear on my plate.

M. Bernard took my hand as he often did. This time, however,
he began to peel off my black lace mitt, finger by finger. He held my
naked hand then, turning it, stroking and studying it, as if it were
of unusual interest.

"So beautiful," he crooned. "And just a little sticky with juice."
He cast me a mischievous glance and raised my fingers to his lips.
His tongue flicked out over my flesh. I gasped as he sucked each
finger. "The perfect dessert."

"Sir!" I snatched my hand back and fumbled to replace my mitt.

He let out his bark of laughter. "Such exquisite confusion." He stood and stretched. "Exquisite, but still I must teach you not to be missish. Shall we stroll through the orchard now? There are many fine fruits to be had."

He said this so pointedly I knew his "fine fruits" had a meaning I wished I didn't understand. If only I could come up with a reason to refuse the walk.

We wandered, with M. Bernard tightly grasping my arm. Mostly I looked everywhere but at him, keeping up a nervous prattle, to which he answered shortly. Sometimes he looked down at me questioningly. He led me from the orchard and along the gravel drive. He paused beside the diseased oak tree, stroking a bulbous nodule with one long hand. He avoided the poison ivy shrouding it, which by now had turned scarlet.

"It's an interesting tree," I said. "Do you find it beautiful?"

"I do," he said. "The uncommon lines please me." He turned to me. "Sophia . . . ," he said tentatively.

"Oh my goodness," I said, breaking away. "I hadn't realized how late it was. I promised to help Daphne with an arrangement this afternoon."

"Tell Daphne—" he started to say through his teeth, then stopped himself and shook his head. "Go, then."

"Thank you for a lovely picnic," I said, moving quickly toward the house.

From behind me, I heard him say softly, "Patience, Bernard . . ."

I went straight to my bedchamber to scrub my hand. His liberties were inexcusable. I must not allow myself to be treated so again. When my family finished their visit, I would depart with them.

◆ ◆ ◆

A few days later I was cozily ensconced on the tufted cushion of the window seat in the yellow salon, sewing velvet posies to a straw bonnet. I wore a dress that rested low on my shoulders, and because the afternoon was cool, a cashmere shawl was lightly draped across them. M. Bernard had cantered off on his horse early and wouldn't return until late, so I was feeling relaxed.

This was the room in which Tara had killed herself. Sometimes I thought I could sense her presence, not the desperately sad one I would expect from a suicide, but rather a—well, a *merry* one. Remembering Tara's laughing, irreverent painted face still made me smile.

George entered. "There is a gentleman come to see you, Miss Sophia."

"A gentleman?"

"He appears to be a preacher man."

I clenched the fabric of my shawl. "Take him to the drawing room, George, and tell him I'll be there directly."

I was torn—part of me squealed, *He came! Mr. Gideon Stone has come to see me!* But the larger part cried, *No, no, no! Not here!* What would M. Bernard say about this when he learned of it, as he was sure to? He would not be pleased. What would he do to me? To Mr. Stone? My legs felt as if they were about to give way. I had to tell my feet, "You move. Now you."

Mr. Stone stretched out his hand when I entered. A smile played about his lips and his gray eyes twinkled. He thought this would be a pleasant surprise.

He couldn't know what he was doing, of course. I wanted to

shout at him, *Run now, before it's too late!* But I could only shake my head slightly so that he withdrew his hand and say, in a cool little voice, "I'm so sorry Monsieur de Cressac isn't in. May I offer you tea, Mr. Stone?" I glanced over my shoulder, trying to indicate with my eyes that Mrs. Duckworth hovered near.

He nodded, looking confused.

"Mrs. Duckworth," I said, "Mr. Stone has come to visit my god-father. Would you please bring us some refreshments and then enjoy them with us?"

His eyes widened in understanding now. He hadn't noticed the housekeeper bobbing about in the doorway.

As soon as she had gone, I hissed, "You should not have come."

"Pardon me? I thought you might be pleased to have a visitor. Besides"—he lowered his voice—"I was worried about you."

"I shall be much more worried about you if my godfather learns we're friends."

"How could he harm me? Have me flogged from the place?"

"Maybe. He'd do that without blinking an eye. He will never, never allow us to meet socially. You mustn't come here again."

It was Mr. Stone's turn to take on a cool tone. "I have no wish to cause you concern, Miss Petheram. I apologize. I won't seek you out again."

I wrung my hands. "No. I want to see you, but not here, not in this house."

"Only behind your godfather's back?"

"Yes, he—" I blushed in shame, realizing how this sounded.

Ducky returned with the tray and sat down between us.

She chatted happily. She enjoyed socializing but seldom had the chance. As she served the tea and cut the apple cake, Mr. Stone conversed in his simple, winning style. In spite of his tall, gawky form, there was a certain dignity about him. I, meanwhile, sat silent. I probably appeared sullen.

"And, Mr. Stone," Ducky was saying, "when you consider the difficulty of training giddy girls to scrub properly, you'll know the task I face."

"I can't imagine how you deal with it," Mr. Stone said. "And yet everything is immaculate and beautiful. You are eminently successful."

I directed a quick look at him, but there was no laughter in his eyes—only sincere empathy. No wonder he was a clergyman. Something fluttered and swelled in my chest. He had come to see me. But then the flutter was stifled; he would never, must never, come again.

At one point he said, "You're shivering, Miss Petheram; may I fetch your shawl? I noticed it out in the hall."

I nodded bleakly, suddenly embarrassed by my bare shoulders. Mr. Stone wanted me to cover up. He found me immodest.

He took a moment to return, and when he brought my shawl, I swathed my upper body completely.

Somehow the miserable half hour passed. At last our caller left.

"Now, why," Ducky said, as she gathered up the tea tray, "do you suppose Mr. Stone came again after his last experience here?"

I lifted my hands. "I can't imagine."

She clucked. "Well, probably such a nice young clergyman

wouldn't want to leave a bad impression. He must have decided to try again. I like him very well indeed. Did you hear how he noticed my ways with the polishing?" She glowed visibly.

"Yes," I said. "He's all a clergyman should be."

She turned wistful. "It would be nice if Master Bernard would allow him to visit sometimes, but it's not even to be hoped for."

No, never. Mr. Stone would never return here. I had told him not to. Everything was ruined.

As soon as possible I fled to my bedchamber and dropped to the ottoman.

Of course Ducky would report this to M. Bernard. She would betray us.

I sat up straighter. What was there to betray? My godfather knew Mr. Stone and I had met. And what exactly did I think he would do to us if he discovered we were friends?

There was no real answer to that, but M. Bernard had the means to hurt anyone he chose to hurt.

Something crackled in my shawl as I pulled it closer. Attached to the inner lining by a small silver lapel pin was a scrap of paper with a scrawled message: *Look in the hole in the live oak where we first met.*

Immediately, by stealing down back ways, I evaded Odette and dashed out to the forest undetected.

I found the oak. The hole gaping in its trunk was so high that I shook my head—obviously Mr. Stone didn't realize how short I was. With a great deal of effort and damage to my dress, I managed to roll a log over to stand upon. Inside the hole was a note.

Miss Petheram,

Please don't be unhappy with me for paying my call. I wanted to see you, but also I wanted Mr. de Cressac to know someone in town is aware of your existence. In the next week look for more notes here. Forgive me if I caused trouble for you.

Gideon Stone

I blinked. So I hadn't chased him away permanently.

Back at the house I read the note several more times before thrusting it into the fire and making sure the ashes were burned beyond recognition.

CHAPTER 22

ANARCHY

My dear Miss Petheram,

I realize I only saw you the day before yesterday, when I paid my solitary-and-never-to-be-repeated call, but something has happened, and I thought, "I want to tell Miss Petheram about this." And so I am.

I have discharged the man who cuts the grass around the churchyard, but he refuses to be discharged. Bobby Moore (the children call him Bobby Mower) greatly resembles the oxen he drives. He is every bit as light on his feet and every bit as stubborn. Ever since I came here, I've had to put up with his swearing and threatening his poor beasts as he works. The children of the town eagerly gather round to listen. Yesterday a little boy tried to feed the oxen a handful of grass, and I raced outside at the hullabaloo that followed. Moore was soundly cursing the poor child, using every ugly word I know and many more I don't, and advancing on him with his whip.

When I stepped between them, Moore turned obsequious, removing his hat and groveling, but I had had enough and discharged him on the spot. He then became *belligerent, so I turned and walked away. The grass could remain shaggy until next spring when I'll find a milder, smaller mower.*

However, outside this morning Moore's familiar bellow bellowed and his sad oxen's lowing lowed. Somehow he was working for the Church once more. I forgot that his father-in-law is an influential deacon. Of course I must deal with it, but before I do, I'm writing to tell you everything, as it makes me feel better to know you'll be sympathetic.

I'm so glad you thought to check the hole in the tree.

Gideon Stone

Three more notes were left that week. Although Gideon (as I called him now in my mind) had only Mondays entirely free, he managed to slip away long enough to deposit them. They related his daily activities, his visits with members of his congregation. One of them was illustrated. Often I smiled as I read, but just as often I was transfixed by his insight, his compassion, his unapologetic goodness.

He certainly didn't resemble the heroes of romantic novels. Far from it. But the very qualities that made him unlike most fictional love interests endeared him to me all the more. Kindness is undervalued in written romances. I imagined someday straightening Gideon's rumpled hair and fixing his crooked neck scarves. I hugged his notes to myself for a short time, then burned them, though it cost a pang to do so.

In return I left letters of my own in our nature-made cubbyhole, describing my thoughts, or a particular memory, or my activities that day. Once I copied a poem.

I told myself I mustn't visit the forest too frequently, but I couldn't stay away. I would approach the grove with anticipation and leave happy if something was there or cast down if it was empty.

I had begun giving Odette little gifts here and there—ribbons or rings or bits of lace; she accepted them for the bribes they were, with a slight lifting of her penciled brows and a shrug. She often allowed me to slip away alone. I wondered sometimes what she did all day. Her duties as my maid seemed so offhand to her, an inconvenient side job. What exactly would she rather be doing?

Probably everything. If I were forced to be a maid, I would rather be doing anything than waiting on some spoiled snip of a girl. Once I caught her coming out the attic door. I wondered again if she were a thief, but as long as she left me alone when I wanted to be left alone, I didn't pursue it. There were more pleasant things to think about.

By the time Gideon and I met in our glade for the third time, I felt as if I knew him well. Which was why I was surprised when he nodded to me grimly and returned to his sketching without a word.

I sat upon my rock again. I had so looked forward to this. I would have been perfectly happy to have basked quietly in Gideon's presence, save for the sense that he was unhappy with me. I plucked a fern frond and began rolling and unrolling it. Once in a while I'd steal a glance at his stern, silent profile.

"Why do you look so severe, Gid—Mr. Stone?" I finally asked.

"I didn't know I looked severe."

"Normally you don't, but today you do. Have I done something to offend you?"

He drew in his breath. Then, so abruptly it sounded like an accusation, he said, "Are you betrothed to de Cressac?"

"What? Of course not. Where did you hear such a thing?" I stared at him with alarm.

"They're saying in town that when his agent spent an evening at the tavern, he claimed you were to marry de Cressac."

"Well, that's the first I've heard of it. No, I would never marry him." I tossed my head and made myself laugh as though the idea were ridiculous, although my stomach plummeted. Mr. Bass could only have gotten such an idea straight from his master.

Gideon's eyes were searching, studying my face. I met his gaze evenly—he must never know that once I had actually been attracted to M. Bernard.

I fired my rolled-up fern at his head. "As a pastor you shouldn't listen to idle gossip."

He caught the frond and smiled, although his smile seemed a little forced. "You're right. I was foolish. The man was drunk, after all. I'll attach no importance to such rumors in the future."

A gray squirrel on a branch above us began to scold and sent bits of bark showering down upon our heads.

I laughed and brushed away the fragments. "Evidently he doesn't like our looks."

"He's an absurd beast, then. No one with eyes could dislike your looks."

I felt a silly smile spread across my face. We strolled through the trees, with me gathering an armful of scarlet-berried sumac. Gideon still seemed preoccupied.

The longer we walked, the quieter he became. Something was on his mind. I thought I knew what it was.

At last he stopped and faced me. "Sophie—I mean—forgive me—I mean Miss Petheram—"

"Yes?" I asked, breathless, certain he was about to ask permission to kiss me or confess he loved me, one or the other. Or hopefully both.

"Is there no way I can court you honorably? If I could speak to Mr. de Cressac—"

I shook my head vehemently. "Impossible. He even banished a servant because he was kind to me. He desires me isolated from everyone."

"Then perhaps to your brothers when they come. If only we could keep company in the proper way."

"That's what I want too, but we cannot. I promise I wish we were both in Boston and you could call at my house and sit at dinner with my family and everything would be as correct as correct could be, but as things stand, it cannot be so." I twisted my ring. "I'm hoping—when my family leaves, I'll leave with them. After that we could correspond. But until then . . ."

He struck his fist savagely against a tree trunk. This uncharacteristic action frightened me. His stubborn goodness . . . I dropped my load and grabbed his arm.

"Gideon, can't you see we're doing nothing wrong meeting here? Our situation is different because there's no way—no way—"

He drew his hand down his face. "I've tried to convince myself of what you say, but being with you like this, I'm putting you in a compromising position, not to mention betraying the deference I owe my calling." He looked down at me, his eyes earnest, pleading for my understanding. I turned my head away. "You're young and innocent and can't realize how wrong it is. I'm years older and should know better. Can't you see that it's best for you if we don't meet again until our situations are different, and then we can—"

I snatched away my hand from his arm. "*Best* for me?" I said in a low, shaking voice. "Why does everyone in this world think they know what's best for me? What's best for me is to continue to get to know a man who is good through and through and who makes me want to be a better person. *That* is what's best for me."

"I wish I were the man you think me." He smiled faintly, and I wondered if he knew how very sad it made him appear. "If I were king of the world, I would make everything different."

I couldn't even attempt a smile.

He gathered up my forest treasure and put it in my arms. "I shall—bid you goodbye now." His shoulders sagged as he walked away.

With burning eyes, I watched him. Jealousy that he could leave and I could not tangled inside me with a yearning to run after him and cling to his side.

When I emerged from the woods, Odette sniffed upon seeing the bundle in my arms, but she picked up a branch I dropped.

I placed my bounty in a vase on my mantel. The room looked warmer with the fall colors lighting it.

Somehow I got through the week, even though I worried when I found no more notes from Gideon. Surely he hadn't really meant what he said about ceasing meeting me? It couldn't be so—not with the intensity of what was growing between us. And why should I expect frequent messages? He had a great many duties. I would see him on Monday. I always saw him on Mondays. I anticipated our next time together all the more. In fact, on Sunday night I awaited the following day with such eagerness M. Bernard accused me of "glowing" during supper. I must be careful not to appear too joyous without a reason I could share.

"I was riding Lily and getting some wonderful exercise," I told him. "Would you like to take Aramis out with us tonight? We haven't ridden together in ages."

Immediately distracted, he agreed and began telling me at length of beautiful foreign places he'd ridden. My mind was able to wander toward Gideon once again.

When the morning arrived, I dressed with care and happily made my way to our meeting place.

He was not there.

For half an hour I waited, and then I tried to seek Gideon out, tramping in every direction until I was ready to drop. Nowhere did I catch a glimpse of the black frock coat and long legs. An echoing hollowness inside me confirmed that he was not coming.

There might be a note. I raced, stumbling, to the tree. Inside the hole was a sheet of paper. With trembling hands, I unfolded it. The message was short.

Dear Miss Petheram,

In vain I have struggled over our situation, trying to convince myself that I can honorably continue to meet as we have been meeting. However, in spite of——or because of——the very high regard I have for you, I cannot reconcile my conscience with the position in which I have been placing both of us. I know you don't agree with this, but please understand that I truly believe it's for the best. I hope our circumstances will change someday. I'm so sorry.

Gideon Stone

I sank down onto a log and stared straight ahead. It was all over. It had barely begun, and now it was over. The meetings with Gideon had been my only joy, my only hope . . . and he was *sorry*. Heat flamed my cheeks. I crumpled up the note and stuffed it into my pocket. *If he felt for me the way I feel for him, he couldn't stay away.* I was head over heels in love with Gideon Stone, but he must not be in love with me. He would forget propriety if he were. He would forget honor. . . .

No. Even as I thought that last, I knew it was false. I would not love Gideon as I did if he weren't the man he was. I thought of the poem "To Lucasta, Going to the Wars": *I could not love thee, dear, so much, loved I not honor more.* I had always disliked that line because it seemed as if the writer must not have cared for the girl if he could leave her so, but I understood it better now. That verse would be my Gideon's creed. He was a man of integrity.

I buried my face in my hands and wept bitterly.

Someone touched my shoulder. I gasped.

"Honey, it ain't so bad as all that."

An African woman stood over me, her face the color of burnished oak, obviously ancient but unwrinkled, with her skin stretched tight over jutting cheekbones. A good witch.

"You best come with me, lil Miss," she said, gesturing with one warped, bony hand. "You best come with me, and I fix you a hot herb drink. It make you feel better right quick."

She turned and stalked through the trees without looking behind, as if there were no question I would follow her. I followed her.

She was a tiny woman, wearing the ugliest striped calico I had ever seen, with an apron of bleached flour sacks. The kerchief she wore on her head was scarlet, and corkscrew tendrils of iron gray hair peeked from beneath. When she hitched up her skirts to step over fallen logs, it seemed a miracle she could hold herself up with such shriveled, scrawny limbs, but she walked ahead very straight-backed. She carried a switch to whip through the undergrowth before her.

"Don't need to step in none of them traps, no sir," she muttered.

She led me to a hovel whose walls leaned so pitifully I tilted my head to take it in. A garden patch, now fallow, surrounded it.

She turned to wait in the doorway and gestured with her switch at the short, saffron stalks poking up from the dirt. "My herbs grow there in season," she said. "I dries them and sells them in town. I makes enough for my needs and a little extra to tuck away." She gave a quick, birdlike shake of her head as she studied my face. "You be wore to a frazzle, lil Miss. You best come in and set."

I stooped to enter. The tiny room was pungent from the scent of dried herbs dangling from rafters. It contained a rickety table with a couple of cane-bottom chairs, missing slats, drawn up to it; a thin bedstead covered with a patchwork quilt; and a lidded crate, which must act as the bureau. On one wall hung an unlikely colored print of an angelic little blond girl romping with puppies. The room was warm from the fire flickering on the hearth, where an iron kettle steamed. My head brushed the herbs, releasing more scent, as I sat down where the old woman indicated.

"My name be Anarchy," she said as she bustled about, pouring hot water from the kettle into a brown crockery mug and sprinkling it with dried leaves she pinched from one of the bundles.

"Anarchy?" I asked, unsure if I had heard her properly.

"Yes, indeedy," she said. "I done used to belong to the Vassars, them that owns Bella Vista Plantation, but when Mr. Richard give me to Miss Fanny, who I nursed from the day she was borned, she give me my freedom papers. I got them still, there in that box. Anthony—my son Anthony who still belong to Mr. Richard—he tell me I supposed to pay the courthouse three dollars every three years to renew them, but I don't pay him no mind. I ain't giving no courthouse no dollars till I good and ready. I got to save to buy Anthony's baby's freedom. She my baby princess. She small and fine and don't got no mama no more—she won't live to grow up if they work her too hard. I gots more'n half her price saved. Mr. Richard say he give me a good deal on her."

The horror of a system where a grandmother matter-of-factly spoke of bargaining to buy her grandchild left me speechless. Luckily Anarchy didn't expect a response.

"I don't worry none about me. Miss Fanny wouldn't let no one bother me here. She give me that picture too"—here she pointed to the print on the wall—"to remind me of my little girl I loved so well. It favors her as a child. Now you sip that. Chamomile to calm your nerves. I done put honey in too, from my own bees. Sweetest there is. You feel better right quick."

The warmth and sweetness and scent of the place wrapped around me until I did feel better. And curious.

"Why didn't you go up North when you received your freedom?" I asked.

She gave a cackle. "If this child ain't asking what folks always ask . . . ," she said to the ceiling. "What they teach these folks make them always wonder that? I say, why should I? I got Miss Fanny and my Anthony and my grandbaby close by. I happy as a duck with a june bug. Anthony, he just made me these squirrel-skin boots I got on. Ain't they fine?"

With a funny little flourish, she displayed her feet, and oddly the boots *were* fine. Anthony had obviously fashioned them with care, the squirrel skin soft and supple, and the fit perfect. Oddly, too, I loved this room, filled with Anarchy's contentment. She had nothing, nothing, and yet she was happy.

"Anthony is a craftsman," I said.

The old woman glowed with pride. "He make all the shoes on the plantation just like his daddy done before him. Miss Fanny, she used to dance for his daddy, so he'd make hers extra pointed and dainty." She cackled again. "Too dainty. She got bunions now. Here. Miss Fanny brung me this cake last time she come, but I been saving it for an occasion. This be it. You eat it all up."

She unwrapped a slice of very old, very dark fruitcake, bulging with hardened raisins, and laid it before me. I choked it down.

"My name is Sophie," I said when I finished brushing crumbs from my mouth.

"Well now, lil Miss Sophie, you be wanting to tell old Anarchy what's got you heartsore, ain't you?" She seated herself on the other chair and waited with shrewd eyes.

I did. I did want to tell her. At first I didn't know where to begin, but soon it came spilling out. I told her of my childhood and of my father's death and of my life with M. Bernard and finally of my misery over Gideon. At some point Anarchy quietly began to rub my shoulders.

"Uh, uh, uh," she said. "You been through a time, ain't you? You been so lonesome and finally you think you got someone good and then he be snatched from you. Uh, uh, uh. All's I can tell you is it'll get better. You got to wade through the pain and the hurt, and when you come out the other side, you be stronger for it. I know your preacher man—he comes round here now and again to buy herbs and honey—he trying to do what he thinks right, but I got a inkling you be with him yet. And that Mr. Cressac—he a piece of work! But you is smart enough to deal with him."

I gave a quavering smile. "Thank you for everything, Anarchy. I'd better go now."

"Yes, you go. But first fix your hair and put your clothes to rights. You look like you been rode hard and put away wet."

I laughed and drew my fingers through my hair. "May I come back and visit you sometimes?"

"Laws-a-mercy yes. I loves company! Have a blessed day."

I started away briskly, but I soon slowed as the warmth seeped out of me. Once more I was absolutely alone.

CHAPTER 23

GRAY DAYS

A gray pall hung over my world in the following days, even with the sunniest skies, as if a film of grime covered everything. Poor Lily stood bored in her stall. Vaguely I hoped Garvey exercised her, but I didn't ask.

I would do anything—anything—if I could see Gideon one more time. If only I could see him once more, maybe I could convince him . . .

The next Monday, nearly without hope, I waited again in the glade, clutching the little silver lapel pin Gideon had used to attach his note to the shawl. Of course he didn't come.

Him and his unyielding male stubbornness. I dashed the pin hard across the glade so that it bounced against a tree trunk.

I scurried to pick it up and clean it off, my sorrow sharp once more.

Somehow I had to make something good come out of this awful experience. I would use it as a turning point to be a changed girl in the future. If I had been a Catholic, I would have entered a nunnery, but as it was, I would be a girl who cared less about pretty clothes and more about important things. I would try to pin down my butterfly mind. Anne would be here in six weeks; she would find me a much older and wiser sister.

And then a disturbing letter arrived. It began in Anne's own pleasant style, but soon she stated her true reason for writing. *Sophie,* it read, *if there were any other way, I would not come to you with this problem, particularly when you were so kind as to send money not long ago, but Harry is in dire straits. He has been running with a fast and affluent crowd, and recently he has been going with them to a high-stakes gaming house. He is deeply, deeply in debt, and so desperate he frightens me, saying things so wicked I cannot repeat them. Please, please bring this Terrible Misfortune to M. de Cressac's attention. Oh, I am ashamed, but I must ask you to do this.*

She went on to name a horrifying sum. I racked my brain for a way to obtain it without approaching my godfather. I couldn't ask him for more. I could not.

M. Bernard noted my shadowed eyes and listlessness with concern. "You are unwell. I will instruct Ling to administer one of his Oriental tonics."

I took the tonic, but to no avail.

At last I developed a plan. I would package up my finest jewelry—the ornate emerald set with necklace, earrings, bracelet, and finger ring—and send it to Anne. She could sell it for more than the requested amount. If only there were a way I could mail it myself, but there was none. I must trust Ducky.

I tied up the parcel with string and sealed it with wax. As I placed it in Ducky's hands, I said, "It's merely a trifle I'm sending to my sister. A small gift I thought she could use before she arrives here."

"I'll give it to George to post," she said.

I sighed with relief. Ducky wouldn't have the audacity to peek inside a sealed bundle.

That evening my heart skipped a beat when my bedroom door flew open just as Odette finished dressing me for dinner. M. Bernard burst in.

"Leave us, Odette," he said. "I must have an interview with Mademoiselle Sophia."

"Now?" My voice squeaked as Odette curtsied and swished out, but not before she cast me a concerned look over Monsieur's shoulder.

"Now." His tone made my blood turn chill.

I knew immediately what had happened. *Oh, Ducky, Ducky, you seem so harmless. . . .*

The cords in M. Bernard's neck stood out and his eyes blazed. He flung the poor little parcel, all unsealed, onto my bed. The emerald pieces scattered, glittering green. "What is the meaning of this? Did you dislike my gift? Is that it?"

His voice blasted me. Would he actually strike me? I had been waiting for it, fearing it, I realized now, for a long while.

I sat on the edge of the bed, licked my dry lips, and said slowly, "I didn't know what to do. Anne wrote saying my brother Harry is in deep trouble. I hoped she could sell it."

"When was this?"

"The letter came a few days ago. I thought the jewelry was mine."

"It is yours, but only to do with as I will. Am I such a beast you did not dare approach me? What did you think I would do? Beat you and lock you in a tower with only dry crusts of bread?"

"No, sir," I said, although that thought *had* occurred to me. "Of course you would have been generous as always, but you've done so much I couldn't bear to ask for more."

"Therefore, you chose to deceive me."

"It was not deception."

"Did you think I wouldn't notice?"

Suddenly I was sick of being questioned, sick of the frequent humiliation, sick of constantly appeasing him. I sat up straight. "Honestly it wasn't such a terrible thing. I simply tried to take care of something without bothering you."

"Apologize for not confiding in me, and then perhaps I will listen to your request." His voice was cold and quiet now.

Did he expect me to kneel at his feet to beg for the money? Well, I would not. I made myself slow my breathing so that the emotion bursting behind my ribs would subside. I must remember Harry. He was what mattered. "I beg your pardon, sir," I said. "I'll never again hesitate to ask when I have a need." Somehow, still seated on my bed, I managed to ask M. Bernard for the funds without dying of shame.

"I will send a bank draft that will cover it," he said when I finished. "It shall be posted today to relieve their minds."

As I reached to gather up the jewelry, M. Bernard's hand closed over my wrist as if in a vise.

I stared up at him, startled.

Slowly he released me. "Remember well, Sophia, if you do not better value my gifts, everything will be taken from you."

"I'll remember."

It was as if a silken net further tightened around me.

• • •

On the following Monday, this time without a shred of hope, I went to the glade for the last time.

I gave myself a stern lecture when, of course, it was vacant. If I continued this way, I should fall into a decline, and I refused to be a declining sort of person. Life must go on.

I worked to rouse myself. I walked in the gardens. I exercised Lily. I stitched away on the tapestry. I made myself focus on the pages of books I read. I continued to study biology, although it pressed on the bruised bits of my heart to do so.

"We need an outing," M. Bernard announced one evening. "Tomorrow we shall drive into Memphis so you may shop for Christmas gifts for your siblings."

I had not left the abbey's boundaries for five months—the excitement I showed was genuine.

The next morning eagerness sped my footsteps as I went out to the waiting carriage while it was yet dark. Despite having endured Odette's black looks because of having to rise early (when I knew she'd go back to bed as soon as I left), I had enjoyed making my toilette today. Over my gown of golden figured brocade I wore a brown velvet day cloak. My bonnet was of amber pleated silk with an ostrich plume that reached down to caress my cheek.

As we rolled away from the abbey, my godfather squeezed my hand. "Oho! *Ma fifille* is eager for a day of shopping. See how her eyes shine."

I smiled. "Ladies do love shops, don't they?"

He soon closed his eyes and snoozed in the corner.

I gazed out the window at the blessed, unfamiliar view. Cotton fallen from the harvest wagons drifted like snow on the sides of dirt roads.

It was afternoon when we arrived in Memphis. We visited a silk warehouse, where I entertained M. Bernard with my canny shopping, crushing fabric in my fist to see if it would wrinkle too easily and whether it was too brittle or too old.

We purchased a length of amethyst taffeta and another of china blue wool twill that would set off Anne's coloring to perfection, as well as silvery satin to make waistcoats for my brothers. From other merchants, we bought a black lace and jet-beaded cape, two beaver top hats, a porcelain-backed vanity set decorated with bluebells, a flask of the violet scent that M. Bernard liked on me, a thick woolen cloak, and I cannot tell what else. The cloak, I thought with a secret smile, would please Anarchy.

"The scent is for you, isn't it?" M. Bernard said.

"No, sir, it's for Anne. She'd like it too."

"I think not. I want no one to smell of violets but you."

I shrugged. "For me, then."

We dined at a fine restaurant, and I could hardly contain my pleasure at not sitting at the end of the long table at Wyndriven Abbey. I absorbed the people and the fashions and the sounds of unfamiliar voices.

M. Bernard leaned back in his chair and watched me with lazy enjoyment. "We shall have to make the trip to Memphis more often," he said. "You are much improved over the last weeks."

It was only as we drove the long way home that I realized I would have preferred a visit to Chicataw. Memphis had been stimulating, but those people were strangers and destined to remain so forever.

In Chicataw I might have made friends. No wonder my godfather chose to take me to Memphis instead.

As we passed through the town, I nearly hung out the window when we went by the parsonage. Even at that late hour, a light gleamed in one upstairs window. Was it Gideon's? It must be.

There came jarring back the picture of his dear face. Had I actually forgotten him in my pleasure over an outing?

As we entered the grounds of Wyndriven Abbey, oppression surged, squeezing around me.

CHAPTER 24

A QUESTION

I had intended to visit Anarchy the next day, to give her the cloak. However, I awoke with a raw throat that turned putrid. I could go nowhere. For two weeks I tossed with fever. Vaguely I was aware of Ducky spooning juice and tea through my cracked lips and of Ling administering tinctures of Oriental herbs drop by drop.

M. Bernard often sat beside my bed and read aloud, placing cool, damp cloths on my forehead and touching my face to ascertain my fever, his eyes anxious. He held my hand tenderly, and I sought his soothing touch, reaching for his fingers again when he tried to withdraw them. I needed the reassurance of someone close by. Someone to take care of me.

I dimly wondered why he didn't call for a physician. When Ducky popped in to bring vinegar in water, I croaked, "Please send for a doctor."

She tucked the coverlet in closer. "Master Bernard does not trust doctors—not since Madame Adele died. He told me so last night. You can imagine how difficult that was for him to confide, as he hasn't mentioned her name since she passed away. Do you see how good you are for him? He's recovering from his losses now, isn't he? And it's because of you."

Her voice came as from a far distance. I closed my eyes. There was no strength in me to listen to Ducky; I was too ill to sort her words.

That night as I lay alone, scorching hot, with the bedclothes crushing down on my body as I was too weak to lift them, I became aware of a pale shimmering that illuminated all the room. Four figures surrounded my bed.

There, there, there, and there. Four women all with ruddy hair. I knew them and tried hoarsely to whisper their names: "Victoire, Tatiana, Tara, Adele." My Sisters. I had almost been expecting them. They stood above me, sad and serene, Victoire wearing emerald, Tatiana sea foam, Tara primrose, and Adele sapphire, just as they did in their portraits. Ghosts.

Wordless voices murmured low, like the sound of a brook bubbling and eddying. A coolness touched me, as of a breeze on my burning skin. I slept peacefully.

From that day, my condition improved. I continued to catch glimpses of the specters. Were they actual, cognizant entities or mere shades, impressions, of those who had lived in this place? Or perhaps I was hallucinating, a remnant of raging fever. I didn't know, but I saw what I saw.

Victoire was one of them. Ducky also had long ago seen her within these walls after she fled the abbey—perhaps she had already been dead at that time?

My mind was never frightened by the ghosts—their impression

was too sorrowful to suggest a threat—but my body was. A chill would creep through me shortly before the mist or flash of color or hint of shadow glided by with an otherworldly smoothness, and every muscle would tense until long after it disappeared.

Good people were supposed to move on to heaven when they died. Certainly my parents had done so—I would never believe otherwise. According to the stories, some great emotion or need must hold these women at the abbey. Could one help the dead to heal? If I spoke to them, perhaps they'd tell me.

One morning I awoke with a start to find Tara standing over me, surrounded by a soft glitter.

"Tara," I forced a whisper.

She smiled a faint, forlorn smile.

"What is it?" I asked. "Why are you here?"

Her silence and her smile made the hair rise on my arms as she faded away.

I allowed myself to convalesce for a week, resting and eating whatever food promised nourishment and strength (even eel broth)—a relapse would be unbearable.

I wondered again why M. Bernard hadn't called a doctor. Yes, I was recovering, but it had by no means been an assured outcome. He had told Ducky he didn't trust physicians, but maybe a doctor would have insisted they crop my hair, which was typical with a fever. I smiled faintly—M. Bernard would never have let them do that.

On Saturday night, for the first time since my illness, I joined my godfather in the library. We sat in our customary chairs, and as he related events I'd missed during the past weeks, I worked on the neglected tapestry. My fingers fumbled—I was still feeble and clumsy in my convalescence, and my mind was on other things. In just a couple of days my family would arrive. I planned how we would entertain them and what we would discuss. They would find me changed. Much water had passed under the bridge since we were last together.

M. Bernard trailed off from the anecdote he'd been telling and looked at me. There was a hunger in his expression that made me shift uncomfortably in my seat, pretending to be engrossed in my stitching. I had to remind myself to breathe. I dropped my needle, and as I reached for it, he grabbed my hand. He kissed the center of my open palm. It lay limp and white as a dead fish beneath his lips.

"Sophia, will you do me the honor of becoming my wife?" The words dropped on me like stones.

For a moment I couldn't utter a sound. When I could control my voice, I frantically snatched back my hand and said, "Please, I'm not ready for this. I'm still not fully recovered from my illness."

He stood abruptly, looming over me. "You cannot have been unaware of my feelings. I have been patient with you, due to your youth, but I will wait no longer. We will announce our engagement to your siblings when they arrive. In fact, we shall hold a Christmas ball to proclaim it to the world." His tone was peremptory. He had thought all this out and assumed it would roll forth as planned, with no contribution from me. "The ceremony probably cannot take place until after the New Year, but our engagement will be pleasurable, *mon cœur*." He moved behind me and pulled aside my hair to nuzzle my neck. "Very pleasurable," he murmured, and I felt the scrape of his teeth.

I shrank, struggling to hide my revulsion. "Sir, I'm grateful for the honor you do me, but I cannot marry you."

He froze as I withdrew, then straightened and returned to his chair, sitting on the edge and facing me. "And may I ask why not?" he said coldly.

Somehow I must answer without insulting him. "There are— there are many reasons. I'm entirely unsuitable. I'm too young and have so little knowledge of the world. I'm penniless. And I care for you as a—as a dear friend and protector who stands in place of a father, but I cannot love you as a husband."

"Are you afraid to marry me?"

"Afraid? No, not of you, of course, but of the responsibilities of being Madame de Cressac and mistress of the abbey."

M. Bernard leaned back and squeezed and released the soft plush of the armrest. "Have you considered your options? On the one hand, you could be my wife, with all the resources I can provide. You would have a husband who adores you, who would strive to do all in his power to make you happy. And I do not believe you are indifferent to me; I have felt your response at times, and we have been affectionate companions, have we not? You have told me time and again you wish you could repay my generosity. I offer the opportunity to repay me in full. I ask only this one thing."

He did not look at me as he continued. "On the other hand, your family is in severely straitened circumstances. If you return to them, you will be a burden. Of necessity you would have to obtain employment, as perhaps a factory worker or nursery maid. You might even be an Odette, scurrying about trying to please a mistress who despises you. In the early years there will be men who will be happy to flirt but not offer marriage." He paused before his next words, as if to give them emphasis. "Especially when it is known you lived here alone with me."

I gave a gasp. "But nothing has happened. We've done nothing."

"Ah, but others do not know that. They will believe what it titillates them to believe, and a word here, a misspoken comment there . . . Things have a way of getting out. While you are young, perhaps you can eke out a pittance to live on, but imagine when you are old and entirely alone. You and your family might well be destitute." He licked his lips, as though savoring the idea. "I ask you to think it over carefully."

"Monsieur Bernard," I said, drawing a long breath. "I don't—"

"I said—*think it over*, Sophia. Upon reflection, you will know we are destined to be together."

I scrabbled together my reels of sewing silk, dropping half and kneeling on the floor to grope for them under the chair. Finally I stood. "I . . . shall retire now."

"*Bonsoir, ma petite.*"

As Odette undressed me, I hardly noticed what she did. When she left, I huddled in one of the armchairs, knees drawn to my chest. I was thunderstruck. Yes, there had been hints. No, I must be truthful; they had been too obvious to be considered hints, but I had told myself M. Bernard was merely being playful in a flirtatious, French sort of way. And early on, when I had been attracted to him, I had toyed with the idea that he might someday want to marry me. I *knew* this was coming, but I had willfully disregarded it as I became more and more disillusioned about my godfather, and even more from the moment I met Gideon. Particularly while I wandered in the daze of loving Gideon and then in my daze of heartsick loss, I had barely noticed anyone else.

Well, Gideon was gone now—since my illness, he seemed a lifetime ago, almost as if he had never existed. There was no more Gideon for me. I could marry M. Bernard in order to help my family and others. Was one life too much to sacrifice for the happiness of so many? M. Bernard could be affectionate and even kind if it suited him. He was interesting and amusing.

But there were his former wives—his bereavement did not excuse the fact that he had made them all miserable and it did not excuse the way he often treated me. I had thought I could manage him better than they, and perhaps I did, but it meant walking on eggshells, and I had been a fool to think I could *always* soothe his abnormal moods.

M. Bernard said we would have a "pleasurable" engagement. I began trembling for what that might mean. It was actually impressive how patient he had been. He could have done whatever he chose from the beginning and no one would have stopped him. Probably I owed it to that fastidiousness in his nature that wanted things done a certain way—he did wish for me to come willingly. At least he was still speaking of legal marriage.

Without knowing it, I had been combing through my tresses

with my fingers. I looked down now, bewildered, at a clump of hair tangled in my hand. How much of M. Bernard's desire for me was this—my bronze hair? It fed his obsession.

I crawled under my covers and wept for all my girlish, romantic dreams. Something brushed my back, soft as a breath. When I opened my eyes a crack, the pale glimmering light of the Sisters bathed the room. I heard one word whispered, not out loud, but neither was it in my mind: *"Runnnnn!"*

CHAPTER 25

STAYING

As I touched the fine linen sheets the next morning, I told myself firmly, "Savor them now, because you are leaving them behind very soon."

During the night I had resisted mindless fleeing, without money or transportation. Even if I could make it to the main road in my weakened state, I would be picked up by the patrollers who watched for runaway slaves and who would be only too ready to return an underage ward to her very wealthy guardian. And even if I reached Anarchy or Gideon, I would put them in jeopardy from the law and from M. Bernard.

Now, in the sensible daylight, I was still determined to leave the abbey, but I knew I must inform M. Bernard and seek his assistance and understanding.

A soft tap sounded on the door.

"Who is it?" I called, terrified it would be my godfather since Odette never knocked. I could not face him yet.

"Me, Miss." It was Talitha.

When she entered, her eyes were downcast. "Please, I got to talk to you. You the only one who might help."

Her expression was so piteous, so different from her usual proud bearing that I slid from bed and ran across the room to her. "What's wrong? What's happened?"

"It be that Garvey out in the stables. Since Charles left, he's after me and after me. He say, 'Meet me in the hayloft' at this time or at that. Always I stay away, but it's getting worse. It be only a matter of time before he catch me by myself, and I so afraid. What do I do, Miss?"

In that moment we shared something, and she was aware of it. She knew the position I was in with her master. I understood that what Garvey intended for Talitha was something much more devastating than a stolen kiss.

I reached out and we tightly gripped hands. For the first time she completely trusted me.

"Leave it to me," I said. "Somehow . . . I'll . . . fix it."

She looked at me intently for a moment, then nodded. We released each other and she ducked out.

I had no influence over Garvey except through M. Bernard. I would have to request him to intervene. But how could I ask for this favor and at the same time announce I was leaving?

Everything in this place led back to M. Bernard. Was I only pretending I had a choice? Was I set inevitably on a path that led to being bound to him forever? Panic rose at the idea, like a little mouse scurrying around in a trap trying to find a way out to save itself.

I dressed and went downstairs early in order to approach my godfather at his meal.

He looked up with a smile so genuinely warm that already my will began melting. "Why, how is it you are stirring so early, *ma petite*? Am I to have the pleasure of your presence at breakfast?"

I shook my head. "I don't feel like eating, sir. I came down to speak to you."

"Well, do not look as if I might bite your head off. Here, take this seat." When I hesitated, he said, "What? Can you not even bear to sit beside me?"

"It's easier to say the hard thing I have to say while standing."

"So it is to be a formidable speech. I shake in my shoes with apprehension. Out with it, then."

I took a deep breath. "I think it's time I brought my stay to an end."

He found my words diverting. "And why would you possibly think that?"

This was not going as I had planned.

I glanced toward George, who stood by the sideboard, and said quietly, "Because if people really will be gossiping, and if you—if you really have those feelings for me, I must not stay because I *cannot* marry you."

"Yes, you told me that before, and I asked you only to continue to think about it. When you have had sufficient time to consider, if you still do not wish to marry me, then we will go on as before."

"But you suggested my only choices were to marry you or to leave."

"You did need to understand the reality of your situation. However, of course there is the third choice—that we shall remain fond companions, with Mrs. Duckworth as a suitable chaperon and visits to and fro with your family. There need be no awkwardness attached. Are you so anxious to abandon me?"

"No, sir."

"I am glad. I have spared no effort or expense to give you all that might make you happy. And your family is to arrive this week; you would pass one another on the road if you left now. I have a good many pleasures planned for them. Would you choose to spoil their visit?"

"Indeed, I would not. It's only that under the circumstances—"

"Bah! 'Under the circumstances' nothing! No more dramatics, *s'il vous plaît.* I am sorry I spoke last night."

"But you said you were out of patience. You said—"

"I said—I said . . . Obviously I made a muddle of everything. I will not repeat my proposal unless you bring it up, nor will I embarrass you with demonstrations of my affection until you welcome them. Have I put your mind at rest? Do we understand one another now?"

"Yes, sir."

"Now I shall spread honey on this biscuit just for you. Sit down here next to me and eat it to oblige me."

I sat down to the biscuit like the good little pet that I was, reeling from the way M. Bernard managed to twist my words and feelings so that, no matter my determination otherwise, in the end I did what he wanted.

After I finished the biscuit, I opened my mouth to bring up Talitha, but I hesitated, unsure how to word my request.

"Is there something else?" M. Bernard asked.

"Please, sir, I also have a favor to ask."

"Anything, up to half of my kingdom," he said, then laughed. "No, I take that back—anything within reason, I should have said."

"Your groom, Garvey, has been bothering Talitha—one of the maids—with his unwanted attentions, and I said I would help. Would you please order him to leave her alone?"

M. Bernard snorted. "I am surprised you continue to interest yourself in the sordid affairs of servants."

"They are people on your estate," I said tightly, "and we have a responsibility toward them. Please, I promised."

"And you have done as you promised. You have asked. And I will tell you that I do not give this"—here he snapped his fingers—"for the dusky beauty's feigned reluctance to yield to Garvey." He threw his hands in the air. "But, only for your sake, I will order him away." He gave a knowing smile—perhaps he thought my concern over Talitha showed I was moving into the role of mistress of the abbey, in spite of my protests.

I thanked him.

And thus I continued my stay.

Garvey's yellow-flecked eyes, filled with undisguised hatred, met mine as Odette and I passed the stables the next day. So, M. Bernard had told him who had requested the order to stay away from Talitha. I had made an enemy.

For Odette, Garvey reserved a lecherous leer and the stroke of his hand down her arm. She blew him a kiss. I grabbed up my skirts and surged briskly ahead toward the woods. They had no respect, to behave so in my presence.

Although Garvey was good-looking in a vulgar way, he exuded

loathsomeness. Odette was either desperate for masculine attention or she must have considered him an unusually entertaining lover. Nauseating image.

Odette caught up with me, now scowling furiously.

"Why do you encourage that vile person?" I asked, not expecting an answer, since Odette had only the once spoken English to me.

"I have use for him," she said shortly.

When we reached the wall, she pulled her shawl under her chin and said, "Be quick. I am cold." She had probably been hoping I had given up such jaunts.

I planned a hasty visit to Anarchy. When the sharp and spiteful wind ripped at my mantelet and shot up my skirts, I briefly considered putting on her heavy cloak, which I carried in a drawstring bag over my arm.

A melancholy weighted the air. The autumn colors had moldered away, the branches stripped and the earth deep in sodden leaves. Fallen trees, which had been sweetly swathed in tall grasses and wildflowers earlier, now lay exposed, their bark peeling and their rotting innards black, like so many decayed corpses.

As I made my way toward Anarchy's hut, I absently braided and knotted the narrow ribbons at my belt. Round and round went my disordered thoughts, with never a conclusion and never an appropriate action step.

"Something setting your mind all a-jumble, honey?"

I jumped. "Oh, it's you," I said, and laughed weakly at my jitters. "I was actually coming to see you—I've brought you something. But what makes you think I'm troubled?"

Anarchy had slipped up from behind. She was wrapped in a

moth-eaten shawl and clutched a burlap sack bulging with pecans in one hand. She put the other one firmly over my own hands to quiet them, then untangled my ribbons. With her chin, she gestured toward a stump. "Set down there and tell ole Anarchy everything."

"Where to begin?" I said, sitting on the edge. "I hardly know."

"Begin with what's got you a-fluttering the most."

"Monsieur de Cressac has asked me to marry him," I said in a low voice.

"That so? And what you be telling him?"

"I said no, of course. He pretended to accept my answer, but he didn't really. He's certain I'll change my mind."

"You scared he try to *make* you marry him?" Lines creased between Anarchy's brows.

"Not by force. At least I don't think so. But he intends to *obligate* me into it. He's given me so much. And not just me—my family as well. He acts as if it's only a matter of time until I relent."

Her frown deepened, pulling her skin tighter across her cheek-bones. She looked up at the treetops. "Listen to this baby, thinking she might owe this man her own self." Now she fixed me with her eyes. "If he a nice man, and if he really cares for you, why you feel squashed under the doodads he give you?"

I considered this. "Squashed" was an excellent word. "I wouldn't," I said finally. "I'd feel grateful, but not squashed. You're very wise, Anarchy."

"Uh, uh, uh. Uh, uh, uh. The good Lord make me so old I know lots of things."

I scooted over on my seat and patted it so she could sit beside me. She dropped her sack and lowered herself rustily.

"My family comes tomorrow," I said, reaching down to replace some of the pecans that had rolled out of her bag. "My two brothers and my sister."

"Why? Why he let them come? The way he sound to me, he like to keep you to hisself."

I began fidgeting with my ribbons again until Anarchy lay her gnarled hand on mine once more. "I don't know," I said. "He must realize having my family here will only distract me from him."

She shook her head. "He plan to get some good out of it for hisself. His kind always do. He show them his fancy house and his fancy doodads and he say, 'See what a fine man I be,' and they shrink all teeny tiny and tell you to marry him. That be his plan, sure 'nough."

"Perhaps you're right," I said slowly. "That might well be the effect he'd have on them. You have no idea, Anarchy, what a powerful nature Monsieur de Cressac has. Well, he shan't have his way this time, not about my marrying him, anyway."

"Lil Miss, you set me a-worrying over you. This man ain't no good. He ain't never *hurt* you, has he?"

"Not really," I said, "although I confess—"

She waited, not speaking.

In the uncomfortable silence I had to voice the terrible thought I had never yet allowed myself to explore. "Several weeks ago I found my cat hanging dead in the woods near the abbey. He was an animal Monsieur disliked, and my godfather was in a strange and terrible mood the night before. But no, I can't believe he could have done such an awful thing."

"Who else you think done it?"

"Some—some poacher or tramp camping in the woods. Or maybe some bad boys from town."

"I'd have known if them tramps or bad boys been hanging round. And the only poacher who dare hunt in yonder woods so close to your place be my Anthony, and he wouldn't never touch no cat. No one else go there on account of the man traps that Mr. de Cressac sets, 'cept the preacher man, and he wouldn't harm nothing."

"Have you seen him lately? The Reverend Mr. Stone?" I could not keep the anxiety from my voice.

"No, not for a long while. Sorry, honey. He never come often and he ain't been to my place since last spring."

I bit my lip. All I wanted now, I told myself, was to hear that someone had seen Gideon and that he was all right.

Anarchy shook her head slowly. "If Mr. de Cressac be a man who would do that to a little ole cat, you best be leaving this place."

"I know. I know. And I will. When my family leaves, I'll leave with them."

"You do that. Now, what else got you fretting?"

"Well, there's Charles—he was a footman at the house. He was good to me, and Monsieur de Cressac didn't like it. He's—well, he's very possessive of me, so he exiled Charles out to work in the fields. I worry about him there, especially since it's my fault he was sent away. He's not made for that sort of labor. I need to fix things, but how?"

"Well, if Mr. de Cressac so jealous, he won't like it if you ask for this Charles to come back, so that won't do no good. Next thing you know, Charles be hanging in the woods 'stead of the cat."

I gasped and started to say that was ridiculous, but I couldn't.

"So . . . you got any money?" Anarchy asked.

I held up my empty hands, then dropped them. "No. Not a penny."

"Uh, uh, uh. 'Not a penny,' you says. Folks think I is poor, but I rich compared to you. I got a hundred dollars saved up in my secret place, more'n half what I needs to buy my grandbaby. Now this Charles, he a young man and trained good, so he probably fetch about two thousand dollars."

Two thousand dollars. Such little value for a man's life, yet even that was out of my reach. I would gladly give back all the "doodads"—at this moment I hated all the "doodads"—if only I could assist Charles. "There might be a way. . . . I know there are people who help slaves escape to the North."

"You got connections?"

"No, but I think I know someone who does."

"Can you get to the person you think you know?"

"I don't—no, probably not." My head dropped.

She patted my knee. "Sometime you got to accept you can't do nothing about some things right now and stop a-worrying till you *can* do something."

"Have you yourself considered helping your family escape rather than trying to buy your grandchild?"

"I done told you I don't want to leave this place, and neither do Anthony and my grandbaby. This our home. I only wants my grandbaby's freedom papers so's she can come live here with me."

I rubbed my forehead with worry and frustration. I couldn't help even one person.

Anarchy nudged my shoulder. "When you leaves the abbey place for good, is you gonna write your preacher man? Let him know you is free?"

My eyes widened. "Why, yes. Yes, I will." A warm little stream of hope trickled through the coldness inside me.

The old woman stood now and hefted her sack. "How about you come back to my place and eat some hot coon stew and sweet potato pie. Anthony brung me a nice fat coon yesterday."

"It sounds delicious," I lied. I could never eat an animal with a black mask and tiny hands. "But no thank you. I need to get back."

"You sure your kin come tomorrow?"

"I'm sure. Oh dear, I almost forgot!" I snatched up the bag. "This is for you. For these cold days."

Anarchy undid the strings and pulled out the gray woolen folds of the cloak.

I helped her place it around her and snugly tied the cord beneath her chin.

"Uh, uh, uh," she said, shaking her shoulders. "Why, if I won't be finer'n frog hair in this. I be the finest and warmest old woman in these here woods! I thank you."

Impulsively I gave her a soft little hug, afraid of crushing her frail bones.

She snorted. "Don't they know how to give no one a proper squeeze up Yankee way?" She gave me a hard, fierce hug that took my breath away.

"Thank you so much for everything," I whispered when I could speak again.

"You take care, lil Miss. Don't you be alone with that man. And you knows the way to ole Anarchy if you needs anything. You think you don't got nobody, but you got me."

"I do know the way, and thank you again." My voice shook a little.

"Have a blessed day, child." She winked and left me.

There was a spring in my step when I turned to go. How could I have forgotten that as soon as I left with my family, I could write to Gideon? I could tell him exactly what had transpired, and we'd have to court through letters, but then we would marry. He could find a church somewhere far away from M. Bernard—perhaps out West, which everyone said was the way of the future. I smiled. My day-dreams could well be reality in a few months; I had only to leave Wyndriven Abbey.

CHAPTER 26

THE NET TIGHTENS

The next day I anxiously awaited my family's arrival. I hadn't seen them in six long months. I had begged M. Bernard to allow me to meet their coach in Memphis, but he refused.

"No, I think not. Mrs. Duckworth requires your help with preparations. I must go to Memphis myself on business; therefore, I shall fetch them."

Despite M. Bernard's words, all Ducky let me do was select flowers from the orangery for Daphne to arrange. I flitted from bedchamber to bedchamber watching the maids airing feather beds and fluffing up bolsters and polishing mirrors and fitting the rooms with every comfort. I placed books my siblings might like on their bedside tables, bowls of oranges on their bureaus.

Talitha approached me as I laid out one of my own dressing gowns on Anne's bed for her use. She shut the door behind her.

"What is it?" I asked when she stood looking at me.

"Garvey."

"He's bothering you still?"

"He say he don't care what Master tell him. He say he can do whatever he wants 'cause he know too much about Master, so Master won't dare do nothing."

"Perhaps M. Bernard has had devious business dealings and Garvey has knowledge of them. I'm so sorry, Talitha. I did try." I placed my hand on her arm. "You've got to get away from here. You and Charles both. Please trust me. I can't do much, but I'll do whatever I can. Maybe—maybe I can get a message to Charles next time I visit the plantation."

"We be going there on Christmas Day. I can talk to him myself."

"You can take my good, thick boots for walking and my black velvet cloak. I'll give them to you right now as a gift."

"And how I explain to the others why I got them? No, I won't take them now, but I get them right before I leave. If I leave."

"I'll try to think what else I dare give you. And you know—at least I'm quite sure—it's the Reverend Stone in Chicataw who will help you." A pale spark of pride shot through me. Gideon would know exactly how to care for them.

She nodded.

"I wish I could do more. I wish I had money. I wish—"

"I understand. Thank you."

"And stay away from Garvey," I said as she turned to leave.

"I try."

I sighed and stared down at the silk of the dressing gown.

As the shadows grew long, I changed into an evening dress and made my way toward the yellow salon to wait there. I shivered as an icy breeze wafted through me. Just ahead, in the dim hall, something whisked around the corner—the wispy train of a primrose gown.

I raced ahead to catch the bright misty figure, who was several inches taller than I, with a cascade of glowing hair down her back. Tara. It was Tara. I would speak to her again. However, when I entered the yellow salon, the apparition faded away with a sound almost like a blown-out breath, leaving only a quiver in the air behind.

At that very moment came the echoes of beloved voices. I ran toward them. In the center of the great hall huddled my siblings, made small by the enormous dimensions of the place, gazing wide-eyed at its opulence. M. Bernard smiled benignly on one side and Ducky bobbed and beamed on the other in her best black satin. I paused—something seemed unfamiliar about the stance of my family—before flying down the vast expanse of checkered marble and throwing myself into Anne's arms, then Harry's, then Junius's.

Junius chuckled and held me at arm's length. "Why, Sophie, you're so excited to see us, anyone would think you hadn't been having the time of your life. And look at your hair, so wild and loose."

"Oh," Anne said, "no one could ever imagine she wasn't doing beautifully. Just look at that dress. Chantilly lace! And those pearls! They fair take my breath away. Here, turn around so I can see the back."

Harry grabbed my waist and twirled so that I spun like a top, and there was laughter when I staggered, dizzy, and M. Bernard caught me in his arms and righted me.

Anne shook her head as if she could hardly believe the sight of me. "This place becomes you. Monsieur de Cressac has been regaling us with little stories of your doings. What a pleasure to have these lovely grounds to roam! We shall have such grand jaunts."

"And," Harry said, "he let me drive his bang-up team of matched bays all the way here. He's a right one, is Monsieur de Cressac."

Obviously M. Bernard had taken pains to begin binding his spell over them.

"Tell me about your trip," I said.

"It was long," Junius said, "and bumpy and bouncy—Harry was sick much of the way—but uneventful."

"Oh, poor Harry!" I cried. "Is your stomach still queasy? Shall I fetch some peppermint tea?"

Harry reddened. "What? Have you grown up so much these last months that you've become our mother now? No, silly little Sophie, I'm fine. Once I was driving Monsieur de Cressac's well-sprung carriage, I felt tip-top."

"How is old Mrs. Whaley doing?" I asked. "And did they ever tear down the theater that burned? I have so many questions you never got around to answering when you wrote—and, by the way, your letters were shockingly rare. How is—" I suddenly noticed the pinched lines around Junius's mouth and realized how exhausted they all must be. "Oh, we'll have plenty of time later for talking. Let me take you up to your rooms to freshen up, although I can hardly bear to be parted from you for even a few minutes. Anne, I'll be your maid tonight, but Talitha will help you after this."

As I took Harry's arm to climb the stairs, I noted his fine buff-striped trousers and new brown frock coat and felt a swift spark of anger. How had he afforded these garments when so recently he was in dire financial straits?

Anne wandered from window to window in her bedroom, taking in the views. "It's glorious here," she said. "How happy I am for you. You must absolutely love it!" She gave a trilling little laugh "Well, who wouldn't? Tomorrow you must show me everything."

"There's a lot to see." I felt a quiet pride in the abbey. An ownership.

My sister held on to the bedpost as I tightened her laces. "Monsieur de Cressac is a perfect gentleman," she said. "Always solicitous of our comfort and so fine-looking. That a man should be so wealthy and still remain easy and unaffected—it's a wonderful thing. And he's so interesting! We discussed a great many subjects, and to my mind, he thinks just as he ought about them. My darling, how happy I am that he's come into our lives!"

I leaned against the bedpost and slowly shook my head.

Anne looked at me, concerned. "What's wrong? Are you troubled in some way by our host?"

"Sister, he wants to marry me." There. It was out. Now Anne would advise exactly what I must do.

She threw her arms around me. "Oh, Sophie, you fortunate, fortunate girl!"

"I told him no."

She gave a dismayed intake of breath. *"What?"*

"There are things about Monsieur Bernard that make me most— most uncomfortable. I told him no, but he wouldn't take that as my final answer." And to think I had expected Anne to be horrified that I was living in the same house with a man who had romantic interests in me. I almost smiled at her opposite reaction.

"Pray, tell me what those things are, and I'll set your mind to rest." She pulled me down to sit beside her on the bed.

"He's been married four times before."

"And they all died?"

"Three died and he's divorced from one." I couldn't bring up my conviction that Victoire was also dead.

"Well, my love, it happens. That poor, poor man, to be bereaved so frequently. It's true he's a good many years older than you, but that only means he already knows how to please a wife. It makes him responsible and settled." She giggled. "Very *well* settled."

"No, please listen. He lets me go nowhere and meet no one. I'm followed by a servant if I so much as set foot outside."

"That's the custom with ladies of wealth. He wants no harm to befall you. He loves you so—he's protective of you, as is right."

"He doesn't even allow me to attend church."

"I must own that surprises me, from one who is such a gentleman. However, I have no doubt once you're married, the love of a virtuous woman will influence him for the good."

Anne stood and I helped her lower her evening gown over her shoulders. She took my hands and patted them between her own. "Now, pray, what else bothers you?"

I gently released her grip and smoothed her skirts over the hoop. "He has a temper. It's boiling just below the surface, and I'm scared of triggering it."

"He's a man who commands a great many people. Naturally he's a trifle high-handed. As his wife you'll learn the little ways to please and pacify such a man. You'll enjoy creating a peaceful domestic haven for him."

In a flash I remembered the letter from Tara's aunt ordering her to be more accommodating to her husband. My own sister might well be penning such an epistle to me in the future if I were to marry M. Bernard. I didn't know what to say now. I had waited months for this chat. I had told Anne my problems and she had dismissed them. My conversation with her was very different from the one I'd had with Anarchy. Anne made my concerns seem light indeed. Were they, in fact? M. Bernard had accused me of dramatics; perhaps I *was* being theatrical. However, there was still one facet of the situation I hesitated to bring up.

"Anne, I've met a young man—a wonderful young man—of whom I'm very fond," I said, casting discretion to the winds as she knelt to dig in her portmanteau for her jewelry case.

She stood and whirled around in one movement. "You *what*? Who is he? I thought you said Monsieur de Cressac doesn't let you get to know anyone."

I couldn't meet her eyes, so I fussed with one of the flower arrangements. "It's true Monsieur Bernard permits me to meet no one. But I became acquainted with this young man when I was walking unattended in the woods. I had—I had shed myself of my maid."

"And he came up to you? It was ill-bred to approach a young female like that."

I turned to face her. "No. I realize how it sounds, but it wasn't like that. Mr. Stone is a well-bred gentleman—indeed, he's a minister—and he worried over the impropriety of our meetings. He would have courted me honorably, but my godfather would never have allowed it."

"Did you speak to Monsieur de Cressac on the subject?"

"No. I didn't have to. I knew he would've been beyond furious."

"So he doesn't know, thank goodness." Anne's relief was palpable.

"He may be aware that I get rid of my attendant now and then, but he certainly would have let me know if he'd suspected I was meeting a man. Anyway, Mr. Stone stopped coming, and I was very—very unhappy for a long while. But I've been hoping I could leave to go home with you and then write to Mr. Stone. Maybe he would—" I stopped speaking at the look of pity on Anne's face.

She put her arm about my waist and brushed a tendril of hair from my forehead. "Darling, you haven't behaved very well, but you know I love you anyway. This is what you must do. You must put away all thought of this Mr. Stone. Your feelings for him will soon fade away as if they never existed. If Monsieur de Cressac knows nothing of him, then least said soonest mended. I've never told you this, but I also once had an unsuitable young man pay decided attention to me. He traveled with a fast crowd, and Papa knew he would come to no good. It was difficult, but urged by our father, I did my duty and sent him on his way."

She thought she was showing me that my feelings for Gideon would soon be forgotten, but instead I wanted to shout, *And look at you now! Are you happier alone and in poverty than you would have been with this "unsuitable" young man?* I couldn't be so cruel, of course. I twisted my hands. Had I been childish about Gideon? It was odd—I had almost forgotten what he looked like.

Anne was patting her cloudy blond hair before the mirror. "I'm sure Monsieur de Cressac, if he learned of your meetings, would understand there was nothing to them."

My lips parted. A sharp stab of fear for Gideon pierced my heart. If my godfather got wind of the fact that Gideon and I had spent those hours together . . . I clutched Anne's arm. "Please, I beg you to never breathe a word of this to my godfather. Not even—not even if he makes you feel confidential toward him."

Her brow furrowed. Embarrassed, I released her.

"Of course I'll say nothing. But, Sophie, do you know—can you possibly realize what your marrying Monsieur de Cressac would mean for us? I haven't written much of this—I didn't wish to alarm you—but we've had a terrible time of it. I've watched Junius age years in these six months. Our father's affairs were in far worse order than at first we guessed. I can't tell you how welcome was the money you sent." She made me face her directly. "In everyone's life there comes a time when they realize they've become an adult and, as such, must make necessary sacrifices. Can it be that for you that time has come?" She stroked my cheek.

My sister's sweet smile had a pinched, pathetic quality to it I had never before noticed. Indeed, now that I reflected, the change I had fleetingly glimpsed in my family as they stood in the hall was more than a stoop to their shoulders; it was as if a shadow clung to them. While I had been enjoying the luxuries of Wyndriven Abbey, they had been fighting for survival.

"Perhaps it has," I said softly. "One thing more, Anne: All his wives had red hair."

She stared for a moment, then gave a merry peal of laughter.

"So," she said, "he's a gentleman with decided tastes. Isn't it fortunate—for both you and us—that you fit his preference? I had wondered why you wear your locks down. Is that a request from him?"

I nodded.

"Well, I don't deny he's an unusual man, but what's the harm in obliging him? Now put a smile on your face and forget that Mr. What's-His-Name. Come, let's go down to supper. I'm famished."

The dinner Alphonse had created was more lavish than any I had ever before experienced at the abbey. There were raw oysters and fried smelts, hare with pudding in its belly and sauce tartare, pigeon pie, quail with truffles, sweetbread patés, roast turkey, potatoes, cheesecake and chocolate custard and fancy cakes.

Junius and M. Bernard ate with relish, Anne more carefully. Both Harry and I picked at our food, although I noticed my younger brother drank a great deal.

My godfather was acutely aware of each of us as he set out to put everyone at ease.

"Harry, my friend," he said, making my brother start, "I am considering purchasing a new phaeton, but isolated as we are, I'm unfamiliar with the current styles. What, in your opinion, should I buy?"

Harry immediately put down his wineglass and launched into a long description of the benefits of different sporting vehicles. As he spoke, my brother seemed his old self.

When that subject ran out, my godfather asked Anne what she thought of certain popular books, and me, of possible changes to the abbey's décor.

He flattered Junius by inquiring into his ideas on world events. They discussed the influx of immigrants and the Crimean War and the railway that might someday connect the Atlantic Ocean to the Pacific. M. Bernard amused us with his description of the government allotting money for camels to be tested for military use.

He had set out to charm my family, and no one could bewitch like my godfather when he made it his business to do so. Whatever his motives, the conversation sparkled.

M. Bernard entertained, Junius and Anne chimed in, Harry drank, and I watched them all.

Despite his fine clothes, Harry was unwell. He looked pale and hollow-cheeked, with dark shadows beneath his eyes. Whatever was wrong with him was worse than what Junius and Anne had been going through. I must speak to him privately.

After dinner Anne and I took up our needles and sat cozily side by side in the library while the three gentlemen smoked and enjoyed their port elsewhere. My sister admired the tapestry I was working on. I myself was not happy with it. The figures seemed to trudge rather than cavort. It was not the lighthearted image I had intended, and yet I couldn't seem to change it.

"What shining thread did you use for the flames in the center?" she asked.

"My hair," I said reluctantly.

"Beautiful. How clever! And how does it stand out so from the rest of the image?"

"Fine wire twisted among the strands."

"You've always been better at needlework than I. And look at your bracelet. It shines like copper, but it must be hair as well."

It was easy to let her believe it crafted solely of my own strands. I would never tell her about the wives. She wouldn't understand.

We met together afterward for a round of billiards. Even Anne and I played, and soon we were all merry because my ladylike sister was naturally skilled at ricocheting balls. The familial camaraderie, the larking, the witty comments, all spread a warm golden glow around us.

No one wanted to retire yet, so next we gathered about the piano, with Anne playing. We sang popular lyrics—love ditties and Negro ballads and folk songs. I took the soprano part, Anne was alto, Harry and Junius tenor, and M. Bernard bass. We blended beautifully. M. Bernard's voice was deep and mellow.

The glow about us continued until I glanced toward the window. Then my throat closed up even as the goose bumps rose on my arms. The shivery glimmering began, and soon a lady was seated upon the window seat, her halo of pale strawberry blond hair brightened by the sea foam hue of her gown. She slumped against the wall, staring desolately out into the black night. Tatiana.

M. Bernard put his hand possessively on my shoulder. "*Chérie*. It is time you retired for the evening."

"Soon," I said, "and then perhaps we should all go."

"No," Anne said, giving me a little shove toward the door. "How thoughtful of Monsieur de Cressac to note how tired you are. Go on up and we won't be long afterward."

I found myself heading upstairs even though I resented being treated like a five-year-old and was too excited by my family's presence to think of sleeping. I undressed but kept the candles lit so I could read.

A soft knock sounded on my bedchamber door an hour later. Before I had time to fear it could be someone else, Anne's voice called, "May I come in?"

I arose and turned the key.

"Do you always lock your door?" she asked, momentarily diverted.

I nodded but didn't explain. "Come in."

As my sister entered the room, her lower lip dropped. "Oh, so grand! And look at those wardrobes filled with beautiful dresses. You fortunate, fortunate girl!" she repeated.

"Did you come to tell me something?" I asked.

She swirled around to face me. "We have wonderful news. I couldn't wait until the morning. Tonight Junius and Monsieur de Cressac discussed Junius's profession and—oh, Sophie, you'll never guess!"

"My godfather says he'll give Junius a start in business."

"How ever did you know? We're so grateful to Monsieur. He'll be the making of our brother."

I didn't tell her it was exactly what I had been expecting. A cold lump settled in my stomach. I suddenly felt very small and insecure standing in my vast bedchamber and could only squeeze out the words, "How grand for Junius."

CHAPTER 27

THE ANSWER

"You may use my little boat if you like," I said from behind Harry, causing him to start.

I had known he intended to rise early to go fishing, and while it was yet dark, I had listened for his door to open. At the sound I dashed to follow the glow of his lantern down to the lake. Toby, a bright-eyed twelve-year-old who did odd jobs about the place, trotted behind him, toting Harry's fishing gear. Evidently my brother had quickly learned the ways of the South.

"What are you doing out here?" Harry demanded once he had recovered himself. "You should still be snoozing for hours like all fashionable young ladies."

I gave a delicate, derisive snort and took his arm as we walked out onto the dock. "I want to have you to myself for a while. You've been here four days and I've hardly seen you."

"Well, you know, we fellows need to hunt while the hunting's good." He touched the curving swan neck of my boat. "Is this really your own? What a beauty!"

"Yes. Monsieur Bernard gave it to me."

"You are certainly in the way to becoming spoiled, my girl." He pinched my cheek, and I swatted his hand away.

Toby held the side of the boat as I stepped in. I inclined my head toward him as he handed Harry the pole and tackle. "*I'm* not the one who needs a poor little boy to carry my gear for me."

Harry laughed. "*Touché.*" He rowed us out to the middle of the lake while Toby huddled sleepily on the pier.

With the black water beneath and the yet-dark sky all around, we were alone in the world within our little island of lantern light. I sat quietly as my brother cast in his line. The silence and the dark settled around us. He stared out with deep-shadowed eyes.

"What's wrong, Harry?" I asked.

"Wrong?"

"Something is fretting you. Is it money?"

With one hand, he scooped a stray pebble from the bottom of the boat and pitched it hard across the lake. "Of course it's money— isn't that always the problem for us Petherams? I shouldn't tell you, since there's nothing you can do about it, but if you must know . . . I'm ruined. If I don't come up with a great deal of cash in a very short time, I'm a dead man. The fellows I owe aren't the forgiving sort."

He looked very boyish, hunched over in the boat with fishing pole in hand, to be saying such desperate words.

"Didn't Anne give you the funds from Monsieur Bernard?"

"Oh, yes. Thank you, by the way. But I owed far more than she ~w. That amount paid my tradesmen bills, so at least they're off Too bad it was a drop in the bucket compared to what I owe the gaming hall. I was a fool—I know that now, but it's too late. Got carried away by the company I kept. I always thought that I could keep up, that I'd land on my feet. And they're devilishly fine fellows—kept me in whoops—but now they want nothing to do with me. Afraid I'll ask for a loan, I guess. Anyway, they took me to their favorite haunt, and I won at first, which evidently is what those places always plan for green players."

My mind raced frantically. I must help him. "And then you began losing soon after."

"Of course. Lost it all, and kept thinking I'd win it back, so I gave my promissory notes, and the long and short of it is, I'm sunk. At least our time here allows me a reprieve. It's hard to forget, though, that those oafs will be lying in wait as soon as I return."

You must marry Monsieur Bernard, a cold little voice in my head stated flatly. I remembered what Anne had said about becoming an adult and making sacrifices. My time had come. "There is a way you can get the money," I said slowly.

"No, I shan't plague de Cressac. As it is, he's done enough I can never pay back. I'm going to take it like a man. Only problem is, I'm scared of how they'll get me. Keeps me awake at night and keeps me drinking the brandy—something else I can't afford—and always I feel ill. There's no way out, so I'll take the consequences."

"Yes, there is a way. If Monsieur Bernard is my husband, he would gladly give the money to his brother-in-law without expecting to be repaid."

"Brother-in-law?" Harry's mouth fell open. "Are you telling me de Cressac wants to marry you? Really?"

"Yes, really."

He ruffled my hair in teasing brotherly fashion. "Hard to imagine you being old enough for such a thing, but I have noticed he acts as if he owns you already."

"He did make me a proposal, but I haven't given him my promise yet. I'll—" I paused, then quickly said the words, "I'll give it to him today."

"No, Sophie. I can't have my sister selling herself for my sake. That would be wrong, unless . . . only . . . do you—do you like him at all? He seems a good fellow."

"Of course I like him," I said, tossing my head. Harry must never know how I really felt, what I feared. And perhaps it would turn out not to be such a terrible thing after all. Surely—surely—if I worked even harder to make M. Bernard happy, my life wouldn't be a bad one. I would learn from his former wives' mistakes.

"Capital, then. That's grand if you really want to marry him. Tell me again you wouldn't be doing it just for me."

"I—wouldn't—be—doing—it—just—for—you, you silly boy." I would be doing it for him *and* Anne *and* Junius. People—my people—were all that mattered now.

He heaved a great sigh of relief, as if he'd been holding it in for days, and looked at me speculatively.

"Our little sister—a bride and a wealthy woman to boot. Imagine! I never dreamed you'd beat Anne to the altar, but you really do seem years older than you did last spring. I saw it first thing when we got here. Not near the flibbertigibbet you used to be. You ought to ask de Cressac for a sea monster boat as a wedding present, by the
there was a brilliantly painted one at Boston Harbor a while

back that would look fine on your lake." He tugged at his line and said cheerfully, "Look now, I've got a bite."

Harry rowed me to shore, and I returned to my bedchamber. Odette dressed me in a morning gown of deep violet. I spelled it m-o-u-r-n-i-n-g in my mind, as violet is a color of half mourning, suitable for what I was resigned to do. This would be the death of so many things.

I placed myself on a carved bench in the hall near my godfather's bedchamber door. It seemed indelicate to do such a thing, as if I were waiting to pounce, but there must be no time to reconsider.

When I spoke to M. Bernard, I would remind him of the ball he had mentioned previously. The neighboring world should know of my existence. I refused to live and die unknown here at Wyndriven Abbey, as had Victoire and Tatiana, Tara and Adele. When we were betrothed, while he yet strove to please, I would make some requests. The ball would be the first, and later I would demand to attend church and pay a few calls. I would carefully tread the balance between giving in to M. Bernard and standing up for myself. I didn't let myself think of Gideon—or rather, *Mr. Stone,* as he must forever be to me now.

Achal eyed me suspiciously as he glided past my bench and into his master's room. M. Bernard emerged soon after, wearing his paisley satin dressing gown. His hair was rumpled and his cheeks showed dark stubble. I had roused him before shaving. My face grew hot; it was too intimate to see him like this. But I'd better get used to it.

"What is it? Is something amiss?" he asked, yawning.

I rose. "No, sir, but I wanted to catch you alone."

"Well then, you have caught me. What will you do with me?" He offered his arm. "Come, let us go down to the library. We can have a fire laid, and we will have one of our intimate *tête-à-têtes.*"

I laid a cold hand on his elbow and we made our way downstairs.

A housemaid lit the fire, and we sat together in the familiar manner, but this time was different. I stared at the tongues of flame licking and curling about the logs.

"So, what is on your mind?" he asked.

I turned and made myself look directly into his amber eyes, his tiger eyes. "Sir, last week you told me—you asked me to marry you, and you were so obliging as to let me consider it for a few days."

"And have you finished considering it?"

"I have. Do you still wish it?"

A smile played about his lips. "*Naturellement.* Dare I hope you have decided you would indeed like to marry me?"

I took a breath. "Yes, if you please. And I should like to be wed very soon—as soon as possible."

"Your eagerness is touching. We will have to consult the calendar to set the date. I am thinking the end of January would give us time for planning the ceremony and a wedding trip. Perhaps to Barbados, hmm? Lots of sunshine and little clothing."

"I've heard that island is beautiful."

He put his hands on my shoulders, and I studied the paisley pattern of his dressing gown. It helped to concentrate on that instead of my new fiancé's face.

He lifted my chin so I had to look up. His expression was tender. "I always be good to you. I want to always make you happy.

This is something I have never before spoken about to you, as it is painful, but I tell you now—my former marriages were terrible mistakes. They were unhappy women. I am not a young man, but all this time was necessary for me to finally know the sort of wife I need, and it's you, Sophia. You, with your spirit of fancifulness and innocence. It took me all these years and all those mistakes in order to wait for you to grow up. This time I have chosen perfectly. These months we've been together—I have never been so happy."

"Thank you, Monsieur Bernard," I said in a taut little voice. "I shall strive to be a pleasant wife and companion."

I wondered how soon I could ask for the money for Harry. I would have to wait a few weeks at least.

"Will you call me Bernard now, without the 'Monsieur' attached? Surely it would be allowed now I am officially your fiancé."

I managed a weak smile. "Yes—Bernard. And there is one thing more."

"*Oui?*"

"You mentioned a ball to announce our betrothal; I would like that—while my family is here."

M. Bernard—or rather, *Bernard*—lifted his arms above his head. "Oho! Making demands already, and her not two minutes engaged." He took my icy hands in his own and said softly, "But of course. I will give orders to Bass and Mrs. Duckworth to commence preparations. A Christmas ball to proclaim our joy to the world. Our neighbors will be astonished—Wyndriven Abbey open for a gala!"

Somehow I didn't know where to look, so once again I focused on the dressing gown. I had done it. I must act happy now. But I wasn't sure I could. I bit my lip. He drew one finger down my cheek.

"Why so serious, *mon mignon?* One would think we were discussing a funeral instead of our wedding."

"I am only feeling a little—a little shy. I don't really know how to go about being betrothed."

"I shall have to teach you. For instance, it is customary to begin it with an embrace."

Yes. You've had a good deal of experience with betrothals. This is your fifth time.

He bent his head down and kissed me gently.

Behind him the face of Tara appeared. This time the lines were sharp and her still-burning vitality was evident, as if she were made of flesh. Her expression was clear. It was one of horror.

"It is also customary," Bernard said, "to close your eyes while kissing."

I closed my eyes.

CHAPTER 28

LITTLE THINGS

Bernard arranged an expedition for that afternoon to the top of a hill on the far side of the parkland. He wished to make the announcement of our betrothal to my family at that place, which was reputed to have a lovely vista.

As Bernard helped me into the carriage, my eyes met Garvey's eyes. The groom scowled and turned away as he finished the harnessing. It was unpleasant to be hated, especially since Garvey seemed the sort of person who would find a way to take revenge. Especially if Bernard could not control him. I would have to carefully check Lily before riding her from now on.

No road led up the hill, and so we rattled off over rough ground. Bernard was in excellent spirits. He had a victorious air. He had triumphed.

I pushed up the sleeves of my gown and loosened my collar, as the weather was unseasonably warm.

"Imagine," Anne said, "this is December, and I'm without a wrap.

Why, in Boston we'd be huddled by our fireside, and here we are picnicking! I'm growing fond of Mississippi weather."

I missed the beautiful New England snow.

Only one gnarled, leafless oak grew on the crest of the hill, the tops of its branches clotted with mistletoe. The clumpy carpet of weeds around it was the color of lion's fur. Acorns crunched beneath our feet once we abandoned the carriage and hiked to the pinnacle. We disturbed a flock of starlings covering the ground like black pepper. With a great beating of wings, they rose and flapped off, weaving in and out in strange undulations of flight patterns.

A crimson cloth had already been spread and cushions lay round about for us to sit upon. In the center of the cloth stood a chased silver samovar filled with fragrant, steaming-hot chocolate, while platters of fried chicken and catfish and ham, of biscuits and yams and gravy and peach pie were set out—a regular Southern feast. There were also a couple of dark bottles that Bernard drank from too frequently. He talked too loudly, smiled too broadly. He sat close, reaching out to stroke my hair, my cheek, my arm. I had to keep myself from cringing. I had to keep myself smiling.

My siblings watched his actions with interest. I inched away from him. He followed me. He plaited a wreath of burnished oak leaves and acorn-clustered twigs, and set it on my hair. "Behold our queen," he announced, bowing to me with a flourish. "Is she not a ruddy beauty? Lithe and dainty, with hair the color of molten bronze."

I peeked over at Harry. He choked back laughter. After all, Bernard was waxing lyrical about his sister Sophie, the one who tried ᷉se her sprinkling of freckles with Dew of Venus lotion.

Bernard continued, "today is a day for celebration. I am

proud to tell you all now that she is mine and mine alone. Your sister this morning agreed to become my wife!"

Only Junius seemed surprised by the news, and he recovered quickly. They all gave delighted murmurs.

"I'm hoping Bernard and I will find you all spouses and careers down here," I said. "So we can live close to each other and our children"—here I flushed a little—"will grow up together."

"Yes!" cried Anne. "That is exactly what I hope for."

We were congratulated, and everyone drank a toast to our future. Bernard kept drinking after the toast ended. Eventually he set down his goblet (it fell over, and golden liquid spilled unnoticed by him onto the cloth), clapped his hands, and then George miraculously appeared from among a stand of trees lower down.

"Fetch my rifle," he ordered. "I left it beneath a seat in the carriage."

"What do you want with a gun?" I asked.

"You'll see soon enough," he said, "my inquisitive little fiancée."

When George brought it, Bernard aimed the barrel up at the top of the oak tree. He fired with a crack that boomed like thunder and made me wince. Evidently he was trying to shoot down mistletoe, but his aim wobbled. A single, pale-berried sprig fluttered to the ground.

"Not much, but adequate for my purpose," he said, and held it above my head. "Now a kiss."

"Please," I whispered. "Not in front of everyone." I pulled away and edged toward Anne.

Bernard's eyes narrowed and his expression darkened. "Come here, Sophia," he said softly, through his teeth.

In order to avoid more of a scene, I obeyed him. He wrenched my arm behind my back and gave me loud, smacking kisses, smelling of spirits, starting at my lips, but then continuing down my throat. "This," he hissed into my neck, "will teach you not to embarrass me."

I shot a painful glance beyond Bernard's head toward Anne and Junius and Harry. They pretended not to see the ugly little display, busying themselves with brushing crumbs from their laps.

How could I bear it?

I suddenly stared wide-eyed at the sky beyond them. A formidable wall of bruised, purplish black clouds rapidly approached.

We helped George gather up our picnic things and scurried into the carriage just as the storm broke with a deafening downpour. I pitied George and Samuel, the coachman, out in the deluge. Bernard drew the curtains, but the carriage bumped so from side to side as the coachman tried to drive swiftly that I peeped out. The rain blew in sheets; the horses reared and slipped and slid in water and mud. One of the horses fell to its knees, and my side of the carriage touched the ground, then sprang back up as the horse righted itself. I gave a little shriek, my sister shuddered, and Junius turned pale. We huddled together while Bernard and Harry laughed loudly at the good sport. We reached the abbey eventually, little the worse for wear.

That night Bernard presented me with a spectacular sapphire engagement ring, edged with ice-bright diamonds. His arm went lightly around my waist, and he slipped the ring on my finger, hold-
~v hand with deference, as though it were most precious and
iy arm still ached from when he had wrenched it.

◆ ◆ ◆

In the days that followed, Ducky and Mr. Bass, who were in charge of the myriad of details involved in the Christmas ball preparations, scuttled about with a preoccupied air. A great deal of correspondence was necessary, as they must hire musicians and order lavish refreshments and oceans of alcohol, as well as send out invitations and receive responses. They must answer to their master if all was not perfection when the evening arrived. Invitations were addressed to all the "suitable" households in three counties. Ducky announced that at least we need not fear our ball would be poorly attended; the countryside was indeed curious about Wyndriven Abbey. The servants bustled to scrub and polish, and the kitchen was abuzz until late each night. The affair was to be held on December twenty-third, when there was predicted a full moon for lighting. This was essential, as the guests would arrive after dusk and leave again in the dark and have to travel through the forest with only the lanterns on their carriages.

Mme. Duclos arrived. She took up residence while she worked on our ball gowns. Although I already possessed one, created last summer, Anne and I sketched out our dream dresses for Mme. Duclos to bring to reality. It was delightful to have a sister with whom to share this fun. What was to be was to be, and I was determined to be a happy person even if my life wasn't taking the turn I had hoped. Little things could still bring joy and comfort. There was still a sweetness in small pleasures.

As all this hummed in the background, Daphne, the flower fairy, hobbled about with her cane to supervise the decorations for the holidays at Wyndriven Abbey. They must be especially spectacular,

since they would festoon the ball as well. She had been drying flowers all the year to decorate for Christmas. The gentlemen cut
boughs of waxy greens—holly and cedar and pine and magnolia.
They carried them into the great hall in overflowing, fragrant baskets.

Daphne showed Anne and me how to tightly weave wreaths and
garlands so they had almost a sculptural quality. Her artistic eye
made our designs echo the architectural elements of the abbey—
arches and round windows and moldings. We bejeweled them with
holly berries, pinecones, dried flowers, lemons, limes, oranges, and
scarlet satin bows. We spent two days at it, though our arms and
hands became pricked and every part of us was sticky with sap.
There was the banister of the grand staircase to twine with green-
ery, as well as so many doorways and columns and mantels and
mirrors and paintings. I loved the atmosphere of the wildwood
brought indoors, but as I worked, my left hand felt weighted by the
great stone of my engagement ring.

I made a special wreath of juniper twined with silvery sage and
misty blue berries to place around the neck of the stone angel beside
the locked churchyard. She looked serene and mystical.

A mountain of Christmas gifts must be prepared for the Negroes
at the plantation and for the house servants at the abbey. These
included ells of calico and ready-made dresses and handkerchiefs
and hats and vests and coats, along with packets of tin horns and
popping crackers, candies and nuts and raisins for the children. Mr.
Bass had done the purchasing, but we organized them. We wrapped
presents for the house servants in white paper with ribbons,

while the plantation gifts were piled in barrels and boxes to be taken there on Christmas morning.

The tapestry, which I had finally finished, was to be my Christmas gift to Bernard. As I spread it out before folding and wrapping, I hoped never to create another such design. All the while I had been jabbing my needle in and out, it had both driven and disturbed me.

"We have a surprise for you," Bernard said one evening after Anne and I rejoined the gentlemen.

He led us to the drawing room and flung back the doors. My sister and I gasped with delight at the sight. A cedar tree stood on the marble-topped table in the center of the room, dazzling from the flames of a hundred waxen tapers wired to its branches. Sugar-frosted fruit and cornucopias of jewel-colored paper and tiny gilt baskets dangled from the limbs, heaped with nuts and sugarplums.

"I've learned of Christmas trees," I cried, clapping my hands, "in the German stories I've read, but I had never hoped to see one. It's a fairy tree."

"Monsieur de Cressac is the genius behind this," Harry said, "but Junius and I helped cut it and haul it in."

"Thank you," I said. "It's lovely."

Bernard beamed. "I have wanted one since the first example I saw in Germany, but you, *ma fille,* are the inspiration that finally made me carry out my plan. Tradition dictates we are to hold hands and dance and frolic about it, but perhaps we can sit on the sofas here to sing and admire the sight just as well."

"You should see my arms," Junius said. "We picked the prickliest tree in the forest."

"Next time," Bernard said, with his deep laugh, "we will borrow suits of armor from my collection for protection, eh? Not to mention swords to keep the fierce squirrels at bay. Who would have thought Christmas-tree harvesting could be wrought with peril?"

We began to speak over each other in our eagerness to spill out holiday memories.

"I can feel it!" I announced suddenly.

"Feel what?" Bernard asked.

"The Christmas-is-coming excitement. Every year I'm scared I won't have it anymore, but I always do."

"We used to tell Sophie," Anne explained to Bernard, "that she'd better keep on believing in Santa Claus or he'd stop coming."

"I have been in communication with Père Noël," Bernard said, "and he knows Sophia's whereabouts for a fact."

We all laughed.

Bernard could cause any room he was in to come alive. His energy and vitality filled his surroundings, making everything more exciting, especially mixed with the tremulous expectancy of the season. Impulsively I squeezed his hand, and he squeezed mine back.

We sang "As I Sat on a Sunny Bank" and "God Rest You Merry, Gentlemen" and "The Holly and the Ivy." Then Bernard taught us French carols while the glowing tree made the room mysterious and magical. When we sang in French, from the corner of my eye, I spotted a flicker of sapphire flitting in the shadows. I realized then that even if I talked to Adele, she wouldn't understand, since she spoke no English. I wondered: In her life with Bernard, did she also

brief happiness in little things?

CHAPTER 29

COVERING UP

I tried to imagine I was in love with Bernard. If I could make believe well enough to convince myself, everything would be easier. He continued to go out of his way to help my siblings enjoy their stay. I was aware, and grateful, that he neglected his work for them. Once the Christmas decorating was done, he and my brothers spent the daylight hours hunting and fishing while Anne and I painted china or trimmed bonnets or stitched our needlework or simply chatted companionably. At other times we would all ride out on horseback or picnic or take in local sights. In the evenings we played cards or charades or music.

When we were with my family, Bernard was affability itself. Still, there was a humming tenseness in the atmosphere.

At suppertime one evening I paused before entering the banquet hall. Only Bernard was seated at the table. Could I scuttle back up to my room until someone else came down?

He saw me.

"Ah, there you are," he said, rising and coming toward me. Then he noticed my gown. "Why are you always wearing these things nowadays?"

"What things?" I asked, trying to move around him to my chair.

"These dresses that make you resemble one of your Puritan ancestors. High collars. Sleeves down to your wrists. Past your wrists actually," he added dryly, since the ruffles of my cuffs trailed gracefully down. "Is it your family's presence that makes you so prudish?"

"It's cold," I said, fidgeting with the lace fichu that rose high on my neck. "It's wintertime, even if it is Mississippi."

He chuckled low in his throat. "Well, your modesty makes you an enticing little Puritan. The more you cover up . . ."

He reached down and slowly, deliberately pulled off my fichu, with a look from narrow, laughing eyes that said, *What are you going to do about it?* Then he proceeded to unbutton my top button.

My hand flew up to his. "Bernard, the servants—and my family—"

George and Ling stood impassive against the wall, but they were stiffly aware of our interaction.

"*Oui.* All the more exciting." He dipped his fingers in his wineglass, spread dripping purple liquid across my chest, and bent his head to lick and suck it off.

I trembled all over and endured for a moment. *What to do?*

Swiftly I ducked low and drew away, frantically buttoning and retying. I babbled, "For me, the anticipation of our marriage is what makes it so exciting."

He growled, but he didn't grab me back, as I had expected. "You'll push me too far, Sophia. You are fortunate I have been a patient man."

Always I was called fortunate. I tried to look up at him adoringly. "And I'm so grateful and it makes me care for you all the more that you respect my honor."

He turned on his heels and strode to the doorway, not waiting for George, who was striding over to open it. He flung the door wide and slammed it behind him, so that the china and crystal on the table shuddered.

When my family finally came, I did more babbling, trying to ignore my sticky bosom and wondering how long I could hold off Bernard. Most of the time my imagination wasn't strong enough to prevent the distaste I felt for his caresses. Distaste edged with uneasiness and—yes—fear.

That night I attempted to lodge a chair under my doorknob. It was too short. The others in my room were too tall. It didn't matter. A chair wouldn't stop my fiancé any more than a lock would, if he wanted to enter my bedchamber.

Less than a week before the ball, Bernard suggested we perform *tableaux vivants,* and we took up the idea with enthusiasm. Scenes from literature or history or paintings were re-created in drawing rooms with great detail. We had heard of such pleasures but had never before participated in them.

All that day we dashed about, preparing our *tableaux.* Chests and wardrobes throughout the house were robbed for costumes and props. Bernard and I were to perform a scene copied from a painting in which I portrayed Salome and he portrayed John the Baptist's head on a platter.

For the performance I wore a garland on my streaming hair, with a crimson robe covering my gown. We placed two tables close together and draped them with a cloth in which Bernard cut a hole so his head could loll to one side, seemingly without a body attached. He looked terribly gruesome, and I told him so. This pleased him.

He took his part seriously, so the evening began badly when Harry burst into laughter at first sight of our scene. I hushed my brother and pacified Bernard, but this boded ill for what might come next.

However, Bernard appeared to be restored to humor as he freely helped himself to brandy. While Anne and I prepared behind a curtain for our *tableau,* he called out, "May I propose the scene 'Nymphs Bathing.' I should enjoy that immensely."

I covered my face with my hands as I thought of Junius's and Harry's embarrassment at the suggestion of their sisters posing nude. I was somewhat used to Bernard's indelicate ways, but my siblings were not. Anne blushed and patted my hand. She understood.

Anne's and my depiction was to be Marie Antoinette and her lady-in-waiting riding a tumbrel to their execution. Anne had procured two gowns from somewhere that she supposed were similar to clothing of that period. Mine was striped in leaf green and gold with a lace scarf, while Anne's was azure. We placed ourselves in our tumbrel made from a table turned on its side with paper wheels and called for Harry to draw the draperies. The curtain opened with a whisper.

For a moment no one said a word. Then Harry asked loudly, "Now, who are you supposed to be?"

"Can't you tell, foolish boy?" Anne said, stung out of character. "We're Marie Antoinette and her lady-in-waiting, of course."

I said nothing because I saw Bernard's face. First it went red, then blanched, and his eyes bulged. I broke out in a cold sweat. What was happening? What had I done now?

"Where—where did you get those gowns?" he gasped at last.

"Why, from the attic," Anne said. "From trunks in the attic."

And then I knew. She had filched them from one of the brides' trunks. The dresses hadn't seemed familiar—I had rummaged through so many that long-ago day—but I, at least, with my vivid hair, must look remarkably like one of those women.

Bernard gave a terrible, wordless cry, dropped the goblet he held so it shattered and splattered, then staggered from the room.

I cursed myself that I hadn't realized what we were wearing. Now that I looked at the gowns closer, they likely had been Victoire's.

"What just happened?" Junius asked.

I shook my head. How could I begin to explain what a mistake poor Anne and I had made? "He—these dresses belonged to one of Bernard's wives. I didn't know, but I should have known. I'm so sorry."

"Well," said Harry, "does this mean I don't have to portray Paul Revere announcing the arrival of the British?"

We all laughed nervously, but I racked my brain to think how I could soothe my fiancé. Now he knew that all his wives' possessions hadn't been burned. What would the repercussions be? Was poor Ducky in trouble?

I searched in vain for Bernard. He must have left the house.

It was late, as I sat at my dressing table, when Anne came in to me.

"Sophie, I'm worried about you." She seated herself in a chair next to mine.

"Why in particular?" I asked. There were myriads of things that were worrisome about me.

"You seem so—oh, I would call it edgy, these days. You start at every sound, you flinch, you give sideways glances as if you expect something to spring out at you. I know now that Monsieur de Cressac can be difficult to deal with; it's him that makes you so apprehensive, isn't it?"

I hesitated. I could make excuses—I had not been feeling well, some such flimflam—but instead decided to speak the truth. "Yes. Bernard's temperament does make me tense. I never, never know what will trigger an explosion. Even when he's happy, I worry about when he'll be angry next. Always treading carefully wears on me. It goes against my nature."

Anne's eyes brimmed with compassion. She didn't speak for a moment, looking down at her hands. "He seemed the answer to all our problems. I thought you'd soon learn to love him. Many wives suffer from volatile husbands, but the men never actually strike them. . . . You don't think he would, do you? I mean, if you are truly afraid, we'll take you away with us. We'll figure another way out of our troubles."

"No," I said. It was more now than Harry's debt. There was no doubt at this point that if I cried off from our engagement, Bernard would seek revenge. He had all the resources of great wealth and ruthlessness at his disposal. "No, it's the right thing to do. Once it's done, everything will be better. Just you wait—I'll pick you out some dashing Southern gentleman for your sweetheart."

My sister put her arm around my waist and smiled weakly.

My skirt shifted as something—someone—invisible edged by. For just a moment I considered telling Anne of the other reason I was jittery: my phantom Sisters, who haunted Wyndriven Abbey. The manifestations were occurring more and more frequently. At times an arctic touch, so soft, brushed past. The warbling murmur of voices often sounded, too muffled to grasp. I glimpsed the Sisters again and again. At other times I simply *felt* their presence—some great emotion hanging quavering in the atmosphere. They were disturbing but not threatening. It was not the dead I feared.

Anne would think me mad.

She rose to leave, and her expression was infinitely sad. "I would willingly take this burden from you if I could. I've never felt true love, so in marrying Monsieur de Cressac, I would feel no lack."

I gave a choking little laugh. "Unfortunately your lovely tresses are the wrong shade."

The next morning Bernard slumped on a bench in the frosty garden, head in hands. The lawns were now dun-colored, and no flowers bloomed, but the cedars and magnolias and boxwood topiaries shone green.

I touched his shoulder and he raised his head. He had not changed clothes since our ill-fated *tableaux vivants*. He was pale, with sunken and bloodshot eyes.

"It was the dresses," he said. "They were supposed to be destroyed."

"It doesn't matter," I said wearily. "You don't need to explain."

Then, as if I hadn't spoken, he continued, "She's gone—she betrayed me with another man and deserted me, but there she was. It was you, of course, but it was her face I saw above the dress." He put his hand to his forehead and stood, swaying on his feet, disoriented. He leaned against a balustrade.

"I understand," I said. "It must have been a terrible shock."

He stared at me now without speaking. His expression was one I had never before seen him wear—wounded and bewildered. I had expected anger. I had expected recriminations. Not this.

I lowered myself to the cold marble bench and pulled him down beside me. He lay his head in my lap, and I carefully touched his hair. "There now," I said softly. "I'm so sorry it happened, but it's only me here."

He stiffened and his hand clamped down on mine.

The *bon vivant*. The beast. The hurt child. Who was the true Bernard? I supposed he was all of them.

CHAPTER 30

THE BALL

We were all relieved that the weather was perfect the days before the ball and that the morning of the great event dawned cold and clear, with the slightest of bracing breezes. A winter deluge could have spoiled everything, making the roads impassable.

Profusions of flowers were brought in from the orangery for last-minute embellishing. Anne and I tucked creamy camellias and roses and lilies like stars among the dark green garlands, and we helped Daphne fashion bouquets of the more exotic blooms in a hundred vases. We cut tendrils of ivy to loop and trail gracefully in our arrangements. Each polished surface glistened. Torches were placed, still unlit, along the drive all the way from the edge of the woods. Wyndriven Abbey was in its glory.

As early dusk approached, a wealth of candelabras and lamps were lit in the public rooms to banish the wintry gloom that lurked in every nook and cranny. I understood the pagans who celebrated the winter solstice with light. There never could be enough light in the abbey.

All was done, but no one could relax, not with the anticipation in the air. We perched ourselves on the edges of chairs while we waited for the time to go upstairs to dress. The rest of us made small talk, but Bernard's conversation was expansive. When at last the musicians arrived and began setting up, we scattered to begin our toilette.

Odette filled the bath, and I used a new cake of Parisian perfumed soap. Mme. Duclos knocked at the door. She came to assist me into her newest creation—the ball dress of my own design. Odette helped me slip into my most delicate cotton batiste undergarments, fastened my hoop, laced me tightly, and then she and Madame lifted the gown over my head.

I gazed at myself in the tall mirror. My skirt had tiers of fine white lawn with long streamers down the back. The bodice had a deep V-front waist and short capped sleeves. It was trimmed with purple silk taffeta ribbons and embroidered white-on-white lace. I wore a necklace of pearls at my throat, and Bernard had sent violets for my hair.

I looked well enough, but this no longer pleased me as it once would have. There was no longer room in me for my old vanity. If I had been homely, whatever the shade of my hair, I doubted I would be engaged to Bernard right now. I also looked young. This was a girl's dress. I could never wear such a frock again after marriage.

Anne entered. Her gown was cut velvet ivory silk, with a pointed waist and pagoda sleeves. For her hair Bernard had sent roses. So thoughtful.

We admired each other. My sister tweaked my tresses, and I gave her a cameo locket to rest on her throat. We then watched out the window, awaiting the first guests' arrival. Twilight fell. A great white marble moon hung low. The torches had been lit. Twinkling pin-points of light that were carriage lamps began to stream in from the woods. Buggies and saddle horses and coaches filled the drive. We opened the casement so the sounds could reach us—horses' hooves, the crunch of wheels on gravel, the rise and fall of voices, laughter. Toby and Tater Bug and Reuben led horses toward the stable, where they would be hitched to posts and cared for by grooms.

Anne took my hand and squeezed it. "Will your friend Mr. Stone be here tonight?" Her tone was grave. "How will you manage if you see him? Have you considered that?"

"Of course," I said quietly, "it's all I've thought about." At sight of my sister's face, however, I gave a quick laugh. "No, that's not true." I twirled my spreading skirts. "I've also given a few thoughts to my dress. Probably he's not invited—Bernard doesn't think much of preachers—but if he does come, he's a gentleman and I'm a lady. We'll greet each other politely."

The first guests alighted, and it was finally time to go downstairs. Odette wreathed a cloud of silvery tulle about my shoulders, and Anne and I descended in a ripple of silk and lawn and the perfume of violets and roses.

Bernard stood beside the massive entry doors, very tall and very elegant in his evening clothes. "I am so pleased to meet you," he was saying as he shook a gentleman's hand. "My travels have not per-mitted me to be neighborly in the past, but I am happy to make your acquaintance now. And so it is you who owns the plantation house with the fine cupola that is visible from the road?" And again and again he found just the right thing to say as he greeted guests. It came easily to him when he chose.

I did not join him. I didn't know how Bernard would have introduced me. The grand announcement of our engagement would be made later in the evening. Although these people were the neighbors I had been longing to meet, shyness suddenly gripped me. What could I possibly say to them, these strangers? I clung to Anne and Harry and Junius.

White-turbaned maids took wraps, and the guests began to spread like water throughout the first floor.

I heard comments. "He brought it all the way over from England"—from a dark girl in flame-colored chiffon. "What a staircase! I must have one like it in my house"—from a gentleman with bushy side-whiskers. "I've heard tell his wife killed herself in one of these rooms"—very low from a woman with a high-bridged nose and badly applied rouge. "He makes his money by . . ." "His morals are questionable . . ." "No children, no heirs . . ." "Dang good wine, though." The gossip flowed like the drink. Ducky had been correct in thinking the curious would pour into Wyndriven Abbey this night.

Shifting masses of people surged from room to room, the ladies graceful in their wide hoopskirts. Their dresses lit by candlelight seemed to glow from within. Inconvenient though the style was, they did make for beautiful silhouettes. I took quiet pleasure in realizing there was no dress I liked so well as my own.

The furniture had been removed from the banquet hall to make room. When the first strains of music sounded, people poured into the hall. Bernard claimed me. He kissed my hand and said, "How beautiful you are. *Je t'adore.*" After that he said nothing as we galloped down the floor in a reel.

I had expected him to monopolize me for most of the evening, but he instead escorted me back to the edge of the dance floor after the first dance. He bowed and led lady after lady out for waltzes and polkas, schottisches and reels. He leaned into them, smiling, in the flattering way that assured them they were beautiful and charming. And some of them looked to be beautiful and charming indeed, with their spangles and jewels, their sleek chignons or springing ringlets, their spreading gowns of silk and lace and taffeta.

I danced a good many dances myself, as did my siblings. Our swirls around the drawing room back home in Boston had prepared us for this. My pearl earbobs bounced and my beaded dancing slippers tripped lightly. I overcame my shyness and talked to the gentlemen who partnered me. In musical Southern accents they teased me about being a Yankee and asked questions about how I found life here, to which I responded with animation. I told the truth that I thought Mississippi beautiful.

Bernard's gaze was often fastened upon me. When I sailed about the floor with older gentlemen, his expression was benign, but when I danced with younger gentlemen, my fiancé glowered. Evidently sauce for the goose was not sauce for the gander—he could flirt as he wished, but he frowned when it was turnabout. I tried to smile at him gratefully when I caught his eye. He must be kept on an even keel.

I retired to catch my breath in a little corner bower and fanned myself with the swans-down fan that dangled from my wrist by a ribbon.

Through a screen twined with garlands, I peeked at Junius speaking intently to a terrifying-looking gentleman near a refreshment table. He had hoped to make acquaintances for business purposes, so that was good. Harry flirted with a pretty blonde with a mischievous smile. Anne danced a second dance with a massive young man. Wouldn't it be wonderful if both of them met someone tonight worth keeping? The movement of the frothy, billowing flounces seemed like the ebb and flow of the ocean. The sound of many voices imitated the sound of the sea. My eyes drooped.

And then I saw Gideon. My engagement ring cut into my flesh as I clenched my hands together. At some point he had slipped in and was now speaking to an elderly lady in silver satin. Seeing his dear face was like a physical blow. Of course I hadn't really forgotten it. He was here—and it was too late.

The music hushed and Bernard stepped onto the musicians' platform. "Honored guests, I have an announcement to make," he said loudly, above the other voices. "Where is my Sophia?" His eyes swept the crowd.

Go up there. I must go.

In a daze I exited my hiding place and made my way toward him. "Ah, there she is." He held out his hand and I placed my chill fingers in his. "Ladies and gentlemen, let me introduce you to my fiancée and the future mistress of Wyndriven Abbey, Miss Sophia Petheram." He continued with praise for me that I didn't hear, nor did I hear the murmur of the crowd. All I knew was Gideon.

His head rose above the others—he was so tall. His eyes were riveted on mine, and there was a shocked question in them. A pang of love stabbed through my heart as, ever so faintly, I nodded. He stood stiff in rigid anguish.

Amid the handshakes and congratulations and introductions

that beset me, I saw Gideon back away, then leave the hall. He headed toward the conservatory.

When I could, I excused myself, whispering to Bernard that a feminine matter must be attended to. I squirmed inwardly as I said it, but I needed a reason to leave the room that he wouldn't question. (Or at least that I didn't think he would question.) He smirked a little, then released me.

Gideon slumped on the edge of the fountain, staring into the water where goldfish darted, but his gaze did not follow their brightness. He raised his head when I entered and barely glanced my way before looking down once more. "Is this a terrible dream?" he asked.

"I wish we'd both wake up if it is." I swallowed. "I'm afraid it's real life, though."

"When I received the invitation, I was so happy to know I would see you again at last. I expected I would meet your family, and you and I would have a chance to talk. I thought maybe, just maybe, we could make our future plans together—since you had said you would go away with your siblings when they leave. I was a fool."

I dropped down to the ledge beside him. "I had no choice in the end."

"A person always has options."

"I used to think so too." My voice was shaking. "But sometimes, given who we are and our circumstances, that just isn't true." He was so close. My whole body ached from yearning to reach out and touch him, to comfort him and me both. I held my arms tightly at my sides. "Instead, you had no choice but to stop meeting me and I had no choice but to find a way to help my family out of their troubles."

"It never occurred to me you couldn't wait a few months." He rubbed his forehead as if it ached. "Did I mention I was a fool?"

My shoulders drooped. I couldn't find my handkerchief, so I dabbed away my silent tears with the delicate top layer of my skirt. "I would have waited for you forever if I could have, but . . . it's complicated . . . I've been so unhappy."

"So have I, but I fought the loneliness by thinking over the hours we spent together and hoping and planning. And now you'll marry de Cressac."

My misery was so great I could scarcely speak. "My family needs the money," I managed to squeeze out.

"I see. You're marrying for money."

I raised my bowed head and said, "No, Mr. Stone, I'm not. I'm marrying for love—love of my family. I'm so sorry."

He shook his head and stood. I could hold myself back no longer from reaching for his arm; it seemed that if I could just—but he was gone too swiftly. He had never really looked at me the whole time we were speaking. I was left with my hand in midair. He halted at the outer conservatory door. Without turning, he said, "Remember, in spite of everything, if you should ever need help, you do have a friend nearby."

He left just as Bernard burst through the other entrance. In the steamy warm air of the conservatory, a coldness wafted. Bernard was scowling. Had he seen Gideon? Had he heard anything? *Please no.*

I ran to him, even though my wobbly limbs nearly gave way beneath me, and put my arms around his neck and kissed him. "I was detained by one of our guests," I said with an arch smile.

"Who was it?"

"Only the funny preacher. He admires your ferns."

"I should prefer that my fiancée not be alone with other gentlemen. Odd that a guest should exit the house in such a way."

"Does it matter how he leaves, so long as he does? What is he to us?"

I lifted my face for another caress, trying to erase all doubts from his mind. His lips met mine savagely, his grip on my arms bruising.

Finally he pulled away. "There. You may dance with whomever you please, but only *I* may do that."

I schooled my features, trying to hide my disgust. "I'm having such a grand time. Do you know, I didn't realize what a fine dancer you were before tonight? And you flirt so proficiently with all the pretty ladies. I was jealous indeed."

He gave a short, mirthless laugh. "Whereas you are not so fine a dancer. I was ashamed. We must see that you practice. Perhaps I shall get you a dancing master. Evidently I was remiss in not providing one early on. Stumbling about with your brothers in your kitchen hardly was adequate."

I swallowed back the sting and put my hands on his shoulders. "Listen, can you hear the music? Dance with me here—just the two of us. You can teach me all I need to know."

Bernard's sardonic curl of the lips told me he knew I was trying to distract him, and he would let me get away with it—this time.

As we danced, a thought came to me: *Gideon and I never had a chance. It was always hopeless. Even if we'd continued to meet secretly, eventually we would have had to leave the shelter of the forest, and always Bernard would have been there, waiting.*

CHAPTER 31

CHRISTMASTIME

"Christmas gift!" First Toby, and then the other young boys, jumped out from a doorway, and I gave them each two pennies as a reward for startling me so. Bernard had warned us of this Southern holiday custom to be the first to say these words upon meeting anyone, and he had supplied us with coins for the forfeit.

I hadn't fallen asleep until nearly dawn. I felt wretched, but I tried to shake myself out of it because it was Christmas morning and my family was here.

A fiddler wandered through the house, playing frolicking tunes. I followed him, running to each of my siblings' rooms as I always had on past holidays. Anne laughed, while Harry and Junius grumbled at the early hour—just as they always had. Little things . . .

Before our breakfast we had a ceremony of making eggnog and dipping the creamy, spicy liquid into tall glasses. Everyone— servants, master, and guests—all drank to each other's health right there in the cavernous kitchen. The place seemed almost jolly.

Our meal was a traditional Southern one: scrambled eggs, slices of cured ham, oysters brought by the barrel on steamboat from New Orleans, fried catfish, bacon, hot flaky biscuits drowning in butter and syrup, several kinds of fruit preserves, cold milk, and strong coffee.

The servants dished up our breakfast hastily. They were excited to be transported out to Wyndriven Plantation for the day's festivities.

Bernard, Anne, Harry, Junius, and I all retired afterward to the drawing room for the exchange of gifts. My siblings enthused over the items I had bought for them that November day in Memphis. Bernard gave me a velvet-covered album; several books; a sparkling, elaborate ruby set; and his new photograph in an ornate silver frame. I thanked him extravagantly, but I privately thought the photograph didn't do him justice. It looked flat; it hadn't captured his vitality.

As he spread out the tapestry I had made for him and praised my workmanship, I was silent. I had done a morbid and terrible thing. What had gotten into me? He must never, never learn what threads made up the fire.

He stroked the flames, and my stomach clenched.

"Amazing," he said, "and dramatic. Such brilliant silks." An odd expression passed over his features. "It almost scorches my skin. What magic did you work into your stitching, my sweet sorceress?"

He put it down rather abruptly and rose then—time to visit the plantation. Thank goodness. Hopefully he would never again examine his tapestry closely, but if he did, I would certainly pass off all the hair as my own.

As we drove, the smell of barbecuing meat and the smoke of bonfires wafted from a distance. In a clearing amid a grove of live oaks, a pit had been dug and a couple of hogs roasted. Girls turned the spit while a woman spooned drippings over them; the juices sputtered in the glowing coals. Several dogs watched the proceedings with interest as running, jumping, overly excited children tossed inflated hog bladders back and forth.

Today the plantation seemed a happy place. There were to be three days free from work—three days of dancing and merrymaking.

Bernard rang the great plantation bell in the yard, and people streamed in from everywhere. We stood beside a wagon and distributed flour, sugar, meal, coffee, molasses, and the fabric and clothing we had prepared. They bobbed their heads and thanked us profusely, which embarrassed me. I wasn't suited to being Lady Bountiful. What had we done to deserve us being in our position and them in theirs?

Aunt Cassie, the "tender" of the children, lined up her charges before us as we gave them their packets of treats and smiled benignly at their delight. Bernard tossed a handful of coins in the air and laughed at the scramble that ensued.

Now the band struck up, with knucklebones and sticks, two fiddles and a banjo, the spritely notes punctuated by the popping of firecrackers. There was to be a wedding and a dance that night in the barn. I wished we could stay to watch them shuffle and jig and "cut the pigeon wing" (which I was curious to see), but Bernard had no intention of remaining for it.

He explained that the slaves' marriage ceremony involved "jumping the broom," since they couldn't be wed legally, as "property" could not enter into a lawful contract. Bernard chuckled over this; I and, from their faces, my siblings were horrified by it.

We sat on planks stretched over barrels and ate yams and ham and corn bread and okra. The simplicity of the meal soothed me.

As I surveyed the crowd, a familiar face stood out. Charles. Charles, who had been arrayed so splendidly in sapphire velvet livery, now wore a much-patched jacket and homespun shirt. Talitha was beside him, her hand tucked in the crook of his arm. They stood slightly separated from the rest, complete in each other. Talitha felt my eyes on her and looked my way. She gave me a faint, expressive smile before turning back to Charles.

I was tired and silent as we drove back to the abbey. All those people, and there was nothing I could do for them. Perhaps it wasn't true, but it seemed as if I were as much in Bernard's power as any slave on the plantation.

Everyone else acted preoccupied as well, looking down at their laps or gazing sightlessly out the windows.

Suddenly Anne broke the silence. "Monsieur de Cressac, in conscience I must speak. How can you justify this way of life? Yes, you give those people presents at Christmastime, but that doesn't make up for their bondage all year round. How can you believe it right?"

Oh no, oh no. I braced myself.

"It is right in the eyes of the law, ma'am." Bernard's smile was twisted, as if he were about to enjoy this challenge.

"Now, Anne," Junius said, "it's not our place to question these things. The quarters look decent and they clearly have food. They—"

He might as well not have spoken. Neither my sister nor my fiancé paid him any heed.

"There is a higher law than man's law," she said quietly.

"None that I recognize, ma'am." He gave her a half bow.

"And that isn't right either. You should not keep my sister from church. From her connection with God."

She should have known no one must question Bernard. No one must challenge him. His tone, the overly polite way he addressed her as "ma'am," the way he leaned slightly forward, all showed his extreme displeasure.

I clutched his arm. "Please—" I whispered.

The tendons bulged in his neck, but he half smiled, and his next words were spoken evenly, calmly, though they caused my stomach to turn over. "Do you know, Sophia, I believe it is time for your family to bring their visit to an end."

I couldn't speak.

"Now, really, Monsieur de Cressac—" Harry started to say, but stopped himself.

My mouth was so dry it was hard to form words. "They haven't even been here a month, and the wedding is in just a few weeks. They must be here for that." I kept my own tone even. Instinctively I knew this was not a time for tears and pleading.

"I do not see why," Bernard said coolly. "You yourself said you wished for a small wedding. We shall have a very small one indeed. All we need is a witness or two and a preacher. Your friend Mr. Stone would do nicely."

"You cannot separate Sophie from her family!" Anne cried.

Oh, couldn't my sister be quiet?

"'Cannot'? You must know that I can do whatever I please. Sophia is my fiancée and she is also my ward. I can keep her from whomever I wish whenever I wish. I assure you I have her best interests at heart."

My gloved fingers were digging into his arm. One by one he pried them off and then imprisoned my hand in his own, so tightly that I winced.

Too late Anne saw what she had done. "I apologize, sir, if I was impertinent. I beg you'll forget my words and not punish Sophie for my mistake. Please, may we stay on for the wedding?"

"No, I think not," Bernard said. "If you will excuse me, I will go now to instruct the servants to bring down your trunks, and tomorrow morning you will be driven to Memphis. Samuel will purchase your train tickets there and see you safely off to Boston."

The carriage had pulled up before the abbey as he spoke. Now he alighted and reached out to help me down. He then turned his back on us all and stalked into the house.

My sister and I wept as we held each other.

"Sophie," Harry mouthed over Anne's shoulder, "um—have you asked him yet?"

I shook my head slightly.

"Well, Anne," he said, "you've certainly made a mess of things."

"Don't blame her," I said, pulling away. "What she said was true, and I should have stood up to Bernard on those subjects long ago, but I'm a coward. There's no way Anne could have known the effect confronting him would have."

I didn't say it out loud, but possibly Bernard had provoked the confrontation so he'd have an excuse to send my family packing. Probably he'd been waiting for such a moment.

"Well, we'd better go see to our baggage," Junius said. "Do you think de Cressac will still allow me into his business, Sophie?"

"I don't know. I hope so. I'll talk to him. And I'll speak to him for you too, Harry. I'm so sorry." I covered my face with my hands and sobbed in earnest now. "Oh, I don't want you to go. I don't want you to go."

Junius and Harry both patted my shoulders awkwardly before going inside with slow, tired steps.

Anne waited until I could choke back my tears. She looked me intently in the eyes. "You mustn't marry him, Sophie. He was so cold. So terrible. Come away with us. We'll get by somehow."

"No." She needed to understand some things, so I pulled myself together. "I have to marry him. He'll never let me escape, and the ways he'd punish us if I tried to leave would be far, far worse than being married to him. At least if I'm his wife, he'll let me do some good here and there with his money. It's enough; don't worry about me. I know quite well how to handle him and I'll be careful." With conviction I didn't feel, I added, "I'll be fine."

Bernard didn't join us for our silent supper. Golden light glowed beneath his office door. Having neglected his business pursuits these last weeks, he now returned to them, shutting us out. My siblings and I spent the evening quietly together and retired early. They had a long day of travel ahead and there was nothing more to be said.

I went to my room and put in action a desperate plan.

Rather than having Odette help me into nightclothes, I brought out my off-the-shoulder gown of plum-colored satin—one of Bernard's favorites. She raised her eyebrows but dressed me and brushed out my rippling hair. I dabbed on the violet scent Bernard liked.

I was reminded of Queen Esther in the Bible, how she had donned special apparel to face King Ahasuerus to plead for her people. Had she brushed out her tresses and used special perfume as well? As I made my way down the corridors and grand stairway to Bernard's office, I thought about her still. According to ancient Persian law, if someone approached the king unbidden and he didn't hold out his golden scepter, the person was executed.

I paused with my hand raised to rap on the office door. Would he hold out his scepter to me?

I knocked.

"Come in," Bernard said.

He sat behind his desk with papers spread about. He looked tired. I breathed a sigh of relief when he smiled and rose, holding out his arms. "And to what do I owe this unexpected pleasure? I was working away, late and lonely, and now you bring me a lovely surprise."

I put my arms around his neck. "I missed you at supper. Weren't you hungry?"

His arms tightened. "Mmm. You smell good. I ate while I added figures. I had abandoned my work too long. Besides, I supposed you would like to spend the evening alone with your family before their departure."

I played with his black silk neck scarf. "That's one reason I came down to see you, besides missing you. I wondered if you would reconsider and let them stay on until the wedding. It would make me so happy."

His arms loosened. "Oho! So that is what you wondered? Well, *ma belle,* you are certainly very beautiful and very enticing, but what you ask I will not do. They have met me, they have seen you are well and realized the advantages of our marriage, and that goal is now accomplished. I want them gone in the morning and you to myself once more. If you all behave yourselves, perhaps they may come again next year."

I looked into his face for one moment to be certain there was no use pursuing the subject, then, with a gasp of exasperation, broke free and swirled out the door.

"What?" Bernard called from behind me. "And I thought you had missed me." Unlike Queen Esther, I had failed. At least the penalty for me was not death.

In my bedchamber I slammed my fist against the pillow. If only it were his face.

CHAPTER 32

OMENS

"He's not a bad sort," Harry said, "but—be careful, little sister. And remember to ask for what we talked about."

"I will. At the right time."

Junius shuffled his feet and looked down at his boots, then clumsily took my hand. "If you're worried about anything—*anything*—write to me and I'll come. I don't care what happens to me, I'll come get you. Remember that."

"I'll remember."

Anne held me tightly. "You have a secret strength he knows nothing of," she whispered. "Hold on to it."

Bernard came out and, it seemed to me, practically stuffed my family into the carriage. I watched until the forest closed around them, then turned without a word to my fiancé and went into the house. I managed to avoid him all that day, keeping to my room and sending a message at suppertime that I was unwell.

• • •

The wild weather that night suited my mood.

Sleet and freezing rain plinked and pelted against my bed-chamber windows, and sharp cracks sounded as trees split from expanding ice in crevices. Great boughs, weighed down by their crystal coating, fell with crashes.

In the morning my room was as cold as a cave of ice in spite of the fire blazing in the hearth. I shivered into my dressing gown and pulled back the heavy brocade draperies to squint at a scene from fairyland—breathtakingly, painfully lovely. The forest was of diamonds, every last twig and blade of grass encased in its own glassy shell. The sun shone brilliantly and the reflected glitter stabbed my eyes like needles. Across the sweeping drive lay several of the cedars, snapped at the trunk. The diseased oak also lay shattered, its black, rotten innards exposed. At least the storm had done one good deed.

I turned the knob on my balcony door, to step outside for just a moment. It was frozen shut, not to be budged.

Trapped. I was trapped in this place.

My siblings were safely on the train heading north, but how was Anarchy faring? And were the feet of birds and squirrels stuck to the branches? I had never before seen such a devastating ice storm; it was a cruel thing indeed.

The laundress, Molly, popped in to bring warm water and to dress me.

"Good morning," I said, plunging my hands into the basin. "It was an exciting night, wasn't it? Where are Talitha and Odette?"

"Ooooh." The whites showed around Molly's irises. "You don't know the half of it, Miss. The whole house gone topsy-turvy. Miz Duckworth be moaning and wailing on account of a vision she had.

And that foreign girl—she gone crazy, talking about leaving and carrying on and won't do nothing. And Talitha done run off! I went to wake her this morning, and her cot had old clothes stuffed in to make it lumpy. She ain't nowheres."

The water turned cold on my hands as they remained frozen, dripping, above the basin. "Where . . . ," I said carefully, "where do you think Talitha's gone?"

Molly nearly vibrated with excitement. "Oh, she run off with Charles, of course. To Canada maybe, but none of us knows for sure 'cause she didn't tell no one a thing. Never did tell no one a thing. Always thought she too good for the rest of us. Master in a fit 'cause his property's gone and in this weather he can't call out the patrollers."

Never before had Molly spoken to me in more than mono-syllables.

"What did Mrs. Duckworth see?"

"Creepy crawlers and noisy black crows and nasty, bad things. We all standing around downstairs and getting her to tell us again and again. You got to hear. Feels like a haunt passing over your grave."

I opened my mouth and shut it. "Thank you for telling me," I said, friendly but dismissive.

As she went out the door, I slowly wiped my hands. Talitha and Charles—Bernard would expend a great deal to find and punish them. Why had they left in such terrible weather when the song had advised them to wait for spring? I could only suppose they were eager to be together and hoped the storm would delay the search for them. *Oh, bless that they are indeed together and that they reach safety. Help them find Gideon and let him put them on the course to follow the drinking gourd,* I said in silent prayer. If only I could speak privately to Gideon— how else would I ever learn what became of them?

I pulled open a wardrobe door. The heavy boots I had offered Talitha were gone and so was the black velvet cloak. I was glad she had remembered to take them, but oh! I wished she had trusted me enough to say goodbye.

I sank to the edge of my bed. I wanted to go to Odette "gone crazy" and Ducky moaning, but if I went downstairs, I would have to face Bernard in a fury, and at this moment I couldn't bear it. When I remembered the way he had treated my family, hot anger rose, strangling my throat. My fine fiancé.

I was too twitchy for any activity. My hands shook so that I dropped the pen I took up to scrawl a letter. I'd never be able to thread a needle. I picked up *I Have Lived and Loved: The Story of a Planter's Northern Bride,* but I stared unseeing at the page. It was a silly book anyway.

A tight little pain throbbed at the base of my skull. What was wrong with the place this morning? Always the atmosphere of the abbey was tense, but now a heavy pressure seemed to be building up to fever pitch. A tremor, a quivering undercurrent writhed. Perhaps the ice storm had caused some electrical charge in the air.

Abruptly I stood, letting the book fall unheeded to the floor. I had to face what I had to face. I stalked into the hall.

Immediately four shadowy figures joined me. They darted on either side like skittish gusts of wind, restless and chaotic, boiling. "What?" I cried out loud, trying to hold them in one place with my eyes. "What is it you want? Tell me!"

They wouldn't come into focus, and I was answered by silence.

Ducky slumped on the sofa in her room while Daphne bathed the housekeeper's grub-white face with a wet cloth.

"I sent away all them slack-jawed girls that was hanging around," Daphne told me. "Ordered them to go do their work, so I hope they doing it. They just be making Miz Duckworth more upset."

The housekeeper raised her face, her eyes squeezed shut in distress. Stringy strands of gray hair escaped from her cap. "Oh, Miss Sophia, I awoke this morning from a most terrible dream."

"I heard. Tell me about it," I said.

Her mouth worked for a moment before she spoke. "I was approaching the abbey from the front when a great many crows burst forth out of the gnarled oak—you know, the one by the drive—cawing and screaming right toward me in a black cloud. Their feathers brushed me and their claws tore at my clothes and scraped my face." She rubbed hard at her wrists.

I laid my hand gently on her shoulder. "What happened then?"

She took a deep breath. "The oak cracked open right down the middle, and the most noisome and noxious insects poured out in a tide of scuttling little bodies. There were cockroaches and beetles and centipedes . . ." She began trembling convulsively, scrabbled at my skirt with her puffy hands, and finally clutched my wrist. I didn't try to make her loosen it. Instead, I clutched back.

When she could collect herself, she continued, "They spread all over the grounds and the house, and they—they spread all over me." She loosed me and rocked back and forth, covering her face with her apron.

Her dream wasn't melodramatic or silly, as I had expected.

Rather, horror slithered down my spine. Along with the crawly sensation of tiny legs all over my skin. I struggled to pull myself and Ducky back to reality.

"Well, actually," I said, "that really happened. Not the insects, of course—or maybe only a few. But that tree did fall over in the storm last night. I saw it out my window, and it's lying across the drive. You must have heard it in your sleep and somehow dreamed what had happened."

"Oh?" Ducky wiped her face on her apron and looked up with hope making her small eyes open wider than usual. "It did fall? Goodness, who'd have thought it? Now, isn't that the strangest thing, that I knew it in my sleep? Why, I was certain it was a foretelling—a foretelling of something terrible about to happen. I've had them before and it felt just like. Goodness. Who'd have thought it?"

I fetched her some tea and tucked a robe over her lap. "Why don't you rest here for the day? We'll come for you if you're needed. Daphne, will you stay with her?"

"Of course, Miss."

As I was leaving, a sudden wail sounded behind me. "But having it really fall is just as bad! It's a sign. A sign!" Ducky began moaning again.

Any comforting words stuck in my throat. I could only shake my head and hurry away before I lost my own composure.

I found Odette in her tiny servant's room, feverishly packing her things in a carpetbag.

She flicked a quick, defiant glance my way. "As you see, I am going now, so it is no use your coming all the way up the stairs. This place and that man—it is all wrong. It has been horribly, horribly wrong for many years." She sniffed suddenly and I thought her black eyes shone with tears, but she turned quickly away. "I know enough now. I will go and you ought to go too."

"You're welcome to leave, Odette," I said, "but just know that Mrs. Duckworth did not have a vision about the future. She dreamed the oak tree fell, and it actually did come uprooted during the night. She heard it in her sleep and that caused the dream."

"That is not really why I leave." She raised her sharp chin. "I only said that to the foolish girls. I leave because I have learned all I can and it is enough."

"Enough about what?"

"This place and that man. And I warn you, if you do not go now, you may never get away."

"Tell me what you're talking about."

She shook her head and wouldn't answer.

"Well, you can't leave today," I said. "No one can get out."

She sat down on her small bed and her hands dropped into her lap. "Maybe not today, then, but soon."

"I'll miss you," I said. "I wish you luck." Odette and I had had a strange relationship from the beginning. Now I felt curiously bereft at the thought of her departure.

A bellow sounded from downstairs, from the vicinity of the library. Bernard was shouting my name. Trapped. I was trapped as if I were in Mr. Poe's story, with the walls of the abbey slowly creeping inward, constricting. I tensed to run in the opposite direction but dismissed that temptation. Eventually I must face him.

He loomed in the doorway, peering down the hall. He turned on his heels when I approached. Evidence of his rage—two shattered vases—lay near the wall where he had smashed them.

He paced back and forth while Finnegan did his own pacing so that the room seethed. Bernard stalked over to the window, jerked back the curtain, and stared out at the frozen landscape.

Not turning, he took several deep breaths and said, "In Mongolia once, I experienced an earthquake. Buildings buckled and split and crumbled. People ran, screamed, stumbled, their faces contorted with fear. Last night I stayed up watching the ice fall in shining sheets. I listened to the cracks and crashes. Not as stimulating as the earthquake, but still it is exhilarating to view nature's destructive power."

"How very compassionate," I muttered.

He whirled around. "What did you say?"

"Nothing."

My eyes locked on his long, white, fascinating fingers when he left the window to hold his hands near the fire.

"Now this morning, bah! I have business to attend to in Memphis and cannot get there and Bass—the fool—does not come. This inactivity drives me mad! Troubles stir at the river docks, and—perhaps you have heard—the slave Talitha has escaped." He began slamming his fist against his open palm, then stiffened and flexed his fingers. "That, at least, I can leave to the ice. No doubt she is dead by now, frozen or crushed beneath a downed tree. The roads are impassable—she cannot have gone far."

I pulled my gaze away from Bernard's hands. *Please let Talitha reach Charles. Please let them get safely away.*

Finnegan began barking at the shade of Tara, who had drifted up as if listening, until Bernard tore at his hair and yelled, "Quiet, sir! Down!" and the dog lay reluctantly on the tiger-skin rug, growling low.

My silence fell heavily in the room. Bernard should know I was upset. I slumped in my chair and glared.

The logs in the fire sizzled and fizzed furiously from the frozen water inside.

Bernard threw his arms into the air. "So, are you going to bore me now with sulking because your family has gone? Is that the oh-so-pleasant order of the day?"

For once I simply didn't care that he was restless and angry. "Do you expect me to thank you for depriving me of my loved ones in such a way? That was cruel. *Cruel.*" I pulled up straight, grabbed the poker, and jabbed at a log, sending sparks soaring.

He hung over me. "Perhaps if you had not ignored me during their visit, they would still be here."

"*Ignored* you? When has anyone in your presence ever ignored you? When have I ever, in the last six months, been allowed to ignore you?"

He dropped his head and took a deep breath as if struggling to hold back his temper. "I know you are not feeling yourself, Sophia. You are upset about your family, and there is an unease in the air—something left by the wretched storm. So, we are left here to entertain each other, locked in our icy prison. How shall we proceed? Hmm?" He squatted down and looped my hair around his hands, watching me with keen eyes.

His breath hit me in the face—blood and meat. I bit the inside of my jaw to keep from screaming. "Bernard," I said in a quiet, careful tone, "would you please read to me? That book by Dickens? It's the only thing I'm in the mood for."

"Very well," he said in an equally quiet, careful tone. "Perhaps that will transport us from our surroundings. He is an amusing author, if somewhat common. And afterward you will be a more attentive, affectionate companion than you have been these weeks."

As I tried to make myself listen to Bernard's beautiful voice reading *Bleak House,* Victoire and Tatiana, Tara and Adele draped themselves over the furniture in limp, liquid, despairing motions.

CHAPTER 33

THE TRUE BERNARD

The ice dripped away as the weather warmed the next day. Grounds-men dragged felled trees and limbs to bonfires throughout the property. A low pall of smoke hung about Wyndriven Abbey, making my eyes water and my nose run.

No news had come about Talitha, except that Charles was indeed also missing. The longer without a report, the better.

I took Lily out in an attempt to escape the haze with a trot on the hillside. Garvey saddled her and insisted, as usual, on accompanying me. Gone were the obsequious, admiring looks he had bestowed upon me early on. Also gone was the smoldering hatred, to be replaced by the impression of a barely hidden smirk, a secret glee. I ended my ride abruptly.

Sitting on a stone bench in the garden, I now ripped at my finger-nails with my teeth. Perhaps it wouldn't be so bad. Perhaps I wouldn't hate *every* moment of the rest of my life.

My absent glance moved across the lawns and caught at the ruins shrouded with dry, withered vines—the folly. The copy of an ancient Indian temple. It couldn't be more than twenty-five years old, yet it appeared a thousand. Suddenly, inexplicably, I was curious. I looked furtively at the house. No one was in sight. How would it hurt if I peeked inside? Slowly I rose and moved toward the building, with its tumbled granite blocks scattered about. From the roof, a stone monkey, furred with mold, grinned down.

I ran my fingers over the indentations in the rock. Moss had collected in the carvings to outline the designs in bright emerald. It was striking and exotic. Bernard indeed had the talent to create objects of beauty. I pulled back the dying wisteria that curtained the concealed door I had discovered on my former exploration, dug my ragged fingernails into the crack, and pulled.

To my surprise, it opened readily, as if on a spring. A puff of cold, fetid air hit my face. The place smelled of rancid dampness and mildew, the floor slimy with mud and lingering ice. I drew back, then steeled myself and moved onward, into the yawning mouth. Scabby, grayish lichen encrusted the walls. A sluggish bubbling sounded from partially frozen water in a fountain up ahead. My eyes were not accustomed to the dim light, filtered from the pierced designs in the stone fretwork and further darkened by tangled creepers.

I walked boldly deeper inside. The ceiling was arched, painted in blurred designs. They might have depicted a slender version of the plump, romping gods and cherubs in the Heaven room.

There appeared to be statuary in dusky corners. Slowly my eyes grew more accustomed to the shadows, and one of the sculptures came into focus. I gasped.

From behind me, Bernard's voice said softly, "I knew that with your, ah, *feminine curiosity* you would find your way here eventually. To my Temple of Love. I have been anticipating it. Garvey has watched to alert me of it."

I drew back and nearly tripped. "I—I—you said once you would show me this place."

"Yes, I did, didn't I? Well, now is the time."

He moved closer. His face was flushed and his eyes unnaturally bright. Was he drunken?

"It's so damp, though," I said, edging away, "we'd better wait."

"I think not. No more waiting."

I tried to bolt around him to the door.

He reached out to snatch my wrist and jerked me toward him so hard my arm nearly pulled out of the socket. "No, *ma petite.* I do not feel like chasing you just yet. Are you game for a little fun?"

I swayed on my feet and would have fallen, but he wrapped one arm around me in a semblance of affection, tight as an iron band. With the other, he grabbed my chin so he might physically turn my head toward what he wanted me to see. I yelped in pain as his fingers dug deeply into my flesh.

"Please," I whimpered, "please, I don't want to."

He gave a short, savage laugh. "I realize that. But no, I cannot oblige you in this. You came in of your own volition, and now you are going to see everything. Besides, it is time you learned something of the pleasures ahead. You are a naïve little goose, you know. At first it was refreshing, but after a time it wearies."

I would have closed my eyes but didn't dare.

The statues and murals were all of couples—some human, some inhuman, misshapen and warped, with too many limbs or heads.

They writhed, twisted, grotesque, naked except for filmy bits of veiling, with outflung contorted limbs, in a mockery of embracing or in flagrant torture. The painted eyes and the blank, blind stone eyes of the statues leered or ogled or rolled back in terror. The lips appeared to be smiling, but on closer look grimaced or stretched distorted in fear or pain.

"It's—disgusting. This—this isn't love." I was shaking, with tears streaming down my cheeks.

Bernard regarded me, partly curious, partly amused, partly angry. "And what do you think love is? All exchanged locks of hair"—here I shuddered—"and poems written to your complexion? *Chérie*, I have been long-suffering, but it's time you learned of passion."

He jerked me toward a pile of mildew-splotched crimson velvet cushions surrounding the fountain and pushed me down. He grasped my arms hard and put his full weight on top of me. "Now I want kisses. Not your missish pecks—long, deep, luscious kisses."

I bit him. He gave me a stinging slap, so that my nose bled.

Then he put his mouth on mine, hard and devouring. I retched from the stench of his stinking breath. He pressed against my chest so that I had no air. His hands scuttled over my body like crabs. I shoved against him, but I was as helpless as a gnat. I kicked, but his legs held mine pinned.

This is happening. This is really happening.

A shout sounded from outside.

"It's Ling," Bernard said, raising his head. With a sort of numb, detached composure, I watched, riveted, as the demon seeped out of his expression to be replaced by concern. "Something must be badly wrong for him to call like that." Slowly he released me and stood.

The muscle twitched beside his eye. "Wipe your face and straighten your clothing. We do not want the servants talking." He disappeared up the passageway.

I tried unsuccessfully to clean the blood from my nose. My teeth began to chatter. Once I was sure Bernard was well away, exhausted and dreary, with bruised lips and face and arms, I dragged myself back to the house and up to my bedroom.

The mermaids on the mantel, the pearl-studded ottoman, the bed—all were unfamiliar. Where was I? What was I doing? Everything must be a dream, a ghastly dream. I buried my face in my hands for several minutes before I could ring the bell for Odette.

"Please bring me water for a bath," I said. My lips felt swollen.

She cast a sharp look at my dishevelment, but she hurried to do what I asked.

When the hot water steamed in the tub, I told her, "I'll put myself to bed after I bathe, so don't bother to come back tonight."

She curtsied, then hesitated, one hand on the doorknob. "He took Daphne there, you know."

"What are you talking about?" I was too exhausted even to look at her.

"Daphne—that one who arranges flowers. Monsieur took her to the folly place. Garvey told me. He thinks I do not understand well, so he tells me things. Monsieur, he was furious over something—Garvey did not say what—oh, a few years back, before he married Adele. So Monsieur took Daphne—her fifty years old, lame, never had a man—he took her there. He beat her and did—other things. Then he gave her to Willie and ordered them to jump the broom. I tell you this now because I am leaving tomorrow, so it does not matter anymore. I tell you this so that man—that monster—will not do to you what he has done to others. You must also leave."

I clutched at the bedpost and closed my eyes. Odette waited a moment, but when I didn't speak, the door clicked shut behind her. I managed to turn the key in the lock and climb into the bath. After scrubbing, scrubbing my skin, I leaned back and immersed even my face in the warm water until I had to rise up, sputtering.

The depravity of someone who would do such a thing to Daphne was nearly unfathomable, but I was learning. The person who could create that perverted folly and take decent women there wasn't a lover or a man. Odette was right. He was a monster. How odd that Odette should have known this even before I did.

And I would not marry a monster. Not for my family. Not for anything. My sense of survival was too great. Bernard's brides had stayed and were all dead now—yes, I was sure now that even Victoire was dead. And even in death it seemed they were not set free.

In the tale of "Beauty and the Beast," the heroine had freely gone to the Beast, believing he would eat her. No sane person would do that. She and her family should have at least tried to flee—as I would flee to my siblings. Somehow I would reach them. We would run to the ends of the earth if necessary.

A knock sounded at the locked door.

"I'm bathing," I called in a hoarse voice.

"I need to see you right away," Bernard said. "I am about to leave for a few days."

I climbed from the tub, dried off, and slipped into my dressing gown, all the while preparing myself to face him, nerve by nerve.

Lucky Beauty! Her beast was a man in beast's trappings. Scarier by far was a beast in the trappings of a man.

He looked even more handsome than usual standing there, a little uncertain, the lock of bluish black hair falling across his forehead. He hadn't bothered to "straighten" himself.

"I must go immediately to Memphis," he said. "The trouble at the docks has escalated, and I have other business there as well. Business that concerns you. I cannot bear to leave you unhappy with me, so I shall tell you that I plan to visit my lawyer and rewrite my will, leaving everything to you. You shall be an heiress. How is that? Does it please you? Am I fully back in your good graces?"

"Of course," I said in a bright, false voice.

"And I shall give you my keys again. You see—I still trust you." He started to hand me the iron ring but paused before releasing it. "With the same stipulations."

"Thank you. And goodbye." I had forgotten how heavy the ring was.

He opened his mouth to speak, thought better of it, and left.

Once the door was relocked, I leaned against it. Slowly the realization of my luck seeped through. These keys and Bernard's absence offered my chance to escape.

One by one I fingered the keys as I made my plans. There must be money in Bernard's office, his bedchamber, somewhere. Could I ride Lily, or would Garvey wake and stop me? Some chances must be risked; it would take too long to walk into town. Once on Lily, I would ride and ride and ride. I would not flee to Gideon. That would be the first place Bernard would look. For Gideon's own protection, I realized painfully that I could never see him again.

In a large reticule I packed a change of undergarments and a toothbrush and hairbrush. I shook my head slightly at the sight of all the opulent gowns in the wardrobe, remembering with dull surprise that once these had thrilled me. I pulled out a simple traveling dress. Nothing that had mattered before mattered now.

In the middle of the night, long after the servants slept, I made my way with one small candle and keys in hand, through the shadowy, echoing corridors to Bernard's bedchamber. I peered nervously about, expecting to see the Sisters, but in this adventure I was alone. I unlocked his door.

Even when Ducky had given me my tour of the abbey, I had only peeked in this room from the doorway, as it had seemed indelicate to enter. I had had an impression of massive, carved, claw-foot furniture, heavy brown velvet hangings, and a general air of masculinity.

There was his washstand with toothbrush and tooth powder, the book *Hide and Seek* by Wilkie Collins lying open on the night table, his familiar paisley dressing gown spread at the foot of the bed, awaiting his return. The scent of his cologne lingered. All too personal.

A faceted amethyst glass jar lay beside the lamp. It was small, no more than three inches across, lidded, and darkly opaque. Because Bernard's room was so free of decorative flotsam and jetsam, this container seemed out of place on his bedside table. It must have a use. It might contain coins. I lifted the lid.

In the dim light I couldn't tell what the pale objects inside were— perhaps beads. They lay on a bed of short locks of hair that had been bound with thread. I poured the things, clicking softly together, out into my hand to inspect closer, and gave a strangled shriek, dropping them. They were teeth—yellowed ivory, scrubbed clean, and pulled out by the roots. Six of them.

Teeth? Could they be Bernard's? No. There were too many. Then—whose? And slowly into my sluggish brain seeped the truth. I made myself think the unthinkable. I fell backward and grasped at things—the counterpane, the bedpost. Finally I leaned against the bed, my heart thudding.

He had killed his wives. The teeth, and the hair, of course, belonged to them. They were Bernard's keepsakes of his ghastly deeds, kept there by his bed so he could inspect them often and gloat. Hints of this had nagged at me through the months, but I had squelched them before ever they came to surface. How could any normal mind comprehend such evil? He was someone I had lived closely with, someone I had genuinely liked for many weeks.

Gingerly I used the edge of my skirt to pick up the teeth and replace them in the jar. A glint of my own terror seemed reflected in the facets.

The very room horrified me, and I was too shaken to continue searching for money. I stumbled to my own chamber. My legs seemed turned to liquid. By sheer force of will, I commanded them to hold me up until I could sink into my chair by the fire. I twisted my hair bracelet round and round as I willed my frenzied heart to calm.

How often had I scorned the stupidity of heroines in lurid novels? Now I understood them—I had been as blind as they. I had believed Bernard had simply driven his women to their early deaths with his selfishness and possessiveness. I had thought I would be stronger. I was a fool. A few years hence and my teeth would be in his bedside jar if I didn't get away now.

I had a little time, though. I must think. It would be a mistake to run hysterically.

It was easy for Bernard to attract women. He was so handsome, could be so charming. Because the devil himself wouldn't truly come equipped with the traditional horns and tail, he must be attractive and charismatic in order to reel in his prey. Bernard didn't anticipate the fate of his wives when he married them. I didn't suppose he intended, yet, to kill me. Oddly I believed each time he married he had hoped for a pleasant future.

Victoire had planned to flee with her lover. Perhaps Bernard had discovered them in the act, and this caused him to take leave of his senses. No, even as I thought this, I dismissed it—the seeds of insanity must always have been present from birth. Perhaps they sprouted after his little son died, and then, with Victoire's betrayal, the monster took over. He watched and waited and then pounced. Neither Victoire nor her lover nor her maid had ever left the grounds. There were six teeth—four for wives, one for a lover, one for a servant.

Somewhere on this vast estate the bodies must lie.

Tatiana allegedly had succumbed in childbirth, but Ducky was away when it happened. It was her husband and not birthing that killed her. I would never know what had set him off—with Bernard's lightning-quick mood changes, it might have been anything. She was buried in the chapel yard.

The accepted story was that Tara killed herself, but Ducky had wondered how she was able to use one of the armory's jeweled knives when it was always kept locked. Tara and Bernard had fought often. It wasn't surprising she had lived only a year—by now Bernard was adept at ridding himself of brides. She was buried at night in the same yard as Tatiana.

Adele had lived with him longer. Bernard took her away to a "healing spring" to improve her health, but she returned to the abbey a corpse.

What if I could find the bodies of Victoire, her lover, and her maid? My weary mind quickened with the thought. If I were to find them, hopefully I would have proof of their manner of death. And what of the teeth? They were evidence as well. I shrank from the thought of going back to Bernard's room to snatch them up, but it was the intelligent thing to do. With the teeth as tangible proof and a knowledge of the bodies' whereabouts, I could go to the police and Bernard would be brought to justice and I could escape without being hunted. I could go to Gideon.

This was what the ghosts wanted of me—to expose their murderer to the world. Bernard liked to say that fate had brought us together, that I was "meant" to come to him. Perhaps, to this end, I was. For the first time in weeks I had not seen a glimpse of the specters all day. Possibly they had withdrawn because they knew the wheels now turned inexorably and the series of events was set in motion.

Or else they could no longer bear to watch.

If the bodies weren't buried in the woods, the most obvious hiding place for them was the locked-up chapel in the locked-up churchyard. Like the "whited sepulchers" in Matthew, which appeared beautiful outwardly, but inwardly were full of dead men's bones. I would at least peek in there and then make my escape. As I made my plans, the trembling that had beset me since I first saw the teeth ceased. If I were called upon to be a brave person, I would be a brave person.

By the time I poured the contents of the amethyst glass jar into my handkerchief and tied it tightly, the black night had become edged with gray. *Hurry.* I draped myself in a thick cashmere shawl and dropped the handkerchief as well as my Christmas present—the rubies set in heavy gold—in my reticule. Hopefully I could sell the jewels. I picked up the key ring and, without a backward glance, left my bedroom.

Down the corridors, down the back twisting stairs I went, careful of the still-sleeping servants, and then out the music room door. In the forest, pine trees mourned. Somewhere a shutter or gate banged—again and again. I picked my way down the weaving, sinuous paths to the chapel yard. No movement showed in the dark windows of Wyndriven Abbey.

Blustery wind rubbed together the leaves of the tattered vines covering the yard wall, sounding like dry skin rasping and rustling. I touched my stone angel, imagining a warmth spread to my fingers from her foot, before lifting ivy away from the gate and inserting the key in the lock. It opened smoothly, as if it had been recently oiled. I replaced the ivy and shut the gate carefully behind me. Anyone walking by would see nothing unusual.

The moon still showed faintly, but by now a low, dim, cold sun also appeared at intervals between shredded clouds. The yard was tangled and overgrown so completely it was hard to make out the four granite gravestones beneath clotted weeds. Why four? Oh yes,

Bernard's son, Anton, would be buried here as well as the three wives. I didn't try to pull away creepers to read the inscriptions; these graves were not what I was looking for and there was nothing to hint at an unmarked grave.

The windows of the chapel were boarded over with thick planks held by many nails. Bernard may have done it to protect valuable stained-glass windows—or perhaps he wanted no one to look inside. A chilling thought snaked into my brain: He might also have wanted nothing to get out.

I struggled through to the iron-shod doors of the chapel, briers snatching and tearing at my skirt and legs. Glancing behind me at the closed gate, I placed the key in the lock and turned it. Again this door opened smoothly. An unwholesome odor greeted me—a mixture of mildew and fungus and mossy stone and decay. Air and early-dawn light filtered in through the cracked-open door and from a hole gaping in the ceiling.

In the ancient chamber slender columns twined with sculpted garlands soared upward to an arched ceiling. Old Testament murals covered the walls, the paint still bright. It was a large room, meant to be a family chapel. Blackened wood pews faced a richly carved altar, while a door behind it led to what I guessed was the sacristy. An ancient peace filled the place and held me frozen for a moment.

Something might be hidden in the sacristy. I started up the aisle.

I did not need to go that far. My hands clenched so tightly my fingernails dug into my palms.

They lay behind the altar and stretched out on the first pew and slumped against the wall and piled with tangled limbs like discarded dolls—all that remained of seven people. Bernard had not buried three of his wives in the churchyard, although I neither knew nor cared what he had buried in their stead. He had wanted these women to suffer the final degradation for defying or displeasing him: to lie exposed.

In his arrogance he hadn't troubled to hide the bodies. Maybe he came here sometimes for little visits.

The Mississippi heat and insects had left no flesh on the bones except a few dried scraps. Some hair clung to skulls—on four of them a reddish shade. Hollow, sightless eyes stared, teeth grimaced. If I looked closer, one tooth would be missing from each. I did not look closer. The clothing fared better than the flesh. Stained and discolored gowns that were once shades of sea foam and emerald, sapphire and primrose, told me which skeleton was which.

Tatiana lay stretched out on the pew, her child in her arms. The babe had mummified, parchment-dry skin stretched over bones. Perhaps it had been born dead, setting off Bernard's maniacal rage. Tara and Adele lay piled together near her, as if their bodies had simply been dumped on the littered stone floor. They had died elsewhere and been brought here.

Something dark and leggy skittered beneath the skeleton slumped against the wall. This was the man, clothed in a blotchy buff frock coat with a dark waistcoat. Mr. Gregg. Victoire and the maid in her gray dress lay behind the altar, as if they had sought protection there. A black and oily-looking liquid—blood?—had dried in a puddle around these three bodies. The trio had been left where they had fallen. Bernard had somehow lured them to the chapel and killed them there.

He would have used his sword stick. A gun would have been too loud and too crass for Bernard.

I wanted to claw out my eyes, and yet I could not stop staring.

I have seen it, I have seen it, now let me leave.

The light had changed. A shadow blocked the opening. In the crack was Garvey's face wreathed in a grin.

I gave a shrill scream and lunged toward the door as it swung shut. Too late. Too late.

CHAPTER 34

TRAPS

I had made a deadly mistake; I had left the key in the lock.

I beat at the door until my fists bled, then clawed at the corners until my fingernails tore off. I screamed until my throat closed. Then I listened. No sound entered from outside. Garvey was long gone, and he would allow no one within hearing distance.

Get out of here before Bernard returns.

As I struggled back to sanity, sick and shaking and driven by a quieter terror, I searched for a way out. The once-lovely stained-glass windows were shattered low down but intact higher up. Gouges and scratches marred the stout, firmly nailed boards behind the windows.

"Did you and Mr. Gregg do that, Victoire?"

Now I was talking to corpses.

The trio—Victoire, her maid, and Mr. Gregg—had spent a night-marish time shut in here before finally being slain by Bernard. The bloodstained slashes in their clothing revealed they had been stabbed.

The three of them—one a strong man—hadn't been able to escape; how should I?

I am going to die.

I snatched up a shard of window glass, wrapped my shawl around it, and jabbed at the hinges of the solid door, but without result.

The twenty-foot ceiling, soaring impossibly out of reach, was stained yellow and black from leaks. Light beams streamed now from the collapsed part of the roof, and a twiggy nest clung to gaping rafters. My boots crunched on the crumbled plaster and shattered glass that littered the floor along with bird and mouse droppings. A few small human bones had been scattered by creatures. I skirted around them.

At the edge of a mound of fallen plaster and slates and rotten wood was a different sort of object. I picked it up and shook the dust from it. A low-heeled lady's shoe of green morocco. The leather had shriveled and cracked from exposure to the elements. Its mate still graced the foot of Victoire's skeleton. An animal had dragged this one here, unless she had cast it off in some mad scramble for her life. I placed it beside its mate.

I would die a lingering death of thirst and starvation.

No. I shook my head slowly in a low arc. That wasn't Bernard's way. He would prefer to pierce my heart with his sword.

A sniveling, whimpering, pleading creature would not move Bernard in a final confrontation. What would? Reminders of my humanity? Of his? Of his former fondness for me?

Thinking like him was impossible. He was mad. His madness encompassed a terrible selfishness with neither compassion nor empathy, a terrible anger, a terrible possessiveness, and a terrible lust for blood.

I was living the nightmare I had dreamed in the orangery, when I knew a ghastly fate approached. In it I had cried out to Anne, begging to know if my brothers were yet coming. In the reality no one was coming to help.

I need a weapon.

There was the broken glass. I carefully picked up a long and pointed shard and placed it near the door. I could use it. I could stab Bernard. If not for my own sake, then for that of the other people he had slaughtered.

I dug at the plaster walls with another glass shard wrapped in my shawl, managing to make only dust. I rammed the boarded windows with wood fallen from the roof, until the rotten slats crumbled to shreds. I prodded and shoved and occasionally screamed.

Hours passed.

Somehow I had spent an entire day here. Now darkness seeped in. A little silver moonlight fell through the ceiling hole to give a soft outline to the altar and pews. To the mounded bodies.

My still companions were merely husks of people, like the shed cicada skins that clung to Southern trees in summertime, or so I told myself. I was not afraid of them.

I took up my weapon and sank down against the wall between the windows, pulling my knees to my chest. From here, I could see if the door opened, although I doubted it would open soon. Bernard was not due back until tomorrow. I hadn't slept all the night before, but I must stay awake, in case.

The series of events that had led me to this fate played out through my head, culminating with Bernard's bestowal of the keys. He knew my curiosity. In some skewed way he probably enjoyed taunting and testing me with them. Twice he had done it, but the first time I hadn't fallen into the trap. Now I had failed the test; now I would share the same doom as his other disobedient brides.

Garvey, of course, had been instructed to watch me. He would be well rewarded when his master returned. He knew what lay here. Had he even joined in the sport? No, Bernard wouldn't have shared that pleasure with his henchman, but Garvey would have helped dispose of the bodies.

An explanation for my absence would be given to the servants. There would be an emergency return to Boston, with my reported illness and death following. That part would be easy. Especially with Talitha and Odette gone, most wouldn't care enough to think twice. If any of them suspected villainy, they would be too afraid of Bernard to raise concerns. Ling had helped me a few times, but he was too weary and too old and too alone to blatantly thwart his master. Ducky—she was not stupid so much as blind to anything she didn't want to see. *Poor little Miss Sophia,* she would cluck, *to die so young, and the master so devoted to her.* My relatives might be told I succumbed to the typhus, which was common here. They would grieve and might raise questions, but they would have no means to pursue answers. He was going to get away with it.

Death itself didn't frighten me. I was secure in my faith of a better place hereafter. There were the beautiful lines in Corinthians, beginning with the hope of the resurrection: "For we know that if our earthly house of this tabernacle be dissolved, we have a building of God, a house not made with hands, eternal in the heavens."

I hadn't realized I had begun weeping. Tears streamed down. Because of the loss of my earthly future. The loss of marriage and babies and becoming finally old and wise and gray-haired. Because I was frightened of *how* I would end here. Of the thirst and the fear and the pain. Of the slicing and stabbing.

No! I wanted to live.

I began to pray then. A litany of pleading for help, for strength, for intelligence and a clear mind. I pled for the souls of the dead. Even in that terrible place, the peace of God enveloped me.

Heavy silence settled down like ancient dust. I slept.

The noise of thunder and pouring rain awoke me, building up to a crescendo of jarring rumbles and booms.

I was still here, with lips cracked from thirst. In the chapel. Waiting for Bernard and for death. I would have begun screaming again if my swollen throat had cooperated, even though screaming was pointless.

Another sound began to rise. This resonating from inside the chapel. A low murmuring swelled and surrounded me. My Sisters. They were not leaving me to face Bernard alone. I listened so hard, trying to catch intelligible words, that my ears hurt.

Finally, both hands clutched over my head to stop the pain, I stumbled to the place where water streamed from the hole in the roof. I opened my mouth for the raindrops that poured down. I stood there a long time, and gradually the moaning died away.

Until it dried, my clothing would hold moisture I could suck on or wring out to drink. But after that, in case the rain ceased soon and in case Bernard didn't return today, I must have stored water. What could I use to catch it? There was my reticule, which was still just inside the door. Unfortunately it was made of cloth, which wouldn't hold liquid. It contained only the underclothing, the tied-up handkerchief, the hairbrush, the toothbrush, and the jewelry. There was not a vessel or any hollowed cylinder in the place except—

Oh, I could not do it.

Lord Byron had drunk from a skull. Bernard must not find me faint from thirst.

Then, thankfully, I thought of the shoes. Distasteful, but not so horrifying as a chalice of bone. I wouldn't drink from them unless in dire need. I was hungry and weakened now, as I'd eaten nothing since the day before yesterday, but not desperately so. It was water I needed.

I collected shoes from the skeletons and set them to catch rainwater.

As I unlaced Tara's kid boots, I brushed against an odd bulge below her belt. She had been carrying something when she died. I lightly touched the tarlatan of her dress, brittle from dried body fluids, then ripped it open. Tara carried a pocket beneath her gown, a pouch with drawstring looped about her waist. It was of leather, brightly painted.

The contents spilled onto the floor.

A flask of smelling salts, a few coins, and a penknife.

A knife. I could almost hear Tara say, *Take it and use it well, for I could not.* Feisty Tara would not have gone down without a fight. Unfortunately Bernard must have taken her by surprise before she could reach for her weapon. Much better than pointed glass.

Once more I seated myself against the wall and, twisting the hair bracelet about my wrist, made my plan.

With my reticule and the opened knife in my lap, I waited.

It must have been late afternoon, but dusky from the cloud cover, when a key rasped in the lock. My heart shot up to my mouth. The weapons had slipped from my hands, but now I grasped them. When he first entered, he wouldn't be able to see well in the dimness. There would be a moment.

But it was not Bernard's voice that spoke. "Sophia," the voice hissed. "I stole the keys from Garvey. Hurry, you must go quickly! Now. He is back."

Odette. She stood in the doorway.

I rose slowly, my cramped limbs rebelling. "You?" I said. My brain was too sluggish from hunger and shock to fathom this turn of events.

"I am the cousin of Adele Lalonde. Always when we were children, I took care of her. She married that man and I could no longer take care of her, but I could come here after she died to learn the truth and then to seek retribution. She is in here, no? I must see her. You—"

Her body gave an odd twitch and her face crumpled, the bright eyes suddenly flat. She fell to the ground, and the man I was betrothed to marry wrenched his sword stick from her back. He kicked her body out of the way.

"She was clever," he said, entering. "I never would have guessed. I had thought Adele had no close relatives. Families are inconvenient." He bent over to wipe the bright blood from his long, thin blade on Odette's dress. Fastidious.

Now! Now was my chance. While he looked down.

Hit him! Hit him! Run! Run!

Instead, a faint whimper escaped my lips.

He faced me, the light from the doorway making his hair and beard gleam so he appeared to have a bluish halo about his head. His eyes held me frozen.

He shut the door behind him with a click.

"*Mon ange,* I was anxious for you." His tone was light, conversational. "I had expected a warm welcome after my absence. But no, you were not in the house awaiting me. You were here awaiting me. And with what strange company."

His tone drew me back to pleasant evenings with a congenial companion. As I listened to his deep, melted-chocolate voice, if I didn't remember where we stood, I could almost forget who he really was.

But I did not forget. My coldness was replaced by a dull rage as life returned to my limbs. I stood wary, ready to leap out of the way if he lunged toward me.

It was hard to see his expression, although I thought he smiled. He didn't move my way; instead, he walked up toward the altar, his boots crunching the debris on the floor. He surveyed what lay there.

"I watched the faces of these whores as I thrust my knife in, and it was beautiful to see the light leave their eyes as the life oozed from their bodies."

"Please, Bernard," I whispered. "Please."

"Yes," he said, stepping back toward the door. "That is what they all said. Poor Sophia with the lovely hair. I used to look at you as you sat there, so small, so easily broken. I could take your arm or your neck and—snap!—break you with one hand. But I never would, I thought. Not my Sophia. Alas, though, first the letters from that boy and then the preacher and always so curious. Why couldn't you leave things alone?" The last word was accentuated by the sword stick crashing down on a pew.

"Bernard," I said quietly, calmly, "you don't need to hurt me. I'll never tell anyone what's here. We'll leave this place tonight. We'll be married. We'll never stop traveling and we'll never come here again. You can forget all about it."

He stared at the floor as if he were actually considering. He looked up. "No, it's gone too far for that." He motioned with his hand. "Come here. I don't want to chase you down. I will do it quickly. You shall not suffer much."

I stirred myself. I moved toward where he stood waiting, step by step, as if pulled by an invisible thread. As he expected me to do.

Closer, closer.

My reticule, weighty with the ruby jewelry, slammed into his face. While he reeled, I thrust the knife at him. I meant to stab, but flesh was tougher than I thought and the blade didn't plunge in; instead, I slashed down his shoulder and arm, and dropped the knife.

For one moment he stared at me in shock. Then, as blood spurted out, he clapped his hand over his wound and laughed. He leaped toward me, but he lost his footing on a bone and slipped. I dashed past him to the door and jiggled at the latch for what seemed ages.

Please make it open. Please make it open.

It opened. I was outside. The cold pouring rain shocked me into speed, and I raced toward the woods. I heard Bernard shouting and expected any moment to be surrounded by groundsmen. No one came.

My boots pounded, pounded, pounded as they hit the ground. Once, just before reaching the forest, I glanced back. He followed, his hand clutching his arm, dark with blood.

I launched into the trees. Their branches wept down.

Which way? Which way?

I leaped from stone to stone across the brook. Evil couldn't cross running water.

Dripping, hanging vines clung wetly, and I slipped on slimy leaves. My sleeve caught on a branch, and my heart seemed to stop because I thought it was Bernard snatching. When I saw what it was, I ripped it away. Twigs plucked at my hair. On and on I ran. He crashed behind me. After making my way deep within the woods, I zigged and zagged. I must not lead him to Anarchy. Once I tripped over a bulging root and fell with a thud. As I lay still in the mud before pulling myself up, my breath loud in my ears, Bernard called from not far.

"Sophia, come here now," he coaxed. "I will not hurt you. It is as you said—we will be married. We will travel wherever you want to go."

Choking back a sob, I picked myself up and ran. I paused for a moment as I broke into a clearing, thickly matted with weeds and briers, the rain striking my face. Where was I? My sixth sense about direction had deserted me when I needed it most. Had I come this way before? Was I dashing in circles?

Hide and wait for morning. Quietly, quietly I could secrete myself in the undergrowth like a small hunted animal. The rain had brought an early twilight. He would not find me.

I lay down and started to wriggle beneath a dense clump of witch hazel.

There I was, flat on my stomach, when Bernard entered the clearing.

He gave a pleased little laugh while I writhed to right myself and tensed to fight for my life. He stepped calmly toward me through the briers. The chase was over. He took one step . . . then another.

A loud clang and a crunch sounded. Bernard screamed.

I scuttled backward on my rear end, gaping.

The glitter in his eye was quenched, replaced by pain and bewilderment. He gasped and shuddered, twitched and trembled.

He had stepped into one of his own man traps.

Shock riveted me to the spot.

He groaned and cursed, wrenching his leg upward while the blood spurted.

At last he stopped struggling and sank to the ground, his leg bent at a strange angle where it was clamped by the long teeth of the trap.

Gradually he focused on me. "Is that you, Sophia?" he said so softly it was almost a breath.

"Yes," I whispered. He could not hurt me now. He was stricken down like the oak tree. Blood oozed from his mangled limb and from his arm and mingled with the rain to pool beneath him. Randomly I wondered if I had hit an artery with the knife. It was a great deal of blood.

I stood.

His face twisted. "It's so dark, I can't see you. Come near so I can see you. You must help me."

How like him. How like him even now to continue talking, to continue to try to ensnare me with his words. "I don't dare," I said.

"Do you think I would grab you and crush your white neck? While I am thus? No, I won't harm you if you'll get a branch and wedge the trap open. You can go free to your family."

"I'll send someone for you."

He sucked in sharply and shouted, "That would take too long! And they wouldn't help; they'd bring a noose. Do I mean nothing to you? Would you leave me here to bleed to death?" He moaned from the pain. And now quieter, almost a whisper, "You are not like that. You are compassionate. Always you would wonder if you needed to let me die. You don't want to live with that on your conscience." He gritted his teeth and closed his eyes. Every part of him shuddered and then lay perfectly still.

Bernard was dead. There was no movement, no breathing. I exhaled and moved slightly closer to peer into his eyes.

Dead.

I shook out my skirts and—in a flash—he *lunged* impossibly far to grab my ankle. The distorted look on his face is one I will never, never forget. The tighter I pulled away, the tighter he held, his fingernails digging into my flesh like the teeth of the trap dug into his.

I screamed and struggled. I sobbed for Anne and for Gideon and for Anarchy and for my brothers.

"I said come," he said, guttural and distorted. He began to reel me in, hand over hand, as he struggled to a sitting position.

I kicked at him with my free leg. He snatched it as well. I clutched at the trunk of the witch hazel bush, holding on for all I was worth.

Suddenly he gave a gasp and loosened his hold. Miraculously I struggled free.

He stared at something behind me.

I scuttled away and followed his gaze.

There stood Victoire and Tatiana, Tara and Adele, watching him with blazing eyes and blazing hair. Straight and strong and fierce, terrible in their beauty. Brighter and clearer than ever yet I had seen them.

"No!" he screamed. He tugged again at the trap, flailed, and covered his face with his arms.

I scrambled up and ran. The thorns tearing at my skin reminded me I still lived.

On and on I ran till I reached Anarchy. The door to her hovel gaped wide. She sat at her rickety table, her dear face lit by a lantern, eating her supper.

"Anarchy!" I stumbled into the room.

She knocked over the chair as she sprang up to catch me. "Honey, what's happened? What he done to you?" Her eyes darted to the doorway.

I babbled nearly incoherently. "Bernard—he killed his wives—all of them, and he killed Odette and then he came after me. I stabbed him and he chased me and he's caught in one of those traps. He's bleeding to death."

"Is he now? Well, good. He ain't going nowheres, then."

"Don't we need to send someone for him?"

"Till he's deader than lots of doornails, don't see why we should. Good riddance, I say. But if it bothers you, what we gonna do is, I'll go on up to the big house while you sits here, 'cause you ain't in no fit state to go nowheres, and they'll send someone into town for the marshal. You ain't scared to be alone, is you? You ain't scared he can still come after you?"

I was, but I shook my head.

She led me to her bed and made me sit on it, leaning against the wall. She covered me with her quilt and thrust a mug of lukewarm herbal tea into my hands and a small, fragrant calico cushion into my lap. "There, that's stuffed with hops and lemon verbena and rosemary. You just smell it, and it'll give you peace and take away your nightmares."

I huddled on Anarchy's bed, swathed in her quilt, clutching the cushion between my legs, and shivering convulsively so that I spilled the tea but hardly knew it. I grieved for myself and for the Sisters and for everyone in the world, even the man who lay dying, caught in his own trap. I grieved for what he should have been.

CHAPTER 35

POSSIBILITIES

"Is Mr. Stone at home?" I asked the formidable-looking woman who answered the door. Mrs. Penny. That was what Gideon had said his housekeeper was named.

She looked at me appraisingly before nodding. "Come on in. You can wait in the parlor."

Mrs. Penny led me through a dark hall and proudly flung back the door to a hideous room, papered in mud-colored stripes. The intimidating titles of ponderous religious works showed behind the leaded glass doors of a bookcase, and the portrait of Gideon's predecessor frowned down at me from above the mantel. It must have been his wife who had worked the knobby needlework on the hard little cushions clustering the sofa.

I smoothed out my gown of black bombazine. It had belonged to the city marshal's sister, who took pity on me. I had taken it in quickly, borrowing her needle and thread, and had hardly glanced at the sweat stains beneath the armpits. However, the fact that I had glanced at them at all at such a time told me the day would probably come when I would care about clothing again.

As I waited for Gideon, I pulled back heavy, dark green draperies. And saw the dogwood tree. The dogwood tree under which Buttercup lay. Its spreading limbs were still bare, but beneath it a hundred daffodil shoots were popping up eagerly.

At the sight of them tears pricked my eyes. I hadn't cried since fleeing Wyndriven Abbey. I had held myself together tightly, fearing what might happen if I let go.

"Spring is coming."

I hadn't realized I'd spoken out loud until Gideon's voice said from behind me, "Yes, it won't be long now, and spring in Mississippi looks like heaven."

I whirled around, and he crossed the room in two strides to take my hands in his own. "Oh, my dear, my dear, why didn't you let me come to you?"

When I could trust my voice, I gently withdrew my fingers and said, "I had to protect you from yourself. You hadn't thought yet how scandal will forever taint my name. Already there are journalists from throughout the South camped nearby. Soon more will show up from distant places. I wouldn't have come today if I didn't need to ask a favor."

"The scandal is the last thing I care about. I can't tell you how many times since the ball I've considered abducting you. Especially after I received a letter from your sister begging me to watch out for you. I should have acted sooner. I was too ponderous. I racked my brain to think what was the right plan of action. I'll never forgive myself for leaving you there to go through what you've been through. So no more holding back for me. You've now had as much time as I can give. If you hadn't come today, I would have stormed the hotel and made you see me."

We were silent for a moment, just looking at each other, until he shook himself and said, "But tell me the favor."

I gave a strangled little laugh because I could almost hear Bernard saying, *Out with it,* as he always did when I hesitated to request something. I quickly suppressed the thought. "I seem to always be asking you to bury bodies. When the examiner has finished with Monsieur de Cressac's victims, could they please be interred in your churchyard? The ones who have been dead for years, as well as Odette. She was my maid, only she wasn't really a maid. She was a heroine. After we've located everyone's relatives and received permission, of course. Monsieur de Cressac's body is to be buried at the abbey beside his son—he truly did care about him, I think—but I'd like the others to sleep beside your church." I twisted my hair bracelet around my wrist. The bracelet would be placed on the stone angel I would move here as well, so she could stand vigilant over the Sisters' graves.

"Of course I'll take care of that. De Cressac is dead, then?"

"Yes. They told me this morning. He held on for three weeks. He'd lost a lot of blood, and then infection set in where they amputated his leg. I'm glad he's out of his misery. That he won't be hung. Is that a strange way to feel?"

"It's commendable you should have compassion for such a person. Your emotions may always be confused where he's concerned."

I rubbed my forehead. "They are—they are. You can have no

idea. I still don't know what was real and what was an act. He might have been a great man if he hadn't been so . . . damaged."

"Thank goodness he's now where he can do no more harm. The Lord will take everything into consideration in his judgment."

I sat down on the hard sofa and picked at a knobby cushion. "How much have you heard about everything?"

"Only what everyone knows now. That de Cressac murdered all four of his wives and you discovered this. The town feels a collective guilt that none of us realized what had been going on. No innocent young lady should have been allowed to go to such a man and be placed in such danger. You're considered a genuine heroine to have foiled him."

"By some, maybe. There'll be others who won't be so kind. Before I say anything else, I need to know—are Charles and Talitha safe? They did come to you, didn't they?"

"They did. They stayed for some time in my attic until the search for them died down and the weather took a favorable turn. By now they should be well on their journey to Canada."

"Will you let me work with the Underground Railroad too? I want so badly to be of service to the people."

"I'm sure you can help."

"And is there a way I can connect with Charles and Talitha once they reach their destination?"

"The different portions of the Railroad are kept in darkest secrecy from each other, but I'll see what I can do."

"Thank you. When we find them, I'm going to do something wonderful for them. I don't know what exactly, but I'm sure they can tell me themselves what would help them best with their future."

He nodded.

"And now," I said, "I want to tell you the whole story, if you'll listen. So you'll know how to—to think of me."

"Let's go outside, then, into the garden. It's so mild today, and for some reason I find this room oppressive."

Now I laughed truly. "Oh, it's the wallpaper. For one thing."

He laughed as well. "You may be right. I suspected it might be ugly, but I wasn't sure. Come on."

I held back as he reached for my hand again. "People might see you with me."

"Miss Petheram—Sophie—haven't I told you I don't care?"

And so I let him lead me into the garden.

He laid his coat on the grass and we sat upon it together—quite close. He smelled of lemon drops. We soaked up sunshine as I related my story, beginning with the day my family arrived at the abbey.

"Do you believe I really saw ghosts?" I asked at one point.

"Of course," he said. "There are more things in heaven and on earth, Sophie, than are dreamed of in most people's philosophies."

"Now, *that's* Shakespeare. I'm so glad you're an unusual sort of preacher."

A numbness took over when I spoke of the horrors. I still couldn't truly comprehend everything, so I related them flatly. The only event I omitted was the one that occurred in the folly. Some things it was better for Gideon not to know. How remarkable that I, Sophie Petheram, once so sheltered, was now protecting someone else's innocence. For a second I felt ancient, but the lovely day and Gideon's presence gently seeped into my soul, growing me younger.

He listened quietly, but emotion worked in his face. When I

finished, he shook his head. "In each instance you managed to do what you had to do. You're a strong woman. And stronger because of the scars you now carry. How could I not have known what was going on? How could I have left you to fight alone?"

Now it was my turn to take his hand. "You had no idea what he was. Neither did I, and I was with him for months. No one really knew, except Garvey. And then Odette. We all did what we thought best at the time with what we knew."

"What of this Garvey? Is he in custody?"

I stared fixedly at the daffodil shoots. "He disappeared before they could catch him. It's my fear that someday I'll look across a crowded street and there he'll be. The valet ran off too, so he also probably knew something. The butler is overseeing the household by himself now, as Mrs. Duckworth is prostrate with grief. Her heart is failing, and they don't think she'll live more than a few days. When I heard that yesterday, I went—I made myself go and see her, to tell her I bore her no ill will for any part she played in any of this, because I don't. Really I don't. But I probably shouldn't have gone."

Gideon's jaw set. "No, you shouldn't ever have to go back to that place. You shouldn't ever have to see those people again."

"That's not what I mean, although that *is* how I felt the first few days. If I ever even thought of the abbey, I had to hold myself back from running and hiding under the bedclothes. But what I meant is that I probably shouldn't have visited Mrs. Duckworth, for her own sake. I nearly killed her off right there and then. When she saw me, she sat up and pointed her finger in my face and screamed that I had ruined everyone's lives and acted as if she were going into convulsions. I left as fast as I could. Poor, poor old Ducky."

"She still can't imagine de Cressac doing any wrong, even after all this has come out. You're right. Poor old Mrs. Duckworth. How did it feel returning to the abbey? If you'd only let me, I would have gone there with you."

"Of course you would, but as I told you, I was protecting you from yourself." I plucked a blade of grass and began carefully splitting it with my fingernail. Gideon started to say something, but I wouldn't let him. "I steeled myself to go there, thinking every room would scream 'Bernard!' at me, but then somehow it wasn't terrible. The abbey existed long, long before he did. He's just a tiny dot in its history. It felt as if I were home when I stepped through the doors, even though I'm just a tiny dot too. I'm going to leave the hotel soon and go back there to stay." I set my shoulders defiantly. "What do you think of that?"

"I think you'd better make no long-range plans for a while. Except for one." He took a deep breath. "You say there's a taint attached to your name. That isn't so, but if it worries you, would you consider changing your name to mine?"

Frantically I plucked more grass. "I—I assume you're asking me to marry you. You can't have considered. We've spent so little time together. You hardly know me. And all this—it might destroy your career. We would be welcome nowhere."

Tenderly he turned my face so I had to look him straight on. "What you do not realize is that most people in this world are sensible and decent. My cousin Richard and his wife have spoken to their friend Anarchy who lives on their property. Apparently she let them know which way the wind blows with us, and they assured me they'd be delighted to have you as a guest in their home as soon as you quit the hotel, if you'd like to wait a while longer before returning to the abbey. And Mrs. Penny whispered just now in the hall that she's devoted to you already. I'm embarrassed my feelings have shown so plainly. Evidently, from the little I've told her in the past few weeks, she knows I'm head over heels in love with you. I have been from the first moment I saw the top of your head down below when I dangled from that tree, and every moment since has only made me more so."

I studied his expression. Was it possible I was going to be allowed to be happy again?

"So do you"— Gideon looked unsure—"do you care for me at all?"

Well, I must simply tell the truth. "Of course I'm head over heels in love with you too."

I let myself be pulled against his shoulder then, where I clutched his collar and buried my face into his waistcoat while my tears streamed down.

"And—and I'm afraid I'm going to be very wealthy," I said when Gideon finally held me back so he could wipe my eyes with his handkerchief. "At first I didn't want it. I panicked at the thought of that horrible money being mine."

"I understand. You don't know how much of de Cressac's riches contributed to his warped personality or how much of it has been accumulated from the misfortune of others."

"Exactly. But then both Mr. Bass and the attorney explained things. They said I could do whatever I desired with the abbey. I could turn it into a museum or a school or a home for unattractive and abandoned cats or some such thing, and lots of people could see it, because it really is a wonderful building, especially once I wipe out all signs of Monsieur de Cressac. I want to turn it into a place that does good. I also have a responsibility to all the people on the plantation and at the abbey. In those first days when all I wanted to do was run as far away as possible, the only thing that stopped me was remembering them. I haven't figured everything out, but the first thing I'm going to do is buy Anarchy's son and granddaughter and give them their liberty. Then I'll find a way to free all the Wyndriven slaves so they'll only stay there working for a salary if they want to. Of course obtaining freedom papers for so many is a complicated business, but Mr. Bass assures me that the money will help to pave the way."

Gideon waggled his eyebrows. "All the neighbors will love that, won't they? But they'll get used to it. Well," he said, stretching his arms in front of him, "it sounds like you've done a lot of thinking, but once again I'd urge you to not make any important decisions without giving yourself time. Except for the one thing I mentioned."

"Mr. Bass has helped me with the thinking. He's really wonderful now that he's not following Monsieur de Cressac around like a dog who's been kicked too often. When Junius and Anne come—I sent them a telegram and they sent one back saying they should arrive in the next few weeks—they'll help too. All this is just what Junius does well. Anyway, to do all that, I really do need to keep the money."

Gideon looked thoughtful. "Yes, you're right. You know, I've wondered if, in the next few years, we ought to emigrate to the West. They need churches built out there. But we won't go without being sure everyone you're responsible for is well taken care of. Now, you still haven't answered my question. Will you marry me?"

"Oh, yes. I thought you already knew. If you'll wait a while. Because I have all this business to attend to first—the servants and the property, not to mention I'm only seventeen and three-quarters, you know. Or perhaps you didn't know that is my age? In any case, nineteen and three-quarters is much older, I think, much more ready for marriage." I smiled at my beloved. "In the meantime Anne and Junius will live with me at the abbey, and I'm going to help my brother Harry get an appointment to West Point Academy. Also, I—I want to be certain I've recovered as much as I ever will from all that's happened. It was so—so horrible, Gideon. There's not a word for how ghastly it was."

"I'm so sorry for all that, Sophie. I'll wait as long as you want." He put his arms around me, and they trembled as he kept himself from crushing me to him. And then he did crush me to him. It was the most perfect thing I've ever felt in my life. We didn't speak for some time. There were a few things I had learned from Bernard that I could teach Gideon. (None of my "missish pecks," for instance.) Perhaps I didn't want to wait two years to marry my darling preacher after all.

Gideon gave a sudden gasp. I turned and followed his eyes. The misty shade of a redheaded woman in a primrose gown stood among the daffodils. For a moment she watched us, smiling. Then the world seemed all of light, she was gone, and I thought I heard a far-off, soft rush of wings.

I leaned back against Gideon, and all sorts of beautiful futures with him flashed through my mind. Because, you see, anything was possible for us.

ACKNOWLEDGMENTS

I wish to thank the Brothers Grimm and Charles Perrault, who told versions of the tale of Bluebeard, which I read (and was disturbed by) when I was a child.

I'm very grateful to my wonderful agent, Wendy Schmalz, and my discerning editor, Allison Wortche, because they recognized the value of this story and were willing to help me make it what it could be.

I am indebted to Ellen Anson, Monica Webster, Carol Trost, Emily VanYperen, Bethany Bailey, and James, Phillip, and Stella Nickerson, all of whom read early drafts of this book and offered encouragement and suggestions.

Finally I express my love and gratitude to my husband, Ted, who allows me to take over the computer, helps with word-processor mysteries, and always lets me spread my wings.

JANE NICKERSON

For many years Jane Nickerson and her family lived in a big old house in Aberdeen, Mississippi, where she was the children's librarian. She has always loved the South, "the olden days," Gothic tales, houses, kids, writing, and interesting villains. She and her husband now make their home in Ontario, Canada. Please visit her on the Web at jane-nickerson.com.